by

MJ Gunn

Bloomington, IN   Milton Keynes, UK

AuthorHouse™
1663 Liberty Drive, Suite 200
Bloomington, IN 47403
www.authorhouse.com
Phone: 1-800-839-8640

AuthorHouse™ UK Ltd.
500 Avebury Boulevard
Central Milton Keynes, MK9 2BE
www.authorhouse.co.uk
Phone: 08001974150

© 2006 MJ Gunn. All rights reserved.

No part of this book may be reproduced, stored in a retrieval system, or transmitted by any means without the written permission of the author.

First published by AuthorHouse 11/1/2006
ISBN: 1-4259-6543-1 (sc)

Printed in the United States of America
Bloomington, Indiana

This book is printed on acid-free paper.

AUTHOR BIOGRAPHY

A typical creative Leo as a youngster Matthew had an adventurous imagination and began writing short stories from the age of seven. As he progressed through education he found a love for both writing and filming, graduating with BA Hons Degree in Film from Southampton in 1997 – where tutored in Script Writing by Seamus Finnegan & in Directing by Ken Russell. Since graduating he built up a portfolio of written work & film industry employment.

Matthew's works include **THREE** Novels:
Stinkin Thinkin, *Gold Dust Memories* and *BritPop* (2005).
And **FIVE** Screenplays
YesterdaY (*In Development with White Lantern Films*).
Sleeping with Fishes (*written&directed*) Premiered & Screened on Propeller TV (part of Sky Film Network), and Distributed by Solarise Records (UK).
Horseman, *(In Development with It's No Joke Productions)*
Dear Prudence (*Proposed 2 part TV series*) and *Trilogy* (*Stage play*)

In the Industry Matthew has worked as a Writer, Director & DOP. In 2002, with three other friends they formed their own production company 'Stray Monkey Productions' to work as a creative outlet for both ideas and freelance work. In 2004 they started a Local Workshop for writers and filmmakers where Matthew taught on scriptwriting and filmmaking. Away from his own written & filming projects, Matthew's worked as Assistant Director & Creative Script Advisor to Award Winning playwright Lance Nielsen on 'Sticks and Stones' and 'Hi, I'm Vince', in the fringe Theatre's of London during 1999 & 2000. Then moved onto freelance work on Short Festival Films, Music Videos and Documentaries, as Writer, Director and DOP respectively over the years.

Matthew can be contacted and samples of his work can be viewed via his Agents Pippa Ealey Associates, please email pippaealeyassociates@hotmail.co.uk

AUTHOR THANK YOU NOTES

Special thanks to his Mum Sue, his Brother Marcus, the Brooks family especially the Lioness, the Holy Trinity (you know who you are guys!), the London & Woking Boys and Emma Williamson (best publishing agent around!)
This book is dedicated to all those people who are told that they don't live in reality by choosing to follow their creative dreams. Believe in yourself and you can achieve anything.

BRITPOP CHAPTERS

PART 1: New Beginnings   August '94 to January '95

Oasis	*(Matthew)*	1
A Week In The Windy City	*(Matthew, Alex, Steve & Simon)*	4
Welcome To The Modern World	*(Linda, Matthew)*	19
Three's Company	*(Alex, Taylor)*	31
Woking Boys		36
Jesus Says I Need To Get High	*(Johnny)*	45
Let Me Take Your Picture	*(Matthew)*	49
So This Is Christmas…	*(Matthew)*	54

PART 2: The Best of Times   January '95 to August '95

Suicide Is Painless	*(Alex)*	61
Carla Part 1		69
Birthday Bonanza	*(Alex)*	78
Nightclub Nights	*(Marie, Charlotte)*	84
Can't Get Out Of Bed	*(Matthew)*	93
The Psychiatrist	*(Linda, Simon, Steve)*	105
Do You Feel The Music?	*(Johnny, Matthew)*	114
Long Hot Summer	*(Matthew, Linda, Alex, Steve, Johnny)*	121

PART 3: Wasted   September '95 to January '96

The Holy Trinity	*(Matthew)*	126
Nexus Nights	*(Keith Reynolds 'The Vampire')*	133
Surfs Up	*(Linda)*	136
Wanna Live Like Common People	*(Johnny)*	139
Sleepless Nights	*(James)*	146
Silence	*('Clarissa')*	148
The Funeral		154
Lord Of The Flies		164
So This Is Christmas… (Part 2)	*(Matthew, Simon)*	170

## PART 4: Madness	January '96 to August '96

Sausage Jockey	*(Steve)*	175
Carla Part 2		184
Blizzard	*(Linda)*	194
On Your Bike	*(Alex)*	200
Tales Of White Lighting	*(Simon, Matthew, Steve)*	203
The Artist		213
Judas		222
Long Hot Summer	*(Simon, Linda, Alex, Matthew)*	228

## PART 5: Moving On	September '96 to January '97

Ghost Town	*(Matthew)*	234
Who's The Daddy???	*(Taylor)*	242
Twins	*(O'sullivan Twins)*	250
The Detective	*(Matthew, Simon, Johnny)*	258
Blair In Magnums	*(Steve)*	263
Merry Xmas Everybody...	*(Matthew, Simon)*	273

## PART 6: The Long Goodbye	January '97 to June '97

Carla Part 3		283
Spot Of Bother	*(Steve)*	294
Hit Woman	*(Clarissa)*	304
Into The Heart Of Darkness	*(Matthew)*	311
The Great Gig In The Sky		323
Long Goodbye		326
The Lost Souls	*(Alex, Linda, Christina)*	335
Oasis	*(Matthew)*	341

## Epilogue:	2005

Tales Of Bobs Barbecues	*(??)*	347

CHARACTER NOTES
Matt Ryan (Main protagonist)
Height and Weight: 5 Foot – 11 inches. Stocky Build, 11 stone.
Hair and Face: Thick Golden brown hair, long sideburns, blue eyes, Liono
Clothes and Style: Typical 'indie' kid / retro'.
Degree Course: Film.
Music: A vast music collection from '60s to '90s, Oasis is HIS band.
Ambition: Wants to be a filmmaker OR maybe do nothing for a while...
Age over the 3years: 20 – 22.   Star Sign – Leo.
Style of walk: Confident a leader but a loner
Drinks: Lager

Alex Page
Height and Weight: 6 foot – 2inches. 9 Stone
Hair and Face: Lanky, ginger floppy hair, 'Shaggy' from Scooby Doo.
Clothes: 'Hippy' necklaces, 'want to be hip' student indie style
Music: Britpop music to be 'cool' and 'in' with the crowd
Degree Course: Film.
Age: 18 –21. Star Sign - Pisces
Ambition: To be hip
Style of walk: Private music in his head!
Drinks: Whatever he thinks will make him look 'hip'

Linda
Height and Weight: 5 foot – 6 inches, 8 stone
Hair and Face: Gel hair products; make-up and appearance vital.
Clothes: Essex girl club clothes
Music: Dance music
Degree Course: RE
Age: 18 – 21. Star Sign - Pisces
Ambition: Perfect appearance and weight.
Style of walk: Get your handbags ready
Drinks: 'Girls' bottle drinks

James
Height and Weight: 5 foot - 11inches. 10 Stone.
Hair and Face: Mousy hair, small sideburns, pale skin and blue eyes.
Clothes: Chequered shirts and blue jeans.
Degree Course: Film Course.
Music: American Seattle music and BritPop
Ambition: Pain.
Age: 18 – 21. Star Sign – Aries.
Style of walk: A shadow merging into a crowd.
Drinks: Bitter

Steve Reed
Height and Weight: 6 foot – 2inches, 12 stone.

Hair and Face: Lanky 'Rodney Trotter' mixed with 'Damon Albern'.
Clothes: Tracksuit tops Blur 'Parklife' era.
Music: Blur and Britpop bands with Tight T-shirts for fans
Degree Course: Film Course.
Ambition: Reveal his secret
Age: 18 –21. Star Sign - Virgo
Style of walk: With a bounce, about to burst into Blurs 'Parklife' lyrics.
Drinks: Lager, Spirits and white lighting

Simon Curbishley

Height and Weight: 6 foot, Slim 'underfed' 9-10stone
Hair and Face: Black hair in 'bowl-cut' style, brown eyes, looks like 'Jarvis Cocker'.
Clothes: Chequered shirts and army jackets.
Music: '60s & '70s drink & drug induced artists, German Kruat Rock.
Degree Course: Film.
Ambition: Nothing… get as wasted as possible.
Age: 19 – 22. Star Sign – Leo.
Style of walk: Hunched down listening to his personal stereo.
Drinks: Lager, Vodka and white lighting

Johnny

Height and Weight: 5 Foot - 11inches. 10 stone.
Hair and Face: Black floppy hair, brown eyes, Mickey Dolenz from the Monkees
Clothes: Chequered shirts, baggy jeans or baggy shorts.
Music: '70s Kraut rock, Frank Zappa and Gong
Degree Course: Film.
Ambition: To be the last person left alive after the world gets taken over by zombies.
Age: 18 – 21. Star Sign - Aquarius
Style of walk: Stoned
Drinks: Guinness

Taylor

Height and Weight: Six foot. Chubby; 12 stone
Hair and face: Long black hair in ponytail, 'chubby' Johnny Depp,
Clothes: Nu-metal clothes
Music: Whatever he hears on the radio
Degree Course: Law
Age: 19 – 22. Star Sign - Gemini
Ambition: To play for or manage Reading football club.
Style of walk: Laid back
Drinks: Lager.

Amy

Height and Weight: 5 foot – 4 inches, 12 stone
Hair and Face: Long blonde hair, pretty 'Scandinavian face'
Clothes: Baggy tops, jeans.

Music: Britpop music and American Grunge
Degree Course: Business.
Age: 18-21. Star Sign - Pisces
Ambition: Doesn't know...
Style of walk: Bored.
Drinks: Lager

Clarissa

Height and Weight: 5 foot - 8inches. Full 'hour glass' figure; 9-10 stone
Hair and Face: Long brown hair down her back and brown eyes.
Clothes: 'Rock chic' look; leather jacket, low cut top, tight leather jeans.
Music: Dance Club style and Rock Power!
Degree Course: Film Course.
Ambition: To live a normal life.
Age: 18 – 21. Star Sign – Taurus
Style of walk: Confident, but her 'past' haunts her reflection
Drinks: Lager and spirits

Jenny O'Sullivan

Height and Weight: 5 Foot – 7inches, 8-9 stone
Hair and face: Long red hair, green eyes – classical '50s actress
Clothes: Erotic clothing
Music: Joni Mitchell, Jazz
Degree Course: Media.
Age: 19 – 22.
Ambition: Take each day as it comes
Style of walk: '50s Movie Star
Drinks: Wine

Marie

Height and Weight: 5 Foot – 5inches, 8 stone
Hair and face: Long black hair, firm figure, blue eyes, nose stud,
Clothes: Bohemian, 'arty' girl style in clothes
Music: Manchester Baggy Scene, Joni Mitchell
Degree Course: Art.
Age: 19 – 22.
Ambition: To create a Muriel of life through destruction
Style of walk: Vampire.

Drinks: Blood?

UNIVERSITY TREE

Matt Ryan – Lead Protagonist

1st Year House Mates
Taylor   (Law)
Alex   (Wanting to be Hip)
Amy   (Esteem)
Linda   (Cocaine nights & causal sex)

Film Course Mates
Steve   (Secret)
Johnny   (Acid)
Simon   (Drink)
James   (Weirdo)

The Holy Trinity
Matt Ryan
Johnny
Simon

Nightclubs and Cocaine Tales
Marie
Charlotte
Linda

Girlfriends
Clarissa
Carla
Jenny O'Sullivan

PART 1

August '94 to January 1st '95

New Beginnings

Part 1: New Beginnings

'OASIS'
August '94

Matthew

Do you feel the music or do you hear the music? Are you a - I am or I want to be person? Bob, real name, Stewart, but he changed his name by deed-pole to have the same Christian name as his hero, is a definitely I feel the music but also an I want to be person, so cancels one theory out with the other and ends up as a nothing, a negative. Still, give him his dues he has passed me over a pint of lager in a plastic glass, as always is the case at gigs in the Astoria.

"Four pound, Matt." Bob aka Stewart, holds his hand out wanting to get paid, obviously he wasn't buying a round. He called me Matt, I hate being called Matt, my name is Matthew, why do people insist on knocking the 'hew' off my name, are people really that lazy the idea of adding 'hew' will take up far too many seconds of the day? No one ever calls me 'Hew'.

I pass the four-pound over to Bob and realise he's sweating like a pig. His 'Self-Portrait' Dylan T-Shirt is soaked to the bone. He's so obsessed with this Dylan album that he carries it around with him everywhere he goes. Some young girl is next to us on the dance floor, she's wearing a 'Rumours' T-Shirt by Fleetwood Mac and even looks a bit like Stevie Knicks during her sexy late '70s look. I can hear Bob speak to this young girl in Dylan style nasal tones.

"Highway 61 Revisited, a psychotics paradise," I join the conversation and dazzle them with my theory on just who Mr Jones is and it is he who kills on the highway.

Some lanky guy, looking like Neil Young, wearing a 'Rust Never Sleeps' T-Shirt, joins us in conversation holding out a petition to get 'On the Beach' by Neil Young issued on CD, saying that if I think "Highway 61 Revisited' is a psychotics paradise, I should listen to 'On the Beach."

"I once listened to 'On The Beach' on a real crusty old tape," I tell the guy. He suddenly wants to be my best friend until I tell him "the tape isn't mine and that I don't even have it in my house." He tells me to just sign the petition.

Am I the only person wearing the band we've paid to watch T-Shirt? Is the band actually playing? Maybe this is a T-Shirt reunion benefit gig and I've paid eight pound for nothing, the day of my A-Level results too. I'm sweating the most in this tight white T-shirt, a size too small, I seem to have grown non-stop since the ages of sixteen to twenty.

"Desert Island Disks?" Bob asks me.

"How many?" I ask.

"Top five," the Stevie Knicks girl replies.

"Let It Bleed, Abbey Road, Pills Thrills and Bellyaches, Highway 61 Revisited and this lot, their album." I don't even bother to play the game with Bob, though I do ask the young girl.

"Stone Roses, Some Friendly, Screamendelica, Dirty, and yeah, these guys," she replies.

I ask if I can start again. "I could have named those too, I love those albums. I always naturally say 'Abbey Road and Let It Bleed'".

She tells me, "It's too late, unless you buy me a drink. Vodka and coke please"

"If you like those albums, why are you wearing a 'Rumours' T-Shirt?" The question had been bugging me for some time, what with being a qualified A Level student in Sociology as well as Journalism and Film. I decided it was the appropriate question to ask and analyse.

"It's my Mum's" she points over to the dance floor, and there is an older woman, wearing this bands t-shirt, surrounded by three or four guys, all putting their hands over her body.

"Oh." It seemed the only logical reply. I might get her to introduce me to her mum.

When's the band coming on? The main act always leaves you waiting. It adds to all anxiety, about everything in my life at the moment, the gig, what I'm wearing, my hair, my stubble, leaving next month. First time living away from home.

The band come on, chords burst out, that front man has got style, the new kings of rock 'n' roll kingdom. They start with 'Live Forever', blaring out of my stereo all summer so the entire street walking past could hear my gospel. These guys playing didn't belong to anybody, their own prince of polarity, not caring what people thought about them. I wonder if this is how my Mum felt when the Beatles first came out, or the Stones? The first time I feel part of a new scene. What was it termed the other day 'Britpop' sounds like a cereal but everyone here seems to know they're part of something. At last we can say to our parents "We was part of that scene, you wasn't there, we was" At last we have a rebuff, all we need now is a new world war.

Part 1: New Beginnings

I feel excited again, better than the last few months, just sitting in my bedroom with an education book glued to my eyes. I kept dreaming that it would pay off, now it has I don't know if I want to leave. I was getting very lonely and secluded this final year; no real good mates, didn't really want to go out anywhere, just study, even my mum asked if I was ok. "Why don't you go out somewhere, let your hair down," she kept saying.

"My hair's not long enough," I'd reply sarcastically, sarcasm is a writer's best friend. My hair flops down to my eyes, a typical indie kid.

"Are you ok?" She'd ask over dinner.

"Of course, why wouldn't I be"?

"Is it because that guy died from that band you liked?"

"You mean Kurt Cobain"

She'd pause and wonder what to say and then one night she finally said it. "You just never seem to go out anywhere"

I just…felt nothing. Though my reasoning to my mum was "Loneliness is under-rated its one of the last few things you can do on your own."

I spent that evening pretending to meet some friends. I walked my hometown alone, went to my old schools and watched from the gates, trying to hear the voices of ghosts from our past if I listened real quietly.

Some guy who I recognised from school was there. "You too?" The guy asked.

"What?"

"I've seen you here before, looking out."

"Hey pal, I'm not a fucking paedophile or anything."

"Phil, Phil Woodhouse," he replied. I hadn't seen this guy since we were sixteen, we used to be best mates, I cant believe I didn't recognise him, I guess I just chose not to. SILENCE.

"You seen me here then?"

"Yeah, I do the same, come out at the weekends when no-ones here, look out, don't know why, just, you know."

"Yeah, I know." I finally look properly at him and its like we're nine again and meeting for the first time. "You know if you're real quiet, you can hear the voices."

The two of us stood in silence.
Looking out.
Gripping the fence.
Listening for the voices.

3

I just wanted so much to escape; escape this town and who I was, live a new life, be exciting, be something I wasn't, stuck where I was. It seemed everyone wants to be my friend cause I'm leaving – where's the logic in that? I'm really confused what to do. I'm really excited about going. I'm really scared about wanting to stay.

Looking around as the band play there's a feeling of freedom of space, escaping from being locked up under a rule of government that advertised daytime telly and singing your name on a dole cheque. Something was changing, a sense of 'self' who we all where standing here. A new generation of one establishment and one order.

I look at Bob, dancing to the tunes; he's getting into the music, broad smile on his face, holding his copy of Self Portrait up high. I look at the girl and her mum, they swap T-Shirts, and neither was wearing a bra. Even the Neil Young guy with the 'On the Beach' petition is feeling the music, is being I am and not I want to be.

We are all 'I am'.
We all 'feel the music'.
  I'm going to University in less than a month...
  The youth of today is the future of tomorrow

'A WEEK IN THE WINDY CITY'
A cold wind is blowing.
And into town they arrive.
One by one.
Drawn to a culture that knows no bounds.
The lost promise of a revolution for their generation.
A queue of excess.
No names but the same faces all believing this is it.
Change the world.
To change the world you must change yourself into that world first.
That's what we all fail to understand.
That's why we all live in Dead Cities.
None deader than one that is alive only when broken promises of youth arrive.

Part 1 ' The House'

Matthew

There's someone else here. I'm not the first one to move in, I'm glad as it might have felt weird, sitting in a house, which now is my new home, alone, waiting for strangers to introduce my life to, whether you like them or not.

Mum begins to cry. I can tell she doesn't want me to leave. Be just she and dad now, they'll be left to each other's own devices, hatred, sarcasm, why are they still married? Divorce is the new love. One by one her boys have gone, freedom at last or a bear naked reality? On the journey down my dad had pissed us both off. "He's leaving home for so many years after being alone" he kept singing, his foot on the pedal so he could get back in time for the pub lunch. I wish this guy would just die.

Looking out of the car, the dark clouds that seemed to hang over Woking dispersed as we drew nearer to Southampton. It got to the point where I couldn't hear my dad anymore killing that Beatles song. There was a silent tone as I stared out the window, blocking out all noises, a smile went across my face each step closer we got to my new house.

"Are you nervous" I finally heard a voice, my mum's over the silence I created.

"Why would I be nervous?"

My room is downstairs next to the living room apart from a bed it's empty. It's a newly built house and has no memories to fill. I can paint my own picture; create my own rainbow to dream over. I place my suitcase on the bed and get my priority's right, taking out my music first, followed by film and band posters. Dad keeps checking the window putting a jinx on it and Mum is looking round the room, probably calculating radiators to put my washed clothes on. What is with parents and buying their sons socks and underpants, do they think we will shit ourselves all the time? Someone comes downstairs, my first new house mate. She's called Christina, petite, Spanish looking, broad smile, thick lips, I wonder what they would look like round…no, stop it now, she's your house mate and you've just met her, show some respect. "I'm going to the local newsagents, would you like anything?" She asks me.

I think about how this could be two fold, look at my parents still in the room and decide to say that - "I'm fine thanks…" for the moment. I'm feeling in limbo, with my parents still here. This is something that I have to do alone; it has to be my influence, my style, and my mistakes. Mum picks up on this and motions to leave, I know she's going to cry.   They leave. I'm alone. I sit alone in a room that seems massive, too big for me, engulfed to swallow what I own as my life in a suitcase, me into a black hole known as my personality. I sit on the bed and try and take it all in. What do I do now? I put on 'Cant Always Get What You Want' by the Rolling Stones, hoping it will impress Christina with my musical taste.

Alex

University the pinnacle of artistic understanding and achievements in the soul of a mind whose parents have created a monster - That monster is me. I blame it all on my parents, I am only what they created me as and so have them to blame for the games I play with people. Dad cheated on mum, I'm now one of the divorced millions of children who can play on their emotions of a confused childhood to milk each situation dry. I'm a rapist of the mind. Back way in. I'll try and surprise everyone. Stand in the kitchen and take it all in, I'll just wait here, for them to come to me. My first catch of the day; a weird looking guy with floppy hair and grungy shirt. "Hi, I'm Alex Page," I inform him, hand outstretched, broad fake grin on my face. I give him my surname to give an ideal of dominance in the beginning of this relationship, mannerisms are very important is what I read during my psychology A Level.

"Nice to meet you, I'm Matthew".

"Hi, Matt." He looks at me like I've just said he's mother is a whore when I said 'Matt' and there is a stony silence.

"Would you like some cold lamb cuts?" He finally asks. Wonder if this is some kind of kinky food game that university people do? My life will be beginning, psychology in principal, black couch lay out, with my dick in hand. I'm disappointed when he actual brings out just that, cold lamb cuts and makes a sandwich for us both, an experiment maybe?

"What course are you doing?" I ask, watching him bite into a disgusting sandwich.

"Film Studies"

"Same as me, what a coincidence," I put on a fake laugh and gently slap his back. "Same house and same course." I take a step back and pretend that I'm trying to take all this in and make some profound statement about religion and fate.

"Are you ok?" He looks at the half eaten sandwich and then me.

Part 1: New Beginnings

Think of something profound, deep, and psychological. "Yeah, just wow!" I hope he wants to be my best friend, maybe we can do everything together... share music, our grants, then our girlfriends... As I bite into a dry lamb roast sandwich, two new arrivals join us in the kitchen.

"Hi, I'm Amy." She introduces herself, a big girl, Swedish face, blonde hair, then she introduces her friend, "This is my best friend Samantha." The name rings in my ears as cupid fires a bow through the coldest of hearts; I am like my father after all. *Let the games begin.*

Six strangers sit in a pub. I don't know what to say. This pub is quiet. It seems even quieter now, since we all sit in silence. "What's your star sign?" that guy Matt asks everyone.

"I'm a Pisces's," Linda replies, gelled blonde hair, Essex girl; I'll try and shag her later on.

"Me too," Amy replies.

"Wow, you're not going to believe this, I am as well," I reply arms out for profound effect.

'Taurus,' Christina says.

"Gemini," Taylor says last, looks like a fatter Johnny Depp. We all go back down to looking at our pints in silence. Matt doesn't even bother to say what star sign he is; he just looks distraught. Frank Sintra plays on the jukebox, an old guy up at the bar begins to sing, they think its Christmas, as they've never had customers before. Where are the other students? I thought it would be bed swapping from hour to hour, people running naked in and out of the house. I thought it would be 'St Elmo's Fire'.

That night, I lay on Linda's bed, locking the door, asking questions for fifteen minutes - "Have you got a boyfriend?" "Are you looking for one?" "What type off guys do you go for?" She asks me to leave.

Matthew

This house is just like 'The Breakfast Club' each of us a different; I'm Judd Nelson, a rebel. Whatever happened to Judd Nelson? At night, I swear I see the ghosts of students past walk the windy city and enter our dreams... Or maybe I'm just pissed? I need a joint bad...

Part 2 'The Course'

This City sure is windy. I haven't got a clue how to get back to the house, I have no sense of direction, just followed the others. Eighty-three people stand on top of the wall, eighty-three waiting to fall. Here we all stand in a room full of strangers where the only faces we truly recognise are ourselves. Its like when you go to a nightclub; a potential meat market, the guys are eyeing up the girls as potential sex, the girls eyeing up the guys as potential dates, everyone eyeing everyone up as potential drug dealers, boffins, drinkers.... future friends for the next three years. There's some guy who looks like Damon Alban, another who looks like Noel Gallagher, another who looks like Jarvis Cocker. Long hair, short hair and no hair. Long legs, tanned, short, blonde, brunette and lesbian. Grungy, unwashed, hipsters, shirt and jeans. The course leader, a Canadian guy, Mark Gammond, looks like a garden gnome, he wants too much to be hip but is an obvious fascist, steps forward and begins preaching from yet another education bible I will break the laws too. "Hi I'm Mark Gammond and I'm your leader." I notice he didn't say 'course' or 'team' just 'leader'.

"If you look at the handout sheets being passed round..." BORING.... I look around the room; Alex is sitting next to me, his face full of eagerness, bet he's a teacher's pet. He laughs where appropriate, smiles and nods when looked at by Gammond, gay buddies already. Not me, I'm a rebel without a clue. The other tutors stay in darkness as Gammond tells the course with pride "I saw Bowie on acid in LA late seventies, so I understand all. Questions?"

The leader separates us into tutor groups. What is this school? Tutor groups, registrar, will there be an assembly? Some hymns? The only hymn I ever liked was 'when a knight won his spurs in the stories of old he was gallant and bold'. It was around that time I started to write short stories about knights, dragons, scantly clad women, loads of blood and gore, real 'Conan the Barbarian' stuff. A friend of the family read one of them and had a private word with my mum, "There might be something wrong with him, these stories are sick for a ten year old"

We sit like authors in hell. Wait in silence to be told that we can make friends and fuck with each other's minds as people always do in the end. I've never met anyone who hasn't been an arsehole at some point. The world hates arseholes but everyone's got one.

Part 1: New Beginnings

"I want you to introduce yourself to the person to your right and explain to them your three favourite films and why," we are told by a nameless tutor, the Ice Maiden.

Everyone seems very enthusiastic about this task we're given; I can't help thinking this is a bad group bonding session that white-collar workers are sent on to understand how pointless all work is. If I wanted a group bonding session I'd be sitting next to that girl with the long black hair, Lyn, very tanned, a bit of a snobbish outlook and nose but I bet she's dirty. Instead next to me is some guy called Kane, shaven hair, scary eyes, more scary then mine, skin more pale than mine, I love the guy already. He's wearing 'skaters' clothes. I'm wearing the same clothes I wore to the pub last night, with my new housemates and new best friends, until the week is out and we can find better people to be around.

Kane tells me three completely obscure films. "Isn't Deep Throat a porn film?" I ask.

"It's a classic." This guy I like, he chats to me about 'skating' and American sports, he is English. "So you like skating?"

"No I like drinking," I reply.

"What about Basketball?"

"I like smoking weed"

"I like your style, real grungy and dirty, that whole sugar scene."

"You mean the band, right?" I hope so, or why else would he think I look sweet? Probably wants to bugger me.

"Have you heard any of Bob Moulds solo music, I'll have to lend it to you. Come back to my room." He wants to bugger me. "What's your name?" He asks me when it's my turn.

"Matt..." I pause and add the "hew" Matthew, that is my name, best not to start lying just yet. "My favourite films are..." I decide to make some up to enliven my bored life, "Hard Cheese - The Sequel, Big Mac – The Whopper Years and BJ Betty"

"All American skate board films," he tells me, a glint in his eye.

The Ice Maiden gets out of her freeze putting her leather jacket on, "That's it for now. Re-convene in the library in two hours for a walk round books."

"Re-convene, what does that mean?" I ask Kane.

"It's a skaters term," he replies, I can tell he doesn't know either and is just trying to cover up.

"Lets blow this joint as soon as and get as much alcoholic

consumption down us as possible" some guy says standing next to us. I take a step back.

"Oh, I'm Richard by the way, I should have said that first, I guess?"

Myself, Kane and Rich, sit in Burger King chucking down food. I look at my two companions and wonder if this is my life for the next three years; sitting in burger king, maybe it will be become our table, we'll never speak to anyone else, just thinking this is freaking me out.

"I've got to go," I tell them, standing up.

"Where?" they say, standing up with me.

I think fast, my stomach is making noises. "Shopping." I couldn't listen to Kane and his skateboard techniques any longer, I'm surprised he hates 'Back to the Future' when I ask him.

"It gives skaters a bad name. He looks like he should be in Status Qu"

"Hey the Qu get a bad rep for no reason Kane, have you ever listened to one of their albums?" Rich butts in. Like I said, I'm freaking out and its only day one.

Don't now how we got to the library. I'll have to follow these two around for the next three years, even to the toilet. I'm extremely worried about how to get home again, feel a bit pissed and paranoid as I downed some pints. Panicked, pissed, with a Safeway's shopping bag of potatoes, cereal and milk, I guess I can always camp outside here tonight as I have dinner and breakfast in this bag. Like a guardian angel of death, I see Alex and stand next to him much to his annoyance. Alex's face turns on me, floppy red hair, trying to be cool hippy clothes and big ears sticking out as we walk back home. "You should have gone round the library with your own tutor group"

"Its just a fucking library, what they going to do - Send me to Vietnam?"

"You didn't see and learn everything about the library. It was very important…"

I just walk and pretend to listen, all I can think about is how my stomach needs some kind of food before I go out on the piss again, no doubt Alex will still be lecturing me about this all evening. I reply at one point that - "I didn't know how to get back on my own"

This then sets him off on another lecture, "What are you going to do, get up the same time as me every time you need to leave the

Part 1: New Beginnings

house? What happens if we have lectures at different times?"

"Then I won't go in," I reply. It makes perfect sense I can then have someone else to blame for being a waster. He is extremely lucky that I don't know the way back without him, otherwise I would have kicked the shit out of him and walked back on my own, but I'm dependent on the fucker for now. My life is not mine, it never was.

I stand in the queue for the government grants, confused, hungover; I can't believe those bitches Linda and Christina woke me up from a comatose kebab state phoning to speak to Alex. He came rushing to their rescue, brought me along for company, telling me, "it will help you learn your way round the streets." I learnt my way round Prostitutes nothing else.

I nod my head at people who I vaguely recognise from the Film Course; no one knows anyone well enough to start intense conversations when we all look this hungover. We stare forward, blankly, waiting for the queue to get shorter, to then form a new queue to pay our cheques into we banks with open arms, to then form a new queue for a bus, to then form a new queue at a bar, to then form a new queue for a club, to then form a new queue for a kebab, to then form a new queue for a toilet, to then form a new queue for the voting of sleep inside your mind. The university of queuing, degree mark 1st.

Behind me is a guy from the course, Johnny, I know he's staring at me, waiting for me to turn round and start a conversation, I can feel him breathing on my neck. I receive a cheque back that says five hundred pound. This is my fucking grant for the next three months. That only covers the rent, what am I meant to buy my drink and drugs with? "I hate my fucking dad," I mutter as I turn around in broken rage.

"All right mate, how you doing?" Johnny catches my eye. He speaks in a strong Manchester accent. Before I know it he has got his cheque already and I'm walking out with him.

"What do you think?" I ask.

"Do you wanna come back to my room and get caned?" He replies.

In what I guess is Johnny's room in Halls of Residence, we walked up various stairs, five floors at least, before we come to a room that finally opens when he pushes the door, he'd tried five previously. I'll never find my way back. Johnny rolls up a joint and we talk. "I want to be in the army, be a cook, that's what I really want to do," he tells me.

"Why you doing a film course then?" I ask.

"You need a degree to be a cook in the army," Johnny replies, so obviously doing a film course makes perfect sense. I hint at what time the banks close and that I should really open an account, I'm starting to feel a bit caned. "Cool I'll come with you, I need to open an account as well." He shows me his government grant cheque of one thousand for the semester, bastard, am I the poorest person in Southampton?

In my caned afternoon state all the students move too quickly, like a busy London rush hour, students, students, students, everywhere, we've taken over the town.

We finish a joint by Natwest so its makes logical sense to open an account with them, poetic license. As I fill out the information, Johnny continues to whisper to me, "I feel really caned", as I put down my reasons for wanting to open an account at Natwest and a thousand pound overdraft – **Drink. Drugs. Prostitutes.**

Back in Halls of Residence, one last joint for the road. "Do you want to buy any weed?" Johnny asks. He pulls out a block of grass that is the size of a brick; you could smell this from Safeway's. "My brother gets it in, he's a big dealer in Manchester, he gave it to me free as a going away present."

"I haven't any money Johnny." I want to get the grass, get fucked, just cause I know Alex, Amy and Linda are dead against it.

"I'll take a cheque," Johnny replies, already cutting the block of weed with a miniature saw in his hand, the guy is like an action man with his little tool kit. He brings out a machine that makes sure the cheque is legit, a true pro.

It's poetic that the first cheque I write with my Grant and Natwest Account isn't for rent but for scoring weed. Johnny begins to collapse on his bed, I'm sure he's packing his end of the joint. "Do you want to do a bucket?"

"I gotta go before I can't move," I reply, the four walls of the prison cell closing in.

"That's the best state to be in"

"Feeling nothing?"

"Being nothing." And he prepares his bucket bong.

I decline his kind offer and walk out. Look left, then right, feeling caned start to walk down stairs, then more stairs, walk out some double doors. Where is the exit? I begin to panic, the whites have

Part 1: New Beginnings

kicked in, I feel paranoid, will I ever get out of here? I run back up the stairs reach Johnny's floor out of breath and stand outside his room. I hear violent coughing into a bucket, now is not the best time to ask him how I get out of this maze. I take a different set of stairs but find myself in the same place.

My life will become a maze. I'm a hamster being experimented on.

"Alright." A guy places a hand across my shoulder; it's someone else from the Film Course. "Matt isn't it?" He asks. "I'm Steve, didn't realise you lived in Halls of Residence?"

"I don't, I'm trying to get to Portswood," I reply practically crying, I may never see my family again.

"Follow me." Steve walks off and for some reason I follow him, practically crawling along the floor. He knocks on someone's door, another guy from the Course - James answers. Are the entire Halls just people from the Film Course? It's like a nightmare.

"All right," James opens the door.

"I'm worried, Matt here is lost," Steve replies all concerned as I'm slouched across the door, ready to pass out.

I should have stayed and done that Bucket Bong.

"We're all lost. Follow me." James steps out the room.

"Don't you want to lock the door?" I ask him.

"Why, its not my room," he replies. Of course it isn't.

"Whose room is it?" I ask.

"I don't know," he replies with a horde of stolen CDs in his jacket pocket.

Reservoir Dogs at the Ocean Village seemed like the logical way to finish of our first week at University. We're asked to leave the waves of creative dreams as James propels himself upside down, hanging onto the rails to stop falling a long way into the sea of change. "Sure looks beautiful," I say looking at the clear blue sea and the stillness of the night, waves of desires rush across my soul, burning fires across the Ocean.

"So you're next then Matt? We've all got to die of something," James replies. I wonder what fires burn inside him?

Before I can begin to run away, a Security Guard from the docks reasons with him. "Get the fuck down from there you idiot!"

"Stop watching me!" James propels himself back up. "You're all watching me, all the time," he says to the guard. What the fuck is he talking about?

"Yeah, stop watching him." I point towards the Security Guard as he gets on his radio to the Police and the first dark cloud of the week pushes over the horizon.

"You understand don't you Matt?" James asks me in private as we walk.

"Yeah, course I do." I reply, not having a clue what language this weirdo is talking.

Back in my house I check the time and decide to make a 2am phone call to my mates back home to boast about what a great week I've been having and how they're stupid wasters not going to uni but working for a living. No-one answers. I stare up at the ceiling; my posters of Mean Streets and Reservoir Dogs stare at me and speak lines from the films. Oasis and Blur start to play tunes, Linda and her wooden leg begin to pound on the floor above. It's been a week; maybe its time I changed my clothes. I get under my duvet it feels warm. The room is spinning with excitement.

The Windy City was full of vibrant colours that dripped with the emotions of a new generation of people, burning with dreams to be fulfilled. The weather was warm outside, and anything seemed possible in the streets of a Town that paraded us with money to be spent. We had arrived to take what our predecessors had failed to grasp

Life.

I feel like I've just started a roller coaster ride that is only going to keep going up…

Part 3 'Halls'

Steve (Halls of Residence)

Inside my room the Madonna posters are winking at me. Kissing the girl on the lips it tastes weird, soggy and wet. She stinks of vodka, I stink of lager, think I might be sick. Shut my eyes and pretend that I'm enjoying this and not think about my truth. The night went so quick, one minute I was on the dance floor, looking at some guy, the next minute this girl, Charlotte I think, as I was so drunk I couldn't catch her name properly, was dancing next to me. I could tell the 'boys' who I've met were waiting to see what I'm made of, thinking that I've pulled this girl, that I'm a jack-the-lad. Got to keep appearances especially this early in the Course, create an image even if it is one big lie. I can't take that risk just yet. "You know you really look like Damon from Blur" she tells me as she

Part 1: New Beginnings

looks at a Parklife poster on the wall.

I finally pull away and sit on the bed, wanting to put my hands on my head and shut this away but it's too late now, I'll have to go through with it as people saw her come into my room. "You like Madonna?" She asks in a kind of way that makes me sound like a weirdo for a guy to like Madonna.

"Yeah, she's great... I love her" I reply, hoping she may get the hint and leave without me having to say anything or go through with the expected actions.

She sits on the bed with me, starts to unzip my jeans and feels my groin. I try and pretend I like it but it's no good, I stand up. "What's wrong?" She asks.

I think quickly looking at her face and my fear hits me. "I'll go down on you...first."

She smiles at this and begins to take up her short black dress, pulling down her knickers, facing me is what has always been the Bermuda triangle. Show a fake smile and put my face straight down in there, her already making gasping noises, after ten seconds of gently licking and kissing I want to be sick, just can't do this, it doesn't taste right. I pull off her. "Wait, I haven't... you know yet...." She says in a mixture of pent up anger and excitement. I stand up and stare at a Madonna poster. "Do you want to swap?" She asks.

The Virgin poster winks at me, now that, I would fuck, cause rumour is its got a dick anyway. "Something more to drink." I say and wink, teasing her. Walking into the kitchen, Simon, from my Film Course greets me.

"How's it going?" Simon asks me in a massive drunken slur; the guy can hardly stand up and speaks like a baby.

"Fancy a drink?" I reply. I get some beers I had hidden at the back of the fridge out and pass one over to Simon. We talk, mumble drunkenly about where we're both from.
After about thirty minutes Charlotte walks in. I nod my head as a casual acknowledgment and go back to talking to Simon, praying she goes away. "So I'll see you then?" She says.
"Yeah, yeah, really nice to have met you" I say, keeping my distance. She just shakes her head and slams the door shut. *I have a secret.*

Simon (Halls of Residence)

It's like the first week at school. People who are you mates one day can disappear the next day. But instead of a playground there's shit loads of vodka, and shit loads of weed. I only came into this room by mistake, thinking it was mine. They sit playing computer games, it was doing my face in watching the screen so I stayed - I want to do my face in, that's the whole point of me coming to University, sure as hell wasn't for the Film Course. Just to get away from my parents. James, sits in the room and we're playing 'Sonic the Hedgehog'. We got back from watching Reservoir Dogs with Matt Ryan. I have a drink and my mouth becomes News of the World with my stories; it's out of boredom of how mundane life all seems. "The end is nigh." We've run out beer, I NEED TO DRINK. Checking the fridge there's nothing to steal, so I make my way down to the kitchen on the floor below, there seems to be some beer hidden. Take one out and open it. A guy from my Course walks in, sweating, Steve, we get talking, he opens the fridge and offers me a beer… it was his beer I had stolen, he doesn't notice, he's as pissed as I am. After a while, I can't understand what he's saying, some girl walks in, and I sneakily place my head into the fridge to steal the rest of his beer hoping he wont notice. It sure is cool in this fridge…*Sleep.*

Magic mushrooms taken with 'The Mad Hatters Tea party' white rabbits, jumping into my mind. There's me, Blonde Paul, Matt Ryan, Steve, this guy from Manchester called Johnny and James explaining how many times his done mushrooms and acid.
"When they kick in, don't get nervous and don't get paranoid." James tells us.
"When do you know they're kicking in?" I ask.
"You'll get nervous and paranoid," James replies.
Blonde Paul suggests going for a walk into Town. "Its always good, freaks you out." We leave the room and go to the elevators. The elevator door opens and James is in there, looking wild-eyed. As we go to step in he presses the button to go down without us. "They're watching us," he shouts. We shut the doors on James who crumples to the floor as the world shuts out his life.
Walking through the Town, the freaks are out, or that's what my eyes tell me, midgets with fireworks. I'm sure I'll be all right; the mushrooms have made me immune to Satan. In MacDonald's, is a guy from our Film Course, Alex. He lives with Matt Ryan and other first years in Portswood. He tries to persuade us to go back there, especially with the state we're in; he wants to experiment on us. He continues trying to do our faces in - " Do you take a lot of

drugs? Are you a homosexual? Do you like your parents?" Steve seems really intrigued by this, says he'll go back, the rest of us decline and decide to go back to Southampton town and its midgets with fireworks.

Steve

They can't get to me up here. I see some people from the Film Course they all walk through the park to get to the Halls of Residence. "Its Damon!" Matt exclaims, knowing full well my name is Steve but determined to keep calling me after Blur's front man. They all stop and look at me. Me up a tree. Holding onto branches like a squirrel afraid to jump. I want to cry. "What are you doing up there?" Matt shouts.

I reply back in bird noises. What am I going to tell them - That I don't who I am? That I'm scared. One minute I was with that guy Alex and then when I said to him that - "I've taken a lot of magic mushrooms, it's my first time and I'm quite scared..." He said, "Lets play a game" and suddenly disappeared. Left on my own in the middle of Southampton Town, full of midgets and fireworks. I started to run, I swear I could see Alex watching me. I got to the park and thought he was up the tree.

Matt climbs the tree, the others shout at him to be careful but he does it with ease.

We sit together up the top of a tree in silence making bird and owl noises as we look at each other. The others just stare at us; they begin to throw stones and beer cans trying to knock us down. "Fucking hell!" Matt says as one hits him and he nearly slips out. I don't hold my hand out as what fool would climb up a tree? "I'll see you later Damon from Blur." Matt jumps out of the tree, landing on his knees, filling with dirt of the Windy City.

How am I going to get down? There are midgets all around the tree, dancing with fireworks waiting for me. I'll have to wait to daylight. Maybe I'll see Alex from here and he'll take me back to Portswood to experiment on me. This is what Parklife is all about. I always wanted to be Damon from Blur but I never thought I'd actually end up living in a park to prove I am him. Freedom is leaving home to live life from a tree. Boys who love girls... ...who love boys? Boys who love boys?

Simon

"Oh yes Simon that's really attractive." Clarissa says watching me fall over out of Nexus Nightclub. I try to stand and then fall flat on my face again. She turns to Matt Ryan and James. "Have you ever seen anyone that pissed?" I hear her say.

"Oh yeah, last Sunday, Simon was that pissed," James replies.

"You going to help him home?" Matt asks.

"No, leave him in the gutter too the vampires," James replies.

I crawl up towards them on my hands and knees, staring up. "I'll be fine." I collapse back onto the floor; face on the pavement, the corner of my eye shows Nexus Nightclub. Puddles all around from the rain, the lights illuminate them and its like I'm in some film noir. The freaks surround Nexus, the Gothic's, the vampires, and the skinheads, "Freaks" I mumble in the puddle and distort their reflections further. The Vampire City. I am crawled along the street by strangers who are now my friends to rob me blind. A Police Van waits as we get to the traffic lights opposite Halls. I can see my room from here, the light is on and I can make out Steve staring out the window waving. What's he doing in my room? Then Blonde Paul and Johnny join him, they all wave. I try to wave back but collapse onto the pavement and throw up. The coppers look at me, I'm convinced they're going to make me spend the night in the cells, is there law against being this pissed?

"We don't like students round here." Good Cop.

"Always going round causing trouble." Bad Cop.

"We got it in for you, we want you lot out!" Good Cop.

They try to grab me but I fall down naturally in my drunken state and curl up ready for a beating. I decide to go to sleep on the pavement, at least if I get the shit kicked out of me if I'm past out I wont feel it until the morning. I hear Alex's pretentious atypical student voice, "Our mate is a bit drunk, its his birthday." It's my birthday? That year sure went quick.

Good Cop, Bad Cop, starts up again. "If we see you lot again we're taking you in" "This is your only warning" "We want you students out!"

Somehow I've got from outside and the police harassment, to inside a room. Matt and Alex are there with James playing on a computer game. I'm collapsed on a bed; face down in a duvet that smells of spunk. "Whose room is this?" I ask them.

"Don't know," they all reply.

When I wake I'm in my room. Clothes still on. Face down on a duvet that smells of sick.

Part 1: New Beginnings

WELCOME TO THE MODERN WORLD
Linda

It's a beautiful Sunday afternoon in what should be a freezing cold October, the phone rings and I know its Mum. "Did you watch it?"

"Yes, Mum, I need to get fit." Our conversation continues along the lines off; getting fit, eating well, the course, the house, when am I coming back for a weekend. I stare in the mirror and the young girl I thought had long gone stares back during the conversation.

"Are you losing weight? You're not forcing yourself to be sick again are you?" She asks me. As every word she says is too close to my reflection, I'm always pretending to be an open-ended book with my parents putting me too high on a pedestal shouting perfection. "Don't you miss home, just a little a bit?"

Long pause, I lie. "Yeah"

"What are you eating? I'm worried about your weight. " I wondered how long it would take.

"I'm normal." As normal as anyone who made themselves throw up last night's dinner.

"Have you got a boyfriend?" They can't live without a society ball of relationships to gossip, she wants an advert in the society mags at the local newsagents.

"No. I'm having too much fun. " I study myself as mum continues to talk, naked and alone. Am I the same as others under this skin and bone?

"You're not taking drugs are you? You can tell me." Of course I can, just like I can tell her that I never want to come home again.

"God mum, you know me better than that."

"I know you're sensible, but what about the other people in the house?" And so starts twenty questions "Don't they like you?" "Don't they speak to you?" Ending in the one all students run away from "Perhaps you should come back home?"

"We all get on, it's just that I don't really have anything in common with them."

"What about that guy Matt? He seemed like a nice guy, asked about star signs." The way to a mothers heart the eternal question – 'what's your star sign?'

"He's always playing music all night, invites people back all hours."

"Can't you do something about it? Have him arrested?" When do parents live in the real world, not something two generations behind? As she continues I stare into the mirror that keeps reflecting the picture behind me when I was a child. She keeps watching me and wonders why I stare for no reason; I guess I am the picture to her, which hangs off balance reflecting the wrong messages to send. "Why don't you come home for the weekend? I'm worried about you." My parents suffocate me. I guess I'm not that little girl anymore with dolls around the bedroom. I continue to listen but pay more attention to the television set.

I spend most of my time in my room now that Matt has taken the TV into his room, only bringing it out when footballs on for him and Taylor to watch just to piss us girls off. They're all taking drugs, I didn't come to university to take drugs, he'll end up wasted, dead, hooked on something harder, I've seen it happen on Sunday TV, there's no redemption for that boy. Always drunk too. Don't get me wrong, I like to go out and let my hair down but not every night. I put some massacre on, as I'm going downstairs to make some hot chocolate. I don't like to be seen without any make-up, not since I looked in the mirror when I woke up once.

Amy is in the living room. She is watching some scary film called 'Carrie'.

"What's this about?" I ask her.

"I don't know its crap!"

"Who's in it?"

"I don't know I'm bored!" The conversation continues along this line, she's a nice girl Amy but she has no self esteem, I'll be glad when its next year and Katie, my new best friend, and I get a house.

I take a shower so I'm fresh for tomorrow morning. It's a tight time schedule – 7am get up. 8am in gym. 9am come back to the house and shower. 10am back out to a lecture. 1pm throw up lunch. Kneeling beside the bed I begin to pray but as soon as my sins are heard the music from downstairs starts up again. I can't believe this, its 9.30pm on a Sunday. I decide I've had enough. I knock on Matt's door. He opens it glazed red eyes, joint in hand, a red dressing gown on that makes him look like a boxer, hair floppy over his eyes.

"Yeah?" he says, doesn't even invite me in, good, because I wouldn't want to go into that den of sin.

"Look its 9.30 mate, I got an early start, 7am, turn the music down mate," I ask him, wondering why there's a cricket bat next to the window.

"What you getting up at 7am for?" He asks me, none of his

Part 1: New Beginnings

business that's what. He takes a puff on the joint and offers it to me; I just stare at him and don't take it. Disgusting druggy.

"I don't," I reply, looking at him in disgust, which is quite easy to do with the way he looks.

"Its only 9.30, not like its 12." He says and takes another hit of the joint, then goes back in and sits on his bed, still not inviting me in. I to have step slightly into the doorway and see that he keeps his room really tidy. Everything is clean, hovered, tapes all stacked properly, clothes ironed and hung up, bed made, posters of films and bands. It's really thrown me; I thought they'd be mess all over the floor, some spaced out hippy girl in the corner wailing underneath a white sheet, needles, bags of drugs, but this is as clean and organised as my room. It make's me hate him even more.

"Look, just turn the music down." I go back upstairs slamming my feet on each step so he gets the picture.

He shouts back up towards me "Happy Mondays, Pills, Thrills and Bellyaches, it's a classic"

I pray for God to get me my own flat away from these sinners.

Work that body. Worried about my weight. Worried that the gel in my hair is making it look disgusting. Worried that my lips are too big, do I have a fish face?

"I can't stand another day," I tell Katie, as I pump my legs backwards and forwards lying down on the machine. I wonder if this is how my legs will pump when I have sex? I've seen it on TV.

"Just keep counting backwards or something," Katie replies, she's got a great body but a horses face, that's why I like her, became best mates, she keeps the attention on me.

"He was playing music till midnight, smoking dope, just a waster" I tell her about my distress at having to live above Matt, though to be honest I call him a 'druggie' but after inspecting his room last night it was really clean, but I don't tell Katie this, I want to keep up the illusion I've created of a den of sin I live in.

As I said the word 'dope' a guy looks over at me. I hope I haven't embarrassed myself, he's really nice, tall, Italian looking, short shaven black hair, working out, great body, I hope he doesn't think that I smoke dope, that I'm a waster.

"I wish I had your smile," Katie tells me as her horses nose drips sweat that wont go down, I don't tell her this, as I see the guy coming over to us and I want her to look stupid.

"I wish I had your arse," I reply and burst out laughing so my

21

smile can flash ahead of the guy. I see a reflection of my hair in the window behind me as I lean back, the black leotard showing my rosy cheeks, flushed, my legs looking firm, the massacre on for the gym, but the hair is sweating over the gel, I can smell it dripping, it smells disgusting.

"How you doing?" the guy asks me more than Katie. But Katie being the 'Essex girl' she is, jumps right in and practically sticks her tongue down his throat, introducing herself before I can speak. Telling him about our Course, where we live, everything he needs to know to become our stalker. She's showing her firm butt off to him, he slaps it but stares at me as he does so, a real gentleman I reckon. He sits himself on my machine as I begin to towel down my sweat; I think this turns him on. "You going to the boat party for fresher's ball on Friday?" He asks me and not Katie.

She has become so obsessed with her own arse that she can't take her eyes of the mirror and hand away from her own buttocks.

I can tell he's well hung. "Yeah, are you?" I ask, praying that he is.

"Yeah, why don't we travel down together?" He asks me.

"We' re getting a coach," I reply pointing at Katie.

"The coach will be packed, why don't you both come down with my other mate, a foursome, share a taxi ride we've got organised there and back?" He smiled with the word 'foursome' he must like double dating.

Katie ever the diplomat and slag, organises this for us immediately and quiz's the guy about what his mate is like, personality etc. "Is he good looking?"

I realise I don't even know his name. "What's your name?"

"Matt," he replies. Another Matt, a million times better looking and nicer than the one I live with, not a waster at all. "Bye Linda" He leans in and kisses me goodbye on my cheek.

I forgot about my stinking hair gel and he has a disgusted look on his face, like he wants to throw up, as he pulls away. Katie joins me on the treadmill. "He's no waster," I tell her.

Feeling queasy, I maybe drunk. The boat is going up and down. Southampton looks a den of sin from this viewpoint on the sea. All I can see are the docks. The wind starts up, and for the first time since I moved down here I feel cold. We're in our own private corner. Katie has her skirt hitched up so, Joshua, Matt's mate, can go into her and lose himself in there. Matt keeps kissing me. I made sure I

Part 1: New Beginnings

got my hair gel right today and it smelled perfect on top but he can't put his hands through my hair. When he goes near I stop him, as I don't want him ruining my hair gel. He tastes of lager and it makes me feel sick. "I need the toilet." I quickly grab Katie, much to her annoyance as she had the guy's privates out.

My head is pushed down a cubicle and Katie is rubbing my back as I continue to cough up. "I can't keep kissing him," I cry out.

"You like him don't you?" Katie asks, a stupid question as I'm kissing him and throwing up.

"I'm not doing what you're doing if that's what you mean?" I cough out towards her, what a slut, she'd only known the guy two hours.

"Well, you wouldn't have to kiss him as much then." Is her theory and helpful hint for me.

I re-do my make-up, foundation, massacre, re-do the hair spray in the mirror. Several other girls come in and we crowd round, all calling one another "bitch" as they leave. I hate most women. I stare into my reflection and I recognise the two girls that come out of the cubicle behind me, Marie and Charlotte, those weird girls whose house we went round and I had to phone Alex up for him to rescue us.

"It's little miss virgin," Charlotte laughs out towards me, wiping her nose.

Her friend Marie looks wired at me, "You want to do some coke china doll?"

Back outside on the boat, in our 'fuck a fresher corner' with a big sign advertising cheap pregnancy kits, Joshua pairs off with Katie immediately and they return to previous positions; privates in hand, both pairs getting wider and closer to an introduction. I turn away embarrassed as Matt stares glassily eyed towards them and then back at me. He reaches into his jacket pocket and pulls out some white powder. "It will help you relax," he tells me.

"I don't," I reply. I then worry that I'm blowing this, that I might not look cool in his eyes, which are beginning to wander round the boat at other girls. "Go on then," I say and take a little pretending to snort it. He places some round his mouth and on his tongue. "He's not a waster, he's not a waster," I keep telling myself. He smiles a crazy smile at me, with white powder all around him like he's advertising Daz, I burst out laughing.

"Why you laughing? I really, really, like you, I want to be with you." Maybe it's the alcohol speaking, maybe some of the cocaine did he hit me, but I reckon he's telling the truth. I look at Katie and realise I don't want to hold on forever, she seems to be enjoying herself. She nods her head as Joshua slobbers over her and motions for me to do the same. Across the boat are Marie and Charlotte laughing at me. I want be one of the girls now. We begin to kiss again; he places his hand up my skirt. I feel too tired to stop him. Before I know it he's pushing his cock out and my knickers have come down. "First time?" He asks. I kind of squeal a yes. "Don't worry, I really like you, I love you," He replies and I believe him. I start to count sheep, seventy-five in all and he collapses onto me and says how much he "Loves me".

Was that it? I'm now not a virgin? How come Katie looks so satisfied or is that what is called faking it? The boat rocks side to side. He stinks of lager. He's not a waster; he's not a waster. I feel tingling round my mouth from the cocaine. I feel wet and disgusting down below. I feel sick. I pull my skirt back down. He collapses onto the floor and passes out.

I look over to Southampton from the viewpoint of the boat. I see her again... that young girl who used to reflect in the mirror at me. She stands on dry land holding a mirror up. I want to reach her, pull her back to me but she's too far away. She waves goodbye and jumps into the ocean. I feel cold.

Matthew

Everything about it is annoying me. It doesn't have any style. It goes like an afro in the wind. It's just bland. I want it to change... I want to change. My first weekend back... Home? As I got on the train at Southampton, I could feel the cold weather for the first time this autumn as I got nearer Woking. The heavens opened and the rain came down. The storm had arrived as I stepped off the train into 'Hells Kitchen'. The richness and warmth in the colours of the Windy City had evaporated into the darkness. "Why have I come back? I don't belong here anymore" As the rain fell across my face, my smile and good memories of the last month in had dispersed, the rain acted as paranoia to my bad thoughts. All that was wrong with me and how I looked hit me like a truck as I came back to this place. Paranoia strikes deep, into my heart it did creep. So I sit in Lugio's and go for the grade two all over. Skinhead. In my minds eye, by destroying my hair, I will destroy the paranoia. I would never have done this back in Southampton. All my self-doubts have returned and I'm only here for the weekend. My Mum has the biggest shock

Part 1: New Beginnings

when I open the front door; I told her I was just popping out to get a paper, not to have a complete facial change. She looks kind of scared at me, like I should be wearing DM Boots and beating up old grandmas. I keep looking in the mirror studying my lack of hair. Running my hand from top to bottom. The more I look, the uglier I look, like a newborn baby. Go straight back out after staring in three different mirrors in every corner of every room of the house. Each mirror and corner makes me look completely different, anything but normal. Hit the train again, find a sports shop and buy a puma hat to wear. Back at home I wear the puma ski hat and try every mirror and every corner again. This time I look like a drug dealer. Start to panic about what happens if I lose my ski hat?

I go back out, my third train journey of the day, back to the sports shop and buy another ski hat. I sit on the edge of my bed, mirror in front of me and begin to cry when I take the ski hat off.

Sitting in the pub with old mates, it seems to be dripping with the intensity of violence, the walls painted red, closing in with my every glance, the blood that drips in 'The Shinning'. I think about going back this evening but the storm is in full swing outside in 'Hells Kitchen', a hard rain is falling that bruises your face. Already I can't stand the conversation, Phil talking about his work for the Tax office. "It's not all bad, I get to go on missions and spy on people."

"Like MI5?"

"No, I basically sit in a car and take notes"

"What on?"

"Song lyrics mainly. We took down Ken Dodd"

Matt Smith, a petty criminal, the classic example of a young person who accepted conservative rule and dole culture at the start of this decade, talks to me next. His life revolves around daytime telly, the pub, spliffs, and the odd football match. The scary thing is it sounds like my life. He keeps talking about players and faces. "There's no faces anymore round here"

"What do you mean, faces?"

"Players. I'm a player." He then spits on the floor and smiles at the management as the walls continue to close in on me. I'm scared I might not even make it through the night.

The rain hits us hard across our faces. We're in the eye of the storm, blinking into a darkness that surrounds us as we try to find cover. We was going to have a joint outside the pub but both Phil and I were worried that we might end up on the end of a cocaine fuelled beating, so we head to the local park which is so badly lit we cant see where we're walking. How adept skinning up in a playground let the kids learn early. Before we can even get to that stage, as I place my left hand down I feel a sharp cut into my palm. "FUCK" I look at my hand with the aid of Phil's lighter and find a massive piece of glass sticking into my palm.

"Jesus Christ mate!" Phil says, he pulls his face away and throws up on his shoes.

As I pull the glass out, I tell him "This is a sign Phil, a sign to never come back. What do you reckon?" He doesn't answer; he's still throwing up. Its left a mark an inch wide and deep, my initial reaction would be to panic but I'm kind of intrigued to know what the inside of my hand looks like, I look in and open the wound slightly. "It looks like mice beef, un cooked." Phil turns away he nearly chokes to death. Welcome home.

Through the front door, my Mum's first reaction is "How dare you step inside without taking your shoes off!" She doesn't say this but I can tell she's thinking it. Blood keeps gushing down as she runs it under cold water, I keep seeing her glance to the floor and she's thinking 'I'll have to hoover later'.

Phil phones his Mum up. "Could she drive me to the hospital?" I ask.

"My mum isn't that type of girl" he replies. Good to have mates.

On the train station in the morning, I had to get out and quick, before 'Hells Kitchen' bled my dry. "I've got to go back, I've got a lecture," I said to Mum

"On a Sunday"

I then said, "I need some cigarettes"

"But you don't smoke," She replied and I run out the door and hear her call down the road, as the hoover starts up, "Will you be back for Christmas?"

The hard rain continues, with me in the eye of the storm. I stare out the train window and watch a heated goodbye to Thatcher's dream in Woking. My glasses are off and no longer blinkered, when you live somewhere for so long its all you know, when you go somewhere different you see that place for what it really is, whether its good or bad. The truth always finds a way of coming out in the end.

As I reach Southampton, the rain ceases and the wind starts up,

Part 1: New Beginnings

but it feels warm, it's home now, safe at last. The colours return to vibrancy and excitement, away from the bleeding of my soul. How can two places be so different in my minds eye?

I wear my ski hat to bed, my hair is fucked, and my life is finished.

Wake up at around 10am. Bandage on my hand from where the glass cut my palm, a scar will be there for life. The room is really stuffy, no air has been in all weekend, and it smells of weed and unwashed clothes. My window doesn't open properly; the guillotine comes crashing down…I sense psychical loss as I realise my little finger didn't get out the way in time. I'm too scared to look to see if it has fallen off, as the Cranberries sing to me 'Do you have to let it linger, got you wrapped around my finger' on Virgin radio. I had asked my dodgy landlord, to fix this window for the last four weeks. Had he done it? "My window still needs fixing." I'd knock on his door everyday. "Weekend, weekend," he kept replying. When they saw me approaching the house, I'd see the curtains flicker and then all the lights turn off, they'd pretend no one was in.

"HELP!" I shout for anyone in the house, there is no movement. Alex is in, listening to my copy of Blur's 'Modern Life Is Rubbish' he borrowed of me the day we met and I haven't seen it since. Once I went into his room and reclaimed it. Later that day he came into my room asking "Have you got my copy of modern life is rubbish?"

"ALEX!" I shout to know avail. I don't know whether to laugh or cry, first my palm now my finger, what with my hair shaved and messed up, I feel like committing suicide. That's the last time I get up and decide to go to a lecture this early. Fucking Course, it's their fault this shit keeps happening.

The baby sitter from next door has stepped outside with the kids. She sees my predicament, and I politely ask her, "Can you fucking help me? I've got my fucking finger caught, fucking fuck!" Like a true superwoman, she attempts to jump over the fence but cannot get her fat arse over and gives it a second try. "Fucking hurry up!" I shout towards her. She finally gets her leg over, which I might later on and tries to pull the window up. "Fucking hell! Fucking push it up!" I shout at her, she's only trying to help, another ungrateful kid to baby-sit.

"Do you mind not swearing, I know you're in pain but there's young kids here." She points towards the young children watching in horror at a red eyed student swearing, wearing a puma skit hat, one hand bandaged from glass and his other hand stuck in a

27

window, welcome to the modern world kids, its downhill the minute you talk.

Finally, she manages to push the window up, the finger remains on my hand, just. "I've never heard so many profanities in one sentence," she tells me.

"Shut the fuck up bitch!" I whisper. Both hands bleed - I know how Jesus felt.

Alex stands at the top of the stairs in a dressing gown holding another one of my albums, obviously crept into my room during the commotion and stole more cd's he can claim are his. The babysitter leaves when confronted by Alex and his undone dressing gown staring from the top of the stairs ready to pounce on her. "Didn't you here me screaming at you?" I ask the ginger one.

"I thought you was trying to wake me up for college so I ignored you," he replies.

"Like when the fuck have I ever tried to wake you up for college?" Such a liar this young man, he continues to speak pretending that I haven't noticed he holds my albums.

"Is your hand alright?"
"My albums?"
"Is your finger alright?"
"My albums"
"Is your hair better today?"
"My albums"
"How fast can a cheetah run?"

"I've never been to hospital before, what should I do?" I need guidance from the ginger one? Is life that bad for me at the moment?!

After ten minutes of pleading he agrees to help me - "If you say these albums are mine"

"Fuck you." He walks back towards his room "Come back... They're your albums." If I could cross my fingers I would, but why bother, I don't care about lying to this guy; violence is the best solution.

We go to an open hospital the next road down. "How did you know about this place?"

"I made sure I was registered with a doctor before I moved down. Didn't you?"

"You're so organised Alex, it makes me sick. Don't you ever just want to get drunk and stoned?"

"I got stoned over the weekend"

Part 1: New Beginnings

"But you haven't got any weed"
"You had some in your room"
"But it was locked"
"It was?" I'm too weak to argue with him, I hold my finger towards the lady in reception like it's a bomb that's about to explode if she doesn't help me. "My finger is going to drop off!"
"Are you registered here?"
"No, but look at me, look at my finger!"
"If you're not registered than we can't help you"
"This is Thatcher's Britain for you!" I slam my cut palm in her face.

After offering more CD's to Alex, he finally gets us to jump in a taxi. "This isn't Thatcher's Briton but John Majors," he informs me in the cab.

"Do you vote Tory?" The Taxi driver asks.

"Yes I do as a matter of fact," Alex replies in his posh middle class privileged accent.

The taxi driver stops and opens the back doors. "Get out my cab you Tory scum!"

We finally arrive at accident and emergency after a twenty-minute walk. "Don't go, I don't know what to do?" I shout as Alex walks away pretending not to hear. "I'm scared," I mutter under my breath. A crazy eyed, long bearded guy stands next to me and imitates my every word and motion. "I'm scared, I'm scared," he mutters to me.

At reception they tell me to go to another reception to inform me that I haven't got my details so to go back to the original reception who inform that I need to go to another reception who inform me with a piece of paper to fill in and return to the first reception, why didn't they just have all this there? "You can take a seat now" They point at a giant waiting ward, a hundred grim faces, school chairs, every bone broken if you piece us all together and daytime TV on the smallest portable you can imagine. A look of sinister smugness on their faces when they realise I have taken all this in and its hit me with a pain that has made my finger seem irrelevant. "So many wait here and find themselves cured," she says to me. "It's the best therapy, to see others in pain, I haven't had a headache for ten years" her co-worker tells me.

Two hours later off smelling death, my name is called. I go into a room with a nurse. I get ready to undress and show her heaven and hope the video cameras will start to roll but unfortunately she didn't have the same idea in mind and pulls out a large needle.

Afterwards, I reach a phone and dial the numbers I dreaded. "Hi Mum its me"

"Are you alright darling?"

"Don't worry but my finger got caught in a window, the nail came off and I had to go to accident and emergency...." No reply, I'm sure I can hear laughter. "Hello, are you still there?"

"Yes, I'm still here"

"The finger's safe. Can you find out a taxi firm number for me in Southampton and I'll phone you back in five minutes...I'll be reversing the charges" I can't even get a taxi without my Mums help. I am beyond useless.

"Alright Matt." A voice beckons me from behind, its James.

"What are you doing here, James, finger stuck in window as well?" I ask, showing my two bandaged hands hoping for sympathy that will involve large amounts of alcohol and weed.

"No, I just like the atmosphere of these places," James replies.

"That's really funny mate," I reply with fake laughter, but he doesn't laugh back his face all serious. "Seriously, what are you here for?"

"I just told you. I thought you understood me Matt?"

I stare at James, then at my hands, then at the hospital receptionists waving at me pointing at the Television set and coffin dodger waiting room. "Got any weed?" I ask him.

"I know you're in there" I shout through Mrs. Singh's letterbox. I see the curtains twitch as usual and I stand with my arms going mad, puma ski hat on, both hands bandaged. "Open the fucking door! My finger nearly got cut off because you haven't fixed that window"

I can see eyes through the letterbox. "I call police," the letterbox threatens.

I shove my broken finger towards the eyes peering out the letterbox. "He either comes to fix it or I'm suing you."

"He not back! Tomorrow, window fixed tomorrow!"

"Today! He fix window today!"

"Tomorrow, window fixed tomorrow!" I feel my finger being bitten, one of the fuckers little kids. A Police car draws up and I can make out the faces of the same two officers who stopped us that time when Simon was pissed. Is that the city force? Two guys who hate students?

Part 1: New Beginnings

In the living room are six strangers I've never seen before with Alex and James, talking about some film with Tom Hanks. I can't stand Tom Hanks. One asks me "What course do you do?"

"Film" I reply.

"Really, we all do film, I've never seen you before."

"I only go in on Mondays," I tell them.

"Why's that?" he asks me. The room fills silent and they all stare at me like an experiment waiting for my answer. But I say nothing and just stare blankly at each of them individually.

"Are you going into the course today, it's a Monday?" they ask me.

"No," I reply. With that they all leave, shaking my broken bandaged hands goodbye, like I'm never going to see them again, they know my fate has already been sealed.

Amy, Linda, Christina and Taylor and his new mate Little Rob replace them in the living room. I am informed by the three witches, sorry, I mean girls, who had a house discussion whilst I was away and they have drawn up a rotary for the TV. I am told this:

1. *We cannot watch Football*
2. *We have to watch certain Soaps*
3. *The girls get to choose what to watch certain days off the week and between certain times*
4. *If there's a film on we have to vote*

The list continues but I switched off after point one about the football. I nod my head at all this, stand up and unplug MY TV and take MY TV into MY Room, where I promptly put the football on. Taylor and Little Rob knock on the door, holding a six-pack of lager each so I decide to let them in. We hear the Witches bad mouthing me in the living room. Unable to decide what to do without a TV they try a conversation but it fails miserably and they realise they have nothing to talk and no reason to even be friends. Welcome to the modern world.

THREE'S COMPANY

Alex

Lying on Amy's bed, Linda and Amy on either side of me, I pretend to close my eyes, drifting into deep thought. "I fancied Kurt," Amy says and my eyes flicker open resting on a giant poster on her wall of the Nirvana lead singer.

"I wish I could have been Kurt Cobain" I reply taking in the photos on the wardrobe, Amy with Samantha.

Linda stands up to leave. "First there was heroin then there was cocaine, then everyone talks about Kurt Cobain." She slams the door shut, hasn't been the same since the fresher's ball, big mood swings, bad news as she's from Essex.

I move closer to Amy. "Why would you want to be him? He's dead because he was addicted to heroin." Amy asks.

"Because he was a modern revolutionary, like John Lennon" I am John Lennon reincarnated in my minds eye though I decide not to share this with her yet.

"But don't you think it's selfish to kill yourself?"

Oh get a life I think, but again decide not to tell her. "But you told me you've thought about killing yourself? Isn't that hypocritical?"

"No, because I wouldn't have to live with the aftermath, I'd be dead. I don't want the aftermath of anyone else's death"

"Maybe that's what Kurt wanted - to see the aftermath, be a martyr in death, he's immortal now" And I swear I can see Kurt Cobain's poster wink at me.

Amy sees me staring at the photos of her and Samantha, so I look towards her lava lamp and closes my eyes again. The joss stick in her room goes out and she lights another one. "I love the smell of joss sticks," she tells me.

"Do you ever think about doing drugs?" I ask her - the time had come for mind games.

"I want to, but I'm scared I'd get addicted. I don't want to end up like Matt"

"Smoking spliffs is ok. I smoked some with Matt the other day" I had to blackmail him.

"I thought you didn't like him. Does he do harder stuff?" She asks with a glint in her eye that is both inquisitive and scared.

I pause for dramatic effect. "I wanted to see things from his point of view." The CD stops and Nirvanas 'Nevermind' finishes. "Listen to this" I say putting on the Elastica album I stole out of Matt's room.

"I recognise this. Do you like them?"

"Yeah"

"Can I burrow your album?"

"Sure" It isn't mine so she can keep it!

"They always play this song at clubs, then that other song that goes 'do you remember the first time' "

"Pulp" I reply, another album stolen from Matt's room. "They're

Part 1: New Beginnings

brilliant, real working class"

"But you're middle class?"

"I want to be working class." Just for a day, then I'd hand the passport back.

"Perhaps I should borrow the album, give it a listen?" She asks wanting to be hip, to be liked, that's all any of us want.

"Sure" Another one of Matt's albums to buy sex with. She's such a musical prostitute this girl a true mercenary. The lava lamp starts to form into Samantha.

"I want to lose weight," Amy tells me looking miserable.

"Why? You are the person you are, a natural beautiful person, Amy, she's lovely." Shall I shag her first then get into a conversation to find out more about Samantha? Or just get to the goal standing?

"It's not my fault, I have an disorder in my body that means I put on weight. I've been to the doctors but there's nothing I can do." She cries looking back towards the poster of Kurt.

"Have you ever thought of dieting or doing exercise you lazy cow," I whisper.

"What?" She replies.

"Its mind over matter, if you convince yourself you want to lose weight you will. You must be happy within yourself first" I smile gently, touching her hand to reassure her.

"I'm fat and ugly" Amy replies, hoping the more she puts herself down the more I'll build her up.

"You're natural and beautiful" I lay my head down on her lap, Samantha…. Samantha…. Samantha… and whisper it continually to myself to keep focus of my mission. Amy starts to play with my hair gently stroking it. The mission is working. "Samantha… Samantha" I whisper by mistake, pretending it's her running her hands through my hair.

"Everyone fancies Samantha" Amy says her hands still rubbing through my hair. "She always got the guys I wanted"

I take this as my invitation - the next sentence must be poetic, must be soul searching, must be the unlocking of the gates. "I think she's fake, she's not natural, all the guys are thinking of you but they're scared to approach in case you say no" Perfect. Perfect. Lean head up towards Amy so she can see the warmth and emotion in the eyes…I'm deserving of an Oscar. Amy leans forward towards me and we kiss. Lying on my back and Amy is going on top, woman in stride. Lay back and think of England I guess is the method *"Samantha…Samantha…"*

Amy's gone away for the weekend and Samantha stays in her bedroom whilst she looks at perspective universities in the south for next year. I rest my head on the bed pretending to be asleep. "I'm really jealous of Amy," Samantha says, hinting that she knows.

"Why? How could you possibly be jealous of Amy?" I reply looking up at the ceiling, beginning to play with my own hair trying to formulate a plan.

"Everything... nice house, new friends, university. I feel like I've been left behind, I feel like she's moved on without me, I feel lost I guess." Samantha replies almost laughing but managing to keep a straight face, what's so funny?

"That's crazy, I think you're great, you're going to go to university, you're beautiful, really natural, to be honest I think Amy is jealous of you." I turn my head and look at her.

"How?"

"Because you're strong, more popular, more beautiful, more confident. Amy has no self-confidence, because she's jealous of you. You are what Amy wants to be." I nearly have me convinced, let alone her, I'm certainly good - this could be my profession, Amy's bed my black couch, a true psychiatrist is a Pimp.

"I know you slept with Amy," she tells me throwing the game out.

I look at her pretending to be shocked "It was a mistake, I wanted to comfort her but I kept thinking of someone else." Wink, wink, nod, nod, now suck my cock.

She smiles, a devils smile, enticing me in. Amy made the move on me – but Samantha will wait for me to make the move on her, I'm in control of this game – and like a rabbit caught in the headlights I do as her eyes tell me to... leans in and kiss. She cock teases me long enough and pushes me violently away... "Alex! How could you do that, what about Amy?" Pretending to play the hurt best friend game is her witch's magic.

"God, I'm sorry" I reply, guilt etched across a face of marble stone. I'm where I want to be - in control - lean in and kiss her, then pull away again and look all confused...

"Amy must never know," she says.

Fucking behind her back, hiding in my room fucking whilst Amy's asleep...this turns me on. I look at the lava lamp and it forms into Amy trapped watching me and she's crying. "Oh Samantha, oh Samantha" I cry out.

Part 1: New Beginnings

"Oh Amy, Oh Amy" she whispers and smiles to herself. *Game Set and Match.*

The door slams downstairs. The footsteps crash up the stairs. I heard the entire argument. She knocks at my door. Do I let her in? "Come in." I'd be stupid not to.

Rachel, Taylor's sixteen-year-old girlfriend, steps in, wearing her usual tight black top and tight black skirt; she's quite chubby though but has a big pair of tits.

She sits on the bed next to me. "Taylor and I just had argument," she tells me.

I know this but I pretend I don't. I heard everything and what she threatened to do. "What about?" I ask, pretending not to be interested as I stare at the TV screen. 2001 Space Odyssey.

"Taylor's so boring, I wanted to go out but he just wanted to sit in front of the TV, that's all he wants to do, watch bloody football, bloody Reading football club," Rachel replies. I heard what she said afterwards though she doesn't say this, that she threatened, - 'to go upstairs and fuck me' - if he didn't take any notice of her and take her out somewhere. He ignored her and she continued saying – 'I mean it'. She's a very sad mixed up girl is Rachel. She's sixteen but has the mental of seven.

I don't care either way; I'm fucking Amy each day saying that it's a mistake and it shouldn't have happened, I don't enjoy doing this but its Samantha's idea. She said if I want to secretly go out with her I have to keep fucking her best friend and then tell her it was a mistake, its crazy but who am I to argue. I just ignore Rachel. I'm not really interested; to be honest I'm exhausted. Rachel doesn't know what to do, I know this, she knows this – she can't leave, as she'll lose face with both Taylor and me. She doesn't know how to initiate this at all, she knows she's made a massive mistake but she's so young and stupid she'll do it anyway.

"Fuck me" she says jumping on me and begins to push my hand onto her breast. I nearly fall off my bed, but my room is so small that I fall back against the wall. As I kiss her I think about Taylor, we've become best mates these first two months, I can't do this to my new best mate, can I? He's only downstairs, he'll hear everything, he'll know. This turns me on...Oh Samantha, you've taught me well, after I fuck Rachel the game will change, and I'll be the master puppeteer. The minute my dick goes into hers I come in one breath, Rachel being the sixteen year old girl she is bursts out with a scream of orgasm, how she managed that when I didn't even penetrate I don't ask, obviously having to decided to throw herself whole heartedly into the project of making Taylor jealous.

"I want to sit up here for ten minutes," she tells me and we sit in complete silence.

Hate in both our eyes, we dare not look at each other's disgusted faces. I go back to the film on TV as she lights a cigarette looking at her watch. "What does it all mean? The evolution or de-evolution of man? I'm going to start taking drugs so I can understand these films." I say to her as after sex conversation, better than a cigarette. Rachel then laughs stupidly; I didn't even tell a joke and slams the door shut. I stare at the TV, as the planet becomes the baby.

Taylor

Matt comes in, sees I'm watching Reading Football club on TV, my new mate Little Rob from my law course next to me. "Where's Alex?" He asks, glazed eyes and looking like he wants to kill him as usual.

"Upstairs fucking Rachel!" I reply.

"Fucking slimy cunt!" Little Rob says, he only met Alex today; an opinion has formed for life.

I don't think Matt believes me; I was hoping he would and kill them both with his cricket bat. Instead Matt just looks at the screen and says "Nationwide League bollocks" grabbing a lighter for his joint and goes into his bedroom.

Rachel comes into the living room and begins to cry straight away.

My first proper girlfriend and she's just slept with my ex-best mate. I hate university.

WOKING BOYS

"Woking Boys here to stay.... Shag your women, drink your beer, we are the Woking... BOYS!" Phil and Garry sing in unison as the car hurtles down the M5 motorway. If it was to go any faster blue lighting would cascade across the bonnet and they would find themselves back in 1955.

Phil between steering checks himself out in the mirror. His short black cropped hair, Elvis eyes, 'Joe Cool' zipped up jumper, designer. He couldn't wait to get down to Southampton, see his oldest mate Matt Ryan, but also get some of this 'squeaker' student

Part 1: New Beginnings

pussy he'd heard about. He hated students but he'd never fucked one, too intellectual for him.

"What do you think of Charles Dickens versus Joseph Heller writings?" he always imagined them saying with a glass of wine and a cigarette holder.

"Er, I like Hugh Hefner" would be his reply.

"Oh, how Catch 22 darling!"

"I've caught what? Jesus, I should have worn a condom. You could have told me bitch, phone yourself a taxi home"

Garry, sits in his black shirt, blue jeans, cropped hair like Phil's, the quieter of the pair, the more sensitive one, but his thoughts as regards wanting some 'squeaker' action was the same. "You're so dark, mysterious, a real man who works nine to five for his living, not like these student guys who dress like girls," he pictured them saying wearing nothing but a bikini.

"I think its very pc of you to wear a bikini in the middle of winter," he would reply.

Welcome to Southampton the sign reads and they prepare themselves for streets of naked students dancing round poles, smoking Indian peace pipes, and discussions on religion and politics. Instead, what greets them is a gust of wind from the windy city and bright blinding sunlight for a cold autumns day. "I can't see a fucking thing!" Phil exclaims, grabbing for his shades but touching Garry's hand by mistake.

"What are you doing? Trying to hold my hand?"

"I was trying to find my shades"

"You was trying to hold my hand, just because we're visiting students doesn't mean you have to start acting like one"

"You wish, you're just too embarrassed to say you liked it when my hand touched yours"

They look out the window. "Where's the naked girls dancing round totem poles?"

"Fucking students, they can't even get that right"

A mad tramp, dribbling yesterday's trash bin dinner down his front hurtles across the road. Phil slams on the breaks and the tramp stares motionless into the car, piss drips down his torn and frayed trousers. "What the fuck are you doing cunt!" Phil shouts out the window.

"Nutters! Two nutters!" the Asian tramp shouts at them and begins to walk with a limp towards the window.

"Wind the fucking window up Phil… hurry!" Gary says, as the

tramp approaches continuing the dribble shouting - 'two nutters'.

The window reaches its destiny as the tramp hurtles his face into the glass, and his features smudge up like an oil painting. Phil sticks up two fingers. "Fuck you mate!" and the car hurtles off down the road. Garry turns back to see the tramp standing in the centre of the main road, limping down, trying to catch the car up, "I've never seen an Asian tramp before"

"Sure this is it?" Garry asks.

Phil re-checks the address, seemed a nice area from outside, they hadn't seen one student walking around, maybe it was wrong? This seemed like normal suburbia.

They reach the front door and just stare at it. Both thinking, shall we turn back?

"Well, fucking knock then!" Phil tells Garry.

"He's your mate, isn't he?" Garry replies.

"I'll fucking do it then you muppet!" Phil taps on the door and then looks at Garry with a look of disdain, "you cunt," he says. Linda opens the door, Phil looks her up and down, too much gel in her hair, just the way he liked it, tart, probably doesn't give out though, his first 'squeaker' catch of the day. "Is Matthew in?" Phil asks, the embodiment of politeness. Linda's face drops with the mention of Matt Ryan's name, opens the door and points them towards the living room, she then runs upstairs, slamming her bedroom door shut without as much as a "hello" or "please come in." "What are you waiting for you cunt!"? Phil motions for Garry to step inside.

"She didn't invite us in"

"No, she didn't invite you in, she invited me in and ran upstairs, what does that tell you?"

"That she went to be sick?"

They step into the hallway following the noise into the living room where the door is open. Sitting down with a joint in his mouth is Matt Ryan, puma ski hat still on and both hands bandaged up. "Matt?"

Matt motions up from the haze of smoke and stares for a couple of seconds, trying to work out who the fuck these people were in his stoned state of mind. He smells the fumes of Woking and boy racers that give a recognised look of 'Hell's Kitchen' and his past.

"Alright Matt" Garry says wondering if he even remembers him such is his glazed eyes, this could be embarrassing if he doesn't know who he is. Phil looks round the living room; it looks normal,

Part 1: New Beginnings

a TV, a sofa, clean carpet, and a radiator with socks on, he was confused.

"Bit cold for those shorts isn't it?" Phil finally breaks the silence as he stares at Taylor in his Reading Football strip on this autumn's late afternoon and then Rachel holding onto his arm.

"Do you not want to know our names?" Rachel finally says. Phil and Gary look at each other and then back at the sofa, feeling like they're part of a circus act and they have to entertain the crowd, staring at them constantly, without ever leaving a breath of privacy to them. "I'm Rachel and this is Taylor" Taylor places his hand up as a salute in silence.

"We need to get stuff from the car" Phil stands up and expects Gary to follow him but he remains staring at the TV set. "I said we need to get stuff from the car" Phil repeats again. Phil walks out the living room and opens the front door and waits by the car. Gary doesn't come out. He walks back into the living room. "Do you want to get your sleeping bag from the car?" He looks at Gary nodding his head.

"Oh right, yeah" Gary finally cottons on, steps outside by the car and opens the boot. "There's nothing in the boot?" Gary says.

"Its so they cant hear us"

"Oh right"

"That guy is a mute"

"What your mate Matt?"

"Not him you cunt! That guy in the Reading football club strip"

"Oh right, yeah, cunt, I agree"

"No. I didn't say he was a cunt, I said he's a mute"

"Yeah, right, a mute." They both nod their heads at one another. "See what I mean then?"

"Er, yeah... er, no, not really?"

"I want to fuck his girlfriend, that Rachel slag, right?"

"Yeah, right, me too"

"But if he's a mute, it must mean she's a spastic as well right?"

"You worried about catching something that turns you into a spastic? I don't think you can, unless its from a toilet seat, I was reading the other day..."

"Will you shut up you cunt! I just don't know how to act among these people?"

"What spastics?"

"Students you cunt!"

Matthew collapses on his bed and lights up another joint. This bollocks he can do without. This bollocks he thought he had got away from. As he lye's on his bed he can feel the walls starting to cave in. It suddenly feels cold in the house. He puts his hand on the radiator, it felt warm, but no heat was circling the room, only ghosts of his past. As he looks out the bedroom window, he can swear he sees the colour of the leaf's change, the sun disappears, the outside world starts to drip with the blood of his soul, and the hard rain begins to fall. They came to visit and brought 'Hells Kitchen' with them into his autumn sun of a different life.

Phil knocks on Matthews door. He opens it with a joint in his mouth and a glazed look of 'who are you? Get the fuck out of my house'

"What's the PA of then?" Phil enquires for the plan of action.

"What?" Matthew mumbles out. "You want to see my sound system?"

"P OF A, Plan of Action, you silly cunt" Phil replies politely.

Matthew just stares for a few seconds, torn between kicking his past out of his world for good or rejoicing with these people in the knowledge he has left them all behind. Spit in the eyes of fools he decides. "I'll take you down the student union bar and then to a club"

"Be fall of students though wont it?" Phil worryingly replies.

"Yeah, it's a student union bar" Matthew replies spelling it out for Phil.

"Any squeakers?" Phil asks, hoping the evening can be saved before it's even started.

"What?"

"Squeakers, pussy, fanny, bitches"

"You mean women?" Matthew replies.

"I'm not sleeping on that sofa, so I want to get my hole"

"Your hole? I thought you was into girls?" Matthew just stares back blankly; feeling like this entire conversation has been alien to them both.

"This place is a mental asylum. First of all there's a mute and no-one says anything, then this…" Phil replies. "I'm going to shower and I don't know how long I'll be, I feel… dirty"

Garry, knocks on Matthew's door and enters. "Alright mate, can I borrow your mirror?" As he stands in front of the mirror, styling his hair, he tries to think of some conversation to start with Matthew, who he can see staring up at the ceiling. "Nice room"

Part 1: New Beginnings

"Thanks"

After grooming himself he waits in silence, sitting on Matthew's bed for Phil to return down from the shower. "Do you like living in Southampton?"

"I love it" Silence.

"This tastes like piss!" Gary exclaims to Phil, a pint of lager in his hand from the student union bar. "I would have got more out of it if I'd urinated in the pint myself!"

"I can't drink this, its tap water" Phil informs Gary and returns the drink to the bar.

"Yes mate?" the barman approaches him.

"I'm not your mate and I'm no fucking student. Give me a bottled beer" Phil informs him. The barman raises his eyebrows, another townie wanker visiting a mate who's now long gone from whatever rock they originally crawled out from. He goes to pour the beer into a glass. "What the fuck are you doing?!" Phil stops the guy's hand. "I drink out of the bottle, I'm not a fucking faggot! Fucking hell Matt, this is shit, it's full of students" Phil looks across the room, not one girl had eyed him up since he'd been in here, he'd stared at all of them until they would look back, but it got embarrassing when no-one would, it made him look deranged.

One girl, who Matt had seen briefly with Linda that first week, Marie, comes up to Phil and asked "Do you need any help?" he was so shocked that she then spelt out "M - E - D - I - C - A - T - I - O - N" Her friend Charlotte then joins her and eyes Phil and Gary up.

"You two don't look like students" Charlotte comments to Phil and Gary.

"Course not, do we look like cunts?" Phil replies.

"Yes" They girls reply in unison and walk away.

Phil heartbroken turns on Matt. "I was fucking in there to get my hole until you looked at them and put them off! It's fucking shit. We fucking hate students, this is shit"

"Why did you come down here then, I'm at university, I'm a student." Matt replies

"Not really a student though are you, you know, you're a Woking boy, you're all right, you're not a proper student, not a cunt"

Matt walks in silence, kebab in hand, wishing he was a piece of kebab meat layered in chilli sauce, it would be a quick and tasty death, rather than being brain dead with these two. He'd only been away for a few months, it was November now, but it felt like he'd been away for years, it felt like a different life, a different person. Since they'd come to visit, the cold had hit him, he felt ill for the first time in Southampton, running a temperature, running from ghosts.

Phil puts his arm round his oldest mate. "Great fucking night mate, I know I took the piss out of the fucking beer and the club and that, but I had a great time, pulled five women and beat Garry hands down!"

"Forget about it" Matthew replies, thinking more about how to get to bed without these two trying to nick his room. Five women? When was that?

"But listen, do you know what would rap the night up perfectly? You letting me use your room to shag that Rachel"

"She's going out with my mate Taylor"

"Yeah but I'm your oldest fucking mate, not that cunt, where's that cunt now? No-where, it's me and Gary you spent the night with"

"You want to spend the night with me?" A confused Matthew replies, he takes a couple of steps back, this was a development he just never saw coming, he knew Phil and Gary were close but this was unexpected.

"You going to let me have that room or not if I pull her, I'll be discreet?"

Matt knew Phil hasn't a chance of pulling Rachel, ever since she shagged Alex she'd been living like a nun, showering daily, even watching Reading play football with Taylor, such was her penance. Every time Alex walked into the living room, Taylor would say – "Time to shower dear". And up she would go and have a shower until Taylor believed her to be clean again. "I want you to name all the Reading players wife's and children?"

Taylor would test her daily, such was her dependence on him, Matt reasoned it was because she was a man and had a sex change. When Taylor was out the room and it was just Rachel and Matt, he went to ask her about her true sexuality at birth but she started to talk before he could - "You know Alex came the very second he put his dick into me, I didn't even feel it, what a disappointment" - she told him matter of fact, like it was an everyday conversation you mention out of the blue like 'oh by the way darling we need more loo rolls'.

Just say yes to Phil, Matt decides and the problem will go away

Part 1: New Beginnings

once he finds there's a dick down there. "Yeah, sure" Get caned and watch Phil crash and burn with a possible transsexual was the best late night TV at this precise day in his life...

...Phil gets his and Garry's sleeping bags out of the car and returns to the living room. He sets his stall out on the sofa then throws a sleeping bag onto Garry's head. "Crashed and burned then, makes us even" Garry says slyly out of the corner of his mouth.

"You've been asleep mate, I banged that Rachel slag on the sofa whilst you was sleeping"

"Couldn't have been very good then as I didn't wake up!"

"She was screaming but I told her to shut up, so not to wake you, see what a good mate I am"

They wake in silence, salvia dropping from their mouths, stinking of lager, kebabs and cigarettes. "What's the PA of today then faggot?" Phil asks Garry as politely as he can first thing in the morning with a hangover. He wonders why he didn't pull last night, they must all be lesbians these students he decides.

"Not doing the same as last night, that's for fucking sure." Gary replies. Nice breakfast will put him in the mood to deal with Phil and his insults all day just because he didn't pull that Rachel bird.

"Lets go down to Bourmouth, make the weekend of it now we're down here" Phil replies, he doesn't want to go it alone, especially now Matthew was no fun anymore, must be something to do with that Ski Hat he wears, its taken away his personality. "I reckon I've got another shot at that Rachel bird, I don't want to leave without leaving a bit of Woking in someone"

The rain hails down across the car on the motorway. Matthew felt it his duty to see off these demons and face these ghosts' head on. He'd hidden underneath his sheets earlier Hiding from the demons in his nightmare he had that night - They chased him through Southampton, the quicker he ran, the more naked he became, until he was just truth and bone. He had felt so cold. The town had no colour, no life. Even if it meant destroying him whole, he couldn't keep going through this state of mind every time friends came to visit, or when he returns home for Christmas. The Jam blares out Phil and Gary singing. "Weller, they should build a statue of the man"

"Do you know what these songs are about?" Matt asks them.

"Woking, you cunt!" they both say back in unison.

"Exactly, its about Woking" Matthew replies, but they still didn't get it. He sits in the back seat, watching the rain and closing his ears to silence. "It's nearly Christmas, what happened to time?" he whispers to himself, away from the disinterested parties up front. He writes in the steamed up car window. As they pass a car on the motorway, a kid looks out, like Matthew from this passing car window, it is him from many years ago, he looks lost, he can see his mum and dad in the front, his brother in the back with him. The kid writes in the window – DON'T LOOK BACK.

Phil and Gary run towards the Arcade and leave Matthew completely soaked outside a hot dog van. He waits there and watches the rain. Smelling the sizzling hot dogs and decides his 'tenner' will be better spent on two hot dogs and a can of coke. He walks up to the seafront, no umbrella, and is soaked to the bone as he eats his only meal for the day, watching the people stare at him like he's insane, wishing the rain will swallow him up and leave him be, away from all these strangers who masquerade as friends blinding his touch and sight.

"We're going" Phil says, he tries the door handle but it's locked. He knocks again, "We're going you cunt!" He knocks a couple of more times; loud enough to wake up the house. He hears movement from upstairs, Linda's room opens, and Songs of Praise blares out.

"Lets just get out of here and fast Phil" Gary motions towards the door. They both run.

Matthew hears the car drive away. He can feel the warmth return to the room. He opens the curtains and looks out the window. The colour returns to the trees.

The rain has stopped and the sunlight glistens through into his eyes, telling him to find a cool breeze and take it easy. No more nightmares, only dreams.

The car draws out of the road and it halts to a stop as the Mad 'Nutter' Asian tramp with a limp appears. "Close the fucking windows!" Gary cries out.

But the tramp doesn't go towards the car; he takes a bowler hat from his jacket and bows before them, moving the bowler hat along the line of the road, to show them the way back. As Phil drives past, the tramp calls out - "Nutters!"

Phil winds the window down. "You weren't wrong mate!"

Part 1: New Beginnings

JESUS SAYS I NEED TO GET HIGH
Johnny

The view is life changing from up here. I can see the entire windy city lit up for Christmas, the bright light illuminating into the city paved with gold. Every colour has a name, every name has its own vision, and every vision seems possible for me in this town. "Johnny, get down" I can hear them shout.

"I'm post box surfing," I shout back. I can feel inside every letter, every word, and every secret thought of you all up here. I'm a superhero, 'The Post Box Surfer'. They'd have to be zombies in it though; I can't stand films without zombies. "Shit!" the giant envelope that is riding me on the crest of its wave across the cities landscape of Christmas lights and gold, starts to enclose on me. Giant lips begin to lick the corners and it begins to fold over, I'm slipping inside the envelope. "Fuck!" I won't be able to breathe, won't be able to escape, doomed inside an envelope with no address. I'll end up back in Manchester. Maybe it wasn't such a good idea. Thinking it would be funny usually means its funny for others but pain for you. They all egged me on - Simon, Steve, Matt, James, and Blonde Paul. The acid what we took had turned me into a laughing jelly, maybe I need to take more and more and more... "I gotta jump before I'm posted back home," I shout to the others and I lose my balance to escape the envelope seal and fall. I won't be taking anything for a while yet. Not after what I've just broken. I don't think the eight pints of Guinness helped. I'm just a microdot on the face of this planet. I reckon my ankle is broken. I thought it would be funny to see the world from up here. Standing tall like the king of all that is written inside. Climbed up there fine, but my balance went when I stood up straight. My ankle twisted and I fell. I landed on my foot and it twisted more as I threw my hands out on the pavement to catch my fall. I feel the gravel inside the cuts; these are going to itch like hell. Why did I do it? Standing on the post box to see if I could surf.

No doctor's note. No medical report. Just a sprain. Still the Course doesn't need to know that. Its nice for November, the sun seems to be permanently out in this city, our spiritual home. Kids full of dope, taking drugs. This place felt like one big park, a return to the sixties hallucinogenic type of crowd, our own Woodstock, a blue print for the decade. Last time I knew a winter like this was back home in Manchester, when Ecstasy came in start of the decade and it became the new designer posh drug. There I was in the Hacienda club just out of school, listening to bad music that this E would change into a work of classical art, Mozart, Beethoven, it was better than working for a living.

Roll a joint and sit in the garden. The weeds look like they could do with some pulling. I'm in my summer shorts and T-Shirt. I can see the neighbours outside in winter jackets staring in; I wave with the joint in my hand and look round the garden. "How you doing?" I ask.

"How long are you people going to be living here?" they ask with a scowl.

"The rest of our lives," I answer in the truth of our world.

I can't be arsed to go to the toilet, maybe piss helps planets, and I was drinking Guinness so I'd be watering the plants with Irish water. The neighbour stares at me as I urinate into the garden, I wave back with the joint and point towards my ankle where the bandage is strapped for the sprain. They didn't even give me crutches; I've always wanted a pair of crutches, gutted. The seeds from the gear I brought need water to but I wont urinate on these, or shall I? It could make the weed a cross between alcohol and grass; that would be a plant everyone would want to buy. I sit back down on the deck chair and work out my grand plan for this new drug. We'll call it 'Johnny'. Self-publicity is the best publicity.

Clem, my housemate joins me. He's a big lad; big face, big man, wearing his black overcoat that makes him looks like a pit worker and surreal rapist. "Alright Johnny"

"Alright Clem." We sit in silence. We've said all that's needed to be said.

He puts on 'Bring it On Down' by Oasis, he loves the line - 'wiping your shit from the sole of my shoe tonight.' Take a sip of my cup of coffee, my fifth of the day. I don't think it's addictive at all; I just need to keep drinking it to stop my shaking. It's medicinal. Clem declines the joint when I offer it. "What's wrong Clem?" I ask this after I finish the joint, as my reaction time is very slow due to the ankle being sprained.

"I think I want to rape your friend Simon"

I roll a new joint and pretend he didn't say what he just said. Keith Reynolds comes into the house, his curly frizzy hair and goatee beard seemed to be tinged with a touch of blood, fake fangs in his mouth. "What's going on Keith?" I ask.

"Occultism Johnny, join us."

Part 1: New Beginnings

"Who else has joined?"

"The O'Sullivan twins"

"I've always wanted to fuck the O'Sullivan twins!" Jenny was the sexier one, but Liana was bigger. I like my girls big, loads of flesh, big tits. That girl from Home and Away, Sally, she's got the biggest pair of breasts I've seen for a girl her age, when she grows up she's going to be my perfect wife.

After knocking on the door to the address Keith Reynolds gave me to join his occult, as I want to fuck the O'Sullivan twins, I am confronted by a girl from our course, Stacy, she is dressed in a black long dress and her face is painted red, she has a long black wig on. She smiles and vampire teeth stare back at me. Usually Stacy has short hair, glasses and dresses very conservatively. "Keith said to expect you Johnny, come in." Stacy turns away and I follow her into a drawing room. Complete Darkness. A stage light comes on and Keith Reynolds is lit like the angel of death.

"The high priestess has shown you to me," Keith Reynolds says wearing a big black cape, face covered in blood, biting into raw meat.

A coffin is used as the dressing table. Fiona, a girl who never blinks is sitting down dressed in white. Across from her is Clem, dressed as he normally is with his black train jacket on, looking like a paedophile. "All right Johnny," Clem nods in my direction. He opens his jacket slowly and he has nothing on underneath but a pair of white underpants, stained. Keith and Stacy take some raw meat and walk hand in hand into his bedroom.

"I thought the O'Sullivan twins were going to be here?" I ask disappointed that I wont get my length.

"They are Johnny, but first you must take the virgin." Keith opens the door to his bedroom and shows both Liana and Jenny O'Sullivan dressed up in sword and sorcery costumes, they wave and smile. "Hi Johnny" "Hiya Johnny"

"You wish to make a doll of Mark Gammond and curse him?" Keith informs me.

"How did you know that?" I reply.

"I know everything Johnny. You must take a lock of his hair and bed his daughters"

"Sounds reasonable"

"I must initiate you joining us," Keith says and locks the bedroom door. Screaming is heard and the slobbering of raw meat. Keith

MJ Gunn

Reynolds's occult is an excuse for him to have group sex with as many birds as he can. Why didn't I think of that?

Fiona motions for me to sit next to her on the sofa. I wonder if anyone's inside the coffin? She places her hand on my crutch. "You must take me, as a virgin I can only be initiated in by a new member." I way up and the pros and cons and decide to fuck Fiona, that way we can see if her eyes ever blink.

Clem sits drinking a can of bitter. "I have bad thoughts Johnny, about your friend Simon…"

The doorbell rings as I start my business with Fiona, she still hasn't blinked, James walks into the living room and takes a seat. "Don't mind if I watch do you Johnny?" He asks. I can't say no, he's a mate, plus he's a fucking weirdo.

Walk the town unable to find anyone I know. It's a Saturday night and they've disappeared on me since I left the High Priestess house. Maybe I'm invisible and no one can see me since I joined the occult? I keep checking my teeth with my tongue for any signs of fangs. I always thought I'd end up a zombie, not a vampire.

"Johnny!" Matt Ryan is across the street and calls me over. I join Matt with his housemates Amy, Taylor, Alex, Linda and some other guy called Little Rob. This is too confusing for me so I decide to pair off with Amy into the club and back to their house as I think she's got the biggest pair of breasts I've ever seen.

Back in her bedroom, nothing is going to happen, she's not up for it, in love with someone else and wants to talk. She's nice enough but I could be getting stoned, or trying to fuck another member of Keith Reynolds's occult rather than just talking, so I decide to leave. She's still talking as I shut the door. "I love him so much, but he fucks me then leaves me. Do you want to know who it is? It's someone who lives here. You know them"

"I don't care," I whisper as I slam the door shut and tears start to fall inside wooden rooms.

I knock on the High Priestess's door; she answers dressed as conservative Stacy. "Yes?"

"High Priestess, is there any action tonight?"

"What are you talking about?"

"Like earlier"

"Earlier?" She slams the door in my face.

Keith Reynolds comes to the door. "What's up Johnny?"

"What the fucks going on Keith?" Keith slams the door in my

Part 1: New Beginnings

face as well.

As I begin my walk to find a floor to sleep on, the icy November air represents a depressing denouement to my boyhood dream of shagging girls in an occult.

I try to sleep in the Halls of residence. I can't get to sleep on Fiona's camp bed. She keeps leaning over and wanting to have sex. I just don't want to shag her again. Ever. I take the camp bed and walk out off her room She is chanting to the ceiling as I leave.

I knock on Simon's door. He is completely wasted. Before he can say no I put the camp bed on the floor and suggest it will just be for tonight. I put Faust on his cd player and press repeat. On the second listen Simon goes to turn it off but I cut him off - "Silent Faust" I light a crafty joint to myself. *Jesus says I need to get high.*

LET ME TAKE YOUR PICTURE
Matthew

It's a Monday so I've gone into college. I'm starting to feel the cold weather now for the first time that I've been living in the windy city. Maybe it's a sign that things are about to change. I walk around for an hour without finding where my lecture is; when I finally do it has just finished. Strangers walk out from my group and nod towards me. "It's Matt Ryan!"

"Alright?" I reply. I haven't a clue who any of them are. I recognise Kane, he walks out holding hands with that sexy rock chick girl called Clarissa. "How's the skating going Kane?" I ask as he places Clarissa on his board and they skate down the hallway without replying.

Martin Pumphrey who teaches me for what I attend on Mondays grabs me. He holds an essay in his hand. When Martin speaks to you he has a habit of standing as close to you as one can without physical contact. His head is nodding up and down; practically head butting me as he speaks. "Excellent Essay" He goes to hand me the essay, I can just make out the mark, 75%, as I go to take it satisfied that my theory of only coming in once a week is working, he snatches it away and nods furiously. My hand is left out like Oliver Twist begging. "Your attendance, is disgraceful" he takes the essay further away and with it my place on the course. His head continues to furiously nod until he realises I have nothing to say and decides to speak instead. "Why, hmm, why? Only Mondays, hmm, why? You still need to make the effort, this is an official warning." He passes over the essay and contradicts himself - "Keep up the good work, the balls in your court, hit me in the face with it..."

I'll play with his head and see if I can get him nodding to the point of combustion. "The grade or not turning up? Or that I get the highest grade but the worse attendance?"

"Interesting theory..." He pauses, "but our leader needs you to turn up"

"Our leader?" I say worried that this is an alien invasion, that when he nods more his head will come off and reveal an alien creature. "The Canadian guy who claims to have seen David Bowie on acid in LA during the seventies? You are willing to be lead by a man who claims something so un-hip?" He remains silent. "Mick and Keith are my leaders"

"Ah, Rolling Stones, 'Let it Bleed', great album, cake on the cover," he replies.

"You know 'Let it Bleed'?" I ask impressed.

"I have all their albums on vinyl up to Some Girls, a great sassy seventies filthy disco album. Why don't you come round my house this week, my wife could do your laundry" And with that he walks away, nodding his head furiously. Why offer to do my laundry? Do I stink?

I'll start going to lectures tomorrow; I had really out done myself by turning up and leaving the house in daylight. I deserve a drink just to celebrate getting this far. I walk into the Angel pub. "Matt Ryan" A girl called Stacy calls me straight away.

"Alright" I reply, "How do you know my name?"

"Everyone knows Matt Ryan"

Sitting at a table as I walk in, deep in conversation are James, Steve and Johnny who was unsuccessful trying to shag Amy the other night. "Matt Ryan!" they all shout. "What are you doing it's a Tuesday, we only see you on Mondays?" Steve asks me.

"What do you mean its Tuesday? Its Monday, that's why I came into the course"

"It's Tuesday, ask anyone"

I walk up to the bar, and wait to ask the nice looking bar girl, with the long black hair and nose stud, Marie, she seems to haunt me. "Excuse me, what day is it today?"

"Wednesday" she replies.

"Thanks" Wednesday? Tuesday? Monday? Best not to argue, just go with it.

"Anything for Matt Ryan" she replies as I turn to walk away.

Part 1: New Beginnings

"How do you know my name?"

"You're Matt Ryan. Everyone knows your name. Every name makes its own sound." Again, I decide its best not to argue. What's the point? I'm just an experiment for these people; in fact the degree isn't a film degree but a degree in my life.

"I got an official warning from Martin Pumphrey yesterday, I mean today, or it could be tomorrow? I got to start turning up, all that after getting the highest grade in the degree" I pull my essay out for the lads, to try and get them to join my 'only turn up on Monday' cult.

"The photography project, have you got a group?" James asks me

"Is it important?" I ask, why don't people tell me these things?

"Goes towards your final mark, wasn't you there on Thursday's photography lecture?"

"We do photography?" I sit in stony silence as I realise I am finished on this course, nearly three months in and I'm finished already. An official warning and now a project I knew nothing about. Back home to cocaine snorting Woking. That's why I felt cold this morning; the Gods are preparing me for my return to 'Hells Kitchen'.

"Why don't you join are group?" James suggests. "We've been discussing an idea and you'd be perfect for the biker"

"Yeah, you look kind of rough" Steve replies. Rough? Biker? Visions flash through my head.

"There is one draw back, you'll have to pretend that you fancy Fiona" James tells me sheepishly like he has just told me to win a million pound I've got to suck his cock.

"Who's Fiona?" I ask, some domestic goddess I shall keep and do some method acting with.

"You've never met Fiona?" Johnny replies his eyes don't blink when he mentions her name.

"It'll be a surprise. All you have to do is wear what you're wearing, pretend that you want to marry her and we'll take the photos," Steve tells me very effeminately, I'm sure his leg has just touched mine under the table.

"Marry her? Photographs?" I begin to wonder if this project actually exists. I am the course, the degree; they are studying me, a reality within a reality. Might as well go along with it, either that or look for a real job three years earlier than planned.

The discussion continues in James's room in Halls of Residence, well, what he claims to be his room, the 5th room I've been in which he has claimed is his since September. Clothes scattered on top of his duvet, ash on the floor, shit stains marked in the carpet, wet smelly towels on the radiators that stink the room out and of course... socks. Every student has a draw full of socks and nothing else. Johnny sparks up another 'owl' and offers it to Steve, who stands at the door, he declines the joint saying - "There's something on News-Round about Madonna" and he runs down the hall like a girl into his own room.

That leaves me with Johnny and James in a stoned silence. 'Led Zeppelin 2' blares out. "Blood On The Tracks is a brilliant album", James tells me. Then once he has had the joint for a couple of minutes, he goes back to being completely comatose.

"I thought we were meant to be discussing the photography project?" I say.

"The project?" Johnny asks, confused as me.

"That's why we're here isn't it?"

"I just thought you wanted to get stoned with us?" Johnny replies.

"I do" These guys are like me; they just want to do nothing. It's the best education in life, because once you know nothing you know everything.

"Get Steve in here" James suggests, jumping up and deciding to roll a joint on a book about Bob Dylan. "I've got ten books on Bob Dylan" he tells me with great pride. I've got ten books about the Mr Men but I don't have a wank over it, the guy has got serious Bob Dylan issues.

I leave the room, with the joint, and go Steve's room.

Knocking on the door, I hear a flustered reply asking - "Who is it?"

"Its Matt Ryan" I reply, everyone else seems to say that as my name.

"Wait" I hear the sound of trousers being put on. Steve finally opens the door, red faced, flustered, doing his trousers up and News Round coming to an end.

He invites me in and I see hundreds of Madonna posters covering the walls, along with Marylyn Monroe. "She's my idol," he tells me. "I'd like to tell you a secret."

Before Steve can tell me his sordid Madonna wanking secret, I leave the room and walk at a brisk pace back to room 101, Steve following me in the shadows. I have enough problems without

Part 1: New Beginnings

sharing other peoples. "Matt Ryan would have listened to my secret" I hear the shadow behind me state.

"I am Matt Ryan, that's my name" I reply like Caine in Carter.

"Are you sure?" The shadow asks.

Meeting Fiona for the first time, she is dressed completely in white. It's her wedding day. Her wedding to me. "We need you to look like you could possibly fancy her," Steve tells me. This is hard work. Her dressed in white, me wearing a black bikers jacket, puma ski hat and haven't shaved in two months. I dread to think what the wedding photos are going to look like. I ask about the story behind the photos, "What's my motivation?"

"To stay on the course." They reply. So I decide to let them get on with it. The first photo is of me looking romantically at Fiona, pulling back her veil, does this girl ever blink? I hope they don't expect me to kiss her. Next to her is Clarissa, who I really fancy in that rock chic way.

"I wanted to play the bride?" Clarissa tells me.

"Are you the maid of honour?" I ask, that way I'll get to shag her, as the usual ritual for the groom is to shag the bride's best mate.

"No, I'm nothing to do with this photo project."

"Then why are you here?"

"Fiona's my friend, if she's getting married I thought I better make an appearance,"

"Its not real, its just for a photo project"

"Its not real? Are you sure?" I look at Fiona and she smiles towards me.

The final photo for my part is lying in bed with Fiona. I make sure I'm fully clothed underneath the sheets and pray to God she is. "Do you like wearing a white wedding dress?" I ask her as the photo is taken.

"These are my normal clothes," she tells me. I can't wait for this to finish. We're under Steve's duvet and it stinks of spunk, there's dry tissue and a crusty sock roaming around. Great, I'm lying where Steve had his masturbation over Madonna.

The photo's lay out in the dark room. Steve and Johnny are in control of the final product of my marriage to un-blinking girl, my survival on the course. "It wasn't a real marriage was it?" I ask worried about what Clarissa kept saying.

"Only if I was a justice of the peace" Steve replies and then smiles like he is one.

MJ Gunn

"Where's James?"

"He couldn't cope with the stress of completing this project, he had to go home"

I look at the amazing production story we have created laid out in front of me -

1. Biker gets married to girl who doesn't blink and is in an occult.
2. Biker gets on his bike and then the real owner arrives and people are chased away.
3. Biker sits in masturbated bed fully clothed underneath duvet of crusty tissues and socks with un-blinking occult girl.
4. Madonna masturbating man hangs from tree long shot & close-up, the same tree I found him living up in one Sunday evening.
5. Hollywood.

The course lecturer for photography, some lesbian tutor looks through our photos. She thinks I'm James and I don't correct her. "Where's Matt Ryan?" She asks.

"He had to go home, he's having a nervous breakdown" I reply.

"Is that him in the photos?" She asks, not being able to realise that it is I, wearing the same clothes and puma ski hat stood right next to her.

I exist in this generation as a name for all to behold and call as their own, but never to be seen or spoken in words. *A generational icon of a waster.*

'So this is Christmas...'

The Princes of polarity await their nations state on Top of the Pops. The sofa wait in eager anticipation for the new single 'Whatever' to start up. The song summoning up the last four months of their lives; free to do what they want, free to be…whatever. No longer did they belong to anybody, no longer did they care what people thought of them. As the band appear on stage, a jam packed audience of fifteen to twenty five year olds seem to fill the television studio, three balcony's move as one generation, a horde of noise plotting the downfall of their restriction and imprisonment of youth. A sense of excitement spreads across the windy city, that perhaps this music was going to change everything. For these people it feels like Christmas everyday before they all return home for a few weeks.

Part 1: New Beginnings

For some this was home now and what was once home is now the 'relatives house', steeped in past memories of a bird long flown. No one wanted to go back, not today, not ever, prefer to stay in a wasted bliss of a generation that had found its most important aspect – *'Self'* This was only the beginning for them. The next steps would define a generation, and every generation has a legend, and every legend has its beginning.

It's December 17th. Matt Ryan gets up early and packs his bags. He's going to watch Primal Scream tonight at the Brixton Academy. He views the carnage in the house; various bodies asleep on sofas, chairs and floors, empty cans and bottles scattered around burnt carpets and crushed cigarettes, broken TV aerials, socks and underpants melted into radiators. The Oasis song 'Married with Children' is playing on repeat. On top of the stereo is a photo of Johnny with a message on the back - Thanks for the memories and Class A Drugs, Merry Xmas -

The photo shows Johnny with a beer and joint in his hand, how did he manage to get it developed so quickly?

As Matt reaches the front door, Alex stands on the stairway. "What about tidying up?"

Matt looks around at the mess. "Why don't you get Matt Ryan to do it? I'm going to my Mum's for Christmas"

"But you're Matt Ryan" Alex shouts back to no avail.

Matthew

I keep dreaming.
Can't seem to move.
What's wrong? I'm asked.
Feeling low. (Don't get so high)
Need to change. (Why change?)

I get into a routine of lying in bed till 6pm. Listening to 'Whatever' EP by Oasis, 'This is a Low' and 'Badhead' by Blur. Then I get up and go out, meet my old mates from back here. My favourite Christmas albums to listen to - Buffalo Tom, Boo Radleys and Stone Roses first album, bringing back memories of previous years and Gary Crowley's radio show on GLR. Before I never seemed to have the education to say the words caught in my mind. But that is my life from the day I left in September, an axis point, before and after. Things will never be the same again. Getting up 6pm, changed and styling my hair now that I've put gel in it. I left the ski hat in Phil's car such was my disgust with it, Dazza picked it up, saying he wanted a memento from the night at Primal Scream. I style my hair in the mirror. I look years younger.

I am someone else. I'm not the person who left here in September.

That train journey back was a fast track of memories. Four months of the windy city speeding through me like a tunnel of visions that merge into one dream. A young girl sat opposite me. She was filling in her university application form for next year.

"Where you going?" I asked.

"Manchester, London, or Oxford" she replied. She had these big red rosy cheeks, innocent. In her innocence was a sense of wonder and excitements, questions of 'what ifs' that will trouble and drive her along until that date with destiny next September, the date you leave for three years. I recognised the look, cause it was the same look we all carried back in September.

"I'm at Southampton, just finished my first semester"

"Wow" her eyes lit up, full of eagerness to ask questions and have an insight into another world. "What are you studying?"

"Film. What do you want to study?"

"Drama, I want to be an actress"

"Isn't everyone" I reply, she looks quizzical at me, then gets what I'm saying, politely laughs.

"What's it like? University?"

I take a deep breath and peer out of the window, try and think of something that will mesmerise her, something that will never make her forget. Instead all I said was - "Life changing" I smiled it was the truth.

"In a good or bad way?" she asked, more tentative, in case I put her off the idea of going.

"Like it?" I pause. "I love it"

"You going home to see your family for Christmas?"

"Home? I guess that's what I'm going to find out. Home..."

I worry about what this gel is doing to my hair, as when I wake up it stinks, this must be how Linda feels every morning. Perhaps her and me will have more in common now instead of just arguing over what time I'm playing my music at; perhaps we'll have in-depth discussion about hair gels? 'Whatever' plays as I put the finishing touches to my hair. It would feel like blasphemy to go out without

Part 1: New Beginnings

listening to the full EP. I've listened to it too much I want to marry it. These days leading up to Christmas I stare at the cover of the EP - the giant field and blue sky. If I look hard enough I can see myself in that field, strolling along with a joint and beer in my hand, smiling. By staring at it, part of Southampton has travelled with me, and rather than the cold days of hard rain that falls upon 'Hells Kitchen', I seemed to have controlled the weather, or at least my reaction to the weather. I can smell the sun on my back and the freshly shaven grass, not the damp of the streets, but the freshly cooking turkeys, and the rain lit puddles, under the street lamps.

Its New Years Eve and I hit the town. I can't help but feel superior to everyone. Its like I'm a celebratory for going away to university. I know a life away from all this and they all want in to be my friend to see what they're missing – My own place. Free Money. Drink. Drugs. Music. Britpop they call it. I'm living it.

Just thinking about the last three months gives me a wry smile, knowing I'm going back and I'm not staying here. For the first time ever back in this one horse town I'm in complete control. For once I'm the one buying the rounds in first. The student Loans you cant beat them. I'm on the pool table and some girl I've never met slaps my bottom and we begin to chat. "Where you from?" she asks me.

I pause before I can answer her. "Southampton" I decide, as that is now the truth.

"I've seen you here before though?"

"I used to live here but I got out"

"You make it sound like a prison sentence"

"Isn't it?" Supergrass begins to play on the jukebox. "We are young, we are free," I sing.

"You're one of these pretentious art students who comes back and thinks they're better than everyone else aren't you?"

"No, I don't study art"

"What then, drama?"

I look around at the people in the bar, all my age, all dressed waiting for that call from the masses, the call that has us finally throwing out post Thatcher, throwing out American consumerism, but a referencing our own culture, our own Britain. "Self" I reply.

Adrian Burrows who I haven't seen for years is discussing going to music festivals next year together. "We gotta go the Glastonbury, and Reading, you'll love them"

"You at Uni then Burrows?"

"I was, but I'm taking a year out, going to change courses"

"Are you crazy, why are you taking a year out?"
"You're a first year aren't you?"
"Yeah, so?"
"You'll see what I mean, once that second year hits in"
"I love it, its ace, I'm never going to leave"
"We all start of like that, that first year, you try and recreate it the next year, and that's where the problems begin, because you can't go back."
"So what are we both doing back here then?"
"Passing through mate, passing the time"
"Don't you feel something big is going happen?"
"Into what? Zombies?"
"You know what I mean"
"Yeah, I know what mean."

We then talk about 'Cloudburst' off the Live Forever EP being the best Oasis song. We argue about what their new album will be like next year. I think- "A master piece," He thinks - "They'll sell out". I go to the toilet and avoid him when I walk back, no-ones slags off Oasis, they're my band, I discovered them and introduced them in the canvas of my mind.

Just before midnight strikes, I look round the room. Something was happening. There was a sense of excitement that music is going to change everything. A new generation had come of age. I can sense us becoming more nationalistic. When midnight strikes, I think maybe I should stay? Maybe just live off my student loan for the next two months back at home and then get a job, 9 to 5. It's been great coming back; I don't think I want to leave these 6pm starts and the celebratory life. The last girl I kiss brings me to my senses. "You can't stay back here, then you'll just be the same as the others"

"Wouldn't you kiss me then?"
"Of course not. I can kiss those guys everyday"
"Isn't that shallow?"
"You're the one being shallow by saying you're going to stay here just cause you've had one good night. Why did you leave in the first place?"
"To get out"
"Out from what?"
"Everything"
"Tell me about university and don't say 'I love it' like all the other first year saps, close your eyes and tell me what you see?"

I close my eyes and let my empty canvas paint its portrait. "All around is new music, new fashions. Bright colours, and its warm and colourful, like a rainbow everyday. And there's a change, not just

Part 1: New Beginnings

in me, but everyone there, we're all part of something, it's like after all those conversations of what 'if', and 'if' has finally happened." I open my eyes and she has gone, if she was ever there at all. Maybe it's time to go.

I'll be forever trying to recreate this last week for the rest of my life each time I come back here now, each time more of a disappointment.

On my bed is a belated Christmas present from my Mum. Bed sheets. That's the present. Fucking Bed sheets. But no ordinary bed sheets. These are of the union jack - red, white and blue. There are various band names written on them. Painted on by my brother. I sneak into the living room where my mum is asleep on the sofa. "Thanks" I whisper and kiss her forehead gently goodnight. There are some presents that money can't buy. I pause at the door and look at her, how could she understand what I'm going through? What I'm feeling? What is happening out there for me? But some how mums always know.

Leaving early the next day on the train I didn't say goodbye, not wanting to wake anyone, I didn't know how to say goodbye this time. I want to get to the house in the windy city and miss the rain that falls on 'Hells Kitchen' each New Year morning. I just want to keep warm watching the world from this train. All the faces that pass me by from the window seem to be friends, inviting me in to scatter the floors. I woke up with the smell of it on my clothes. There's limitless sophistication, try my hallucination...

"Hello" I stare up from my minds eye and that same girl on the train who travelled back here with me those two weeks ago is opposite me again, her fresh rosy cheeks more eager of anticipation of the world that awaits her next year.

"Fresh rosy cheeks" I say.

"Fresh rosy cheeks?"

"Yeah, that's what I keep thinking of"

"Did you found out where home was?"

"It's a canvas"

"What's on it?"

"Whatever I desire." We both look out the window and envision our separate dreams.

Just get up. (Don't cry)
        I'll see you someday.
                When everyone else fades away.
                        (I wont fade away)

PART 2

January '95 to Summer '95

The Best of Times

Part 2: The Best of Times

SUICIDE IS PAINLESS

Alex

Portishead's album paints me a picture of sleeping bliss. Curl up inside the duvet. Floating away, staring at the ceiling trying to take my life in. What a difference a year can make. I welcome 1995 in Southampton, staring at a white ceiling that would suffocate others but for me it's my psychotic's couch. What have I achieved? I've fucked Amy to get near her best mate Samantha. Rachel became my next couch suspect, to fuck over my best mate Taylor. Why do I this? The darkness of the Portishead album allows my mind to run wild with accusations and I dream of a lonely walk I take on a cold January morning where the roads are frozen over and each time I stare at these people I mentioned their faces freeze over.

My parents were officially divorced on January 1st. My dad played away from home, we repeat our parent's mistakes, it's in our genes and nothing can stop our fate being theirs. Everything in this place, in our lives seems to go full circle. I know I've fucked people over but I blame it on my parents, you can only live what you witnessed as behaviour.

"I just want to know who I am?" I said over Christmas dinner after too many Sherries.

"Why do you have to analyse everything Alex, why can't you just be?" my sister asked. If it's true about becoming your parents, my mother's fate awaits her.

"Because I want to learn what makes the human mind tick"

"Perhaps you should start with your own first before you fuck up others"

I'm glad to be back. It's warmer here. It's the only place I feel truly safe. There's a smell in this room of heat, sexual heat, thinking heat, dreams of heat. The room is a temperature cooker that I control through the dial of my thoughts. Taylor rushes into my room, crying. "Its Rachel" He looks distraught, a panicked expression of a child whose lost his parents out shopping.

"What about Rachel?" I pretend to say all meaningful, that I actually care about her; I'm hoping she's killed herself then Taylor and me can bond again.

"She's tried to kill herself!" Taylor cries out. A grown man crying, I'd never do that.

I stand up in all my morning glory at midnight, Taylor just looks through my naked body, I pause and look into his eyes, to see if he likes what he sees, but his eyes are lost. Sometimes you should be careful what you wish for. "Is that a new Reading football kit?" I say to break the silence. For the first time since we met, he doesn't even acknowledge his first love, Reading Football Team. She must be dead.

Following him downstairs into his bedroom, Rachel lye's there on the bed, crying, and a bottle of pills empty in her hand. "I want to die," she cries out, a child without its security blanket.

After all that's happened, me shagging Rachel, Taylor turned to me. "I don't know what to do?"

I am a better man than my father. "How many has she taken?" I ask. If she had taken the lot she'd been passed out, she's still awake; she's playing us for complete falls, well, playing Taylor for a complete fall. I've never seen a guy so naive over a woman.

"I don't know, we had an argument, and I left the room. Then when I came back the bottle was empty"

"I don't want to die" Rachel begins to scream, she begins to hyperventilate, she's a good actress, I'll give her that, but I knew that from our liaison in my room.

"Lets take her to the hospital" I say.

Rachel loves this, gives her a chance to be the drama queen. "No, no, I'm not going to a hospital, Taylor…." She then starts to scream for her Oscar, "TAYLOR! NO!".

"Jesus, what shall I do?" Taylor turns to me, holding the empty pill bottle. The scene of the crime is cold.

I've never known any room in this house to be so cold, its winter now, but each month in the windy city has felt like an Indian summer, our duvets are shields.

"This room is freezing," I tell Taylor. Welcome to the winter of out discontent.

Taylor grabs me. "What do I do?!" the bottles of pills fall from his hand and hit the floor. The glass doesn't break, Taylor kicks his foot onto the bottle and it flies across the room, hits the wall in the centre of Reading FC club photo for the season, still, the evidence doesn't break, it bounces back off the team and into Taylor's hand, like a magicians trick. Exhausted from his magic trick he collapses onto the bed next to Rachel. "Don't die!" he says, holding her hand, two suicides in one day. I feel like this must be a joke being played on me, but I realise he is serious, he honestly thinks she's going to die, love must be blind.

I stare at the virgin suicides and wonder if my father is to blame for these. What makes a person want to end their life? Maybe it's

Part 2: The Best of Times

something I should try myself, if I am to fully understand. If I cannot understand, does that make me less of a man? Taylor stroking Rachel's hair looks towards me, helpless, the child who has lost his way home. "I'll get a taxi number," I finally say.

"Alex," he shouts out towards me as I reach the door out of this frozen ice cabin of death, "don't tell anyone ok, I don't want anyone else knowing"

"Sure, you can trust me" Just like he trusted me when I shagged Rachel, like Amy trusts me and I trust Samantha that she takes that morning after pill.

Into warmth of the living room and standing by the radiators along with underpants and socks, taking the events of ones life and fate into my head. Linda is on an armchair discussing hair gel with Matt whose sitting on the sofa, Christina next to him, they've been spending a lot of time together this first week back from Christmas, must be his new hair cut. I'll soon cut him down to size though. "Do you know a taxi number?" I ask, more to spy on them and their budding friendship then to get a taxi number, I know plenty. I hope one of them asks me what all that screaming is about as Rachel starts up again.

"I'm trying to watch Once Upon A Time In America, the greatest film ever made" Matt replies, looking pissed off at me and then towards the noise from Taylor's bedroom, as Rachel's pleas for attention turn into a massacre horror flick.

"What's all that noise?" Christina asks.

I want others to know how pathetic this girl is, perhaps then they wont hate so much for shagging her. "Rachel's tried to kill herself"

Matt doesn't care and continues to watch the TV, as does Christina. Linda has various hair gel products on the table that she is modelling for Matt, they don't believe that for one second Rachel has tried to end it. Takes guts to kill yourself, and Rachel is a coward.

"Well she seems to be making a good deal of noise for someone whose meant to be dead" Linda finally says breaking the monotony of the screams serenading from the ice room.

"Must have been her choice of hair gel" Matt Replies.

"Pills, a bottle of pills" I say, holding my head like I'm an actor on the stage awaiting my next dramatic line to deliver to my loving crowd. After various minutes waiting for them to continue to ask me questions, so I can milk the applause of my public, there is nothing but silence, perhaps my performance wasn't up to scratch? I dial a taxi and wait in the living room for a couple of minutes, trying to get my head round everything. Robert De Niro is on the screen, I should have guessed, Matt only watches films with Robert De Niro in.

"Have you seen Heather's?" Matt finally breaks the silence.

"What's it about?" I reply.

"Christian Slater and Winnoa Ryder kill people at their college and make it look like suicide"

"I didn't kill Rachel"

"Soon suicide becomes the pc of the college and if you kill yourself you're hip"

"What are you suggesting?"

"You tell me, you're the one always wanting to be hip, Alex"

As usual Taylor and Rachel claim to have no money, so I pay for the taxi. She's been getting Benefit cheques to arrive at our house, which she's put down as her legal residence. As for Taylor, he comes from extremely rich parents, they give him an allowance of a thousand pound a month. I get a small allowance as well, but I don't tell anyone, as my parents are divorced I get the full grant; I prefer to keep up the idea of a working class hero to everyone. I'm as rich as Taylor, if not more, Samantha knows, as I felt like she might leave me.

Rachel cries in Taylor's arms in the back of the taxi, I sit in the front and eavesdrop their conversation. The girl is disjointed, why did I ever fuck her? Because it made me like Dad, that's why, fucking anyone that offers it up. We are what are parents make us, since the start of man to the end of time.

"I don't want to go, what if they find something wrong with me?"

"What's going on?" the taxi driver asks.

Rachel begins to freak out, "Don't say anything Alex, I'm warning you, I'll do it, I'll do it" The taxi driver watches them from the rear view mirror, if we're not careful we'll end up walking. I wish she would have taken more pills finished her self off.

"What's wrong with her?" the taxi driver asks as we step outside to the hospital entrance

"She tried to kill herself" I reply, looking for the exact money, I never give tips to these working class foot soldiers.

"What with?"

"Sleeping Pills"

Part 2: The Best of Times

He bursts out laughing, I go to pass him over the exact money, and his face turns all serious. "If she really wants to do the job, I can help her"

"What do you mean?"

He pulls out a blood stained wooden club from under his seat. "Sometimes I get customers who want to end it, usually students."

"End it? You mean you kill them?"

"Only if they ask me" He keeps staring at my hand, with the note waving in the air. "Or they don't tip me"

In the accident and emergency department, Rachel is whimpering now she's in public, not brave enough to throw a complete fit but still acting enough to whine and cry in Taylor's arms. He bravely rubs her shoulders telling her it will be all right; he is sadly disillusioned, if that would have been my girlfriend sleeping with someone I knew upstairs I would have kicked her out.   I wonder What Samantha's doing?

"These places always smell of swimming pools" I try to make conversation.

"Yeah" Taylor replies, too hooked up in Rachel's acting performance to listen.

"When I was a kid, I always wanted to be a doctor. You know like Dr. Kildare, help people"

"Yeah"

"What happened to that dream?"

"Yeah"

"Look at the lights, like in the theatre, a separate spotlight for each injured person. The theatre, swimming pools, isn't strange how two completely different activities can merge into a train of thought, in a place like this"

"Yeah"

"Swimming pools and death, that's what it smells like"

"Great"

"I had a friend who died in a swimming pool"

"Alex will shut the fuck up!" Taylor shouts back at me in tears.

Looking across the waiting room I could have sworn I just saw James walking around in a doctors uniform, the shadow of my friend stops by two girls I recognise from the second year, Marie and Charlotte, both dressed as nurses. I really want to fuck that Marie. I decide to investigate, hoping its some kind of doctors and nurses game. "James what are you doing here?" I approach my friend, dancing side to side with the music of my mind playing to look hip.

"Making a movie" He replies, "I haven't got time to speak Alex, this is costing me" and he leads the two girls away, I see him put some money into Charlottes hand.

"Wait" I cry after them, "I could be a patient" but its too late, James has disappeared back into the shadows.

Rachel, finally, is called, if she had tried to kill herself she would have been dead by now. That's the state of the British Health system, would never happened under Maggie. I fancied Maggie, as well as Diana. We stand in a dead silence. Awaiting a morgue report that will confirm our worst fears that we're all dying from the minute we're born. "What happened?" the nurse asks, her face has turned from caring mother nature, to the fury of hell, all by examining Rachel, some people have the effect of the eye of a hurricane on people.

"I tried to kill myself," Rachel says.

"She took some pills" Taylor replies and hands over the bottle.

"Did she empty the bottle?"

"I'm in the room you know. You don't have to speak like I'm already dead. I took them all."

The nurse looks sceptically towards Rachel, then at both Taylor and I, knowing that she wouldn't be awake if she took the amount of pills to empty the bottle.

"How many pills did you actually take Rachel?" The nurse asks. Rachel looks away, the game is up. The nurse gets verbally irate. "How many pills did you actually take?!" she says.

Rachel speaks up, holding back tears of a clown. "Two" she croaks out.

"Is this a joke?" The nurse escorts a crying Rachel out of the hospital.

"But I want to kill myself" she screams out.

"Come back when you try properly next time"

"I'll do it, I swear I'll do it, I want to die!"

"Good"

"I'm sorry," I say to the nurse as Taylor and Rachel wait in embarrassment for a taxi. "I think she needs professional help"

"I think you do," she says towards me, does she know me?

Up at the ambulance entrance I catch a glimpse of James running towards the exit, holding a small video camera, he disappears into the shadows yet again but where are the nurses?

I feel a tap on my shoulder, its Marie, Charlotte next to her, still

Part 2: The Best of Times

dressed in nurses uniforms. "James said you're going to pay us," Marie states.

"Pay you for what?" I reply.

"Time is money pal, do I look like I want to be dressed in this uniform in the middle of winter?" Charlotte butts in.

"Yes" I reply.

Marie slaps me round the face, "You need to read more" And they walk away. I think I'm in love.

In the taxi back we have the same driver as earlier. He is reluctant to let us in at first, seeing the psycho that is Rachel quivering under Taylor's arms. I offer him some extra money for the journey and he lets us in on the promise that - "Any sign of trouble and I'll leave you stranded." Rachel has an apocalyptic effect on the world.

"I thought you might leave me," Rachel cries over Taylor's shoulder, quivering like she's been found nearly drowned on an ocean where her life was meant to finish and we have rescued her from the fate she drew out.

The Taxi driver gently pats the wooden club underneath his seat and stares at me in the front with an evil smile. "Students are my favourite notches"

"Notches? You keep count?"

He passes the club onto my lap it weighs a ton. "See those marks?" I can see knife marks on the side I count twenty. "Each one is a customer"

"They didn't tip?"

"Some didn't tip. Some sick in the back. Some didn't have the money. Some, I just didn't like"

I place the club in my hands. "What if I turned this on you now?"

He bursts out laughing like before and then turns all serious. "Do it" He continues to drive the taxi, never taking his eyes of the road, he doesn't even look at me, his potential attacker, not giving me a second thought, or time of day in his mind.

I place the wooden club back under his seat he doesn't flinch. "Aaahahahah" he begins to laugh, "Students, I fucking love them! Oasis, Blur, Supergrass, I'm your fucking man!"

Taylor and Rachel go straight to bed once we're back in the house. "You wont tell any of the others will you Alex?" Taylor asks me.

"Course not" I reply, just like I didn't shag his girlfriend that time. I need a cup of tea, just to set my mind back analysing. What did that nurse mean, "I think you do?" And Marie saying, "I need to read more?" Its really bugged me.

In the living room Matt sits still watching the TV. On the table is a Christmas card with a photo of Noel Gallagher wearing a Christmas hat, looking really drunk. I pick it up and inside is signed autographs from the band, dedicated to Matt. "You got a Christmas card from Oasis? How?"

"Didn't you?" He replies.

I notice Christina has left, blown Matt out no doubt, that new hair gel will only get you so far, just look at Linda. "Where's Christina?" I hate the thought of something going.

"Bed"

"You two seem to be getting on really well," I say suggestively, just like Dad got on well with his Sectary. He doesn't reply. "Nothing, just saying," I continue, I want to know his secrets.

"I'm trying to watch the film Alex, its bad enough I got disturbed because of that psycho trying to kill herself, suicide is meant to be painless you know"

"Isn't that a song by the Manic Street Preachers?"

"It's a cover of the theme from MASH"

"Is this is the same film you was watching earlier?"

"Yeah, its four hours long. I thought you didn't like Robert De Niro?"

"I just think he's overrated, he's always playing the same character"

"What? You can't say that?"

"He's always being a gangster"

Matt begins to roll a joint, enthralled by the discussion. "You know Alex, I just think you like having arguments with people"

I smile, Matt I get on least with in the house but he knows me the best. "Like you"

Matt smiles, I think I understand him the best. We are two sides of the same coin at times. "You wanna joint?"

"Cool." I'll get stoned for free, makes up for paying for that taxi ride.

"So what was it with the psycho?" Matt asks.

"She took two sleeping pills and hid the rest down her jacket" I sit in silence and picture it when I fucked her. Her orgasmic cry of pleasure the minute my cock entered her, I don't even think I penetrated her.

Part 2: The Best of Times

"Cant believe you fucked her" Matt says reading my mind, it must be the joint.

Matt leaves to go to bed. "Aren't you rolling a joint?" I ask wanting more weed. They smell of the joint had finally killed the smell of the hospital, swimming pools and death. All I could smell now was oranges and bar stools. "You know a friend of mine once died in a swimming pool"

"You're a jinx"

"We dared him to see how long he could hold his breath, I guess he won"

"Another notch for you Alex"

"What was that you said?" I remember what the taxi driver said.

"Another notch of someone's life you've messed with"

"I wonder what its like? To die?"

"You know next time she wants to pretend to kill herself, I reckon we should help her, give her the instruments and let her go through with it"

This leaves me thinking.

Before I go to bed I put a kitchen knife wrapped round a piece of paper and write left handed so she wont recognize my handwriting

TRY THIS NEXT TIME

And I place it under the door of Taylor's room where I can still hear Rachel whimpering.

Picking up the phone at 5am, I decide to call Samantha from the living room.

She tells me she's missed her period.

Maybe I do believe in fate after all.

CARLA PART 1

Matthew wakes up and feels the cold bite of winter finally falling upon the windy city which had previously been laid full of gold dust memories that had now left the streets bare. The sound of silence beckons. No music from the stereo. No shouts from inside the house. No hard rain to fall. A fly moves around the British flag duvet, marks the silence in respect and ghosts around the room treading on water.

For the first time since he'd been here, Matthew felt nothing. He sits on the edge of his bed. The floor is a mess of a world created by torn skins, tobacco; the smell of weed lingers in the air. Fresh air would do the room good, ability to breath life back into him. The window still hadn't been fixed, it was cold outside, winter was biting his body pale white. The frost forming on his skin making him scratch. This room that was embodied by dreams for some reason was the embodiment of a prison cell at this moment where time seem to have stood still. "4am" he says to himself. He couldn't get back to sleep though. Time was waking, tapping on the window. Fresh air would be his one saviour in a withdrawal he faced, to leave the warmth of his duvet, the protection of his country's flag, and descend into the night, like a vampire.

He gets dressed and thinks about watching the daylight from the docks, seeing the sun glisten over the sea, where a thousand memories have been washed ashore. He wanted to do something different, to do something that morning that would break the routine of drink, drugs, lectures and sleeping. He wanted to do something that would be personal, that only he would know and he himself could remember. He wanted to see himself reflected in the city.

His jacket is on a chair in the living room, the lights are off, but someone has left the TV on the exploits of the culture of late night television. As he goes to switch the TV off he hears a voice. "What are you doing?" He ignores it, his mind playing tricks on him, as he's in a state of purgatory, half awake, half asleep, this maybe a dream. He could wake up at any second; find himself safe and warm under the British flag of bands that protect him from demons that come to haunt him at night. "Leave it on I'm watching it" the voice says again.

This time Matthew follows the trail of the voice and sees movement underneath a duvet on the sofa, a head is outside, this time he psychically jumps. As he stares hard enough in that spilt second between being frightened enough to run, or just standing still to await your fate, he can make out the face on the head, James. "Jesus, James! You scared the shit out of me!"

"Sorry, but I thought you was going to turn the TV off" James replies.

Matthew's heart returns to his body, and his blood begins to pump at a normal rate. He pauses, confused, is this the right living room? Is he in the correct house? Has time moved forward? These are the stupid questions you begin to doubt in yourself when it's the twilight hours of the night and you are awake. Nothing is real.

Part 2: The Best of Times

Nothing is ever what it seems. Just shadows that meet silence to conspire for possession of your soul.

"Why are you staring at me like that?" James asks, feeling sensitive to Matthews gaze.

"I wasn't... I mean, what are you doing here James?"

"Trying to watch TV"

"How long have you been here?"

"All night"

"You came round to watch TV?"

"I was on my way back and it was too cold to walk anymore, I had to stop, rest up" James's eyes don't leave the TV. There are women gyrating round poles, then dancing on top of men. As he stares in silence, the only noise is the fake orgasms coming from the television speaker that rattles and becomes muffled. "Cultural viewing," James comments.

"Doesn't do anything for me" Matthew replies repulsed at himself for not being able to take his eyes away from the television set.

"Its the art of pain" James smiles and finally makes eye contact with Matthew, as the TV switches to a sado-masochism room, where a guy is whipping a girl.

"Is this on a normal channel?"

"It's my video, very own private collection."

"You're a sick man James"

"Why? Cause I'm finding pleasure in pain. Look around; this place is full of pain."

"Its not the same"

"Least with physical pain the scars heal, emotional pain the scars are only visible for the person inside"

"Have you been taking those mushrooms again James?"

"I've been taking pleasure in pain tonight"

"And where exactly was you tonight?"

"With someone."

"With someone? Someone we know?"

"No-one you know. Then again you might, what streets do you walk down at night Matt?"

"What do you mean?"

"Its 4am and you're going out, not coming back. Perhaps you and me share the same tastes"

"What the fuck are you talking about?"

"Derby Road, by the end of the street that leads into the market, towards the hospital."

"Who was with you James?"

"A lady of the night I frequent, you're lucky to ever see the same girl again as the street changes its attire so much"

"You were with a prostitute?"

"Don't be so shocked. They make their best business out of us, student discounts with a NUS card, it's like any other business, you corner the market with better value deals"

"You paid to have sex with someone?"

"Who said anything about sex?"

"What have you done James?"

"Nothing you haven't thought about doing every time you see some girl you like but cant speak to because all that bollocks of what's the correct procedure is in the way."

"And what is the correct procedure?"

"Money. Its buys whatever you desire"

His head hurts. He had a migraine and it was bad, he always feared these, they'd taken the life of his grandmother, his mums mum, she got them too, it was hereditary. With a cold biting winters wind, it felt like a needle shooting up his temple with each step he walked outside. He didn't know what he was looking for. He never realised how fucked up James was, it went to show, you don't truly know anyone inside, only yourself, and most of the time that's covered in armour, so we cant let anyone in, the fear of getting hurt far out weighs the high of being loved.

The more he walked, head down, thoughts of 'nothing' reeling through the waters of his mind, the less assure of the surrounding he was. And then it hit him. He stood in the centre of a T-Junction, a crossroads, down the street of the name 'Derby Road'. Why had he ended up here? He had wanted to walk to the docks, to watch the ocean bring up the sun and dawn in the new day, to feel what it was like to be alive when you witness the miracle that is the passing over of a new day. That each breath down by that river, watching that miracle would cleanse him and help find out what he was missing inside. But somehow, he had ended up at the fermented street James spoke about. The lost town. Tramps decimate the night outside subways. Corners are populated by ladies of the night. Windows are broken where screams are heard. And different colours look on with suspicion at one another. Bolted up front doors. Wire mesh fencing over the walls, glass covering the bricks. This is what they don't show on the prospectus. This is what they try and pretend

Part 2: The Best of Times

doesn't exist. And the longer it goes without recognition, the more it will spread like a wild fly catching its wings deep in. This was Thatcher's Britain. Best forgotten and left to destroy itself in time. The wind whistled across his face and shoot its needle full of empty drugs into his temples, it brought his eyes to water such was the harshness of the wind that had found its way down this part of the city. It wouldn't blow him backwards, or forwards, but keep him rooted to his spot on the street. The street was silent but of eye of the storm, the centre of a hurricane he had walked into, he was that eye now, he tried to feel for his face, to make sure he was here, hoping against all hope that this was another dream. He was just cold in bed that's all; if he could feel his face, he'd feel the duvet by his chin, and he'd wrap it round himself. But he couldn't feel his face his fingers were too numb.

He can hear a young girls voice sing down the streets, a sad song, that floods the pavement of the forgotten parts despair. He looks up, through the dust that blows in his eyes and sees a part of the street that is empty from all this hell, empty from the storm, empty from the rivers of blood, she was oblivious to all around here, it could not touch her. She is an angel, on a street corner. He stares, afraid to approach, afraid to ruin such a vision of beauty. The one pure thing he had seen since he'd been here. He could feel redemption in his soul, what did he have to redeem himself for? It was obvious; he had to redeem himself for looking at her. Closing his eyes, she surrounded him in every thought he battled. She notices him and looks away at first. Then puts on a mask of her job, and confidently strides forward.

"Alright" she says, the confidence pretence, she was new to the work.

Matthew turns his head away, pretending he was looking past her, and then across the street, pretending that elsewhere is a better place for his mind to be. Never in the present. But the just before the dusk of the sun brings a chill to his eye and makes him stare harder towards her to avoid the freeze.

"Its cold" she says and puts her coat round warm across her naked shoulders, her black top cropped to show as much bare nakedness of her soul without freezing her to death. Her skirt hanging above the bottom of a perfectly formed petite cheeks, long black stockings, forming shapely legs, Venus D'Milo of the streets. Her jacket her armour, provocatively places open when a punter arrives and pulled to when business is elsewhere. She had long blonde hair and the bluest eyes. "Do I know you?" she asks, as he continues to stare.

"The wind, I can't focus properly, I'm sorry…"

"Its ok" She pauses and looks up and down the street, it was empty, quiet. This guy seemed harmless, she wanted to get in from the cold, even if it wasn't a punter, she needed it to look like a punter to walk away. "You want to come inside?"

Matthew steps inside a small room, bare, the bed is neatly made with red sheets and red curtains by the window. Red carpet. "You like red?"

"Its easier they say, to clean any mess away from the sheets or carpet"

"Do you get a lot of mess?"

"No so far" She sits on the bed. Matthew remains standing. "What's you name?"

"Isaac" he lies.

"Biblical name. Your parents church goers?"

"No. Yours?"

"I don't know, I never met them"

"Count your blessings"

"What would you like to call me?" Silence, he shrugs his shoulders, his mind a blank canvass of names to be painted over. "Why don't you sit on the bed, it would be more comfortable?"

"I don't know what I'm doing here" He finally speaks again.

"Its ok, we don't have to fuck, you get a lot of people who just want to talk I guess"

"Really?"

"I guess"

"How long you being doing this?" He asks her.

"A while now"

"How old are you?"

"Twenty one"

He looks into her soul and sees she too is hiding behind a masquerade. "How long you really been doing this? It doesn't matter to me, I just want to talk like you said"

She looks up to his eyes. "This is my first day"

"I've never picked up a prostitute before. Am I your first punter?"

"Yeah. I don't really know what to do either" She admits and smiles a beautiful smile that is her natural persona. Matthew feels more relaxed and sits on bed. "Do you want to start?"

"How old are you really?" He asks again.
"How old do you think I am?"
"Fifteen"
"Sixteen. I'd say you're in your early twenties"
"Twenty"
"So we're both just out. First perceptions are often wrong."
"What did you think when you saw me?"
"Student. Out after a late night, wanting to have sex"
"Are there a lot of students who come looking?"
"The girls tell me that's their biggest clients during the winter"
"I wasn't out late, I just couldn't get to sleep"
"Why? Pressure?" She says sarcastically.
"There's nothing for me to worry about, so I was awake worrying that I don't feel anything"
"What like for other people?"
"For everything"
"Do you have a girlfriend?"
"No. I'm a student." He pauses trying to understand the meaning to that statement to a conversation that had no meaning. "Don't you girls have a life story?"
"I can make one up with you if you wish, to pass the time"
"Are you charging me for this?"
Long pause. "No, I invited you up here, get in from the cold"
"You could be missing out on business"
"I could also catch hypothermia"
"So why invite me up?"
"I thought you might want to have sex if we got speaking, but I was wrong"
"Do you want me to go?"
"No, its nice just to talk too"
Silence returns and spreads across the city. Matthew looks out the window as the sun beckons to dawn the life back into the empty streets. "It weird, when someone says they're enjoying talking, it always goes silent, I never know what to say, the pressure to entertain"
"What do you study?" She asks him, genuinely interested.
"Film"
"You make movies?"
"Yeah"
"What type of films do you like?"
"All sorts"

"I like vampire films."

"What like eighties horror?"

"Yeah, and those British ones with those old guys... Cushing and Lee"

"What makes you like vampire films?"

"The ladies always look so beautiful in them, regal, I think in a past life I was a regal lady"

"When people talk about past lives why are they always someone famous or rich from our pasts? Why not just a poor guy? Or a soldier who died an un-heroic death?"

"Maybe I was a vampire..." She gets up and moves towards him, opening her mouth, "I vont to suck your blood" They laugh and he touches her skin, smooth, she smiles. "I like that, it's gentle" He stops and looks back out the window. "I didn't ask you to stop" She puts his hand back on her arm and gently moves it down her body.

"Is this your selling technique?"

"I won't charge and I won't bite"

"Why?"

"I just don't want to be alone" She finally reveals the truth behind her beauty.

"Me neither" And he reveals his lost soul.

As he pushes himself into her, she feels very tight down below, she makes a gasping noise that it hurts, and he gently recoils back and smoothes her below, "that's nice" she gently arks her neck back and gasps, when he puts himself back in.

"I don't have to, if it hurts"

"No I want you to"

He places himself back in and her eyes wince in pain, but she stares still at him, an angel. "Here" he says and gently moves her on top of him and begins to move her waist up and down, in a nice steady motion, she enjoys it more, the pain is less, she can control when it hurts. She starts to gyrate against him, her pelvis throwing back and forth, ignoring the pain, he holds her hips back, arching her back, moving his hand onto her stomach and then her chest, helping ease herself back. And then he comes. And she smiles.

She remains on top of him, unsure whether to get off or not. "Should I move off?"

"Does it hurt?"

"Its nice, I can feel you inside of me. The guy who looks after us, he breaks us in, but he wasn't gentle like you, with him it hurt and it was over."

"I'm sorry"

"I just closed my eyes"

That fly from earlier in his bedroom, had somehow followed him into this room and perches itself on the red duvet sheet. "Oh god" she turns away, and laughs innocently.

Matthew flicks at it and then it fly's away, it comes back and he catches it, in his hand. He goes over to the window and lets it fly away, alive, like he felt. He sees a man staring up at the window, tall, long black crombie jacket, shaven hair, and light stubble. "What does your pimp look like?"

"Tall, always wearing this long jacket, even when he broke me in, he wouldn't take it off. Why?"

Matthew returns to her side. "No reason"

"Would you like to go?"

"I'd like to stay if you want me too?"

"I want you too"

He goes back into the bed and stares at her.

"Do you want to go again?" She asks.

"I just want to look at you, naked, is that ok?"

"You don't want to fuck me?"

"No"

"Did I not do it right?"

"It's never felt so right," he gently kisses her lips, she sits back up on the bed but he stops her. "No, you stay on the bed, just lye down and close your eyes"

"Close my eyes? But you might do something"

"Only look into your soul"

"What if there's nothing there, what if I'm a vampire like we said before?"

"Then I'll be one too now"

"We could live eternal life, roaming the streets I work to feed"

He stares into her. Still. Unable to move. Encapsulated by her beauty. "What's your name?" he finally speaks, his mouths dry, nervous, like a first date.

"Carla"

Minutes pass. Silence is broken by her voice. "Can I open my eyes yet?"

There is no reply. She opens her eyes a little, a child playing hide and seek. The more full her eyes open, the barer the room is. He has gone.

MJ Gunn

She walks back out on the corner, confused. Her pimp approaches her, she worries that he may realise she had disappeared, gone to the flat and not charged. He reaches her. She takes a step back. He raises his hand. She flinches as his fingers touch her cheekbones. "Good work" he says.

"Thanks" she replies, confused.

"I like it that you asked him to pay me, shows you know whose boss, that you know you'd be doing no favours by trying to rip me off"

He paid you, she wants to say, but she plays along with her pimp, she smiles a stoned cold reaction.

"Look happy, it gets easier" he walks away.

She stands on the corner and feels the bite of winter in her naked body. Why did he pay him? She didn't want it to be tainted; she wanted it to feel like her first time.

Matthew watches her from a side shop, watches this Angel of mercy out in the cold, witnessing her face change, her attitude becoming alive to the cold light of day. If he were to keep her pure, he would have killed her very essence of the breath that breathes fire into one so young. By pretending to devalue what had happened, he not only protected her, but also protected himself from what he feared more than anything, falling in love.

BIRTHDAY BONANZA

Alex

"Lets play war, lets play war!" Simon shouts at the top of his voice, jumping up and down like an excited child on Christmas morning who can taste his presents before he opens them, just the smell is enough to set the pulse racing.

It was a good idea of mine, to come down to the New Forrest to celebrate my birthday. Showed everyone how popular I am, James had to get his camper van for us all to travel in. There's me of course, the Robin Hood of the Forrest, I don't steal money from people but peoples confidence. I don't steal and give to the rich but I give to my own mind and persona.

"What exactly do you do Alex?" Linda asked me in Rhinos during Amy's birthday.

"I sell confidence"

"What does that mean?"

"I tell people the good things they need to hear about

Part 2: The Best of Times

themselves"

"You mean you lie?"

"I distort the truth"

Amy only had a handful of people a couple of days ago for her birthday; I can tell this is upsetting her. She didn't even want to come out originally she laid in bed in her dressing gown as James drove up in his camper van. "It wouldn't be the same without you?" I reasoned, as it wouldn't, it would be better.

"We didn't do anything like this for my birthday" she whined.

"That's cause I thought it would be a double celebration, both are birthdays." Like I said, I tell people what they need to hear. I'll play with her mind some more later tonight whilst I wait for Samantha. She's not in the New Forrest, she's coming later, a birthday present to be smuggled in my room by James, who knows my secret along with Steve's, and Amy knows both our secrets. The world is fall of secrets. Its what makes us who we are - Secrets & lies, lies & gossip. Samantha's been a bit weird since the night of Amy's birthday; I think she wants to tell Amy the truth. Every time I go to touch her, she pulls away, saying she has a headache.

"You had one last night?"

"And I'll have another one tomorrow" she replied.

As Simon jumps up and down, "Let's play war, lets play war," claiming teams, he slips on the log he was standing on and cuts his hand. "Yeah Simon lets all play war"

"Shut up all of you! It hurts" Simon retreats back to James's camper van with a tissue over a small graze, my first causality of my birthday I want plenty more. The new forest is wet; it was raining all day yesterday. It's a picturesque landscape, something out of a Vietnam movie just before the artillery is called in. It feels warm for February, the sun shines bright, and the green that forms a maze around us, seems endless. As I stepped out of the camper van and onto the first blade of grass, I looked around, pretending to be deep in thought, holding my hand up to my head, taking it all in, waiting for someone to ask me what was I feeling so I could reply, "I could lose myself here"

"It's fucking freezing you idiot! Why did you want to come here?!" Matt's voice shouted. There's a camera to record my celebration to cherish this in years to come. I press play, there's footage of Matt putting a hair clipper across Rachel's hair grading the back and sides as Taylor sits on the bed watching 'Vanessa' on the daytime TV. "Don't cut too close! Do you know what you're doing?" Rachel is screaming out in her apocalyptic voice.

"I cut peoples hair all the time" he replies. I decide to keep this incriminating evidence, I've needed something to use on Matt for a while now.

Everyone is standing in the forest, drinking cans, looking bored. I hear Little Rob start the mutiny - "I could be doing this somewhere warm with good music to listen too, not out in the freezing cold, it's a forest, wow, now lets go home".

"Look at the beauty of the place, take it all in" I reply. There are a few moments of silence, as they take in the beauty of what I've helped create in their minds. I'll be treated like a God for discovering this Forest of dreams for them.

"Trees, the colour green, a freezing cold sun"

"And why's it called the new forest? What happened to the old forest?"

"Are you rolling a joint?"

"My hands are too cold to skin up"

I couldn't see who was talking. Voices just came shouting out from various directions. "Who spoke?!" I shout out, "I demand to know who is descending in the ranks"

"It was the forest, they say its haunted"

"You're quoting directly from Robin Hood Princes of Thieves"

"Everything I do, I do it for you"

"I brought that record"

"You sad bastard"

My head spins round and they all stare in silence. "Who was speaking? Tell me!" What is obviously needed is a game, as war is not on the agenda; I need some kind of magic trick. "Everyone hide behind a tree and then when I say walk, you've got to all walk out" I set the camera to record. "Ready" Someone passes someone else a joint between the trees. "Who passed the joint? Who?"

"I did you twat" Johnny replies.

"This is fucking stupid, lets just hurry it up then get the fuck out of here, back to the house and get caned to some good tunes" Little Rob shouts out.

"Ready..........go" Everyone steps out from behind the trees and walks towards the camera like it's a funeral march, am I the only person who can see the fun in this game?

"Wow, that's amazing Alex, people walking out from behind tree's, now you've got what you wanted lets get home" Matt suggests.

"Do it again!" I shout, "Put some effort into it"
"TWAT" Someone shouts out.

James sticks up for my idea. "Thanks James" I say. It was his idea to come down here. "How many times have you been here James?"

"A few"

"On your own?"

"Sometimes alone. Sometimes with women"

"I bet its romantic in the summer"

"Who said anything about romance" James replies, and as he walks with the camera I notice that his feet are seeing how firm the ground is, as if something's buried there.

Little Rob, who had driven here as the extra car, ignores James and begins to walk back to his car. Why did he bother coming if he doesn't want to partake in the fun?

"I'm serious, we do this Camera trick or there's no lift back" James states, "everyone but Alex as it's his birthday" James keeps informing everyone - "You can freeze to death out here. There's plenty of spaces left to dig holes but the shovels are in the van" How does he know this? "Lift back? Freeze to death? Or dig a hole?" James continues.

They all look at each other with fear. Matt passes me the video camera and I believe he's going to be next. I look for a big rock to throw at him but he just walks towards the car park and ignores James chants of - "No-ones getting a lift. You'll all die"

Matt sits in Little Rob's beaten up car, smoking a joint out of the window that hardly rolls down, rust on the side of the car door.

"You didn't go across, James will make you freeze out here," I inform him, still holding the rock I want to throw into his face.

"James is a fucked up guy, I don't think any of us realise how much" Matt replies.

"You'll be lucky if this car gets you back to Southampton. Look at the rust"

"Hey man, rust never sleeps" Little Rob pipes up and Matt passes him the joint to smoke for a lift, no principals that guy.

Inside James's camper van, Simon is collapsed on the floor from his injury, with his hand still grazed and a tissue over it. "My hand hurts" he cries out like a child.

"Why are you collapsed on the floor like you're dying?" James asks.

"Shut up! What would you know; you didn't slip on that log did you? I could have tecnus? Or worse still aids!" Simon replies.

"Aids? How can you can catch it from a log?" Steve pipes up.

"I don't know, but I don't feel well"

James puts the keys into the camper van, turns the ignition on. Everyone smiles with relief, then James turns to face us all like a school headmaster about to give out detentions. "What is everyone doing? Only Alex can get a lift back"

A serious argument breaks out between the others and James. Simon leading the way "I'll fucking kill you James, I'm just not in the mood"

"What's the matter Simon, did you cut yourself playing war?"

"I'm fucking serious James! I'll drive the camper van, I'm warning you James!"

"Have you ever killed someone before Simon? Its not as easy as it looks"

"I'm happy to start! I'm dying here!" He holds his cut hand, like it's a spliced heart.

"What would you know about dying?"

I step out of the camper van as the argument ensures. Matt has stepped out of Little Rob's car and is looking across into the New Forest. Obviously time for one of his and mine 'we hate each other but we could be best mates' conversations. "I've got video footage of you cutting Rachel's hair, do you want people to know you cut hair? Like a hairdresser?"

"Sure, I charged Rachel five pound, as I did Simon and James" He replies.

"Right, will you cut mine then?"

"You know Samantha came onto me the other night"

"Trust me Matt, she wasn't after you, I told her to dance with you in the club so Amy wouldn't realise there's anything between me and Samantha. She wasn't going to go with you, its why she left on her own from the club just after you did. She wasn't after you"

Matt stares at me like he's thinking, trying to work it out. "You're right, she left after you went, I was left on the dance floor alone," Matt says but he smiles towards me with a devious grin, like he knows something I don't. "Besides, anyone can tell Samantha is wrapped up in you" He walks towards the car and has a big grin when he gets in. I wonder why he's smiling at himself? For being a fool of course. Like Samantha was really interested in him, she left the club just after me and followed me back about thirty minutes later, she was a little wet though but she said she'd had to pee in the

Part 2: The Best of Times

street. "When was the last time you had sex with Samantha?" he shouts out from the car window.

I haven't had sex with her since that night. She's always had a headache. How would he know? I bet he listens outside my door. The only action he'll ever get.

The party is in full swing downstairs but I'm upstairs hidden in my room with Samantha. The walls are closing in with the conversation. I've never noticed how white those walls are, almost blinding, no wonder Samantha has headaches. The more the conversation continues, the lower the ceiling seems to get, until it's on top of me. "Are you sure?"

"I'm pregnant Alex, I've done a test"

"Well, let me do a test with you"

"It doesn't matter cause I'm not keeping it"

"I want to make sure, that you're pregnant"

"Don't you trust me?"

"Its not a case of trust, I just want to make sure, before we do anything else"

"I don't want a baby with you Alex"

"Maybe not now, but what about the future...?"

"My future is going to university next year, having everything Amy has now"

"And us? We could come clean, I'm tired of all this sneaking around?"

"Us?" she sounds confused, like I've said something dirty to her.

I've never really noticed the smell of Samantha before. She smells like she's wet herself, a smell of dry urine. I want to be sick. The wall has collapsed onto me, suffocating my breath, the only air I take in smells of her betrayal.

There's a knock at the door and Matt enters. "People are beginning to wonder where you are. It's getting obvious you know. You need to make an appearance"

"We're talking" I reply gasping for air from the open door, anything that smells fresh. All that hits me is a chain of dope smoke, wallowing into the room, circling like an Indian rain dance.

"Alex go downstairs," Samantha pushes me out of bed; I fall onto the floor, having just had the air kicked out of my life with our conversation. I stand up and put some clothes on, in full morning glory for Matt, like I had done previously for Taylor. But unlike

Taylor, he doesn't look through me, he looks directly at me and then smirks towards Samantha, who opens her mouth, about to speak up for my prowess I hope - "Matt can keep me company"

As Matt sits on the bed, I notice Samantha seems to chirp up, but he ignores her and takes my Modern Life is Rubbish CD back. "I'll take this back?"

"Do you want to borrow it?"

"Its mine Alex, I own it"

"I'm sure its mine"

"I've been accepted into University for next year" Samantha says to break up the double act.

"Not here?" he replies rudely. I stand and listen to the entire conversation, she had never told me she'd got accepted, I don't speak up though, embarrassed it would look like Samantha and I don't share anything in our relationship. I stand there pretending I knew all this, as I get dressed, my head knocking back and forth to the imaginary music that is permanently playing in my head to make me look hip.

"Portsmouth, I'll only be down the road"

"What are you studying?"

"Pharmacy"

"What the fuck is that?"

"Drugs for animals"

Matt's eyes light up. "Perhaps we could do some business"

I step out the bedroom door and go to pull it too, but Matt is walking with me. "I thought you was going to keep me company?" Samantha shouts out towards Matt, sounding gutted all of a sudden. Matt doesn't even reply but smiles; I see his reflection in the mirror.

"Why you smiling?"

"Nothing, just you and Samantha, you're perfect for each other."

NIGHTCLUB NIGHTS

Marie

Girls will be girls. And Boys will be Boys. Sometimes girls will be boys. And boys will be girls. Boy-girls? Girl-boys? When it's cold I wish for summer nights. When it's warm I wish for winter nights. I'm never satisfied. But who is?

Perhaps when we die that's when we reach a state of satisfied bliss,

Part 2: The Best of Times

but they also say you meet souls you've met before so if it's someone we really didn't like how do we end up satisfied. 'Unsatisfied', a great song by The Replacements.

Itching in my tight fitting top indoors. Summers round the corner. And I'm neither hot nor cold in these Nightclub Nights. New York's, always sounds like Frank should be playing as you walk in, a club of go-go girls and gangsters the cream of the artistic crop. Unfortunately, this is something I would love but it's anything but. Handbags and glad rags at dawn, music with a thumping bass but no substance unless you've taken a substance. But that can create any music, you could be listening to Abba and it would sound like a marching band in your body thrusting and bursting out of your seams. Still, all the kings' horses and all the kings' men couldn't put Charlotte back again. I watch her, dancing round her bottled spirits with lime, her Gucci handbag and two-hour made-up face. As much as we fuck each other I really do hate her, hate her more with each night we share together, perhaps that's the attraction? Hate is stronger than love, love is hate, two words written with a biro for tonight on either leg for all to see in my flowery skirt

LOVE
HATE

I'm out of place here but I'm loved here - The hipster artistic girl with the 'in' crowd but too cool to be one of them full-time. It's an act I've mastered to perfection in my two years at university and something I shall get a 1st degree in when I graduate next year. I don't think it matters who I really am as long as I'm not Charlotte.

"The best thing about New York's" - this guy tells me - "is that its not got any 1st years, no fresher's, just us more mature students." This guy's been talking to me for the last hour. He has brought three drinks and I still cannot remember his name, I think it maybe be twat or prat. "Definitely more mature," he continues nodding his head round the club like there's a private party in his neck. "Have you ever been fucked with coke sprinkled on the tip of a cock?"

Oh real mature. "It will make your dick limp," I inform him.

"Now you're talking, it took three bottles for me to buy you but lets fuck"

"How much money you got?"

"What? Are you a prostitute?"

"You said it took three bottles to buy me, you tell me?"

Charlotte is dirty dancing with some guy on the dance floor, he looks like a Spanish dancing teacher, his real name is probably Ian and he's probably from Birmingham but has spent all day under a sun bed paid for by his parents in his members only gym which Charlotte is after a card to join.

I hate this place. Young, Posh and Cunted. I decide to leave.

The guy grabs me. "Where you going?" His eyes are full of violence and fear; fear that I'm going and fear that he has to pretend to be violent and firm to keep face with his friends. Those two go hand in hand, violence and fear. Love and hate, rhubarb and custard.

I turn the tables and grab his bollocks whispering "come on, come on" and start to unzip his trousers then and there, getting his limp dick out.

"Jesus Christ," he laughs, thinking I'm joking, stopping my hand and pushing me away. He is trying to put his cock back in without anyone in the club noticing it. He's embarrassed, fear is replaced by embarrassment and that walks hand in hand with pride. Pride comes before a fall, as he falls on the floor with my push.

In the cloakroom of the club is that girl from earlier this year, Linda, who Charlotte and I picked up for a foursome but they didn't cotton on being fresher's. She looks awful, half smiles as she passes me my brown feathered Yoko Ono jacket, and I can see the bags under her eyes, the daze of a white powdered discovery taking over her mind and becoming her universe. She looks like she's hit the ground running with her new life and the faster you run the more skin you shed, the harder it is to stop until you're just skin and bone. The bare necessitates. So many first years travel a route, Charlotte was where she was for a while and then I picked her up and helped her slow down, helped her to learn how to jog and look around the scenery. Burn the candle at both ends doesn't have to mean exactly that – an end - it can mean endless. Balance. That's all we are underneath it all, just skin and bone.

It's 5am, I lye in bed on my own and for the first time in two years it feels nice, it feels right. I'm tired of sharing a pretence in a bedroom; it's either awkwardness as you've only known each other for a few hours and you really want him or her to go so you can get some sleep and forget what they look like or it's an attachment, where him or her are regularly here and you feel like you're being trapped. You want one without the other and crave the other when you have the one.

Cannot sleep, as I know Charlotte hasn't come back. The front door creeps open, she's alone, there's no laughter, I tip toe over to my bedroom door and gently turn the lock. "Marie?" I don't answer and curl up in the womb position by the bedroom door. "Let me in"

Where was she till 5am? Why am I feeling like this? It was only meant to be a bit of fun, a bit of sexual flirtation. Once I felt this way for a guy. Now once I felt this way for a woman. I don't know which I prefer but I hate both feelings the same.

"Fine" Footsteps walk away and I remain on the floor, curled up like a baby.

I think about last year, my first at university, my first year of being a grown up, first year away from home. Certain songs bring certain memories, happy memories and some tears too. But you can't have one without the other. How can you know what is happiness without knowing what is sadness. Or what is sadness without knowing happiness. Two sides of the same coin both you touch in the palm of your hand everyday. What came first the chicken or the egg?

Stone Roses first album is still amazing. They could have been as big as the Beatles.

Maybe its better to burn out rather than fade away, so Neil Young sang.

Charlotte

Cocktail hour. JFKs. I wonder what he was like? Wonder if he would have slept with student girls like Marie and me? Maybe together at the same time, a JFK threesome, that's a good name for a cocktail.

Ever thought about the name cocktail? Break it in two, its -
COCK
TAIL

So it's a cock with a tail. That rhymes with female. God backwards is Dog. Live backwards is Evil.

Why doesn't Marie sleep with me anymore? It's almost put me off cocks, knowing that my tail doesn't entice. I understand it now, the cocktail.

COCK = MALE
TAIL = FEMALE.

The cinema crowd in JFK's, Film and Art students. It was Marie's idea to go down here. She sits at the high court table like Yoko Ono in a white sheet screaming obscenities. We haven't slept in the same room now for over a week. I miss her.

I prefer having sex with guys, the penetration, the coming, the sheer animal instinct of two species tearing each other's bodily functions to the height of ecstasy and pain. I like S&M. But with girls I just want to lie in bed and hold her, Marie, hold each other and feel content before the alcohol kicks in the next evening and my cunt starts itching. It sounds sick talking about it like this but I've had a few JFK cocktails and they are making me be honest and expressive the only way alcohol can do.

I worry about next year, my final year, doubts of what will happen, do we all just leave at the end of three years and go back home? Will I see any of these people again? Do I go straight into a job? How could I keep a straight face in an office and sit there for nine hours a day with people who don't know what I know? Because anyone who has lived this would never think about working in an office, so what do we do? My degree is business, what does that mean?

Damon Albern, well the guy who looks like him, the guy who went down on me in that 'fuck a fresher' week and then disappeared into the halls of residence kitchen, Steve, he's here with some fat girl, and a ginger guy with big ears. He walks straight over and begins to chat like nothing happened that night, like I didn't feel completely humiliated and felt like a whore. Why did he stop and walk out? Am I not attractive? Does Marie not find me attractive anymore either?

"I love this time of year for films, reminds me of being a kid" Damon, or Steve, tells us all. Marie sits under a white sheet still screaming lyrics from Sometime In New York City Album by John Lennon. I don't like the music she does; perhaps we're drifting apart.

"I like Grease" I reply.

"Grease, that's my favourite film. That's the only film worth watching, anything's better than Robert De Beardo," Amy says, then laughs at her own joke.

"A typical girls film, Grease. If you just learnt to sit down and watch a film, try and analyse it you'd get so much more out of it and possibly learn more about your life" Alex tells us.

Marie stops screaming from her white veil and silence drops amongst us as she stares at this guy. "You're very anal aren't you?"

Marie can be so cutting at times. I wish she'd let me sleep back in her bedroom. She never wanted to sleep in my room, hated the music, and liked her own stereo. I want to be like Marie. Every girl she meets does. These cocktails are burning my insides. These people are boring my brain. Standing at a crossroads where the wilderness is a beast that has no sex.

Marie

      The music is bad.   The alcohol is watered down. Even the pills are duds.
A cheap night.   A cheap pick up.   A cheap fuck.
Why go there?   Why do that?   Cause we can.
     Charlotte and me.   Charlotte and I.
        KAOS
Dancing.   Flirting.   Drink Water.
Tab of speed.
    Dancing.   Bored Flirting.   Tab of speed.
Dancing.
     There's a girl dancing by me and it's not Charlotte.
She's with that anal guy with the FA Cup ears.
     He dances with me, or so he thinks.
Smiling.
    "Hi, there" it greets me.
     Dances like his body is apart from his head that's on the moon.
    Charlotte's here now, is dancing with him.
     His friend, is quite small, short hair, she looks like a true lesbian, not a swinger when the mood takes me, a weekend lesbian like me, a fake lesbian like me.
    Kasbahs.
The lesbian, or so I think, Lauren introduces herself to me.
     Charlotte is with Alex, but Alex wants to be with Charlotte,
He is still dancing. She is looking embarrassed.
     "It was just a dance," she tells him.
He continues to walk on the moon.
     Charlotte takes my arm.
"Lets go next door"
     I want to take Lauren with me.
"You want to go next door?"
     She looks away embarrassed.

MJ Gunn

"Hey, lets do it, be my first time" Alex says.
"Sorry it's not my scene" she replies.
Alex tries to cajole her.
I go to kiss her goodbye, kiss her lips but she moves so I hit her cheek.
She dresses like a lesbian, looks a lesbian, but isn't a lesbian.
Neither am I.
I'm just bored with students.
I want to play games.
Magnums.
No Tom Selleck.
But plenty of Queens.
Plenty of straights.
Here the queen's look at the straights in the same way the straights would look at the queens in the outside world
The world away from this darkened enclosure that is hidden in this town like a tale of debauchery
It's basically round the back of Kaos
Quite adept I think, round the back of a shit nightclub.
Sometimes Charlotte and I come here with other friends, just to get away from being hit on
It's nice to go somewhere without having to worry who you'll get off with, if you'll have to take them home, if they'll have to get you drunk
Girl's night out
I can still feel the speed from Kaos
And the rejection from that girl Lauren
Is it possible to be bi-sexual your entire life?
Or is there a choice we all have to make?
Is love not just love after all?
The word is four letters

So is -	FUCK	CUNT	SHIT
EVIL	LIVE	DICK	COCK
TAIL			

Part 2: The Best of Times

"Four letter words are the rule of are language," I tell the JFK crowd who have joined us
"The bible of everyday spoken life"
"The words, which are spoken in private and in whispers so our peers don't fear"
FEAR   HATE
I add these to the party
"I'm not gay, I just find the best looking girls come here," a guy called James tells me.
Dan not the Man sits with him.   A regular here.   Always following that guy around who looks like Damon Albern, who disappointed Charlotte that night
These first year film course artists
Linda, she is a true hetro-sexual but she tells me her preference is for women
"And do I want to?"
"No"
Her mate Charlotte.   A model type.   Tanned. Long legs. Big Nose though.
She's never and never will.
Experiment that is.
I'm bored with this experiment.
I'm bored with life.
I'm bored with university.
Blair Larry from the TV Game Show comes in.

Charlotte
          Men.
               Women.
                    Marie.
                         Me.
                              Night Club Nights.
"Rhino's interior is so bland" Marie tells the boys; she has her white sheet round her head this evening. Since when has she been an interior designer? She begins to move the furniture around, painting the walls with her make-up. Some band playing a new indie Britpop anthem, Northern Uproar, sits with us. The bouncer's do nothing, thinking its part of Britpop to design a local dive. They played the Joiners Arms tonight, Marie and I went, I dressed out of place ready for New York's, she dressed as Yoko Ono. They followed

her like a piped piper down into town as she wailed in her white sheet. Sitting at the table hanging onto their every word is a some guy who looks like Johnny Depp called Taylor, some guy called Little Rob who looks like he should be in Countdown, and a guy called Matt who wants to look like Liam Gallagher but failing.

LIVE   SONGS   IMPROVEMENT   A L L THIS MUSIC IS ALIEN

Back at the house and I have to choose who I want to 'cop' off with as Marie has taken all four members of Northern Uproar into her bedroom and locked the door. I can hear 'Sometime In New York City' playing by John Lennon and Marie wailing to the music crying Yoko's name. That used to be our song.

I sit on the sofa. Next to me is the Johnny Depp look-a-like Taylor; he's very quiet, very shy, which could mean he's wild in bed. Next to him is the Countdown contestant, Little Rob, he's very intellectual and every sentence must become a discussion and then an argument for him. On the floor is my best bet, the Oasis obsessed guy, Matt, he's acting the DJ in the living room and playing some funky tunes which is winning my vote.

"What course do you do?" I ask like a first year virgin to the Johnny Depp guy.

"Law" he replies and then he says nothing, is there a wind up mechanism on his back to get him to talk? Are his batteries low?

The countdown contestant pushes himself next to me, so I'm in-between the two. "It's easier to talk to you from here, I don't like speaking to people if I cant see them properly"

"Great" I reply. I look to Noel Gallagher but he's engrossed in the music. Next to me Countdown guy, tapping his fingers, making conversation, silence Next to me also Johnny Depp, complete silence.

There's a knock at the door.

"I invited some mates round, you'll like them" Noel, I mean Matt, tells me. He opens the door TO MY HOUSE. In walk two guys and two girls complete strangers into MY HOUSE I hear Yoko in the bedroom wailing. I sit in silence, between a rock and a hard place. Everyone knows everyone else. I know no one. THIS IS MY HOUSE

I go to say something in MY LIVING ROOM but the countdown contestant who tells me –"listen to the tunes" and looks at me like I've been very rude to speak in my own house whilst music is playing shushes me.

"Jimmy Quinn, he's my hero," the Johnny Depp guy tells me.

Standing to leave and go into my bedroom, no one says goodnight, no one notices me leave. It took me an hour to work up the courage just to stand up to leave the room. I stand outside Marie's bedroom and hear her wailing to the live cd disk 2 on the 'Sometime In New York City' album, screaming "Kroko" with the rest of Northern Uproar. She wont fuck them I bet, just cock tease them, a night of Marie pretending to be Yoko in a room with a flashlight spinning round, her under a white sheet wailing, joss sticks filling the air and a magic carpet ride is better then sex for these guys. For most of Southampton it would seem.

Alone in my room I hear laughter from the living room downstairs I'm glad they're all enjoying themselves in MY HOUSE. Wonder if they'll still be here in the morning, permanent residence, and permanent debris in the carpet.

No sex.

No body next to me.

I'm alone.

I touch myself and begin to frig myself off down below. As I come I feel sick, disgusted with myself for doing what I just did, like some sad 13-year-old girl who wasn't kissed at the school disco. I smell my hands and it brings vomit to my throat and I throw up on the carpet.

I'm not coming back to university next year I've decided.

I'm going to get a job, work 9 to 5, find a nice guy called Garry or Phil.

CAN'T GET OUT OF BED

Matthew

Who's that knocking on my window? Ignore it and pull the sheets back over my head. Ever since I got the union jack duvet it protects me from all intruders into my mind, who want to discuss and distort my dreams. It's so hot in the room, the duvet could warm ten of us in size, the radiators are permanently on, and I still cannot open my window without the fear of my hands being chopped off. All that smoke of marijuana, all that smell of alcohol related evenings, all those hazy memories locked inside. No wonder I'm burning up, I'm suffocating in my own den of sin, and I love it. I'm never going to get up again. But it happens again. Can't you hear me knocking on your door? This knock rattles the walls, the

Oasis poster comes alive and then goes back into their living room of memorabilia, the Blur dogs from 'Parklife' jump out and take a bite at my duvet and I cower under the sheets, afraid to look back up, then when I do, Harvey and Bob are sitting on my bed, Mean Streets fallen down to my side, my protectors, two bit hoods with a line for improvisation.

I can hear voices as the knocking and banging continues - its Mr. Singh my landlord. "I can't believe they could still be in bed at 4pm on a Sunday, it's fucking disgraceful"

What do I do? Hide in bed in silence pretending that I'm out? Or turn up music pretending I can't hear them? The opening guitar rift of 'There's no other way' breaks in, it returns the rattles of the walls to outside. I hope it's made them fall to the floor, clasping their ears pleading for me to -'Turn it off! Turn it off!' 'Go away and I will'

"I can hear awful music being played" My landlord says directly outside the window. There's a shadow behind the curtain, the haze of sunlight, the type that arrives at the end of winter to bring in the spring, blazes a trail through my curtain, reflecting an eye of my landlord into the room. The shadow of his eye is reflected onto the walls across the posters, a giants eye, watching my room and all that I posses. "Get up, come on!" The eye moves with the words.

Why should I get up? Is the house burning down? If so, I'm in the safest place, no fire would dare enter this room; the lack of air for months would dampen the wildest flames from hell. After five months that 'well dodgy' landlord has finally decided to fix my window. He has no idea how stuffy it gets when you're smoking loads of weed and you can't open the window as you're too stoned and worried about losing a finger. Should have sued him, taken him to court but I thought I'd show race relations. He lives directly opposite; should have pissed up his cars, mugged his wife, tortured his kids, sold them class 'A' drugs and got them hooked.

Or just taken my revenge my cutting their little fingers off in my broken window.

Pull the duvet back over my head, fuck him, how dare he try and fix the window when I'm trying to sleep. I haven't left the house or got dressed in over ten days. I can't get out of bed.

"What shall we do Mr. Jelly?" Another voice comes from outside. What is the landlord's name? With the unpleasant business of meeting him for the first time he introduced himself as Mr. Singh. We pay our rent to him as Mr. Ray. And his friends who come round pretending to fix the shower and the mushrooms growing on the

Part 2: The Best of Times

carpet call him Mr. Jelly.

"Ah, good mushrooms this time of year." They proclaim to us at the fungus growing round our wet feet.

"Would you like to buy some?" I asked once.

"Mr. Fish grows his own" he replied.

"Who is Mr. Fish?"

"Your landlord"

The next cheque I write will be to Mr. Jelly Fish Singh Ray

I get up. I've had enough. I can hear them quiet outside my window.

"At last" the shadow of the massive eye says.

Change the tape, couldn't stand another second of listening to 'Leisure' it was really depressing me. Go back to sleep, listening to the Charlatans sing 'Can't get out of bed' to me. Hopefully this will give my landlord the hint.

Someone's having a telephone call directly outside my room. FUCKERS. First Mr. Jellyfish stingray wakes me up, now an intense telephone conversation outside my room, I say intense as that's what I am twice in one day. Last time I felt this intense was during the 1990 World Cup semi-final during the penalty shoot out against Germany. Often wonder if Chris Waddles ball has come back down yet or is it still orbiting the earth? Wait…. what day is it? The alarm clock and Mickey Mouse point towards 9am. It must be Monday, what happened to Sunday? I must have fallen back to sleep. Shall I get up? No, go back to sleep.

It's Rachel's voice on the phone it carries like a pig squealing before its shot. "…. Yes I'm contracted and paying rent at this address. How long will it take for the Housing Benefit cheques?" The crazy psycho has been getting unemployment cheques sent here and now she's claiming Housing Benefit?! She doesn't even pay rent. She was meant to be staying for a long weekend six months ago and has been here ever since.

The worst thing is I'm wide-awake now to being fucked up the arse by Rachel and Taylor. She gently puts the phone down, trying to hide the conversation and I hear her sneak back into Taylor's room. I pull the duvet off me and try to formulate a plan. I decide the best plan is to pull the duvet back over me.

There's a knock on my door. Great, who the fuck is this?
I ignore it. The knock happens again this time with a voice. "Matt?" It's Christina.

"Yeah?" I think about getting up and letting her in and she can come under the duvet and we can get really close like we did after Christmas but nothing happened but I'd like something to happen now, but then again, it seems like a lot of effort, I'd rather stay in bed and sleep.

"Can I have a word?"

Fuck it. Jump out of bed and put my dressing gown on and check my hair, completely lop sided, haven't washed it for a week, its been growing back, but its got to that stupid frizzy stage again which made me get it cut in the first place. Not long enough to be floppy or curtains and not short enough for gel, what should I do? I pick up a pair of shades and put these on - like that will cover up my hair. I open the door to Christina, her dressing gown on, one belt holding her firm great tits Spanish prostitute figure in place. One move of that belt and I could be fucking her on the carpet, maybe getting out of bed was a good idea after all. "Come in" I say and open the door, then realising I haven't let any air in for over ten days this is a big mistake.

"Its ok I'm about to have a shower," she replies, smelling the sin inside, a disgusting look of realisation crosses her face. Must remind her of those Spanish whorehouses she worked in back home.

"Even better," I say underneath my breath and step out into the hallway.

"What?" she says.

"Nothing, what's the problem, you want the TV right?" I had left the television in my room for the past ten days, much to Amy and Linda's annoyance. That's part of the reason I did it.

"No, well, yes, but did you hear that phone conversation?"

"Yeah" I look at Christina's lips, perfect fit.

"It's taking the piss. It's been the longest weekend stay in history. What are you going to do about it?"

What am I going to do about it? What the fuck is it to do with me? Shouldn't she be having this conversation with Taylor? Unless this was just excuse to knock on my door? Please, God, please, be an excuse just to knock on my door. "I know, I know, I'll have a word with Taylor" After I fuck you Christina is what I forget to say afterwards.

"She's got to go"

"I know, I agree, its too much now, she's got to go, its taking the piss like you said" I really want to throw that dressing gown off and do it on the stairway you filthy bitch.

Part 2: The Best of Times

"I wouldn't mind but she's not even all there really is she?"

"I know, I know" I undress Christina in my mind and see myself fucking her in the shower, unfortunately she's starting to walk upstairs but perhaps I am going to be in luck, as she turns on the stairway seductively...

"Can you put the TV back in the living room?" Then she disappears.

Back in bed, I get some tissue ready and start to have a wank about Christina having that shower. There's another knock at my door, it might be Christina and she could finish me of. I put the monkey back under my dressing gown, throw my shades on and even decide to gel my hair back. I'm ready....

At the door is Rachel; she is crying, "Don't you and Christina like me" Her face is puffed up red, for a minute I thought Taylor had hit her, I was so angry, I would have gone straight into Taylor's rooms and said – "How dare you hit her alone, we could have all joined in."

"Of course we like you." I cross my fingers behind my back, usually I would just tell someone what I truly think of them, but this girl is psychotic, so best to lie.

"I heard what you both said, you said you didn't want me here no more." She is now crying massively, I can hear Christina listening outside the shower. Maybe she wants me to come up and wash her back?

"You cant stay here and claim money, we could all get into trouble" I surprise myself with my clarity of thinking, maybe ten days of sleep gets the brain recharged? Maybe Einstein would sleep one year and work out pointless anal theories the next year?

"Only if someone told," a whimpering Rachel replies, like a schoolgirl getting detention.

"Its not the point, it's the principal, we all pay rent and live here, you've been staying rent free for months." Its time for my Robert De Niro impression to end the conversation, its far too cold outside my room, I'm only safe under a duvet in this world. "You know you've got to go home to Reading. Pack up go home." De Niro style pauses and then repeat – "Pack up go home, you gotta go back home to Reading, back home" After doing the De Niro trick of repeating sentences twice or more, I even raise my eyebrows in his style and stare directly at Rachel, nodding my head up and down.

"I thought you all liked me?" She goes running into Taylor's room. She's hysterical; wonder if she'll take three sleeping pills this time, another amazing suicide attempt.

Back to bed, pull the duvet over me and put the Charlatans back on. Another knock on my door. "Yeah?" I reply, getting myself ready about thinking of Christina in that shower.

"Can I come in?" It's Christina's voice.

Fuck it I decide, an imagined wank is always better than the real thing with someone like her.

"I'm sleeping," I say.

"Well done with what just happened."

I don't even want to have a wank now. I just want to sleep.

I'm awake now. I get up and into the kitchen. I want some breakfast. My two pints of milk have been stolen. MOTHER FUCKERS. Who drinks more milk than anyone else in this house? …Alex. Cricket Bat in hand. Smash Alex's bedroom door open fuck knocking.

I hold the bat over his head. "Where's my fucking milk?"

"What milk?"

"You steal my fucking milk again and I'll fucking kill you!" I slam the door back shut and go back downstairs, back to bed. I feel better after that burst of violence.

I hear a knock on my door. 6pm. Nine hours sleeping. "Where's the TV mate?" it's Linda's voice, I don't even bother to respond. Surely she's got better things to do; like gel her hair, go to the gym and snort the white powder her face bleeds dry.

I try to go back to sleep. Another knock on my door. "Matt, it's Rachel" Great, she's probably got a kitchen knife and is going to stab me to death cause of earlier. I decide not to open the door. "I stole your milk last night so I could have some hot chocolate. I thought I better tell you as Alex told me what happened. Also, you might let me stay if I'm honest with you"

I'm awake now cause of that bitch. I get up and changed, maybe I need some fresh air? I lock my bedroom door so they can't take my TV. Alex is in the living room. "I think you owe me an apology for earlier" he says, head moving to side to side with that imaginary tune that seems to be permanently played in his head.

"What are you listening to?" I have to finally ask him.

"Its my CD, not yours, you cant have it" he says covering up his ears.

"Why would I want to listen to the CD of your fucked up mind?"

Part 2: The Best of Times

"Are you going to apologise?"

I ignore him and go to the outside toilet to have a shit. I hear the kitchen door lock, Alex laughing. The bastard has locked me out. Fine, I'll just go round the back, when I finish. The light has gone in the outside toilet. I can't see anything. But I can feel what's crawling round my feet. Spiders, I turn my face away and it hits a cobweb, I pull away at it, panicking. I start to shiver, this toilet is freezing, no wonder no one ever uses it. I can see shadows go across the garden. A shadow tips its hat and throws money into the garden pond.

As I start to shit I realise there's only one pull of loo roll, shit on my hands, a stained arse. Pull my trousers back up and knock on the kitchen door where Alex's face is pressed up against the window. How does he shag so many women? "I've run out of toilet paper, open the fucking door! Hand me some paper at least"

Taylor joins Alex there. "Can you hear anything Taylor?" Alex says.

"No" Taylor says.

Walk down the outside side passageway - Condoms, needles, and pair of Y-fronts. Nice. Haven't got my key so I knock on the front door continuously. Both Taylor and Alex ignore it, telling Christina not to let me in. Ha, ha, this is so funny. I hear Linda turn her Songs Of Praise video up louder to drown me out. Finally Amy comes down from her bedroom. I thank her, "Bout fucking time!" before slamming the door shut and walking straight into the kitchen past Alex and a quivering Taylor who thinks I'm going to kick the shit out of him. I wash my hands, flick all the water at Alex and say nothing; the guy doesn't deserve my words.

"Not so funny when the jokes on you." I hear his voice vibrate all the way through the house as I smash the door to my room, contemplate the cricket bat but decide to change my pants. Alex's voice still calling out to me - "Cant stand the heat get out of the kitchen" That guy is really starting to piss me off. Maybe I'll shag Samantha after all. Then again, she's as fucked up as him. They deserve each other.

Where is everyone? I hadn't been out the house for ten days but you'd think that at least one of Simon, James, Steve or Blonde Paul would be in their rooms. Even Johnny's not slouched across a hallway somewhere in Halls. I need them to be around so I can complain about those fuckers in my house. "WHERE IS EVERYONE?" I shout.

"Hi Matt" I turn around to see Clarissa, off my course. I fancy her in a real dirty way, she has a black leather jacket, a tight black skirt, she's quite voluptuous, long brownish hair, big tits, low cut top, a real rock chick, according to James she's always asking about me.

In Clarissa's room and I've got her tits out, caressing them, a fair size, her hand giving me a nice motion on my cock. "What about Kane, don't you go out with Kane?" I ask her, before wanting to take this any further. He's a bit of psycho I reckon so I don't really want to end up stalked by him and run over by a skateboard for fucking his girl.

"Yeah but its an open relationship, we both fuck who we want" Clarissa replies and she starts to gyrate harder on my cock.

"I heard that Kane likes to do quite dirty things to you?" I ask this knowing the reaction is two fold; get out or come on in with bonus points.

"You want do the same?" She asks me, a come on in with bonus points, and a Christmas wish. It's going to be a long night...

...I stare up at the ceiling. It's the first time I've slept in Halls of residence. The rooms are tiny, with Clarissa and I on the floor, a sheet underneath us, and the bed behind us, there's no room to move in. We sit in silence, both of us wondering what to say next? "I'm not looking for anything serious." She breaks the silence, stating her intent, that was meant to be my line, but she got there before me.

"Me neither"

"Have you got anyone?"

"What like you have Kane?"

"Yeah, like me and Kane"

"No, there was someone I met the other day..." I think of Carla, "but it was a once off"

"Why the but?"

"Her style of life is different from mine"

"Do you love her?"

"I only met her once"

"You're not answering my questions"

I think of Carla for the second time, an angel. "Yeah, I love her"

She leans over and turns the radio on. I take this as her excuse to get me to leave.

"Sorry, I'll get up and go"

"No" and she lye's back next to me on the floor. "Stay. Its just two friends talking, that's all"

Teenage Fanclub come on the radio, 'The Concept'. "I love Teenage Fanclub, they are the ultimate summer band" And with that, the sunlight begins to shine through the drawn red curtains, and the room fills with warmth. Her next to me feels warm, spring has arrived, and the cold of winter disappears as Teenage Fanclub work their magic to welcome in the long hot summers into the windy city. "She wears denim, wherever she goes, she's going to buy some records by the status Qu," I sing along to the music.

Clarissa stands up naked, opens a closet door and pulls out a denim jacket and places it over her naked body. "What do you think?" she spins round and laughs. "You like Denim!"

"The song could have been written for you"

She lye's back next to me, both of us staring at the ceiling. "You're not getting serious on me are you?"

I gaze secretly towards her and think she'd be nice to have as a girlfriend, have someone steady for once. "Of course not" I reply, why can't I ever be honest with any woman I ever have sexual relations with.

"What made you come back to my room?"

"James"

"You thought James would be here?" She asks, looking disgusted.

"He said you always talk about me, ask where I am"

"I do. I always wanted to have sex with you"

"Does Kane know?"

"Yeah, I told him I'd fuck you one day"

"What did he say?"

"He likes you, thinks you're a cool individual. He said rather you then someone like James"

"What made you say that, someone like James?"

"Don't know really, he's strange you know"

"Yeah, I know what you mean. He talks about strange things some times"

"Sometimes I know he's watching me, I'll be in a lecture, or walking back through the park at Halls and I'll see him, just staring. I'll have to say, hiya, then he'll stop staring and go back to being normal and start talking to me"

"Do you get the impression he may do bad things?"

"What like we just did?"

Sit in silence and await the next song.

"Do you ever think about death?" She asks me.

"When I was younger, I'd worry about there being a nuclear war. I saw this TV programme called 'Threads', and I'd worry every night that the bomb would drop"

"How old were you?"

"Seven, eight."

"Your parents let you watch that?"

"Yeah, The Omen as well, that freaked me out at the same age. My mum figured there was no point in getting someone to go to bed if they weren't tired, let the kids stay up till they get tired. Made sense to me. What about you, did your parents let you watch those programmes?"

"My dad's dead. My mum is a playgirl"

"What like in the magazines?"

"No, a 'playgirl' stupid. She's a rich bitch, who jets around the world, taking blokes for their money, I've had at least two step fathers since my dad died"

"I wish my dad was dead"

"When I was younger I was kidnapped. My dad's heart never recovered and he had an attack the day I came back"

"Are you serious?"

"I don't care if you believe me or not. Its such a ridiculous story, I tell people cause I know they wont believe me, but I know its true, so that's all the matters. I mean being kidnapped, that happens in the movies, not real life right?"

"I believe you"

"Tell who you want, I don't care, walk around saying that's the girl who bullshits about being kidnapped"

"I'm not going to tell anyone. As you said, who'd believe me?"

"Why do you believe me then?"

"Who would make something like that up in the first place?"

"I've told you a secret, now it's your turn"

"That girl I love. She's a prostitute, her names Carla."

"You said her name as you came, I thought it was all a bit weird, so I didn't say anything." We both go onto her bed. She opens the curtains and the sun shines through. We stand naked by the windows, her with her denim jacket on, watching the world go past. "I guess there's still so much we both have to let go," she says out of the blue, almost as an after thought to herself, but she's right.

"What happened when you was kidnapped?"

"They didn't harm me, or abuse me, it wasn't like in the films.

Part 2: The Best of Times

All I can remember vividly is how I escaped"
"How did you escape?"
"I'd have to kill you if I told you"
We stare in silence and watch spring enter our world.

I'm asleep in my bed, dreaming of the summer, late nights, mornings, the smell of newly cut grass, and I see Carla across the grass, she is dressed in white, I try to reach her, then I'm disrupted by a weight on my bed, the weight of the world. I open my eyes and Alex is staring at me. I forgot to lock the door. I wonder how long he has been there but decide not to ask him; some things are best not known. "What?"

Alex sits on my bed. Is he trying to come onto me? He takes out... Jesus I can't look...

...His credit card, is he going to pay for this? I'm not that cheap or easy... though summer is coming. "I want you to hide my credit card" he passes me over his Barclaycard. I look at the signature, seems easy enough to copy.

I take the credit card and close my eyes. I open them again and he is still staring directly at me. "What?"
"Samantha's pregnant"
"Congratulations. I'm trying to sleep"
"She's going to have an abortion"
"Why are you telling me all this?"
"I haven't told anyone else, we don't always get on but I trust you more than the others"
"You know who the father is? You can borrow the cricket bat if you want?"
"I'm the father. She's always been faithful to me"
"You want to talk?" Why did I say this?

Asleep. A lecture at 9am but I need to sleep. There's a knock at the front door. 8am Mickey Mouse tells me. This knock continues and continues. Taylor is right next to the front door why doesn't he open it? Perhaps Rachel has killed herself again, one can dream, umm, dream, sleep, duvet. The persistent knock on the front door continues. Fuck it! Get up out of bed, dressing gown on and as I reach the door I see Linda on the stairs waiting. Her face is gaunt, blotchy skin, eyes caught in a blizzard. "About time you got up to open it!" She shouts at me and then slams her bedroom door shut. What the fuck. Why didn't she open it? Out of hair gel and massacre to open the door with? Maybe I'll go to a lecture today… or a walk down a certain street, or see if Clarissa wants to have lunch, in bed, nothing serious of course, just, I don't know, just sleep…together

My journey wasn't fruitful, in fact I just walked to Southampton Common and sat down on a bench for 4hours and thought about this last year of my life, it made me tired, need to sleep.

Straight to my room. Glass is all over my bed. The window has smashed finally. I cannot even sleep in my own room now. The TV has gone.

I walk into the living room, where the TV has been put; Amy, Taylor, Alex and Linda are watching it. "What happened to my window?" I ask.

"Don't know mate" Linda replies, "the TV license guy came"

"You better hope you find that licence cause I'm not paying it" Amy says.

"Neither am I" Linda replies.

"I haven't even got a TV" Taylor says.

"But you're all watching my television. You've all watched it since last year"

"Not our problem mate, its in your name and its your TV, you'll have to pay it"

"It's a thousand pound fine"

I go into my room and look at the smashed glass. Whoever took the television – LINDA – must have smashed the window by accident – LINDA. Probably wants to sell it to get money to feed her white line habit. Jesus is telling her she needs to get high. Alex has followed me in, looking at the broken glass, mesmerised by the cut pieces. He wants to talk about Samantha and the abortion. It sounds bad, but I don't want to hear it. "Where the fuck am I going to sleep? I can't sleep here can I?" I shout in disappear.

"The spare room" Alex replies

"What spare room?"

"Christina's old room"

"Christina's old room? When did Christina move out?" You sleep for ten days one day merges into the next. Everyday is the same.

Part 2: The Best of Times

THE PSYCHIATRIST

Linda

Lost little girl looking for a place to hide. There she is again, the child I was once, and the rag china doll is falling apart. Sitting round the courtroom table that is Sunday dinner with the family – a public bar that only the rich ski holiday set frequent in the city of dreams... or nightmares as is the case as the walls close in. Their eyes look at me like its my first day at school and I've brought back a best friend to play with – Katie. They cannot see the tales of excess that I fight on a daily basis.

"How you enjoying university Katie?" My parents ask their new adoptive child, I want to commiserate with Katie that she'll now be looked upon as the sister they always wanted for me to play with like a dolls house off a family. I do not even hear what Katie's reply is – she knows the best answers and ways to act for all such social proceedings, the fake nods of 'how hard the work is' but there's 'always time for fun' but 'nothing like those crazy stories you hear'.

As I look around the pub I notice it's full of students with their parents visiting. Grinning in our 'we know better than you know' splendour that life is meant to be lived not suffocated in a Alice in Wonderland past created by parents a generation behind. Always with the blame they say our generation is – pointing the fingers at those who brought them up, but the cycle will continue with our children – the blame is laid at home because its easier than looking at your own reflection. Us students having chosen this bar by choice – out of the cities reach of student culture but not out of the pull of habitual routines. "Will you back for summer?" All the tables' parents ask simultaneously and it's an answer that leads us all to the biggest generational queue of the decade – The toilet to score.

My eyes awaken from the onrushing bright headlights of my parents eyes, now I'm hidden in the cubicle with Katie as we each draw a patterned line across a small mirror reflection, its part of our make-up bag. The relief of escapism hits through every sleeping vessel and the joy of being alive compared to the dead wood of pretence I had put on shoots through like a train. It's all in control. Just ask any of the mystery guests behind each cubicle door.

"Your parents really love you" Katie tells me as I reach for my first smile of the day.

"They suffocate me, they live in some pretend social world of happy families, social gatherings like barbecues and dating the boy next door. Are your parents like that with you?"

"I come from a family of four sisters and a brother, what do you think they'd be like?"

"Don't they spend time with you?"

"Yeah but you have to spread your love around and that's a lot of equal measures for five kids in twenty-four hours"

Stepping out of the cubicle I circle my reflection – left then right – right then left – content that I can now handle any questions that are fired at me from my parents.

"You seem very quiet Linda, is everything ok?" Dad finally asks.

I look around the seating area and see all the other students nodding to their parents and pretending to listen after visiting their own private cubicles to deal with what gets them through such meetings. "I'm fine"

"You just seem a little lost" Mum continues, it would have been her who asked Dad to bring the question up in the first place – I've never known a man so under the thumb of a woman's rule. If its true we become our parents than that awaits me – the female matriarch who breaks balls of men to get gossip for a weekly column. "Is it boyfriend trouble" My mum thinks anything that might be wrong has to be with the opposite sex, I think I'm a lonely child because they only had sex the once.

"I don't have a boyfriend" I reply.

"I bet Katie has a boyfriend" she says to me rather than Katie.

"No, we're both so busy with our activities to have a long term relationship" Katie replies, I begin to laugh at these 'activities', how can Katie keep a straight face?

"I'm sure your mothers the same, you cant help but be worried" she replies to Katie. "John, why don't you mention who was at our barbecue the other day?"

"What?"

"You know..."

"Oh right, yeah, a psychiatrist who works at your university" Dad states bluntly and Mum gives him the evils. "What?" he says. Katie's face is etched pure stone but I can tell she is laughing non-stop inside.

"Psychiatrist... you think I need a psychiatrist?" I ask disgusted, is there no privacy anymore.

"No, of course not, he just seemed a really nice person and said that loads of students go to speak to him about all different sorts

Part 2: The Best of Times

of problems, doesn't mean they're mad" My mum states drinking from another glass of wine, I don't envy dads drive back with her and then continues to speak as I have no reply... "I spoke about you and he said if ever you needed anything then you should maybe see him" All I can think of is does 'anything' mean he can score me some high quality cocaine? "Will you see him just once for me Linda, please?"

"There's nothing wrong with me" I reply, it's them who need to see someone.

"The Jones's son sees one at his university, half the barbecues parents told us how educational that all their kids have one." She reasons back. So my business will be all common knowledge for the 'family' barbecues back home and mum can say with pride how her daughter is like the neighbours children and has her own resident psychiatrist. Katie then sneezes, wiping white powder from her nose.

I thought they'd be a big black couch for me to lay on and tell the world I wasn't held at birth and that's the answer to everything but it's a hard chair I sit on, opposite a boorish brown desk and a guy who is short, black hair, a light stubble and wears an Armani suit. "Did you want to come here or was it your parents?" He asks me, and he stares at my legs, the black tights I'm wearing. Behind him is a full-length mirror that reflects the entire brittle bones of those awaiting treatment in the 'patients' chair. The reflection begins to show me gaunter, for some reason I keep thinking I'm in a brothel with this red light - psychiatrist's offices and brothels, two sides of the same coin - one fucks your mind the other your body.

"Can't you do something about the light?" I ask him and he turns to look at me staring at my reflection in the mirror that turns gaunter with each passing wasted breath of the day.

I decide to re-cross my legs ala 'Basic Instinct' style, he smiles and says - "It's a true light" and with this the young girl I once was holds the broken china doll in the seat as my reflection.

"So what do you want to hear?" I ask him.

"You tell me" he replies.

"Oh very clever, maybe I'll just sit in silence and let my parents pay for wasting your time"

"If you want to leave Linda that's up to you, you came here not your parents."

"But at the next barbecue I'm sure my mother would bleed it

dry out of you"

"You came and saw me and there was no problems is what I'd say. I get loads of students who come because their parents don't feel complete unless their kid is in therapy, its like the new tea and cakes set" he tells me and laughs, picks up a magazine and ignores me.

I try to move but something stops me inside. "You know I snort shit loads of cocaine, I took some the day my Mum asked me to come and see you and she hasn't got a clue."

"How does it make you feel?" He looks at my tights again and wipes his brow.

"How do you think? You ever done cocaine?"

"Yes"

"Then why even bother asking. If mum knew it would kill her in shame, that's maybe why I'm telling you"

"Part of you wants her to know?" he asks, again he looks at my legs, so I re-cross them and take out a cigarette just like Sharon Stone in the film, he leans across and lights it for me.

"People like you always ask questions with questions, its because you don't have any answers."

"I never said I did" he replies, lights his own cigarette and looks into the reflection again where the young child with the broken china doll stares back at him.

"Answer me this then - I have this recurring dream that I'm the child, I'm in my bedroom back in my parents house and I lay on the bed with all my childhood memories but my favourite is this black china doll that I'd take everywhere with me but its broken. Then I feel the walls closing as I try to mend her before my parents see its broken, the closer they get to the room the more I suffocate and the doll breaks into pieces" I wait for a reply. "So?"

"So?" He replies back, again looking at my black tights.

"Lets cut to the chase, do you want to fuck me?" Fucking the psychiatrists whom my mum begged me to see would be an even better buzz than snorting cocaine over lunch with her.

"Not particularly" he replies. And the china doll in the reflection breaks and the walls begin to close in. I cannot breathe.

Simon

Dear Mark Gammond,
I apologise for not turning up to lectures and not being able to hand certain work in on time, I really need an extension on my essays. I'm going to be honest with you - I have a drink and drug problem.

Part 2: The Best of Times

I have never lived away from home before, hardly drunk or taken any drugs, then all of sudden I'm in an environment where I am living on my own, learning to cook and clean and be responsible for myself but I have found drink and drugs easy and cheap to come by. I've taken all these to the limit and I realise I have become dependent on them. I can't leave my room in halls unless I am stoned or unless I'm going to get drunk. I'm really scared about what I might do, I feel really depressed.

The depression of being like this just makes me stay away from the course even more as I feel like a failure to both you, the other tutors on the course, all who have been welcoming to me and most of all to my parents, I cant tell them this as they would be so disappointed. This just adds to my depression, of being away and having this addiction. To cure the depression I keep drinking and taking drugs to make things better but they are just making things worse. I have seriously contemplated harder drugs in this last month. I know this is no excuse for not handing in the essays on time but I need help. This is a cry for help, I am pathetic, I am worthless, and I am drunk.

Yours Sincerely, Simon Curbishley

Steve helped me with part of the letter, saying his letter was about the same thing and it got him an extension in his essays and a date with the resident psychiatrist to help him instead of turning up for lectures. I think I can bear that if it means an extra reason not to turn up.

Mark Gammond asks me into his office. I expect my marching orders from the course. He puts his glasses on and sits on the desk putting his arm on my shoulder like a caring father would. "How are you Simon?"

"I got locked in a closet, it took me a day to get out, that's why I wasn't able to come in yesterday"

"There's a film in that Simon, think about it, there's film" I think about it.

"You know Simon, if you need to talk to anyone I'm always here for you, you're not alone. I want you to know you can approach me whenever you want. It's not easy being away from the home for the first time. When I first left, I went to see David Bowie in LA, I took acid, you know what I mean don't you Simon?" I nod my head and let him continue. Still thinking about how I could make a film about being stuck in a closets? "I get a lot of bullshit excuses from people unable to do essays, but I've been able to tell for a long time you was troubled. You're an intelligent young man, I wish I could have known your problems earlier and helped them, but I'm here for you now. You want to talk? You need an extension on an essay? You just come to me first, no problem, we can't sort things out. If you need sometime back home, no problem, it won't affect your grades and attendance. Just don't want you to think you're alone, you're not. I used to drink, I took acid seeing Bowie in the seventies, I know man, I know what you're going through, kindred spirits, right Simon?"

"Right." I reply, imagining being stuck in a closet with a film camera. He gives me a cuddle.

No long black couch. No shelves off books speaking in the silence of the room as the pages open to me. Not even a maze of the Institute, like Nicholson in The Shining. "The maze is the lay out of the hotel you know? That's how the kid knows his way out." The psychiatrist tells me, sitting on a chair reminiscent of Captain Kirks in 'Star Trek'.

"How did you know what I was thinking?" I reply, sitting on a cold wooden chair, reminiscent of something from Sunday school.

"Its what all the students think when they first come in here," he replies, and smiles, showing big black stained teeth from the roll ups he smokes in his hand.

"Why haven't you got a beard?" I ask him, he's clean-shaven, has short hair, he doesn't look how I'd expected a psychiatrist to look.

"People have such a strange notions of psychiatry as white fuzzy haired bearded people, who wear tweed jackets with elbow patches. See this jacket, its from Next, four hundred pound for the entire suit" He stands before me, looking like an Italian gangster. "You want to touch it?"

"No"

"Of course not, maybe later. Once you accept why you're here, then you'll be wanting to touch it all the time"

"No I wont"

"Just admit it, Steve, you're a homosexual"

"Steve? My names Simon"

"What? Shit, er, you're not Steve Reed"

"No, he's a friend of mine, he's waiting outside, we swapped appointments"

"Forget everything I just said. Excuse me please" He steps behind a hospital curtain rail that is drawn behind his desk. Looking round the room, there are posters of Madonna and Marylyn Monroe. He steps back out, dressed in a tweed jacket with elbow patches, a white

Part 2: The Best of Times

frizzy haired wig and a fake beard. He tears down the posters of Madonna and spends the next ten minutes erecting bookshelves and filling them with long titled books on psychiatry.

I sit in silence. The longer I sit here, the more likely I'll miss my next lesson. He sits down and takes out a pipe. He rocks back and forth. And finally speaks in an American accent. "So Simon, what seems to be the problem?"

"Nothing" I reply. *And that is the problem – I feel nothing.*

Steve

One-man leaves, one man enters. "What was it like?" I ask Simon.

"He thought I was you" Simon replies.

Fears rush through my confused mind. "What did he tell you?"

"I don't know I was really stoned, just kept wanting me to touch his suit"

Sounds interesting, I hope its from Next or Top Man. I enter into the dark surroundings and find a man of average height and middle age removing a fake white beard from his face and then a white curly wig from his head. "Don't look at me!" He shouts towards me in the fear that I have seen his secret identity like a superhero – The Psychiatrist.

Dear Mark Gammond,

I apologise for my lack of attendance and handing in essays late. I know I always ask for extensions but I really do need some time to adapt to being away from university. Please let me have this opportunity to come clean about my problems, I hope you maybe able to help me come to terms with them as I am truly struggling. Before I left to university I was having certain personal issues with my sexuality, I haven't told anyone this, especially my family, who would be heartbroken. My father is a violent man, an alcoholic, who is very biased against any such same sex relations.

Without having anyone to talk too and now being thrown into an environment where I don't know anyone and don't know who I truly am, I struggle to do myself justice on the course at present. I struggle to even get up some mornings; my confusion is not helped by the fuelled student life of casual sex, easy drink, accessible drugs and free money.

I think I am gay. You are the first person I have told. I don't know what to do and where to go to next.

I know this is no excuse for not handing my work in and having bad attendance but I hope that you can maybe see it from my confused point of view and possibly advise me to what I can do to rectify my personal situation and help me come to terms with this.

The course is all important to me, it is the only thing that I understand in my life at the moment, please don't take it away from me, I don't know how I'd cope without it.

Yours Sincerely, Steve Reed

PS: Please keep my secret a secret.

The psychiatrist having changed into a Next suit, then his appearance to - short hair with light stubble, stops reading the letter. "Tell me about this letter Steven?"

Whenever someone's being serious with you they always use your full name. "I figured if that doesn't give me essay extensions I don't know what will." He doesn't reply and just stares at me, I hate this, I feel uncomfortable in the silence...god, someone talk please. "Don't you believe it then"

"Doesn't matter what I think. Matters if you think your secret is true or not"

"Who'd make something like that up?"

"You make it sound like your secret is wrong"

"Everyone seems to treat it like a disease. All the women I know say they want to cure me. It's not a disease. I'm not dying. It's who I am. Maybe?"

"Do you only tell women?"

"They're a couple of guys I've told as well"

"Boyfriends?"

"No, straight guys. Well, they say they're straight"

"Seems like it's not much of a secret."

"I tried to tell a mate of mine called Matt Ryan yesterday"

"Ah yes, Matt Ryan"

"You know him?"

"Everyone knows Matt Ryan. How did he take it?"

"I said to him – 'I have a secret that is a Greek tragedy oiled in mythology.' He replied 'what the fuck is it with you and the oils'?"

"What is it with the oils Steven?"

"I haven't finished the story yet." I stare into the giant mirror behind me and picture myself naked in a bath full of baby oil.

"He then said to me that he had a secret as well, when I asked what it was he said – 'its wanting everyone to shut the fuck up and just live in silence'. I then asked if he wanted to know mine but he replied if I was fucking deaf and didn't hear a word he said"

"Sounds like he has issues."

"He has issues with his father, he wants him dead."

"You mention your father in the letter…"

"Here we go, I was wondering when this line of thought was coming."

"What line of thought?"

"One time my dad came to pick me up, a weekend back in Brighton. I saw his car pull up and I headed downstairs into the courtyard of halls of residence, where he was already swearing and looking pissed off. Walking towards the car, I hear a smash and a broken plate is next to my foot, surely he's not throwing things at me already I thought. – 'Fucking hell Steve Boy, its raining plates' – my dad said pointing to the sky. A stream of plates come down, smashing round the courtyard, they are thrown from a window and I follow the stream of plates and recognise the faces – 'See you later Steve Boy' – Simon, James, Johnny and Blonde Paul shouted throwing plates towards me – 'You fucking cunts! Come down here and I'll kick the shit out of you' – My Dad said and he opened the boot… I knew he was reaching for his axe. How can I ever tell him what I've written down in that letter?"

"Your dad carries an axe around with him?"

"The guy carries an axe everywhere, even public toilets. He chased me before with it down Brighton seafront; people thought they were watching a film being shot. So, all this pent up frustration my father shows and hatred towards all men especially any mention of gays is really him trying to find hide his own feelings that he is…gay." My father is gay? "Wow, my father is like this because he is gay and that explains why I'm gay, wow how did you do that?" I ask the superhero psychiatrist.

"I didn't do anything?"

"You worked out my father is gay"

"Why would an axe chase and hatred feelings towards other men mean your father was gay do you think? Is he the same with your mother and sister?"

"Of course he hates everyone."

"What does that tell you Steve?"

"That he's not gay? Perhaps he's a-sexual and that's why he hates everyone? Guess you want to know if I hate my father?"

"All kids in therapy hate one of their parents, it's why their parents beg them to come"

I stare into the giant mirror behind him and look at my reflection, a clown stares back doing juggling tricks. "Nothing in my life makes any sense. The only sensible thing I've seen all day was two white birds flying across the water, urging one another to fly deeper and swim across the surface. Then as they went back up, water dripping from their beaks like the touch of a holy grail, they charted off into distant lands heading towards the sunset over the city park. Hand in hand."

I sit there out of place in a world that questions everything I feel inside.

DO YOU FEEL THE MUSIC?

Johnny

As you get to know people their names seem to suit them perfectly. Each name has its own sound. It's the same with drugs, a pill to revaluate your death and live-forever. Getting a third person involved seemed important, with just James and I taking them it could have been a bit boring, you always need a third, a 'holy trinity'. Bad idea. I could see the state Steve was in; very emotional, looked like he had the weight of the world on his shoulders, never a good time to do what we're doing. Living forever wasn't high on his agenda tonight, and his face was crushed with lines before his time. When he came in and said - "I'll do it with you" and practically snatched the pill from my hand, there was no hesitation in his grasp, no panic in his touch, just pure emotional wreckage.

As he swallowed the pill he looked like the survivor of a train wreck from his day, something that he'd never get over and the pill would help him forget. His tracksuit looked beaten, his eyes welled with tears. But James and I ignored this and just thought selfishly that he could complete the numbers and form a circle, well, a triangle. Never give someone acid when they are at emotional low. You need to be relaxed, you need to be level headed and just go with it. It makes you face yourself at your worst and ugliest. If you can't laugh at the mirror but analyse and cannot look away, then you're in trouble. And what the mirror was showing of Steve's problems was too much for him. "I can't get out!" Steve is crying, tears flooding down his face, a fountain that no-one wants to play in. James and I cannot bear to watch.

James doesn't help matters, he tries to analyse what's going on, thinking it will help to do Steve's face in. "Can't get out of where

Part 2: The Best of Times

Steve?"

"The TV, I'm in the fucking TV!" Steve isn't laughing, he is shaking; he really thinks he's inside the TV. Fuck.

"What you doing in the TV Steve?" James asks, he laughs a nervous laugh and hopes that this is all a bad joke. You can tell it's making him come down because of it, he's trying to keep it up but Steve is seriously losing it. This is no joke. Ignore all this and concentrate on the music, Stone Roses 'I wanna be adored' it doesn't fit the situation well. The more you try and help, the worst he's going to get, the worse I'm going to feel and come down. Like James I'm trying my own way to not come down, to ignore the situation but when that situation is in your room and sitting on your bed its kind of difficult.

"Its like you're all watching me, I'm a fucking show on TV!" Steve's eyes are all over the place, neither in the same direction at the same time, but both showing his captive audience the same signals. He has lost it. And it's going to get worse.

"Then switch the channel," I suggest calmly. If I can act calm, I won't start to come down myself, it's each man for himself in this situation. The last thing Steve needs is us all inside the TV, then we'll all be lost in a soap opera that mirrors are lives.

"Yeah, just change the channel from yourself to Eastenders and Arthur Fowler's allotment" James says all serious for the first time tonight. I've got the feeling that he's on standby at present and one false move he'll be next to Steve on the channel of our lives.

Steve is silent for a minute. I can see him physically trying to change the channel in his mind, this isn't good, the more he tries to change it, the more he is shaking, hands up to his head, rubbing his face, eyes alerted by any movement or sound. I've had the tunnel before, running down trying to reach the light, sewage water streaming across your feet, the sound of rats biting at your laces, but I've never been stuck inside a TV. At least with the tunnel you can run, but how you can run inside a small box? I'm just glad the TV is in colour. "I can't! I'm fucking stuck! I can't get out!" Steve stands up panicking. "I can't get out of the TV!" He tries to walk round the room, knocking into things he's hyperventilating. "I can't get out, I can't get out...what am I going to do, fucking hell"

I roll a joint, but as Steve heads towards the door I feel I should stop him, if we don't stay with him I fear for his life. This is bringing me down really bad now, I've got to stay with it for Steve's sake, James isn't going to help, he's the worst person to be with when this happens. Laughter doesn't solve everything, what's needed is calm, someone who isn't on the acid, someone who can take care of Steve whilst James and I continue on our own trips and paranoia. If not we're all fucked, we'll all be inside the TV. James steps up to leave. "Where you going James? Don't fucking leave me!" Steve is panicking, holding my TV control, and pressing the buttons. "Its not fucking working…." He checks the batteries, rubs them with his hand and places them back in. "Its not fucking working!" The next stage hits; the tears of acceptance. "I'll never see my mum or sister again, I don't care about my dad"

The TV control is staring at me, if I press a button, I'll be inside. Always as a kid you can't help but do what you shouldn't, you want to see what will happen. "Take the TV control with you," I tell James.

James looks tentatively towards the TV control. Someone has just stepped on his grave. "No fucking way. I'm not touching it"

"Why wont neither you touch the TV control?" Steve asks. His face is all serious, the panicking and acceptance have stopped, welcome to the most dangerous stage paranoia against your friends. Steve becomes suicidal. "Fucking hell, you're all leaving me. I want to fucking die, if I can't get out I want to die." I make sure there's know sharp instruments that can be used in his suicidal bid to get out of the TV.

James and I sit on the park bench outside Halls. We've hit rock bottom. It's 4am and we have only managed to walk two hundred yards in over three hours. Each step on the pavement was a miracle of mind over matter. I held the TV control, wearing black gloves, that way it couldn't touch my skin and infect me. "Do you think he'll be all right?" James asks me. He keeps looking across at the phone box in the park and then turning pale.

I look at Steve; he has climbed up the same tree he climbed as before when people found him on magic mushrooms. He is curled up, next to a bird's nest; at least he has stopped crying. "I'm not going to get him down, are you?" I get to the point with James.

"No" James replies.

"Do you want to know my secret?" Steve shouts out towards us. And he shouts out to all who can hear, some secret, I'd imagine all of the Halls of Residence heard.

"I hate myself. I want to fucking die." He says at the end, after revealing his mask behind this masquerade. He should never have taken the acid when this confused about life, about family, about

Part 2: The Best of Times

himself. Being inside the TV, unable to change the channel, unable to get out, it all makes sense when he reveals his secret. He's scared to come out.

James and I both sit in silence. A shadow comes across the trees, at first we think its Steve, but we can still see his shadow hanging from the skyline above the tree. The park has street lamps, as they'd been a few cases of girls being attacked on their way back to halls, through the park. Now it's lit with streets lamps, shadows move across the fields, the park has become even more dangerous to the naked eye. Playing tricks on all you fear. The shadow enters the phone box and takes out a bag of money. Without a second thought he throws it up in the air and hundreds of pounds fall down over him like the first flake of snow on Christmas morning. When it does snow at Christmas? Never. When do people throw hundreds of pounds up in the air? Never. Exactly, that's my point. The last of the money falls from his long black jacket, onto the phone box floor, the notes sit with nightclub fliers, sex chat lines, and a torn phone book of numbers. The entire world of our mass culture basically. It was some statement for the shadow to make and as he disappears into the night, the shadow turns to James and I, tipping his hat "What do you reckon?" I break the silence, staring at the phone box.

"You do it, not me" James replies, turning a whiter shade of pale by each passing breath that comes from the phone box and its contents of society we bleed dry.

"What's with you and the park tonight, James?"

"Sometimes in this place, when you're in the shadows you can hear the entire planets conversations."

Finally, Steve climbs down from the tree. Neither us bother to help him down. He walks up to us on the bench, ice-cold stare, and a broken soul. "I want to go back"

I don't mention the TV, if he's still inside or needs the control. We walk back in complete silence. Steve goes straight to his room. Scared he may still be suicidal I go into his prison cell with him and make sure there's no knifes or anything else lying about. "I'm ok now"

"Good" I reply.

"Thanks Johnny" The door locks.

James returns to my room and we light up a joint. He presses play on the stereo and 'I Wanna Be Adored' plays. I get a flashback of events and immediately skip the track.

"What did you do that for?" James asks.

"We never listen to that song again." It will be a good month before I'll even think of touching acid again. A pill to revaluate your death and live-forever.

Matthew

Do you feel the music? Something is changing in this country. 'Some Might Say' got to number one in the spring. The Tories got trounced in the council elections; it was all over the news. The music is capturing the mood of the moment… it's the best years of our lives. We can live together, with dreams and fantasies of a better life, they've invited me into an inclusive group. "Come and join us," they sing to me. They're not snobbish or snooty, they don't care that my jumpers are tatty, that my jeans are baggy, that my trainers are old, that my hair is unkempt. They've created their own club, where if you look a smart boy, you're not coming in. The faces in town are the faces of the students, the faces of freaks, the faces of 'what ifs', and now we have centre stage, voices want to be heard. We can make a difference.

If only we knew where to start, if we had the education to speak. It's a nice notion I paint, a nice empty canvass to be filled by dreams. As I stand in HMV with too many CDs to buy, seeing the masses like me with a student loan that needs to be spent ……Sod revolution, I want to buy the sales. I want to get stoned. I want to get drunk. I want to get laid. The revolution can wait for tomorrow.

I spot Simon; he has got his German army jacket on, looking like Jarvis Cocker. He has about five CD's already in his hand. "I could do with some weed for tonight you know mate?" I say, hoping he has some on him and will share it with me. He doesn't reply. "Really need to get stoned before seeing the Boo Radleys tonight," I beg him.

Between us we buy in the three for twenty pound section:

Neil Young – After the Gold Rush (Simon), Sebadoh – Bakesale (Simon), Charlatans – Some Friendly (Simon), Talking Heads –Fear of Music (Simon), REM – Monster (Me), Mazy Starr – (Me), Happy Mondays – Pills, Thrills & Bellyaches (Simon), Velvet Underground – Velvet Underground (Simon), Doors – LA Woman (Simon), Teenage Fanclub – Grand Prix (Me), Ride – Going Blank Again (Me).

James comes over empty handed. "Do you feel the music?" I ask him.

"I don't understand what people want from me?" James says, his eyes blazing a trail of emotion and confusion. The two fit like hand to glove.

Part 2: The Best of Times

The people in this house haven't brought any weed since I've lived here; they live of the dregs of mine. It's like living with the 'weed tramps'; even Amy smokes now, the girl who "didn't come to Uni to do drugs". As for Linda whose opinion was the same, her eyes and face are a cocaine blizzard. The poor girl hit the ground running, still least she doesn't complain about my music being too loud late at night anymore now she's pre-occupied with her habit.

In walks Alex. He doesn't say a word. Just goes straight for my CDs and looks down them. Then stops, turns to me and looks at my clothes. He then looks down my closet. "What the fuck are you doing?" I finally ask him. Most people would have asked straight away but with Alex he's so odd this is normal behaviour.

"My credit card" he replies.

"I hid it in my wallet"

"No its not there. I took it back and used it when you was out and then re-hid"

"You gave me your credit card to hide, I hide it for you, then when I'm out you find it, use it and then re hide it my room where I wont know where it is but only you, who wants it hidden from himself in the first place?" I've now got a headache after saying all that.

"Yes, but if I don't know where its hidden I cant use it when I need too, can I?!"

"Get the fuck out of my room!" The radio begins to talk about the WAR. I can't stand this bullshit anymore and I leave my room, with Alex still inside searching high and low through all my private possessions for his credit card. I don't care anymore, as there's a War going on apparently, maybe we'll all be called up to the front line of the respective record company offices. Sitting in the living room the Nine O'clock news has a main story about -

THE WAR. BLUR VERSUS OASIS.

The main news guy with a straight face talks about the massive WAR going on and how we must choose a side. We all watch hundreds of people going into record shops and being interviewed about what song they prefer and why. This is the main news? Nobody died? There's no threat of nuclear attack? There are no political upheavals? What about the new labour leader, Tony Blair? Oh, there he is, giving his opinions on what song he prefers. What some people will do for the student vote.

"Your right this is stupid" Linda says. I pause in stony silence, the cocaine fuelled Essex girl has agreed with me for once in this house. I could kiss her but she looks really disgusting with all that hair gel. "Blur will win easily as Damon's really sexy," she continues. There you have it - The Golden era of British pop music: Female Musical Prostitution.

    Leaving today. Going back home. But where is home? Here or there? Maybe its no-where. My bag is packed. My parents are here to take me back to a different form off insanity from what I've known here. I wonder how I can go back to that town now after the year I've spent. I don't mean to sound superior but the people back there wouldn't understand. Wouldn't know the fucked up state of joy and fear I have felt these past nine months.

    The most important thing is my deposit; my dad wants it back so he can get pissed on it. I fail to mention the burnt table from the Barbecue we had yesterday. I got stoned and pissed last night at the Barbecue, awaiting the paranoia of my parents seeing and invading what is now my world, now my home. All the posters had come down. Take one last look at the room that I slept so much in. Such a massive part of my soul remains in here. I wish I could stay in it for eternity, stay this age forever, and relieve that first year each day. Each final look brings a different memory, eternal faces, spoken sentences and a different fear.

    I don't bother to say goodbye to anyone in the house. I hate goodbyes, scared of what tomorrow may bring. Sitting in the car with a year of my life packed into a trunk and a back seat, I see Linda returning from the shops, looking jaded and lost. "Doesn't she live with you?" Mum says. I tell them to get the car moving. Linda glances up and puts half a hand up to wave goodbye but I turn away and pretend I didn't see her.

    I can feel myself changing into that person of twelve months ago as I go back in the car. My Mums speaking to me, my Dad is moaning about wanting to get down the pub in time. But I'm oblivious to what they both say. I just watch the road; the places that have become my new home and memories fill up. And a smile reaches my face. BritPop they call it. BritPop I'm living it.

Part 2: The Best of Times

LONG HOT SUMMER

Matthew

Bored. It's only been three weeks and I'm already counting the days to going back to Southampton. I have crafty joints to myself in my room and open the window fully hoping they wont smell the weed. My parents don't even know I smoke. That's what I tell myself. The new 'Underworld' album hasn't left my stereo this summer; it will have to be surgically removed. 'Woowie, Zowie, by Pavement has been my other summer album, stoned bliss, inane babble, my personality in a nutshell. Britain has become exciting again; I know this cause I read it in the NME. Magazines are fleshed out with glamour models, a return to the swinging sixties, where culture surrounds music. Kate Moss is pictured everywhere, looking moody, eyes that tell us we want more. A few days ago, I watched the rain from my window, and marvelled as it fell across the street. I wanted to be like the rain, and arrive falling from the skies in a random place, then slowly travel across the wet streets and see where it would take me. So I left the house. Left the protection of a world outside my window for the first time in weeks. I left the city. I travelled down to the big city, paved with gold, where the excitement is pictured in so many magazines, with so many faces. Our faceless peers with hearts of revolutions in their head. I go to visit 'The Shark' - Damien Hurst. What does it mean? What does it say? Looking at its skin, looking at its dead eyes that are full of life and vengeance. I could be looking in a mirror.

"It's a shark" a guy stands next to me, it's him, from 'our nations' band. "I guess you want my autograph?"

"Yeah" I reply. The truth is I don't but it would seem rude to break the guys ego.

I understood that shark, the feeling that we can all go that bit further, that anything was possible. Sitting in a beer garden, I'm pissed already. People around me, they're talking about old times but it doesn't annoy me like I thought it would. It's almost like being back in Southampton. Back home, as that's what it is I realise now. And I'm going to stay there after the course finishes. This long hot summer has taught me that.

Linda

Next year I'll be different. The year starts in September and ends in June. July and August are 'nothing' months. I never thought I'd be happy feeling nothing but the truth is I do. I'm sitting at home in my old bedroom what a year ago was my life. I feel cold, isolated and out of place in what was once my sanctuary. The room was untouched by my parents. It was like I had died and they were too emotional to touch anything. On the wall are posters of boy and girl pop acts, my teddies of comfort on the bed and floor. This isn't my room anymore but a young girl who had dreams. The only dream I have at the moment is to feed my habit. I need some coke. Especially lying here with a pure past and a reflection of a girl who was once happy staring at me. She's here you know at the end of the bed. There she stares with an innocent look of wonder and excitement at what awaits her. She wants to ask me what has happened? I'm too ashamed to speak. And she disappears.

Staring at the ceiling counting the hours till Garry comes round. My parents think he's my boyfriend. They think he's a nice clean living boy I met at university. They leave me alone to score what I need from Gary and I ask him to stay for longer so my parents don't realise that he's my dealer. They wouldn't know what a dealer is "A car dealer?" my dad would say.

September this year, it will be different. It will be Katie and I in a house together. No more music from Matt's room. No more weird talks with Alex. No more moaning from Amy. Katie came to visit last week for a few days. She doesn't seem to have a problem taking the class A's that I do. She can turn it on and off when she wants. Just like she can with sex. I've got an itch down below. I've got a blizzard up above. I pull the duvet over me and hide away. The young girl appears under the duvet all smiles and goes to kiss me goodbye

Alex

The post arrives and it's the letter I've been waiting for. My father's best friend has died. He left his house in Tottenham to me rather than my sister or dad. I own the estate. All those days of telling him what he wanted to hear on his deathbed paid off. "Father cheated on mum, when he left us we had nothing" I fail to mention the house being in mums name and it was dad who started with nothing.

"How could he do that you Alex?" He wheezed out, as I sat there praying he'd last the night so I could get him to change his estate.

"Mum was suicidal. I had nothing at university no money, I even contemplated becoming a rent boy" I failed to mention the student loan, full government grant. I don't lie I just distort the truth. I'm just telling a dying man what wants to hear; that the man, my father, who he trusted and loved like brother, was an arsehole, and that he, my fathers best friend, can redeem himself for all his own sins and prove himself a better man than my father is.

Best I don't tell anyone for the moment. Maybe tell Samantha and we'll have a new secret to share and keep our relationship built on deceit going. A rich deceit this time that she won't be able to resist. I dial Samantha's number.

"Hello?" I don't answer. "Hello?" I don't answer. "Fine" She slams the phone down.

I press redial. "Hello?" I don't answer. "Hello?" I don't answer. Let the games begin.

Steve

I tried to tell my parents. That's a lie to a certain extent as I tried to tell my Mum. Asked her 'hypothetically speaking' what she thought of gays? She laughed and said she was glad that I wasn't one. When I started speaking about gay rights my dad turned on us all. "What's the matter are you a fucking queer?"

"No, I just think they have as much rights as everyone else"

"What the fuck do you care?"

"Alan, there's no need to start an argument"

"Shut up you fucking bitch" My sister starts to laugh. "You can shut up as well you fucking whore, you and your boyfriend fucking away in this house, you're not even eighteen"

"I wish I would never have brought it up"

"You're fucking trouble maker Steve, sticking up for fucking faggots"

"I can't wait to go back and leave you. Wanker" This was not a good move on my part.

"Well lets make sure you fucking leave then"

Dad chased me outside and picked up an axe. I if I told people this they wouldn't believe me, just think I had watched the Shining too many times. As I run as fast as I can down the hill and towards the beach with my dad fifty yards behind wielding an axe shouting 'fucking bastard" Mutley our dog runs alongside me thinking it's some game we're playing and has a look of joy and excitement in his stupid eyes, his tongue hanging out, turning to wag his tail towards Dad with the axe and then catch up with me again. Must be great to be a dog.

Johnny

Five essays to re-do over the entire summer. I start all five with a week to go. Get stoned. I finish all five with six days to go. Get stoned Surely they wouldn't really kick me off the course? Get stoned.

PART 3

September '95 to January 1st '96

Wasted

The mushroom season will soon be upon us.
Walking the fields in the late summer that dawn into the Indian autumn.
Magic is in the air.

THE HOLY TRINITY

Matthew

The streets are empty and I stand-alone. Engulfed by giant buildings of the windy city. I recognise the faces that peer down onto me, they point and laugh but I cannot hear their words, only the silence of the in-coming storm. What was once bright and full of warmth turns violent but I cannot run. The rain is cold but it burns my skin as it falls from the coldest sky. Why can't I move? The violence washes from the storm towards me, stuck in the centre of a crossroads. I feel nothing. I don't even want to move now. But accept the fate. It swallows me hole into the eye of the hurricane and I do nothing but stare into the abyss...

...I wake up with a start. Sweating from a dream of a city that for once I saw as a nightmare. Today I travel back to 'The Windy City'. Home?

The wind seems more violent then the year before as I walk from the station to my new home. My hair, which is now floppy over my ears, touching the tip of my nose, waves in various directions. I cannot see anything past the hair, distorting my sense. The 'windy city' is not pleased to see me for once. The sun is blinding but cold. It blinds me as it reflects into the puddle waters that lye in wait like bombs left by past soldiers who have walked the same road, and were struck down by the blinding light of their grizzled reflections.

Putting the key into the lock I pause. An Irish tramp, green hat, duffel bag, food ridden beard, sits on the subway wall watching me struggling with the keys and the demons of the nightmare I had dreamt this morning. "The key to the entire street you hold there" he says, and takes a bottle of white lighting into his dead liver. "Join me for a drink?" I ignore him. He has replaced the Asian Nutter Tramp, a higher class of verbal bollocks in the area.

As the front door opens the first thing that hits me are two complete strangers in the hallway staring at me. One guy, one girl, they look no older than sixteen. Have I got the keys to the right house? "Alright" I say to them. Maybe it was next door that I was meant to go? The key for this house opens every house in this street, the tramp told me. Maybe it opens Kaos and Kasbahs as well? Could be very useful.

"This is Taylor's and Rachel's house," I'm told by this spawny sixteen year-old whose voice hasn't broken. That figures. Rachel. I thought she'd be long gone this year. Not another year of fake suicide attempts, psychotic behaviour, screaming at Angel Heart, stealing milk, illegal Benefit cheques and no rent being paid. This has put me on a downer already and I feel the need to get pissed.

As I sit on Taylor's bed, he explains to me that him and Rachel have broken up. I can't help but wonder why she is naked in bed next to him then? But I don't ask as Rachel's exact words are - "I'm going back to Reading to live full-time. Got a new boyfriend there and a job. Will you miss me this year?" I don't reply but just smile.

I unpacked automatically this time without a second thought, knowing exactly where each personal possession will go, don't feel scared or excited just the need to get wasted again. It took precisely thirty minutes and the ideal I created of concentrating on the course, arriving late and being more secluded away from everyone has gone and I just want to get drunk and stoned. I have no will power, but fuck it, I'm at Uni. I've only got two years left before the world swallows me up into its vacuum of mediocrity. Soon I'm greeted by each member of the house, coming into my room to say hello and the age old horrible question – 'How was your summer?' It's like a hairdresser asking you if "your going anywhere nice your holidays?" No one really cares about the answer; it's a polite pleasantry we feel we have to ask everyone.

Samantha comes into my room wearing her pyjama's says - "Hi, how was your summer?" and lays on my bed, not seductively but just collapses for no apparent reason.

"I thought you was going to Uni in Portsmouth?" I ask her, not remotely interested if she is or doesn't, just want her to get out of my room. I sat alone most of the summer, living of the memories of that first year. It's now the only place I feel content. I want to be alone again. Live the memories for the next two years and maybe time will stand still.

"I am next week, I thought I'd spend this week with Amy" she replies, making sure not to mention Alex, the games those two play, oh the hilarity. I leave her to it and go downstairs into the living room, where Rachel has now joined her primary school mates sitting on our sofas. I can't help but ask immediately, "When are you leaving?" trying to sound all sincere but it comes out as I truly mean it – "Get the fuck out of this house you psycho"

When I return back into my bedroom, Amy and Lauren now join Samantha collapsed on the bed. All three in their pyjamas, do I share a bed with these three?

"Are you living here as well Lauren?"

"No" she replies. I decide not to ask her why she is sitting on my bed then in her pyjamas.

Next to join the party on the bed is Simon, looking extremely hungover, a joint in one hand, can of lager this early in the other. Luckily he's not wearing his pyjamas. Where there is one, there is always the other not far away. Johnny appears in my room on the floor with a McDonalds drink and meal. "Are you going to put that in the bin Johnny?" Already I'm worried about the state of my room. At last I have a room upstairs, but it means that everyone convenes in it, on the way to the toilet. No one wants to be left out of my pyjama welcoming party where I invited no one but everyone came bearing gifts for themselves.

"They've kicked me off the course, those wankers" Johnny begins to roll a joint, tearing rizzla paper across my floor, and tobacco into the carpet.

"Are you just here to make a mess of my room? Of my life?"

"When did you become so anal?" Johnny replies to me. He's right, when did I?

I collapse onto the floor next to him and start to roll one up with his gear. "Can you feel the cold?" I ask.

"I said I was kicked of the course, but no-ones asked why?" And no one does again. The inevitable is always boring. "I don't think they found my film funny"

"What did you do film?"

"A shit being flushed down the toilet with an impression of Mark Gammond" Silence. How do you follow up such an emotional statement of human awareness? The only way Johnny knows how too - "I can't go home, my parents think I'm still on the course, they've given me loads of money as I said I'd sorted myself out. I got no-where to stay, can I stay here?"

That night I dreamt I was falling from a great height. I couldn't stop myself as I didn't care enough, too wasted to move, my mind was stoned, my body was drunk, my eyes blinded by my hair. There was no ground to hit. It was eternal.

It didn't take long. The 'Holy Trinity' is formed. Simon, Johnny and I are the only one's willing to buy weed in the house and who can skin up. There seemed nothing else to do. The clubs were the same clubs as last year, this time with new people, looking innocent with wonder, fear and suicidal, all the looks we carried with us. This depressed us, not that they've taken over our places, but that we

Part 3: Wasted

cannot ever get those feelings back of a new world. The once warm windy city, with friendly bright colours, had turned into violent colours that would stop and start on us, give us excess in one hand and then depression in the next. Excess that would leave us locked into a form of complete madness. We had achieved too much, too soon, now it would be harder to get back those feelings. Every joint paints its own picture. Mine is the cold autumn nights, there has been no Indian summer this time. Just wanting to be indoors and do nothing. Feel nothing. Later would take care of later. Each day to merges into one - nothing. Welcome back to my empty portrait.

Who the fuck am I?

Back for three weeks now and I've left the house only to score weed everyday between lectures. In three weeks, the 'Holy Trinity' has brought on average an eighth a day between us. This in the third week has moved to a quarter a day.

I cannot move.

Lauren's Sega play station wakes me up as Simon and Johnny sit in my room playing on 'Sonic the hedgehog'. "What time is it?" I ask, hoping they will tell me it's 4pm and time to score some weed.

"10am" they reply, both have a joint each and pass them simultaneously towards me.

The room is stuffy; it's the only way to keep warm. It doesn't rain outside, but there seems to be a constant storm, with no calm before it. The 'windy city' is living up to its billing. It's safer inside with the radiators on, the joints keeping me warm. I don't want to step outside and go out for the night. It's too cold. "This is our education, wake our life up each morning with medicine. Sitting in our holy circle where we feed our education. Our black couch says we're psychiatrists in this perfection. But do we stand as tall and pure as our medicine?" I rhyme.

Aren't we taught that life should have routine? 10am smoke weed until 2pm. 2pm go into lectures. 6pm score some more weed on the way back home and begin to smoke. 10pm still smoking weed and maybe go to a club, usually Nexus, as they don't mind you skinning up. Stay till 2am and go back to the house and smoke till 5-6am. Go to Sleep. Wake up 10am. Sonic the Hedgehog. Get those magic rings

I Seemed to have spent the last three weeks between my room and Simon's sitting on beds that are covered in tobacco packets, rizzla's, roach material, bread and biscuit crumbs, all inside a hazing ring of smoke that protects us from outsiders but wont let us ever leave, the holy trinity getting caned all the way to heaven. In my dreams are Frank Zappa's 'Lumpy Gravy' and Captain Beefhearts 'Trout Mask Replica'.

"Alright" a stranger walks in, it could be any of the other housemates. What do you say back? What is there to discuss? "Don't you guys ever want to go out?" another strangers voice, this time a female asks.

"I'm warm here. I'm safe here" I reply.

When I'm alone I stick on the new Oasis Album I brought this week, 'What's the story, morning glory'? I keep looking in the cover of the Oasis album. I love the smell of new albums; it breathes life back into me. The princes of polarity have come back, and they will re-motivate me to get on with my life. The reviews gave it thumbs down in NME and Melody Maker but I reckon it's a classic. They all gave Blurs 'Great Escape' top marks. Musical Prostitution started with the journalists and it will end with them. They will bring down our culture in the same manner they built it up.

At night I pretend to sleep away from the prophecy of my nightmares, where life is wearing me thin, I feel so drained; my legacy is a sea of faces just like me. I listen to the music, trying to remember why I'm here, try and remember the joy I felt all year previously. Oasis and The Verve don't leave me stereo at night, 'Northern Soul'; I even share a joint with Little Rob without telling the other's when they're not around, listening to musical desperation.

Getting ready for lectures I haven't finished my cup of coffee and so decide to take it with me. The new house is only a five-minute walk from the lecture rooms.

It's at the start of town and is so much easier to get to than last year; otherwise I would never have turned up. I hadn't started drinking coffee till the start of this 2nd year. Now I cannot see how my life would survive without it. Walking down the subway directly at the bottom of our road the Irish tramp greets us a good morning drinking his white lighting. "All right you fucking arseholes, have a great morning" I clink my coffee cup with his bottle. "Sit down for a chat sometime?"

Walking into the lecture I carry a cup of coffee from the house. Steve carries some very dry toast Simon carries a glass of vodka from the house. Wasters.

The lecture room is cold; people sit wearing jackets over jumpers, over shirts, over t-shirts. It's not just us then who feel the change this year? The rest of the course does too. All of them with a look of desperation and confusion. What are we doing here for another year? Why doesn't it feel the same as last year? Why can't we move on? Why is it so much colder? And every friend a stranger? James sits at the back of the class. He sits alone all the time now. He doesn't want to speak to anyone anymore. Doesn't even nod his head in recognition, just walks as a shadow behind us all, watching.

Amy, Little Rob and Taylor have finally decided to form their own Trinity and buy some weed. We have to buy it for them, with Little Rob coming along as insurance for their 'gang'. It's like its some major kidnapping plot for these three. Our mood spreads through into the house; a depression of wanting to see how far you can feel nothing, how bottomless is the hole where your personality is kept. Until any of us know that, we cannot move forward. Little Rob examines the block of solid and even wants to do a test burn and have a free joint sample before completing the purchase. This isn't doing our creditably with the dealer any good. Already Little Rob lays down the ground rules. "You can only smoke after lessons are finished for the day, say between the hours of six and eight before we go out. There has to be all six of us present in the house. No smoking in the morning as I'm not doing that and no getting caned in the clubs but maybe one or two when we get back, on average should be smoking five, six joints maximum a day from it"

Johnny opens his mouth to speak and I know he wants to say - Each? We usually smoke that much in an hour. Simon, Johnny and I - The Holy Trinity – look at each other but keep quiet, too stoned to really make a statement.

Within forty-eight hours we sit in Simon's room smoking the quarter of solid to its last burning millimetre after we stole it out of Little Rob's room. Usually I don't go with doing over mates with things but we couldn't survive without it. Enough was enough, is my justification in being a cunt. The more weed I smoke the more my mood changes. I just want to keep getting stoned, the more stoned I get the more stoned I want to feel. I'd always lived a kind of imitation of life, fearing there was no one home, dreading having no personality myself. We're all terrified that we aren't somebody. Fears, that's all I'm doing, hiding from my fears. What's wrong with that? Everyone does it. When we drink. When we fuck someone. When screw over a friend. A life without fears is a life that would have no meaning. Unless you know what fear is, how can you ever know what happiness is? You need one to feed the other and teach you. We just have different ways of dealing with fear.

Alex, Slimy Alex he has been re-christened by Taylor, Little Rob and Amy who hate him, knocks on Simon's bedroom door and enters dancing into the room. Both Simon and Johnny have decided to hate him as well and don't even look at him as he dances round the room picking up CD's. "Hey guys how's it going?"

I feel sorry for him. Only Steve and I talk to him. "Take a seat" Simon and Johnny look at me like I've committed a cardinal sin, but I wont pass the joint to Alex though. Not cause of his new hated standing in the house but because he doesn't inhale. He soon dances backwards out of the room in slow motion to the way he came in. He really is cracking up. Steve told me that he keeps driving to Portsmouth at 3am and parks outside Samantha's Halls and watches her room until a light is turned out, convinced she's fucking people behind his back. Which she is, she keeps leaving him but he bursts out crying begging her not to leave. Alex has really fucked his life up here. He really is unstable but I'm too caned to do anything about it. Karma, what can you do.

As we pass the last joint round, Amy comes in, followed by Taylor. "Is that our drugs? You've smoked mine and Taylor's drugs?" she screams out.

I seem to remember there were six of us buying it.

"You never want to smoke any" Johnny replies.

"Well I did now and so did Taylor. That's fucking bad" and she slams the door on us.

Taylor remains in the room and Johnny passes him the joint. "I can smoke my five pounds worth with this joint?" Taylor asks.

The Holy Trinity says nothing too ashamed.

"Sorry" I finally mumble out of my stoned state.

"I don't mind really, I brought it so I wasn't left out."

"Can we have the joint back then?" Johnny forever the diplomat asks, but I was thinking exactly the same.

The prophecy of my dream has come true. It has only taken a month but I don't know who I am anymore. I don't care too either. I just want to feel nothing. It's safer.

Wasted

Socially isolated
Computer games

Falling
Excess

Our nations state – the revolution of our minds

Part 3: Wasted

NEXUS NIGHTS
Keith Reynolds (The Vampire)

It's these autumn to winter nights that feed me. Nexus Nights. Before daylight and we have to hide behind our shades and clothes, we look for new membership into our sin, into our way of life that knows no bounds. Nexus is the den where we feed, sleep and hunt our pray. Jarvis plays our anthem 'Common People'; he is one of us, postured along the darkened passageway to save us from the light that will burn. All as one in Nexus Nights, they all stand and sit in the filth on the floor, a red carpet mixed with the alcohol of blood and the burning of your throats. I see you; the hippy chick girl, the indie girl, the rock girl, the metal girl, the out of place girl, the wish I was somewhere else girl. I see all, my heart starts to beat and my eyes turn to red for the chase and passion that those naked bodies bring. Undress you with a bite on the neck and the promise of eternal life with me, I see you all.

"Madam Priestess have you found the one for you to ordain for tonight's feast of sin back in the tower?" I ask Stacy, whom stands before me dressed as a slapper in black. Sometimes I wonder if I put those marks in deep enough as her wish to sin for the eternal passage seems to contradict her wish to be normal and get laid.

"I like Matt, he reminds me of you with his hair" she replies, looking over towards the Matt Ryan super posse, all of them burning their throats on a different planet.

"A taste of his blood would poison us," I tell her. The chemical reaction wouldn't be a good idea so I wave my cape away from her and disappear into the dance of the living mortals.

The sweat pours off each of you as your bodies beckon me in, beckon me to move closer to destiny and offer you the chance of blissful harmony, sleep. How do we leave the wreckage of our lives? One kiss can throw away the memories that make you cry. Fiona stands before me, still wearing her shades, she never will blink again. Clarissa with her, she has taken Clarissa into the group, taken her powerless into the sight we dream during the day, she too wears her sunglasses. They remain on during the day, to stop us burning. At night they keep our true self from revealing the treasure we hide in our soul that has no reflection anymore. It is our signature – the shades – the darkness – Nexus - no one needs to be afraid – just hide from the light – and create our own light of night

The vulture finds his prey, preying the kiss will shoot away my minds despair. She is dressed as Marylyn Monroe, I recognise her

MJ Gunn

from nights at JFKs before they threw us out for life, taking life out of the fake souls that drank from its fountain of lies. Before she was in a white sheet, Yoko Ono. I always believed she was the High Priestess but she knocked back advances and walked hand in hand with a member of the same breeding.

Stacy, the chosen High Priestess joins me on the dance of sweat to entice our bodies to bite. No doubt she can feel her place being threatened and will continue our afterlife search together. "I'm going to another club with Matt" she tells me. Matt stands in the background next to her, his eyes glazed over, like an onrushing hurricane that he is in the centre off and the headlights wont go out and he cannot move.

"Are you going to feed?" I ask worried about the hurricane's poison.

"No, I'm going to fuck" she replies and walks out with the Hurricane.

The coffin where I sleep, the tower where I feed, the darkness that fills eternal light, otherwise known as my rented house in the Polygon area of Southampton.

The rich area, only rich people understand and have the realms of power possible to enact this style of life and richness in its disregard for human life as mortals.

'The Lost Boys' plays on a giant projection screen. Fiona and Clarissa sit at opposing chairs in the room like gladiatorial guards protecting the nest where the master will dine. Their shades on leaving a blink less trail of no personality underneath.

The O'Sullivan twins, Jenny and Liana, are naked on the rug of fire, breathing the flames of magic out into the naked air. Their bodies form into one and they are two bats hanging upside down waiting to watch their master take another soul.

And Marylyn, Yoko, but she is Marie, sits scared next to me, the surroundings making her shiver, her heart beating faster, her eyes not lying, her Monroe wig has turned white and the clock strikes and it is time.

"Time to feed" I say as I turn my fangs towards her and leer onto her neck.

Marie pulls away. "Vampires, that's so last year"

"You're not afraid?" I ask, "But your heart is skipping beats, your hair is white and your eyes do not lie they have turned the colour of death... A death that awaits for you to join us"

Part 3: Wasted

Marie starts to laugh hysterically. "Do you really want to be a vampire?" she asks me, and her Monroe wig turns complete white, her eyes that were cold go black, and she leans into me with fangs from her mouth…

"Fuck!" I jump up, my fake fangs fall out, and I think I've pissed myself. "You're a real vampire!"

I run from the room, run upstairs, I can hear screaming from downstairs… The bitch is a real vampire, fuck.

I storm into Clem's room without knocking. He sits on the end of the bed with just his underpants on. Johnny is skinning up at a table.

"What's all the noise downstairs?" Clem asks me, just his underpants and fat belly staring at me.

"Vampires" I reply.

"Are you still running that occult then Keith?" Johnny asks me.

"It was a joke, just to get laid, but that bitch downstairs, she's a real fucking vampire…

I mean she's a fucking vampire!"

"That'll learn you to muck around with the spirits" Johnny replies.

"Isn't there a lock or something? Why aren't you scared? She's feeding downstairs, we'll be next!"

"No-one woman's going to come in here with me sat on the end of my bed in my underpants are they?" Clem responds.

I look round the room; stale food, bread, dry tissues, porn on the TV, Clem sitting in his underpants, the smell of a dead rodent fills the room.

"How can you sleep in here?" I ask Clem.

The living room door opens and I push my hand through, expecting to see the blood shed of my followers, skin and bones laid out bare for me to feed and become a vampire for real.

Instead the O'Sullivan twins are now fully dressed watching late night Letterman.

Fiona and Clarissa remain either side of the room blocking the doors.

"Where's the vampire?" I ask.

"She turned into a bat," Fiona says.

"And flew out the window" Clarissa continues the sentence.

135

SURFS UP

Linda

"I love that film, 'Big Wednesday', class," I'm told by this guy who claims to be a DJ, James, I think he used to be mates with Matt Ryan. He picked me and another girl, whom I recognise, last night in New Yorks. I was interested in listening to his DJ'ing on the decks he has got upstairs and in the amount of cocaine he could pass over to me. He puts on 'Easy Rider', whilst listening to his mate Johnny's babble about his limited success at being a dealer claiming - "I don't need the hassle" - when it's really a case of he's lost all the money as he smoked the weed himself. The other girl finally arrives, Charlotte. We're shown into the living room for five minutes of 'Easy Rider' and a chat with Johnny, so we can feel suitably disgusted with his appearance, hasn't washed that hair for weeks, or changed those clothes; he really is on the edge of a breakdown.

We sit on the edge of James bed. Charlotte more confident, cropped black hair, fur jacket, short black dress that has a cut hole round her belly showing her piercing. She has the look of she's done this before. I'm more nervous, keeping my jacket pulled tight, hair gelled flat on my head, made-up rosy clown cheeks to hide my gaunt face in this light.

James dims the bulb and put the red lampshade over it, giving it a sense of an erotic film. "So do you girls like surf films?"

"Lets just cut to the chase" Charlotte says.

"We're here to listen to your DJ skills aren't we?" I ask.

"And?" He says.

"Score some cocaine" My gaunt eyes speak.

"And?" He says again.

"Maybe you'll have sex with one of us" I answer again through a blizzard life.

"Or maybe both of us" Charlotte cuts to the chase again.

"I want you both to take your clothes off and then fuck each other," he says.

"And what are you going to be doing?" Charlotte asks.

"Playing the DJ tunes you came to listen too."

"And?" She continues the role reversal.

"Feeding the cocaine"

"And?"

"Watching you girls"

"Good. I just wanted to you to say it." This Charlotte sure hits the mark. She takes the initiative and takes off her fur jacket, and starts unravelling her dress. I watch Charlotte and take my jacket half way off then stop, as I'm unsure to continue.

"I want you to take each others clothes off" James tells us to start his musical portrait.

I feel apprehensive. "Wait. I cant, I mean I haven't done this before"

"Do you not want to?" He replies.

And with that the choice is laid out before me. Every girl thinks about it. Every girl looks at another girl and finds them attractive. So I study Charlotte, and lean in to kiss her. Again I stop. I need the blizzard. "Wait. Sorry. Have you got something?"

"Sure" He walks over to his 'decks' and pulls out of the draw a couple folds of the white powder. My eyes immediately light up, and I take to the cocaine like it was my last wish before life takes me, the last meal I had requested.

For a moment I sit sombre, taking the surroundings in, and what is being asked, the actress in me washes back over. The actress in Charlotte I'd imagine was already there. "Ok" I say and I lean and kiss Charlotte. She can tell it's the first time I've kissed another girl; I'm tentative, unsure if the lips and feel are the same as guys.

"Its ok, just let me take the lead. You'll enjoy it" and with that Charlotte takes over and my tentative steps are now over powered by a raw emotion inside, an ambiguity that is now coming to life.

"Another notch to bowl of your blizzard." James states like a poet. "Start to undress each other" James says, as he studies our faces to create sounds. We start to undress each other and he begins to play music on the decks. At first an eerie trance mix, that makes it seem like some futuristic noir movie.

"What course do you study?" I ask Charlotte trying to pretend this is an everyday occurrence.

"Business. Whatever that means. You?"

"Religion" There is a stony silence.

"I'm an artist." James tells us girls. "I don't study art, I don't know what I'm studying, but what I create in this room with this music is art"

"Shut up and let us do the talking" Charlotte says. "Do you have a boyfriend?"

"No." I reply. "Just fuck buddies"

"I have a girlfriend, Marie. I want a boyfriend now though. Marie treats me like shit" Charlotte reveals with a scowl in her voice.

We're both now naked but for our boots but James stops us,

asking to - "Keep the boots on, and, Charlotte, I want you to keep your fur coat on. Linda, completely naked." We start to make love to each other without the masculine penetration. "Poetry in motion" James says as he watches the beauty of two naked souls, form one Venus D'Milo of the stars. Charlotte takes the lead and I'm now a willing accomplice, weather through the white powder or the power of inquisitiveness.

James starts to talk incessantly about us, like we're not in the room, in third person -

"I don't fuck them. I watch them to create the music I play. To inspire the tunes in my head through their souls. As I said I'm an artist. I create the tunes of a generation to fuck to. The greatest surf movie. The greatest crest of a wave. We ride it together, with the power of the unknown, that's not aloud. What's right becomes wrong, and the norm becomes bad social etiquette. This is our time. It won't last forever."

He stares into us as we start to cum together, numb, writing down in a black book what he says, like he's watching a movie and writing a script, Charlotte and I the stars - "I play some thumping tunes with loud bass through the decks. I can hear the floor rattling. They start to vibrate. Louder the better. Fucking them both with my music. Music. Coke. Sex. Surfs up boy. Surfs up"

I look at a photo on the wall, a collage of various sins in life put together.

"Wow, that's amazing, what is it, an art project?" Charlotte asks.

"No, it's my life, I carry it around everywhere I go, as that way I don't forget my past, my present and what I want in the future." James replies. "If we're all going to die I might as well get as many under my belt as possible." He continues.

"There's a vampire on there" I say.

"Yeah, I like the nightlife" He replies.

I stop completely. "Have you heard the stories, about the vampires in the city?"

"I know one. I used to go out with her" Charlotte replies.

"Its hip not to be one" James tells me.

Part 3: Wasted

WANNA LIVE LIKE COMMON PEOPLE
Johnny

It's been nearly two months since I got kicked off the course and I still haven't done a days work. I joined an agency but they always phone me at a ridiculous hour like 9am and the phone is always locked in Alex's bedroom for some reason. The Benefit agencies send me the unemployment cheque. It gave me the idea to get Housing Benefit cheques as well, I ran the idea past Simon and Matt and they were cool with it but wasn't too sure how the rest of the house would take it. "Why? It's not like I've got my own room". Perhaps I should leave, it's not much of a life really is it - Sleeping on the mattress in the hallway. There's two doors either end of the mattress so I can shut myself away from everyone, my own private prison cell. To make it more homely I've put up some paper clippings and old posters that Simon and Steve lent me; Marylyn Monroe was his gift, merging them with separate dialogue, making my own form of print. People stop by the wall standing on me whilst I'm trying to sleep looking at my work of art, my media collage.

"What does this say about today's society?" Alex asks me each morning.

"I'd say it's the room of a serial killer" I reply, hoping this would make him leave me alone.

"What is the room of a serial killer in today's society?" The guy just wont stop, he's lonely, no one speaks to him. I know what it's like to be an outsider.

There was a long period of time where things and people on the dole were considered marginal, all of us 'pieces of turd'. But the country is getting caught up in a wave of youth'ism, and suddenly the pieces of 'turds' have moved centre stage. My voice to this revolution of my youth is this wall Muriel, where nothing makes any sense, no picture fits any words and everything means nothing. I'm in-between Little Rob's Bedroom and Steve's bedroom an interesting contrast. Little Rob's room stinks for some reason. As for Steve, I awake every morning to his Madonna records. Still when he's out in Magnums behind Kaos trying to pick guys up, I go into his room, rest on his bed and watch some porn. Though his porn is boy on boy porn and it's not something I can wank too. So far it sounds ok, but the real problem is the mattress is at the bottom of the stairs, every morning people step on me to get to the front door, or kitchen. I can tell they're starting to get pissed off when they say – "fucking hell Johnny!" One time even Matt kept kicking me as he walked past, pissed off about something. It was his idea that I slept here.

I think about phoning Mum and seeing if I can live back there for a while, though I know she'll just be having goes at me and nag me so much that I'll be quite happy to return back and live on a mattress in a hallway. "Hi, mum its me"

"What do you want Johnny?"

"Why do I have to want something, I'm just speaking to my Mum" Silence, she's put the phone down on me.

I'm starting to itch; I think the mattress has got fleas. I've been having bad shits as well. The entire house isn't healthy; I've never lived in such a pig stile, no one cleans up. There is a smell coming from the kitchen that goes through the walls into my corridor. Ghosts come and visit during the night. "Isn't time you cleared up?" they stand over me.

"Its not my mess, fuck off back to the afterlife" I reply, lighting a joint. Whenever I offer them it they disappear and Steve is standing in front of me.

"You're not going to believe what just happened to me" he'll say, grin on his face, walking awkwardly.

"I can believe that's why I don't want to know."

"Who were you speaking to when I came in?"

"The ghost. It was complaining about the smell from the kitchen"

"Next time you see him, ask him to do something about the slugs that crawl in my room from under the sinks"

"Why do people naturally assume a ghost is a man? It might be a woman?"

"Or a hermaphrodite. I met one tonight" I knew he'd get to tell me the story some how, some mouths aren't meant to shut naturally.

Piles of rubbish greet a good morning in the kitchen, the smell of unwanted food and half eaten kebabs. The living room has become an extension of this. The rubbish and fungus is spreading. Dry rot is forming on my Muriel. Amy is one of the worst culprits, I thought living with a girl they'd clean up but it doesn't make a difference. Taylor and Little Rob don't clean up just throw stuff around and say - "If no one else is cleaning up why should we?" Steve is too busy in Magnums living his double life that's meant to be a secret but half of Southampton knows. Simon, Matt and I are too caned. As for Alex he's constantly going for drives at 11pm and not returning till 6am, what is he doing? Where is he going? "Adventures" he keeps saying to me, "come on an adventure with me" I always decline. I want to

Part 3: Wasted

finish 'Sonic Hedgehog' before I go anywhere. Before the ghosts of the house stop coming into my corridor for midnight joints to share and the fungus drives them out and turns us to zombies.

We're in Thursdays, on a Wednesday, and this girl is talking to me. She looks great, long blonde hair, quite rounded, great figure, big tits, but I can't understand what's she saying. When she speaks she sounds like a spastic, she's speaking through her nose and chin, it's weird, it's not bothering me, in fact it's turning me on. "dodsfoijsdfokjsdklf" she asks me.

"Yeah" I reply, hoping that was the right thing to say as I didn't understand what she said, hoping that I'll get to go back to her place so I can have somewhere to sleep. I can't exactly invite her back to mine room - a hallway with a mattress.

I lean in closer so when she speaks my ear is practically next to her mouth, both for sexual reasons and to hear what she is saying. "Stone Roses and Oasis" she shouts down my lobe.

"Yeah I like them too" I reply, I lie, well, I do like them, but I prefer listening to Lick My Decals of by Captain Beefheart. That Oasis album is starting to annoy me, everywhere I go I hear it being played, loads of townie idiots singing along to it, though when I told Matt I hated it for this reason that's why he kicked me I think. "Why don't we go back to yours and listen to them?" I suggest.

"xflkgdsfljglsk" she replies. I lean directly in so her tongue hits the inside of my ear with every letter she spits out, "I live at home with my parents" Guess she will be sampling chez 'hallway' mattress after all.

Trying to have sex in a hallway on a mattress as people return back late at night is very difficult. She was initially upset, Daisy, I think that's what she said her name was, that I didn't have a stereo in this hallway, she didn't seem to mind fucking in the hallway and actually said she liked it, 'it was homely' and didn't question why I sleep under the bottom of the stairs. "I wanna be adored...." I keep singing to her as I'm trying to fuck her but this puts her off and she says she needs the real thing. I borrow the stereo from the kitchen and as luck would have it, the radio station plays 'Fools Gold' by the Stone Roses as we're going at it, followed by 'Roll With It' by Oasis and finishing with 'Common People' by Pulp. After various interruptions I finish my duty.

Those songs sure did the trick and she leans in and says, "dlskghdsfhgkjshgkjs" I just want to sleep but she keeps nudging me and repeating, "sgfaskjhglksadjglksaj"

"What?" I finally say.

"It was like fucking Ian Brown, Liam Gallagher and Jarvis Cocker with those songs playing" she was saying. Both naked on an itchy mattress, between two big wooden doors, by the stairway, people tread on us as they walk through but it doesn't bother her, she says - "lgjlsdkgldj go again?"

"You want to fuck again? Sure"

"No" she screams out, like I had forced myself on her.

Slimy Alex appears on the hallway getting ready for one of his adventures. "Are you alright? Did he try anything on you?"

"I'm fine" she replies, for some reason when she speaks to Alex I can understand exactly what she is saying.

"Alex ask her what she meant when she said 'again'?"

"Only if you come on an adventure with me. Both of you." His eyes light up companionship at last for him. The eyes of someone who is socially isolated and walks up and down in his room till 3am, we all hear him, listening into others phone conversation, ear to the floor boards. I start to think of Shallow Grave.

"An adventure, sounds fun" Daisy replies, then turns to me, "ghldfjgklsjgi" why does it make no sense when she speaks to me?

Daisy sits in the front of the car with Slimy Alex. I sit in the back, rolling a joint. The car is parked outside a Halls of Residence in Portsmouth. "ghdfjghjkdfhgkjsh" Daisy says.

"She wants to listen to Common People by Pulp again." Alex tells me. He then turns to her, "It's the perfect encapsulation of Britpop aesthetic"

"dkhjdlkjhklfjhlkj"

"She says she is that girl from the song"

"dkjglkfdjglksdfjsdfjglk"

"She wants to see how common people live. That's probably why she fucked you Johnny"

"You don't have to tell me everything she's saying you know?" Great, another middle class rich girl who wants to see and live working class culture, desperate to say they had been hanging around with the 'we' people. "Its shit being working class."

We sit in silence as Alex points from the car directly under a room, where a light has come on.

"You see that room?" he asks.

"lskgjdskjgdsfjg" Daisy replies.

I look up and see Samantha in that room.

"That's my girlfriends room"
"kgjsldfjgldsfjglksfj"
"No, she doesn't know I'm here."
"Why are we just sitting here watching her? It's freezing, why don't we go up there?" I ask him, the joint has an icicle on it.

Across the window comes the shadow of someone else. Another guy.

"That's my girlfriend cheating on me with another guy. How do you like that?"
"dsklhgdsfjgsdfjgklsd"
"What are we doing here? Why don't we just go home?" I beg Alex. I can't feel my fingers.
"We can't leave until she sees me"

I lean into the front seat and push the car horn. Samantha looks out the window and sees the car. Alex waves to her. "There she's seen us, lets go"
"Not until she's had sex"
"Alex, what's wrong with you?"
"I want her to know, that I know" Samantha begins to kiss the guy by the window; I can see her devil smile towards Alex in the car. The guy begins to take Samantha from behind and she presses her self up against the window, for all the night creatures to see. I have to admit, it's turning me on. "We like to play games" Alex tells us.
"ds;lkjgoksdjglksdjfglkjs"
"Do you want to know a secret, Daisy?"
"lgjlksjglksdfjglks"
"dlskjgldskjgldsfjg" Alex replies, telling her his secret, in her own language. They both nod their heads and stare up towards the window; she waves to Samantha this time as well. I feel left out and decide to join in, waving.

Tomorrows World is on tonight. My Dad is going to be on it. He wrote a book called 'The Sperm Wars'. Everyone was thanked, his many illegitimate kids, all of them but me, the black sperm of the family. My dad looks like the pervert you'd imagine to write such a book; big black beard, long thinning hair, big disgusting anorak on, if he wasn't a published writer he'd be an arrested paedophile. He remarried a woman, I say woman, more a young girl, who is only two years older than me. I find it a real problem as I think I fancy her and tried to fuck her last Christmas when I was really drunk. "But I'm your mum" she kept telling us, laughing, flirting, hand on legs.

"Only in name" is what I replied.

The silence that falls upon the house is deafening after my Dad leaves the TV screen to no doubt find an even younger bride with his new televised popularity. Finally Matt speaks, "He looks like he'd make a good Dr Who" As I try envisage my Dad in the Tardis with the youngest 'assistants' the shown has legally seen, my Christmas dinner thoughts are disturbed by an irate Taylor and Little Rob.

"Whose left the bloody oven on?" Little Rob shouts into the room.

"Oh fuck," I say, " that was me"

"There's no food in it, are you pre-heating it?" Taylor shouts at me. They are both like demons, destroying my stoned state, oh yeah, I forgot to add, I'm completely caned it was the only way to watch my dad.

"No I finished my food" they see my empty plate, "can you turn it off"

"Fucking hell Johnny! All you do is use electricity!" Little Rob is so angry his glasses fall off.

"We're pissed off living in a shit hole. This house is a fucking disgrace. The kitchen hasn't been cleaned, there's rubbish all over the floor, me and Rob aren't living in this state anymore!" It's hard to take Taylor seriously wearing the Reading football club kit for the season, isn't he cold in those shorts? "Oh and Amy's shoes all over the floor" Taylor follows up.

"Oh fucking hell! That's right have a go at my shoes when Johnny's the one to blame" even Amy is getting on my back now. They all go into the kitchen to examine the scene of the crime, I can hear them argue about me – "All he does is use electricity." "He still hasn't even turned off the oven" I feel gutted. It's time for me to leave.

Matt says nothing. He finally turns to me all serious, "Do you think if your dad was given a script and a small budget he'd consider doing a trailer for me as the new Doctor Who?"

I step into the kitchen when the coast is clear and see they still haven't turned the oven off. Well if they can't be arsed to do it, neither can I.

My bags are packed. The train ticket is booked. I haven't told anyone yet, fuck 'em. They can use all the electricity they want now. Sitting with Simon, smoking this strange solid we brought, got to finish off before I go, not leaving a last crumb. It smells strange,

it's not like getting caned, it gives you a hangover. Something's not right. There's a knock on the door and before we can answer, praying it's not Alex dancing into the room wanting to go on another sexual adventure, Matt and Steve have entered the room; Matt looks white as a sheet, rash up his arm and even Steve looks concerned.
"He has got meningitis," Steve informs us.

Simon's initial reaction and mine is to kick him out in case it's contagious. Matt start to take his shirt off, I turn away in disgust, I think he has been hanging around with Steve too much these last few weeks, wonder if he knows his secret? Perhaps he's part of the secret? It's all over his arms, onto his chest, everything but his face covered and that's only cause his hair is getting quite long now and is down to his mouth like cousin 'It'.

"I don't know what to do? Fucking hell, meningitis? Do I go to a hospital or what? What do I do?" Matt sweating, his getting whiter by the minute, a picture of panic and fear that today might be the last day of his life, as he once knew it. A face that paints every students picture. What have we really achieved in life? Nothing. What did we excel in? Doing nothing. What are your aspirations? Nothing. Then death comes for you and you want everything.

"Meningitis is a killer, there was that student who died from it above the room in Kaos" Steve informs us with pride.

"Fuck, James moved into that room, he said that they hadn't changed the bed"

"He might just be a carrier, some people only carry it. If you've got it, it can effect you for life, wear away"

"Steve just shut up!"

"James isn't alright."

"What do you mean? His got the disease?"

"No, he's not alright is he? He's kind of strange these days"

Silence as we all think of James. Moving into a room where someone died. Sitting by himself in lectures all the time. Never coming out anymore.

"What's that got to do with me and this fucking rash?" Matt cries out.

As we wait for Matt in the doctors, I constantly check my arms, scared that the rash might be on me now, might have moved in the waiting room like an alien life form to another being. Perhaps Matt will come out and be possessed? 'Invasion of the Body Snatchers', or a zombie. At last I can live my dream of the world ending with zombies and only me alive like Charlton Heston in 'The Omega

Man', running through each city with a massive samurai sword cutting the heads of the zombies until I've wiped all them all out and then commit suicide myself as there's nothing left to do. On returning from the doctors room, the rash has left Matt completely and he was told it was a one-day rash that a lot of students in the area who smoked a lot of weed had got. This really disappoints Steve, he's psychically upset to see Matt back, hoping he would be cordoned off and we'd have to visit him in those suits they wear in ET. But to Steve's joy, Taylor comes downstairs with exactly the same rash, perhaps him and Matt have been kissing and that's why Steve's upset.

That night I repack my bag and check the train times. It's nothing to do with them saying I pay no rent and only use electricity. I just don't want that rash. I leave a note.

ALL I DID WAS USE ELECTRICITY

"Where do you think you're going?" The ghost has sailed into the corridor; he has a gas mask on, breathing away from the stench of the kitchen and dry rot that is circling my corridor cell.

"I'm out of here, before someone dies"

"Someone is going to die, they've made preparations for their stay here with us"

"What there's a house load of you in this place?"

"There are thousands of lost students in purgatory."

"You were a student?"

"Yeah, I was the one who died in that flat across the road, above Kaos"

I take a step back from him afraid I might catch something. "Someone in the house is going to die?"

"No. It's someone you know though"

Goodbye Southampton. No farewells, no tears, no money. For eighteen months it's been the best fun. But I'm so wasted and nearly dead. I couldn't keep living like that – on a mattress in a hallway; I'd end up being the ghost of the student past.

Hello Manchester

SLEEPLESS NIGHTS

James

Sweating. Sleepless nights.   Bad thoughts
Loose roving round a mindless mind
They've taken all my chairs. Moved them without asking. Who

are they?

Lay on my back and the ceiling is my campaign for time.

That has no beginning or end

I just ended up here...

I hate a lot. I want to change others.   I'm not the problem

Stare beneath the wings of an angel and I'll make you the shadow of a saint

Wake up and sleep walk through a day that holds no bounds. But the limitless of my ambition. But what if my ambition equals nothing?

The ceiling is suffocating me. I wanna change, I wanna change, I wanna change

Change into what or whom? Sit on the end of my bed. 4am the clock says.

Alone

If we had no family who would we celebrate Christmas with?

We're all the same when we sleep

Depressive thoughts can lead you into bad thoughts that lead to a life of bad karma

What's the point? Don't we all die?

I don't eat. I don't fuck

I consume all that is dark in my soul

I hate my friends

Everything and everyone annoys me

My head hurts

Headaches... hands are cold... head is hot. And bothered in a chain of events

I keep dreaming the future. I'm famous for a day. And then I fall onto a sword that is made of plastic. Like the personalities that I seem to inherit around me

When is it New Years? Why do we believe in Christmas?

Lying on the bed my feet outstretched to each side nailed down

My hands and arms outstretched bleed in by imaginary nails

Crucify myself. Real power.

All the kings' horses and all the kings' men couldn't put me back together again

Edge of the bed is my mind's eye

I have no home but my pride

| Can't sleep | My head hurts | What time is it? |
| Sweating | Bad thoughts | Sleepless Nights |

'SILENCE'

Clarissa

Silence...my favourite sound. I never listen to music in my room when it's a cold autumn evening like this. Stand at the window in my one bedroom flat, and watch the rain fall, dreaming of the outside world, seeing other people run from the tears of heaven, the sound of the rain on the window makes me feel safe and secure.

My favourite film star is Bette Davis; I've always admired the amount she smoked. It is here by the window I act out the final scene of 'Now, Voyager', "why reach for the moon, when we have the stars" I say, cigarette across my lips. There is no reply to my question, I am alone, and it's the way I want it on days like these. You cannot share silence with someone else. Listen to nothing but the wind as it whistles the outside worlds love and hate around us. The rain falls across the window, making the sound of a constant heartbeat that will slowly stop and die away. Each storm makes its own sound. Today I could feel one was coming. I shiver from the window at the world outside. Someone stepped over my grave. I had blocked it all out. Now it would return. You cannot hide forever inside silence.

Most people would stay away from such a storm. I wanted to walk into the eye of it. I start my walk into town for no reason but to meet my fate head on. I had the same feelings back then, all those years ago when I was just a young teenager, something had made me walk out that day and when I finally returned, I was different, my father then died. My life was no longer mine but owned by the hand of fate, which had returned today. I know this because the storm is making the same silent noises as back then. No umbrella to stop the tears that fall. I walk in the centre of the streets, letting the rain and wind engulf my soul fully, carry me to a distant shore, the mother of my past, the days when I was free, but this is the true colour of the world I had left behind. People watch me from under the covers of shop doorways, shaking heads and pointing at the girl who walks through the town; letting the rain fall across her, letting the wind blow her into different directions, but how she remains calm, still, oblivious to the eye's around her. She is me. I am her. Again. I knew today would come. I dreamt it last night.

I head down towards the docks, towards the ocean, where my sins will be in full view of a sea of change that never lies in its reflections. The streets are well lit and I know nothing will happen here, a game to ready myself, to return to what I fear. Each street lamp is a guardian to those who walk alone, the rain is beautiful to watch across a street lamp, falling like a Christmas night, colouring what we try and hide from, the beautiful picture that paints an after glow. When I was younger I would travel to the ocean on my own and watch the waves as the sunrises and sets. As I stand this evening, the waves crash back and forth, fighting against each other, fighting the contents of each memory that is lost when people come to forget. All those memories that are our after thoughts, do we ever really stare at the ocean, or just stare at our past?

Behind me, is the JFK crowd, a party full of people in the bar. I decide to enter, but I can't help but feel alone in a room full of people, most of whom I know or recognise. The smiles of recognition, they are unsure to invite me to join them for the party, their recognition is followed by concern of knowing the rain soaked lost girl who stands in the centre alone in a crowded room of friends. I studied one of the girls, I recognised her, Charlotte. She seemed very pretty but overly anxious and nervous, timid. I wondered if life had dealt me a different set of cards if our roles would be reversed, if we would be friends even. What worries does she have? What traumas the daily grind of the world throws at such people, if only they knew, how close they are standing to death. For she has returned.

Before starting the walk back into the eye of the storm, I can feel the shadow behind me, the presence that stepped on my grave. Not a professional but more than an amateur. I decide to go into the empty coffee shop, wanting to warm my heart, find an easier solution, I'm not stupid, I could freeze to death out there, but tonight wasn't my time, not yet, it was someone else's. When I was younger, before that fateful day, after watching the sunrise over the ocean, I would drink coffee alone and watch the sparkles across the sea, the lights of a golden texture that would make the world seem content and beautiful for a few moments. The silence would make me feel content; I've been forever trying to recapture it.

I'm not alone in the coffee shop. I can make out another person watching the ocean from the window, like I was. As the person turns our eyes meet, a smile of recognition, it is Matthew. A silence of what do either of us do next? Do we talk? Do we ignore each other? Do we just walk away? This only happens with someone you've had sex with someone, but hardly spoken to since. It was a nice day, we confided in each other, but what does that mean to two people on a night like this when all are strangers. He slowly walks over to my table. "Hi" he says, his hair over his eyes, wet, his face drawn, gaunt, aged since we were last together. He looks like the eye of the hurricane. Too embarrassed by his appearance or the situation to look me in the eye.

"Hi" I reply, trying to catch his eyes, behind the face he now wants to hide away. He pauses unsure to sit with me or not. Instead we both look out of the window and watch the ocean.

"It's some storm out there" he finally speaks.

"Yeah. You'd have to be crazy to want to come out"

The silence returns, only sex can do this to people.

"How are you?" he finally says.

"Good." I lie. "You?"

"Yeah, good." He lies. His aura carries that of a person who has set his heart on one thing that he cannot have, and to live with it, knowing you will never have what you desire the most, you walk into the realms of 'wasted' and bury your soul deep into the excess you can afford to keep that desire from your thoughts. I know this, as I was once there.

"Gotta go" he says, eyes still on the ocean.

"Bye" I say, and I hold my stare on him. He finally looks back at me, and I can see his eyes, red and bloodshot, broken by something or someone. But he's not too far gone, he's not past the point of saving, he's at that stage where he can save himself, and the last few months of whatever pain he is running from will be immaterial if he takes that step. I want to tell him this, I want him to sit with me, I want to help him.

"Bye" he says, looking his eyes away in embarrassment of what I could see.

Begin the walk back through town. Had no last look at the ocean, I'll be back there this morning, to watch the sun dawn in, now my past has swept back ashore. The wind has eased, now it is just rain, covering the street lamps reflecting the true warmth you can only feel when you know you're nearly home, and you secretly wish for one more street to walk down, to stay that bit longer and marvel at the world, marvel that we're alive. Kids run through the town in Halloween masks. And all the time behind me I know is that shadow, following me in the corners of shops, keeping its distance, before it reveals its true attentions that will effect both our lives from that point on. I sit in the park outside Halls, a damp bench, even the tramps have relinquished this tonight, they could smell the fear and decided to sleep elsewhere. It is here where girls have been attacked over the last fourteen months, walking back alone, followed by the same shadow that waits for me in the corner. I can hear the screams

Part 3: Wasted

of their fears, the ghosts of each of those nights. Am I to become them? The shadow breathes behind me. My hair at the back of neck stands on end. What is 'it' waiting for? It is waiting to smell my fear. But I know no fear. Not since Clarissa became Clarissa. Every name makes its own sound. A smile goes across my face. I want the shadow to see this, to know that I know. Stepping up from the bench, it expects me to run, but I walk, at a slow pace, not towards the light, but towards the darkness of the park, where we all stand equal as nothing can be seen.

As I thought, the shadow would not follow me in. Confused that someone was welcoming the danger towards her. Back home is where fate demands it. Life always goes full circle.

Step into my flat, I leave the door unlocked. Anyone could walk in, but I didn't want anyone, I wanted the demon. I don't turn the light on. Darkness is what binds the shadow and me. I turn the TV on, the sound up loud, to drown out the commotion that will occur within minutes. It is set up perfectly for him to enter, I know it's a him; I've always known his name too. I feel disgusted with myself that I have waited till now to act, waited till now cause it is my life that is in danger. What about the other young girls who were made to suffer before me? They're not alone; I had to suffer once too. From the window the rain rattles across it, spelling words as the tears race down the sill. I see my reflection in the window, hair wet, matted onto my face, clothes damp. The TV flickers in the reflection, illuminating the room. The tear drops off past victims stop falling on the window and spell the word for me

F   E   A   R

I see the shadow behind me, goblin mask on, dressed in immaculate black, down to his gloves. I begin to laugh, the shadow stops in his tracks, tilts his head to one side, confused. "I'm sorry, I keep thinking of the milk tray man," I tell the goblin. He finally moves his hands up towards my hair, gently pushes it away from my neck. "I've been waiting for you," I tell him. The goblin grabs my neck; I pretend to struggle enough, backing up into him, twist and turn, so he will throw me to the floor. As my head hits the carpet, he pushes himself onto me; his legs on my knees, his arms holding back my arms, he pauses, confused, why I don't scream. He slaps my face and waits for a reaction, nothing. This ignites his anger further; a victim who welcomes this, a victim or does not know the procedure to act. He kicks away at my jeans, violently pulling them down with his feet and hands, still no reaction, he grabs my hair with one hand and pulls it tight and stares into my eyes, still I give him nothing.

With his loose hand he unzips his trousers, then I give him something. Something sharp. Something I had prepared earlier for him. And then it happens, what I had run for, returns... again. I relive the moment as it goes into his lung – I was thirteen, dressed in cotton white when they took me. The first day was the worst, I cried constantly for my dad. And they took away the cotton white dress he had brought me on my birthday and invaded all that was pure. I stopped crying then. I stopped being Clarissa, daddies little girl, I became nothing, a non-eternity –

As the goblin falls, his shadow spins round the room, illuminated across the walls, showing posters of famous people from the screen, he can see the flash of photos taken as they were for them, "over here, over here" he hears the voice cry out, and spins round for another flash off the lives he took, a show that doesn't end. His eyes end on Bette Davis, cigarette in hand and he falls to the floor.

I sit up, leaving my jeans off and walk towards him in my knickers. I touch the knife in his lung, the goblin mask looks up towards me, I can see the eyes through the eye slit, the look of fear, fear of dying, praying in its eyes that I will save him, and remove the knife. I push on the handle and press it deeper in, the masks eyes turn bloodshot, and I pull the knife out violently. I sit back on the floor and stare at the TV screen, an old episode of 'Steptoe and Son'. The shadow begins to cough and removes his mask. I stare directly into the face, confirming what I knew already.

James.

"I knew I was going to die today" he coughs out blood, collapsed in an upright heap against the wall, his eyes becoming more bloodshot, his skin paler.

I look back at the TV screen, I cannot bear to watch them die slowly. "I knew I was going to kill again today"

"Again?" he begins to laugh. I turn to see further blood disappear from his lungs and onto his black jumper. "I should have guessed. I had a dream last night... I dreamt all the girls I had attacked, were sitting at a table in my honour..." he continues to cough with his laughter, eyes going more bloodshot. "In the centre of the table was a banquet prepared but the main course was hidden. And then someone I couldn't see arrived at the table, I didn't know who it was..." he stops, his eyes roll over and he is silent. Then a whisper comes from his voice, "the shadow showed the hidden meal, it was me, laid out along the table, then I could finally see the shadow... it was you"

"I had a dream last night too" I remain staring at the TV screen as I speak. "I dreamt of a young girl, no more than thirteen, she was playing in the park, wearing a white cotton dress and then she stopped, and the girl became me." I turn to look at James. His eyes are focused on the Bette Davis picture. His skin is pale. The same white as the cotton dress I once wore. He has breathed the last breath. He'd done me a favour, he didn't bleed over the floor.

No one would walk these streets on a night like this; the storm was my ally, as was silence, my best friend. The streets are dead. The windy city was asleep. I reach the garbage skip by the subway and go to lift the black bin linear into to it. "Wait" a slurred voice, says from behind me. I turn to see the regular Irish tramp, bottle of white lighting in his hand, next to him the famous 'nutter' Asian tramp with a limp. The Irish tramp walks up to me. I drop the bag to the floor by his feet, so my hands are free if it becomes a necessity to use them. The tramp looks at me and passes me his white lighting bottle "hold this".

What can I do? Kill the tramps as well. Domino killings, why not kill everyone.

The tramp moves down and tears open a part of the bag, revealing James's stone face, he turns to me, then back to James's face and spits into it. The Asian tramp limps next to his friend and points at the dead face, "Nutter! Fucking nutter!"

"Put him with the rest of the garbage" the Irish tramp says. The two tramps take either end and throw him into the garbage. "Move along" the Irish tramp bows his head to me, taking off his green fisherman's cap. I begin to walk. I don't look back. Shadows move in mysterious ways. "Wait!" the Irish tramp spits out. I stop in my tracks I can feel him stumble behind me. "My bottle of white lighting" I breathe a sigh of relief and pass it over to him. "You can get your fucking own" and then he disappears back into the shadows with his friend, shouting 'nutters!'

Back inside my flat, the window still reads   F E A R   In the tears from the heavens.

My clothes burn in the corner of the mirror. I stand naked. Silhouetted by the TV and my reflection that shows me just skin and bone. The phone rings. No one knows this number. It is them. I answer it. "I wondered when you'd call"

"A professional job Clarissa"

"How did you know?"

"We know everything" The TV blacks out and then comes back on. The picture shows me, as I stand now, naked, in the living room, holding the telephone. "You work for us again"

"What if I say no?" The phone clicks dead. The picture remains on the TV. I watch myself.

Watching 'them', watching me. 'They' always were. They're watching you right now.

The world returns to my favourite sound.

Silence.

THE FUNERAL

The first death of their generation. The first casualty of their Britpop years.

"Did you get them?" Matt asks.

"Of course" Samantha replies.

"How much for how many?" Matt asks.

"I can't believe the two of you are talking about this?" Alex buts in.

"Why not? James's of all people would have appreciated the demand for a new quality merchandise," Matt reasons.

"It's his funeral" Alex pauses for profound effect. "Doesn't that mean anything to you?"

"You're not going to start analysing death again are you?" Samantha asks Alex, she couldn't stand another day of that.

"Suicide." Alex again pauses for dramatic effect.

Samantha ignores him and turns to Matt. "What price range were you thinking of?"

"How can you discuss that type of business, a friend of ours is dead" Alex pauses and holds his hand to his head like a theatre actor. "What makes someone take his or her own lives?"

"Did you ever see James on mushrooms, he went up and down the lift, freaking out. Then that time on your birthday he kept talking about death, holes dug in the new forest" Matt remembers that James was as fucked as the rest of them put together.

"He knew he was going to die, take his own life. That must be some experience," Alex says, holding his eyes on his profound statement.

Part 3: Wasted

"I saw him once staring into the pond in our house last year, he just kept saying 'they're waiting'" Matt raises his eyes.

"I wonder if he saw death come for him, and that's what he meant?" Alex replies.

"He was drunk, he couldn't handle his drink, and he couldn't handle his drugs"

"Just cause people cant consume as much as you, doesn't mean they should kill themselves. You make it sound like a competition," Alex reasons.

Samantha has had enough. "Jesus Alex, stop trying to analyse it."

"Our friend is dead and you two act like you don't care" Alex turns away in disgust.

"Care? What for?" Matt says. "He hadn't spoken to anyone since the course started again, sat at the back of the lectures, giving everyone evil looks. He had turned into Travis Bickle, kept making gun fingers at the back of my head and winking."

"What makes someone kill him or herself?" Alex again asks, speaking his words theatrically.

"Being friends with you," Matt replies.

"You want to play psychiatrist do it on your own time, Matt and I have got business to discuss." Samantha takes out some pills from her pharmacy degree she stole.

"I always said I'd never wear a suit, now look at me, I'm wearing a black suit for a funeral," Matt says looking like he should be going to work. "If he would have any respect for our friendship he wouldn't have killed himself, forcing us to wear suits, I feel like I'm going to school, or church"

"You are going to church" Alex replies. "The eyes of the lord are going to judge you"

"Here. Is that enough for a test sample?" Samantha holds the pills out.

Matt takes the pills and swallows one. "I'm not going to sell anything I haven't tried myself"

"I'll take one too. I need it to get through today," Samantha replies.

"Where you and James close?" Matt asks.

"No, I can't stand being with Alex," she replies.

"I can't believe you're both taking animal drugs on the day of James's funeral" Alex cries.

Matt touches Alex shoulder to calm him. "It was James's idea to start to sell them. It's the one thing he spoke to me about since we came back. That and if I had any shovels"

Steve wonders why he is the only one walking in this storm, what a horrible day for a funeral, if there was ever a good day. His suit, which he had brought for a wedding is getting drenched, he might as well buy a new one. More money he hasn't got. They all ran to the cars, to run from the rain, why does no-one own umbrellas? He tried to get in each car, but the doors locked and smiling faces pretending to mourn a loss waved goodbye as the car's screeched off down the road. Left alone, by the gutter, wondering if this was as low as James felt when he took his life. Alex's car drove back, a lift? But he just wanted to ask Steve to go in the off licence and get something tasteful for the reception. "A bottle of wine for the family"

"It's not a dinner party Alex" Matt says from the back seat.

"Where's the money?" Steve had demanded.

"You'll have to pay, my hands are full"

And as he sped of, he splashed water over the curb onto Steve's trousers. "CUNT!"

As he walks the streets, life seems the same; the windy city is cold and violent since they came back. He wonders if all the people he passes know James has died, or even knew of him. Today people he knew would be upset, by next week, he'd just be another forgotten face, and a story of what happened to someone they once knew. Their own death amongst a group of friends. What great dramatic effect this story could hold for Steve. Images and visions run through his mind, a starting point; my friend, no, wait, my best friend, killed himself at university, committed suicide. In death James could bring the correct tune to each party that he never did when alive. It gave him more depth and interest than he ever had breathing, his perverted tendencies and talk of suicide. This was gold dust. Images of being by James's grave talking about his secret in weeks, months to come, and the mourner, recounting the day he told James his secret. "Never speak about this again you said. If only I could understand the sorrow you felt inside"

Drama Queen City.

When Simon heard that one of his friends had died, his initial thought was Johnny. He had disappeared on them all, it would be poetic licence that only Johnny could conjure up and do justice too

Part 3: Wasted

- by next time they see him, he is lying still, with a open-ended look on his face, knowing all the answers. He'd sit beside the luminaries of his generation, before the demand of excess would hit one of the Gallagher's. That was the problem with the British bands - they started a generation, a voice, but none of them were willing to go the whole nine yards and become martyrs. A Jim Morrison or Hendrix for the Britpop generation, taken before their prime, and held in such high esteem that the revolution would be complete. But there was no revolution. Only in death is there a true conflict of masses. It's something none of us can run from, Simon reasoned. Maybe that's what freaked James out. Along with the 'oddness' and decline of his behaviour over the last eighteen months. But was it a decline? No one had known him before they arrived. We could all be wearing masks and hiding are true personalities. When he first met James he seemed normal enough, then came the mushrooms and tales of acid and bullshit, then obsession with certain girls, Charlotte, Clarissa, then staring saying he was 'waiting'. Followed by unwanted discussions on death and the private video collection of S & M tendencies. When you look at it from an outsiders point of view he must have seemed fucked up. From a students point of view, he seemed normal, healthy, with all the above. Drugs can do weird things to your mind. What made him so special that he thought he'd be a martyr in death?

Simon left earlier than the others, wanted to find a pub, drink, not to be deep or anything, he couldn't get through any day without a drink or drug. They'd be running a book on whose next, it wouldn't be worth the money to claim back on him being the next to go, not that he'd commit suicide, but he couldn't operate unless he was under the influence of something. The Britpop generation, more like, the Excess generation. James wasn't the type to commit suicide; he'd bore others to death, but wouldn't take his own life. Then again what's the type? People who want their egos to out last their lives, which was James. Maybe he was the type. He looks around the bar, looking for the type.

"Going to a wedding?" the Irish tramp sits next to him.

"Funeral"

"Murdered?"

"Suicide"

"No-one kills themselves, they're all murdered," he points to his brain and then his heart, "murdered in here" That was the type, those who thought too much. He'd place the odds on Alex being next.

A circle forms round the grave, funny, how everything in life becomes a circle. A circle to smoke dope too, sit in restaurants or tables with a group of friends in a circle, karma, what goes around comes around, evolution process, the world is one big circle, everything spins. A circle for life. A circle for death. In this time at university they all spent twenty four hours a day in bed, laying claim to the legends in their heads. And seeing the coffin of one of their own, they realise that the statue they bow to isn't made of gold but stone, that every memory they have conjured was brought and sold, nothing was pure or real.

The sermon starts, family, friends. Death always awaited others, never oneself, until it happens to someone you know, and then the fresh doubts of your own mortality drive up.

Did any of them really care about James? Not enough to weep. But to see one of their own being buried makes them think. That was James's purpose in the friendship – make them question the truth.

Steve turns up drenched. "Thanks for the lift you fucking cunts" he shouts across the service.

"Jesus Christ Steve, they'll about to put James in for the count"

"Oh fucking hell! Shit sorry, I mean, heaven, not hell, he's going to heaven" He stands there drenched, smiling towards the family.

Simon turns up and stumbles through. Red-faced glazed eyes. "Sorry, I needed a drink"

"We all need a drink," Matt replies.

"I can't sleep unless I have something to drink" What happens afterwards? Simon begins to wonder. Is that it, you die and then no more? You wait for the worms to eat your skin? Is that even a body in there? No one has seen it. Who says James is even dead? Perhaps we're the ones dead? No, that's stupid; the dead would be too clever to stand in the rain. Never been baptised? Does that mean don't go to heaven? Simon looks at vicar, wondering if he gets the sack if he someone in his congregation isn't christened, "Does God sack people?" he asks.

The rain falls, making the sound of a heartbeat on the coffin. Family members cry, his sister looks quite sexy, Matt thinks, can't help but think maybe fuck her? The sound of despair, not at death of someone close but despair of their own lives. And he disappears. Away from our lives to wreck whatever hell he created on here. It was as easy as that. "Is that it?" Matt asks.

Part 3: Wasted

"Yes" Alex replies.

"I wore a suit for that bullshit?"

"Show some respect" Alex demands

"Out of respect for him I'm going to get pissed and take some more pharmacy pills." Matt reasons. Before they leave to the reception, Matt sees Clarissa. "I'll walk, let Steve get in this time"

Matt joins Clarissa by the grave. She stares, motionless. "I missed the service"

"You're saying goodbye now."

"Goodbye, yeah, I guess. Are they all reminiscing about what a great person he was, a great laugh, a ladies man?"

"I've got no memory before the rain" Matt replies as it falls across his skin.

"Me neither" Clarissa says as the rain falls hard across them both.

"You don't have to stay with me," Clarissa says, looking at the grave.

"He was fucked up. He was in to all sorts, don't think we ever realised who he really was"

"Why are you telling me this?"

"Just thought you might like to know"

"I didn't know James, he was just someone we go to college with"

"I thought you was upset, that was all." Matt begins to walk away.

"Wait." She calls out. "Death is upsetting, it reminds me of when I was younger"

"With your dad?"

"Yeah, with my dad"

He walks back and the two of them stay and watch the rainfall across the grave. "Suicide they said," She finally breaks the silence.

"Yeah, so they said"

"You don't think so?"

"James was too fucked up to kill himself." Matt then pauses. "Others maybe..."

"What are you trying to say to me Matt?"

"That I understand"

"You know don't you?"

"Does it matter?"

"You tell me?"

"All that matters to me is getting caned, getting wasted, I care for nothing".

"Do you work for them?"

"Them? I do I look like I could work for 'them'? Whatever that means?"

She looks at Matt. "No, you don't"

"Would you like me to wait, we could share a taxi?"

"I'm not going to the reception."

Matt waits regardless as Clarissa looks into the ground and sees all the faces that have haunted her. "I wanted to say my own farewell" She puts her arms through Matt's and they walk like a couple; him stoned and wasted, her cold and controlled. "You scared of dying?" She asks.

"I will be until I can get drunk, get stoned, then it wont matter, cause I'm untouchable then."

"Must feel nice?"

"Feels like waiting in a queue that doesn't move"

"How much will it cost?" Simons asks.

"The first sample is free," Matt replies.

"What does it taste like?"

"Nothing"

"What side effects thus far?"

"Nothing"

"What animal was it meant for?"

"Horses." Matt looks at Simon and stares at him, like his soul is in possession of the horses that have taken the giant pill. He wonders what it would be like to roam wild; across the funeral reception have James's sister ride him in his saddle.

"Give me two," Simon holds his hand out. "How do the horses take them?"

"They're shoved up their arses" Samantha informs them.

"Who would have thought James would commit suicide?" Steve says. "I need to be christened"

"You got a lot of sins you're trying to redeem?" Alex asks. "What makes you think being christened will help you. There's no cure"

"Cure? Why does everyone keep going on about cures, I'm not sick!"

"From points of view in society you are sick"

"Shut up, Simon and Matt are coming over they don't know... Alright boys." Steve looks at their completely blank faces. "It's hit you guys quite hard"

Part 3: Wasted

"Very. I feel nothing." Simon replies.

"I wish I could feel nothing, but I feel why suicide? I feel like I want to know the secrets James had," Alex says.

"Who's talking about James?" Matt asks.

"Don't know, I was talking about the Horse pills," Simon replies.

"Fucking hell! You've taken pills at a funeral?" Alex shouts at them.

"Horse pills" Simon replies.

"They'll be two more deaths, have a joint funeral," Lauren speaks for the first time this day.

"We're all getting away from James. This day is meant to be for James" Alex reasons. "Suicide. Makes it seem profound"

"I think it's selfish. Killing yourself and leaving the others to deal with it," Amy moans.

"I doubt he didn't think of that, he was very alone," Steve thinks of stories to tell to strangers.

"I've thought about killing myself"

"Why Amy?" Steve asks her.

"I'd be popular in death. James is the most popular person in the city now"

"Be great, to see you're on funeral" Steve reasons.

"I feel bad that I should have done something to help him," Lauren says.

"We all could have helped him" Alex holds out his arms for a group hug.

Matt looks at them, "James was fucked up, and we all knew it."

"How can you say that? It could be me next, committing suicide, or any of us" Alex replies.

"Fucking suicide, you make it sound like it's the new cocaine," Matt says.

"I'd take pills," Amy says.

"Hang myself," Steve says.

"Bullet to the head" Simon says.

"Who do you think will be next?" Lauren says.

"Hope its me," Alex replies.

"You want to die?" Lauren asks him.

"If it's going to become a fad. Suicide. We should all try it" Alex says to the group.

Matt walks away and moves into the kitchen, staring out of

the window. Members of James's family are crying, others getting pissed, the younger ones having crafty joints to themselves outside, just an excuse for another party. A celebration, not for James's life, but for everyone else's immortality, he thinks.

"How well did you know James?" his sister has come over, sexy, the one he wanted to fuck.

"Not well. I'm Matthew"

"Meg"

"Sorry for your loss"

"The expected thing to say, how many people have said that, a pound for each pays my overdraft off. Tell me what you really feel?"

"I don't think that's a good idea?"

"He was an arsehole. I'm pretty sure he fucked a lot of people up, not just himself, and as for this suicide business, he was too much of a coward to kill himself"

"You don't think it was suicide?"

"He'd signed onto a donor deal, saved someone else's life. In death, James becomes a hero"

"Whilst in reality?"

"You tell me."

"Why does everyone think that I'm some expert on what your brother was really like?"

"Cause you look like death"

"Thanks"

"Fuck social graces. I'm glad he's dead, aren't you?"

"You're a real nice person"

"I'm a fucking bitch, that's what you want to say"

"You're a fucking bitch, there said it"

"You also want to fuck me don't you?"

"You're sick"

"You do though, you kept looking at me at the funeral"

"I was looking through you, there's a difference"

"Just say it, before I'm bored with you and walk away, and you'll lose the chance to fuck me"

Matt begins to think about this and she continues her torture. "Got you thinking now haven't I? A guaranteed fuck."

"Yeah, I want to fuck you"

"I don't think so. It'll be no fun now that I know you agree with me." She walks away.

These horse pills really made him feel nothing for anything.

Part 3: Wasted

He'd reach the lowest ebb his drug taking could take him too, the storm of the last few months, was now at its height. He couldn't get any more wasted. Couldn't get any colder. Negativity breeds this. He had a choice. That's the one thing this funeral had taught him. As the reception moves into the winter evening hours, the more drink consumed the more honesty prevails at its lowest level. A wedding reception that was next door is joined up with the funeral service and a karaoke machine is the order of the day for life's celebration, in death and in birth united families by grief and greed - Marriages and deaths - Both have ceremonies, both have receptions. Both end in tears and drunken slurs, which later cause families to stop speaking to other members, until they are united by the same ceremonies. The only difference was on the certificate.

In the hallway of the house a new member joins the ghost...
"Hi, I'm..."
"You don't need to tell us, we all know your name"
"Where is this?"
"Student purgatory"
"What's it like?"
"Hundreds of students doing nothing" The ghost leads the new arrival into the kitchen. At the table are a number of student girls.
"Take a seat"
"Its my dream I had before I died. Are they all ghosts? I didn't kill them all."
"You don't have to kill someone to take their souls. They'll never be the person they was before they met you, only here did that version go to when that part of them died."
The ghosts sit down at the table, awash with memorabilia of the Britpop generation. Each has a mask of their favourite band member on their dishes. A union jack tablecloth spread across, fountains of snow in the bowls and big banquet dish in the centre. The top is taken away and the new ghost sees himself lying flat as the main course.
"Is this my punishment?" The new member asks.
"I prefer the term redemption, it sounds more biblical"
And as the night dawns in, the storm holds an hour of calm for all to return to their respective homes. The city streets return in colour, to the excitement and blossoming of that first year of promise. The windy city offers stillness, a mark of respect for the passing of one of its own that had walked the streets in various

guises and states of address. The emptiness as the past whispers memories in all the places they had all visited. For that one-hour there is no past, no future, no present, just a city that wanted to sleep. Worn out from a wasted generation.

LORD OF THE FLIES

The flies swarm round the head of the garbage, more food and rot to feed the entire family for a year. The Lord of the flies stops and beckons them into the food. As they circle, smell and drop in like vultures, the top of the mountain becomes shadowed, and something big to swallow them whole, dropping with fluids and chunks of food, falls towards them, and builds the mountain higher. The lord of the flies leads his family out of the mountain, but some are trapped underneath the shadow, immersed in an eternity of food they wished to steal. The Lord of the flies stops, remorseful, but directed in the knowledge that casualties are always taken when you fight for survival. A human figure looms above the mountain, a giant, and the hole in its face opens... "Take a seat"

Phil looks across the room. At the bottom is meant to be a sitting area, joined into the kitchen. There is a brown beaten sofa, its stuffing falling out, two torn armchairs with wet clothes draped across them. The floor is sticky and garbage has made its way from the door. Various shoes, block the path. "I'll stand" He goes to lean against the cooker, and feels his coat stick to the back, like a resin that will not let go until it has connected together for lasting life.

"Yeah, I wouldn't lean against that if I was you" Phil heeds Matt's advice, he turns his jacket round and it is now stained. He takes in the cooker properly - black tarred, grease dropping from the grill, a burnt strip of foil. The hobs are suffocated by past food of the last few months, never cleaned away. "It was originally white. You want something to eat?"

Phil starts to feel psychically sick. The best was left to last, Matt had blocked the doorway, where the man made mountain stood in all its glory. Rubbish piled up on the bottom, stuck into Asda bags, then the bags had dried up, and the rubbish had been thrown on top of the previous bags, nothing to support it. A mountain of food, drinks, cigarettes, joints, bottles, stacked from the floor, reaching just below his waist but higher than his knees in height, and half his body in width. "Jesus" he whispers to himself, he had never seen anything like it.

"There was an argument over who's turn it was to buy bin bags, so no-one brought any. Its going to be Christmas soon, we wont be here"

"What about when you come back?" Phil asks. The room falls quiet. He looks across the ashen faces of the house, sitting round a table sewn with rizzla's, bottles, tobacco, and the smell of burnt brains. "What's the smell?"

"The flies, they feed off the rubbish," Matt informs him, as Phil sees the flies march around the mountain of rubbish. The leader of the pack, the lord of the flies, whizzes past his face and Phil flicks a hand out to it. "Did you get it?"

Phil looks round the club, Nexus, Steve talking about James's suicide and some fake story about how it has affected his thinking. "He was my best friend and I did nothing. James and I had a lot in common. Secrets"

In Nexus, the floor was covered in beer stains and tobacco driven in by marching feet of freaks. The room felt damp, full of a dry rot. The light was low, hiding peoples truth, souls hidden behind obscure clothes, faces cut open through piercing and make-up on both sexes.

"How long have you guys been coming here?" Phil asks Matt.

"A lot this second year. They let us skin up"

"Don't you ever go out somewhere nice?"

"There is no-where nice"

"What about all those places you took me to last year when I visited?"

"That was in the first year, things are different now"

"What's different with all of you, was it James's death?"

"James?"

"Yeah him killing himself, you seem in mourning, Steve was telling me that..."

"Everything just seemed colder when we got back in September."

"Don't you guys go out places? This is full of vampires"

"So?"

"What about your house, don't mean to be rude but its fucked mate"

"So?"

"Do you all just sit around and do nothing?"

"Seems the only thing left to do. Get wasted"
"What about the course?"
"What course?"

"Do you not want to get stoned?" Matt says to Phil back in the house.

"No, I'd rather just get some sleep" he replies. Matt starts to walk away, eyes gone completely. Its 3am, they'd been smoking since he arrived; then when they finally left for the vampire club, they carried on smoking there, smoking on the way back, now back at the house, they continued to smoke. "Where do I sleep?"

"The sofa"

Phil lye's on the sofa, keeping his eyes away from the mountain of rubbish, the dearth of rot and indignations on the floor. He remains fully clothed. The room is freezing, next to the back door. He thinks about turning the gas on, to keep himself warm, but is scared it may cause an explosion. What was he doing here? What happened to these people? Can a place and people really change that much in the space of a few months? Coming to visit Matt had been a big mistake. He had left the house this morning full of excitement, hoping like Matt had himself said – "to recreate the first year." But what he found was drawn eyes, burnt souls, and a wasted education of nothing. They were all waiting for life to happen around them, whilst they sit in a holy circle, a council of wasters.

He feels something on his face as he tries to sleep it drops off. He jumps up like you do in twilight of your sleep, scared if this is real or a dream. His face is fine. He can see a crack in the sofa, where his head had been trying to lay and pretend to sleep until daylight. Afraid at first, but inquisitive, to justify his next action, he puts his hand down the crack and pulls out an age-old kebab wrapped in paper. He runs over to the sink, crying to be sick, nothing comes out but fear of choking. The tap runs and Phil splashes himself with water. Pouring himself a pint in the one rinsed glass on the side of ten. He downs it, gulping every drop to cleanse himself of this shit hole he was trying to sleep in. A noise scuttles across the bin bags and he is frozen.

"It's the rat" a voice comes out from the hallway and a shadow stands by the doorway.

Phil turns to face the voice. It is Alex. "Jesus, you scared me." Alex is nodding his head back and forth like there is some music in his head, a dancing motion in his body. "What you listening to?"

Part 3: Wasted

"Nothing. I cant hear any music, can you?" Alex dances his way into the kitchen.

"I just wondered why you was dancing?"

"Cause I'm high on life. Its good to be alive"

"How come you didn't come out with the rest of the house?"

"I don't spend much time with them anymore."

"I take it you don't like getting wasted all day then?"

"Not really, there's loads out there"

"Thank fuck for that. I thought the house had been taken over by zombies or something, glad to see one of you is still normal"

"I go on adventures, would you like to come?"

"Where to?"

"Portsmouth. Its where my girlfriend is"

"Its 4am"

"That's the best time to watch"

"Watch what?"

"My girlfriend have sex"

Phil looks at Alex, the guy was dancing to a tune only he could hear. His face was lonely, like he'd been talking to himself a lot. This guy was the next suicide. "I'm going to the station" Phil replies. He had made his mind up as he said it. He wouldn't have another minute in this place before he found himself dragged into the same routine of nothing. It seemed an easy existence. No turning back. No goodbyes. He'd have to wait couple of hours on a freezing cold station to get a train back. As he walked through town, he could see what Matt had said earlier to him. It was different. It was colder. The colours were grey. The windy city was falling into darkness, where once it lit up their dreams.

Simon, was shaking, he'd continued into the afternoon, he stood now a chemical imbalance. He hadn't turned up for the course since November. At one stage he admitted to forgetting what he was actually in Southampton for. It had seemed a different lifetime when the course was the focus off attention. Everyday was merging into one, and it didn't seem to matter as the money was constantly coming in from government grants, from student loans, from bank overdrafts, it was free, who mentioned a course to study, it was free money to get wasted in and do nothing whilst awaiting the next cheque. Simon takes two pro-plus, the shaking increases, and his eyes wild. But for some reason it seemed essential that he join Matt in attending the film screening. They reach the lecture theatre, nearer death and the promise of sleep when they collapse. Most importantly they had done it. Made the effort.

Martin Pumphrey, hides in the shadows and pounces out of the doorway. "Simon, need word, yes, aha, yes, Simon, word" his head nodding furiously, as he speaks.

This was it for Simon. There was no turning back. He had to explain himself for the last few weeks, and as Martin Pumphrey's head nodded furiously, awaiting an answer to why he hadn't turned up recently, he searched what was left of his mind on that evening to come to the conclusion he new the day he started the course. "I want to leave"

"What? Leave? We don't need to be that drastic"

"No, I want to leave the course. I hate it." It felt like a weight had been lifted of his shoulders; he longer had the responsibility of turning up.

"Do you want to change to another course?"

"No I hate education"

"Well, lets wait and see after Christmas"

"I've left. In fact, I was never really here"

Matt Ryan sits alone in the lecture theatre. The room is full of people but he is alone in his thoughts. Paranoid reasons to why no one sits next to him, that only being this permanently wasted can create. Being wasted is two fold he reasons; you have the ultimate high each time which you need to keep going further, then when you're not at that ultimate point for the rest of the day, everything is wrong - the way you look, the way your clothes hang, the way you smell, the way people talk to you. He has an entire row to himself. No-one spoke one word to him or acknowledged his presence as they waited for the lecture to begin. He looked around hoping to make eye contact with them, so they would nod a hello, but it was like he had escaped from all existence. Not even Clarissa saw him. She sat at the side but as people spoke to her, replies were limited to a fake smile, her thoughts on something else that weighed down her shoulders. As the lecture starts, he is left looking at the cover of 'Select' magazine through the corner of his naked eye, where a union jack stands tall. This style of the flag had always been associated with racists in the seventies, but now, it was being reclaimed through Britpop and the political culture that was sweeping through the student masses. He puts his walkman on, headphones hidden in his ears, Noel singing 'Don't Look Back In Anger' down to him. And he could see it, what it meant for these last eighteen months, the culture was cool to be an outsider, the mis-shape, and the outcast. And as he looks around the room, at the middle class expensively educated around him, trying to portray themselves as working class, he realised it wasn't just them that was being patronising, but his ideal of the 'outsider' wasted to his hearts content, was just as bad.

When the lecture ends, everyone leaves the theatre room, but Matt. He remains sitting, staring at the silence of it all. He didn't want to get stoned. He didn't want to get drunk. He just wanted an answer. Confusing this addiction with his need to fit in.

As Matt walked the streets, he wanted to look at 'wonder' at the Christmas lights, the excitement of those around him. He wanted to feel what he felt when he walked the parade of shops this time last year. When it felt anything was possible.

He wanted to recapture the magic of Christmas - looking into the shops, as the bright lights beckon you in, the tinsel falls from the heavens, the smiles on faces of all ages, the warmth of the street lamp, and shop lights, the calm of events.

No memory before the rain, he'd told Clarissa at James's funeral. There were memories; just he'd chosen to hide them away. He was fucking his life up. A person with drawn eyes, hair damp and tangled down over his face, gaunt cheeks, tired posture, reflects back at him in the Christmas lights. A Santa Clause goes around wishing Merry Christmas, to all but him. He had failed to exist outside of a wasted world. Social isolation. Suicide. He'd never contemplated that; it was for the Amy's, Steve's and Alex's of this world, the attention seekers, the drama queens and the manipulative. Once you're at the bottom, the only way left way left was up. That was the challenge for him. For a second he sees a reflection in the window, its James, he shivers, tingles down his arm, someone has stepped on his grave.

"Hi" the reflection says.

Matt looks down, and then back towards the window, the reflection is Clarissa. "Alright"

"Been better," she says.

"Me too"

"You going home for Christmas?"

"Maybe, I don't see the point"

Clarissa leans into him and kisses both cheeks. "Merry Christmas" and she walks away.

The lord of the flies, brings his family back together, the giants had all dismissed themselves from their place of realm for a period of time, and the man mountain, that crumbled across the floor, kicked from one end of the room to the other by the giants as they left. The lord lets his servants roam and pick from the food, and the liquid on offer, their Christmas would be grand, and they would be treated like kings in their land, bringing gifts for the chosen one.

Then the lord of the flies stops, as he hovers above the centre of the mass of wealth, and a shadow of a giant closes in, scraping up all the rubbish in the gulp of some machine that swipes at the floor. Then fresh air comes not from the broken window, but from another machine, that sucks up the lords family and followers, into a vacuum of the never life. His choice is to follow or to stand-alone? Another shadow of a giant has joined the destruction. This shadow goes to the broken window, the lord of the flies' one chance of freedom, and begins to put in fresh glass.

No escape. No wealth. The kingdom he ruled upon under the guises of the giants has now been destroyed and repaired to its normality.

SO THIS IS CHRISTMAS... (PART 2)

Matthew

Opening the door back I'm not to sure what it is I'm expecting, where it is I'm going back to, but most important of all, who or what I am? Standing on the station earlier, my Liverpool bag over my shoulder, full of unwashed clothes ranging back three months, the smell leaking across the station, no-one again sits next to me, they keep their distance. My hair floppy over my face, big curtains, big afro, frizzy, lying over my eyes, down to the bottom of a nose that seems to have a permanent cold, no style, no nothing, the Bee Gees meets cousin 'It'. I'm not healthy at all. Itching, that house made me nothing but itch. Sitting on the platform, I need a joint, but I dare not take any back with me. Women look at me, but it can't be through looking good, mothers point, suits stare. Paranoid. My usual routine, at this time, 6pm, rush hour, I'd be on my 7th joint of the day, starting a new session. The world was built in six days; God had a day off on the seventh that must have been some weed he smoked.

Open the front door. It'll be Christmas Eve tomorrow. My Mum greets me with a big cuddle and kiss. I greet her with unwashed laundry and a drugged ugly son. She looks into my eyes and can see the fresh faced of my youth'ism all but disappear. She knows... I can tell she knows. Afraid to ask me how much and how far I've taken a road down. I want to tell her all this but I have trouble speaking sentences

Laying on my bed all evening, the TV on, it's blank and fussy what is clear to anyone else. I'm trying to search for my mind, search for some dialogue, search for something that is a conversation and not something that burns on my finger tips with the light of my throat later.

It's all so very blank. Nothing, I feel absolutely nothing

"Yeah" is about my conversation at the dinner table this evening, its drooled out with a deep huskiness like I'm acting in a hard mans movie by choice; this is not by wish but my medical condition. My Mum and brother ask me questions and give each other deep concerned looks I see through the corner of my eye when I don't answer, as I didn't hear what they said, my mind elsewhere in a big black void.

Paranoia. I'm so scared of what I've become. The worst thinking that I'm so cool doing this, sarcasm my new best friend, quietness and smugness my two soul mates, nothingness my wife.

Christmas Eve, I sit in the local at the end of my road. 'Don't Look Back In Anger' ablaze in the minds of a new generation of followers. The speaker rattles with the entire album, not one pub goes without it, hand in hand with a generation that knows no bounds at present. But that's my problem I know no bounds. An old friend, Matt Smith, next to me up at the bar, he seems to have calmed down a bit from his 'faces' and 'players' who he was around. He's talking about going to university. He's really taken the straight road big time, he's talking about a future, when a future before for him was a jail cell waiting with his name tattooed into his cellmate. "What do you think? University?" he asks me...

"Yeah" I drool out.

He looks at me to carry on. I'm trying to think of something to say, something to come into my mind but I think nothing. I can tell his eyes are burning into me thinking - 'waster... waster... what happened to this guy' I don't want to be like this. I really don't

"You'd advice going to uni then? And don't just reply yeah for fucks sake" he asks me.

I pause, trying my brain with any number times theory that will equal an answer of my past eighteen months, what am I studying and for what reason?

All I can tell him is the truth, "it's all free..." I pause, I've completely forgotten his question, what did he ask me?

He looks away in complete disgust and whispers under his breath - "fucking waster"

Who am I?

Please....

Christmas lunch.   Questions. "Yeah" is my reply drooled out again?

Pickled Onions.   T w o different cheeses

Questions. No reply as I can't answer

Just got to focus on the food it may bring back my mind from the enclosed cave with the caveman who has set up campfire by my lifeless body

Salmon.   Ham.

Bacon

Mum and brother talk and laugh. I don't understand what they are saying. Lips move and smile nod and talk. But my mind doesn't collect what my eyes see. I smile back and my mouth opens to comment but...what crackers, Ritz? Bread, white or brown?

"Would I like a glass of wine?" I make out along the washed shore where as I stare at my food I stand naked by the ocean, thick blue that will drown and suffocate me, I've got to go in though to cleanse my itching body. Waves wash over me, my first words at the table. "No... thanks...." I wanted to be offered a joint, the ocean sucks the air of each breath I've taken from several class A and B hits. I don't think I can carry on. I want to tell Mum and get her to help me.

New Years Eve. Last year I could handle it all. Smoking. Drinking. Free money. No debt but what I'm paying now. Twelve months down the line in mind and pocket. I would lye in bed till it was time to get up and go out at 7pm. It felt great, it all fitted into my place, everyone wanted to know me, and everyone wanted to kiss me. Now I lye in bed frightened. I try listening to the same songs as twelve months ago - 'Parklife' album and 'Whatever' EP but they seem out of place. I'm the one, who is out of place in their world, that I've embraced too full on. I smiled contented last year when sleeping till 7pm. Now I stare scared into the mirror till 7pm.

In the pub, it's the same faces as last year. The same girls I kissed. They all ignore me this year. Am I not the same person? The mirror says not. The eyes never lie. Old red eyes is back.

Midnight chimes and I stand alone in a crowded centre where all around me embrace and rejoice with bodily fluids. I stand in the middle, deluding myself that I'm better than this.

One girl approaches me. "Have you got any speed?" she asks.

"Do I look like a drug dealer?" I reply.

"Yes"

"I'm never coming back. I hate this place, I'm never coming back," I've never prayed to God but I do tonight. To help me in this hell I have built around me through my personality. I just want to get well. My addiction gets worse with time, blind my next hit, a drug or drink, taking it away from my mind, without I don't feel safe anymore. It's my only friend. But it is never true.   Limitless is the most dangerous aspiration an egomaniac can boast for. Cause I don't know what's right. And I don't know what's wrong.

Simon

Walking back through town, down the long winding country lane my parents live down, I hear voices. I see colours. Shadows scuttling across the pavement. No cars I stop by a bench. The bright light under me. Colour of the rainbow

What the fuck is happening? What am I seeing? Is this my first acid flashback?

"Craaazzzzzzyyyyyyyyyyyy" a voice next to me says.

I'm afraid to turn round but my head does so, like a child told not to go back into that cupboard but can't help himself.

A clown sits next to me, just like Tim Curry in the TV film of IT. I hate that film. I get up and don't think about it, walk away from the bench and don't turn back. Keep my feet walking quickly down the road. My house must only be a few minutes away. I'm almost there.

Out of a hedge comes another clown. He blows his horn and points down the road for me to hurry up.

In the centre of the road are two clowns pushing pies into their faces and laugh

I reach the front door of my house the key doesn't fit. I see a light upstairs and hear footsteps coming down. I hear footsteps down the driveway; the clowns are closing in on me. "Open the fucking door" I shut.

The door opens and my Mum is dressed as clown. "What time do you call this Simon?" Next to her is a midget with a firework. They say that flashbacks get worse with time. It's only been eighteen months...

PART 4

January '96 to Summer '96

Madness

SAUSAGE JOCKEY

Steve

Debt. Financial debt and personal debts to pay. "I need more money," I beg in tears of desperation to the lady in the bank. I'm sure she's smiling she must fancy me. I'll be sure to get a loan if I give her inkling I could be interested, though I much prefer the guy sitting next to her. He looks a bit like Alex James, I look like Damon Alban, we could form a band.

"What do you need it for?" She asks like my mum did when I needed money for new clothes.

"Cigarettes, alcohol, lottery tickets" I reply, forgetting I'm talking to a personal bank manager assistant and not my mum.

"I'm sorry?"

"I need to get my hair cut as well, the wind is blowing it all over the place"

"Let me get this right, you want an extended overdraft for abusive substances and a hair cut?" She looks at me still smiling. I'm sure underneath that rough guise of headmistress pretence of power she wants to get me in bed. Even the guy next to her is staring at me now he wants to get me into bed as well. The entire population of the windy city wants to fuck me.

"I was only joking" I say and smile first at her, then erotically move my eyes towards the guy like they do in those gay porn films I watch. "It's to pay my rent"

"Oh, that's fine, just fill in this application" she says matter of fact, bringing out an application from her desk like it was magic, an everyday occurrence of students who beg for more money. "We just needed to hear you say 'rent' it doesn't matter what you spend it on"

"That's it?" as I pass the filled application form back. "When will it be in my account from?"

"Next working day."

"Tomorrow?! I need the money today; I've got to pay rent today!" I spend the next five minutes going back to begging, tears streaming my eyes, tales of landlords with baseball bats. "He'll break my fucking legs. I'll have to leave the course, leave the city. You gotta do something... GIVE ME SOME CREDIT!" The story of my life, all I want is some credit.

Sit and wait for thirty minutes, panicking that the shops will close by the time they give me some money, and I wont have time to buy that new top I saw walking into town, that made me want to get the overdraft extended in the first place. The zip up black Next jumper, winked at me in the mannequins eyes, beckoning me and promising sexual advances of the greatest wealth. Finally a stern looking small man with glasses and one hand smaller than the other walks over to me. I put on my 'ugly' face torn and broken. I'm one pound away from being a street victim, sleeping in a box with the Irish tramp as my dad and the 'nutter' tramp as my uncle. "Mr. Reed," he greets me, no handshake, just a look of disgust, "The best we can do is give you an emergency one hundred pound in cash, which will then be taken out of your account once the overdraft is put in tomorrow morning"

"That's all I need." My face lights up, spend, spend, spend.

"Do you have enough for your rent now?" the lady asks me, I know she's building up to asking me out for a drink.

"Rent?" I asked confused, surely they mean that Next jumper? "Oh, right, yeah"

The three of them don't move from their positions, like the mannequin in the Next shop window that beckoned me in here. We all stare at each other waiting for a Mexican stand off, for someone to draw first. I really want to know if that guy would like to come out for a drink, but its her whose been coming onto me. I'll have to ask her, and she'll bring him. "Would you like to come for a drink?"

"No" The guy and girl reply in union. He's gay; he just doesn't know it yet. She obviously said 'no' cause she realised I was gay, and didn't want to embarrass herself.

The first fifty goes on the 'Next' zip up jumper, my new 'pulling' method. Zip up to the neck, to only reveal more, when zipped down, all the way. If I've got a new top, I need to buy some new jeans, another thirty pound. The next ten goes on five lottery tickets and five scratch cards. I'm destined to win it's the law of averages. I win two pound from the five cards this is obviously fate. "Another two cards" I tell the lady behind the counter. She passes them over with a look of disdain, that will be rubbed off her face in a bout of emotional rescue when I win the jackpot and she begs me to share some of the winnings with her - "Smile like a mannequin, then I might" I'll reply, before laughing in her face. "I want another card?"

"We're closing"

"You said five minutes, two minutes ago. That's three minutes. I could always take it up with the manager"

"Fine, she's right behind you"

"I won a pound, I want a pound, no, another ticket," I tell a stern

Part 4: Madness

looking pregnant woman.

"Take the ticket, then please leave," she replies.

I begin to panic; what happens if there's nothing on this one, but the one after it has the jackpot? They may have fixed it? I could be one card away from being rich, from buying my own car, my own house, my own clothes shop, and my own gay porn production company. "Give me another five tickets," I tell the lady, passing over a five-pound note. She passes them over with a look of 'loser' written on her face. She turns the cash till off, and a security guard is now standing with the manager behind me. "I'll show you" I mutter as I slowly walk towards the door, scratching frantically, I want to wipe the smile of their faces... Nothing.... Nothing...Nothing... Nothing... Nothing... One pound. I run back up to the till. "Give me another card"

I feel a big hand grub my shoulder, "We're closed," the security guard tells me, his hand feels quite nice.

"If I win I'll buy you a drink"

I trip over into the street, the security guard standing by the window with a fist out, as the doors to WHSmith shut. Like Indiana Jones I try to sneak underneath the closing doors, holding out my one pound winning scratch card like Dr. Jones does his hat, but I don't make it, the scratch card does though. "Give me my winnings!" I bang on the window. The security guy picks up my scratch card and tears it up from behind the closed doors. Feeling into my pockets, all that's left is a five-pound note from a hundred. Do I buy cigarettes or alcohol?

Running into the house, I'm greeted by Taylor saying - "Where have you been? The landlord was here earlier, you still owe him rent"

"Put the lottery on, hurry up" I reply.

I sit next to Simon he too is holding a number of tickets. "This is it, no more money worries," he tells me.

"It wasn't just the landlord, he brought two heavies with him" Little Rob informs me.

"They're going to break your legs Steve" Amy continues.

"Not once I've won the lottery, I'll tell him to fuck off, that I'm buying my own house"

"That's nice what about us?" Amy, as ever is feeling left out, "forget about your friends?"

"No, be a house we can all live in, I'll be the landlord, you'll pay the rent to me"

"You'd make us pay rent?"

"Yeah, of course, nothings for free in this world"

"Like lottery winnings?"

"That's different, they owe this to me"

"Who the fuck is 'they'?"

"This country." I open a can brought for my advanced celebration.

Simon and I sit on the edge of our seats. Our eyes searching furtively round numbers.

"Someone write the numbers down, write them down, its going too quick" I can't check all the tickets simultaneously with each number.

"9. 13. 17. 27. 29. 40"

With each number on each ticket, dreams disappear and reality kicks back in. Simon has already given up the ghost and is burning his tickets.

"Careful Simon, they might catch my tickets alight"

"You haven't won anything, you're just hoping that the numbers will change if you look hard enough." He's right. I haven't won. Not one fucking number. But they don't know this. I stand up with a giant smile across my face it hurts. "You didn't get one number did you Steve?"

I keep up the pretence, but its no good, they know I've lost, again. I'll have to ask the bank for another loan now. "I'm never doing it again"

"You will Simon, you will" I say it like the Yoda in The Empire Strikes Back. "Still" I say, "It's not all bad, I've got my new clothes"

"But you haven't got any money?" Taylor reminds me.

"I got an emergency overdraft extension from the bank to pay my rent"

"So you can pay your rent?" Little Rob asks.

"Not now. I brought these clothes with the money"

"You brought clothes with the money for your rent? What the fuck is wrong with you?"

"I deserve some new clothes!" I start to undress and model the new clothes for them. "What do you think?"

There's a violent knock at the door. "Oh yeah, the landlord said he was coming back to get your rent Steve" Taylor finally decides to tell me.

"Fucking hell! Why didn't anyone tell me?!"

Part 4: Madness

"Well, you just said you deserved some new clothes" Simon reminds me.

As the front door opens, I run out the back door and down the side alleyways. Some guy has another guy pinned up against the wall, giving him a blowjob. "Alright Steve" the guy getting the blow job nods his head towards me, "How's things?" And it gives me an idea how to pay my rent.

Southampton Common in January is a painting that you want to look at but not be in. The leafs have fallen onto the frozen icy grass, as the orange lights from the lamps that stand tall next to the bare naked trees, illuminates an orange hazy due across each person. I shiver waiting for my first chance of making money. My first adventure into a way of life I had contemplated before but often as I walked the Common at various seasonal nights, I stayed in the shadows and watched others participate, trying to find the courage to enter into the paid arrangements. It's only now, as I freeze in my new 'Next' zip up top and jeans, that the intuitiveness, the 'dare and danger' of actually doing something when I come here has become a necessity to starve off an angry landlord.

I watch in the shadows, as I see car's draw up by the darker areas, both sexes, male and female appear from out of the hazy orange due of the lights, and go into them. Sometimes, the driver steps out entering into a dark walk and doesn't return for a number of minutes. When he does, he walks alone. "Hello." A voice is next to me in the shadows, my hairs stand on end of my neck. If I turn around I enter a new world that may bring me riches at a psychical price I cannot afford later in life.

Fuck it, I decide, I need the money. "Hello" I return in the same posh accent, if I'm going to sell my arse, I need it to give the idea that it's an expensive arse. Silence. Do I wait for him to speak, or do I do a hard sell? I try to think of those prostitutes down Derby Road, so I turn in a female way, hand on hips, then realising as I see my shadow across the light onto the frozen grass that I look ridiculous. I put my hands into my jeans pocket, the Oliver twist scenario. "It's a lovely night." I break the silence and look into the guys face. He looks know different from anybody else you see on the bus, in a shop, in the street, who smiles a good morning. I always thought they'd be freaks, have something wrong with them; pocked mark skin, shady hats, long over coats, in disguise, to hide them from the sordid acts they come here to perform. But he looks like he's come straight from work.

"Aren't you cold?" He asks me, looking at my lack of clothes, just the new model from 'Next'.

"I'm ok actually. They're brand new"

"I can tell" And he steps in and touches the jumper.

"Really?" A man of taste I decide. He could become my sugar daddy; I could become a kept boy. This could be my lottery ticket.

"Yes, the labels are still on" and I see where his hand is on the jumper, on the label staring at the price. "Fifty pound, did you get it from Next?"

"It was free. I'm a catalogue model for them." Telling the truth about my day would have seemed too desperate, a student selling himself too obvious. A catalogue model sounded higher class of standards than the other shadows that step out.

"Do you enjoy it?"

"Yeah"

"Which do you prefer, the modelling or the Common?"

"Maybe I could show you?" I can't believe I said that, its like I'm in some bad porn film, taken over by the spirits in the Common of rent boys past they are speaking my sentences.

"I'd like that." He places his arms by his side and makes the bulge in his trousers become prominent. He is slightly embarrassed for the first time, looking shyly towards his crotch.

I take my lead and unzip his trousers, taking out a large firm penis. Before I put it into my mouth I decide now would be a good time to ask an important question. "What do you do?"

"I lecture Art at Southampton Institute." I pretend he didn't say that, the consequences of future meetings could be disastrous. I close my eyes and take his cock into my mouth and begin to suck. "Ease my pain," he keeps repeating to himself.

I want to get this over with as quickly as possible, it tastes disgusting, sweaty, I try and pretend it's an ice cold lolly on a hot summers day, but its no good. The faster I swallow it whole, the quicker he pushes my head down, muttering to 'ease his pain'.

He comes. I swallow. Hopefully that means I'll get paid more. He does his trouser zip up and I stand back up, searching for some tissue in my pockets to wipe my mouth but there's none. I'm worried that I might begin to dribble onto the new jumper and ruin it with someone else's seamen, mine I can accept but not a strangers. "Have you got any tissue?"

"Sure" he passes over a hanky from his jacket, I forget about any germs that are being passed over and wipe my mouth. "That was my first time," he says with a glow of satisfaction.

I take this as the ideal opportunity to offer other services for more money. "Would you like to do something more?"

"God, no, I get sex at home," he replies.

"Home?" I bet he has got a married boyfriend and he wants an affair.

"I just wanted my cock sucked. My wife, she wont suck cocks"

"Your wife?"

"Married ten years." He takes out his wallet and shows me a picture of his wife, long blonde hair, and two kids. "That's my son Ian, and the little girl is my daughter Kristen." I study the picture, the wife, and the kids. I've never felt this low in my entire life; I want the ground to swallow me up. "So, how much do I owe you?" he asks.

"Twenty?" I say more as a question then a demand.

"Cheap price," and he pulls twenty out past the photo of his family and puts it into my hand. "Well, goodnight then." And he walks away.

Me, I follow the yellow brick road home, keep on walking and don't look back.

Suitably drunk, as always in Thursdays on a Wednesday. It's time to tell Matt my secret. Since he came back from Christmas he's stopped smoking weed. Simon said exactly the same, he too wouldn't go into details, but I get the impression over the Christmas period the 'Holy Trinity' really caught up with them both. As for Johnny, no-ones seen or heard from him in over two months, he just disappeared.

"Matt I need to speak to you," I lean into his face, on tiptoes, breathing onto him.

Matt is practically falling over, leaning back, away from my face. "Not now Steve" he replies, as he always does when I go to tell him my secret.

"It's really important, it's about someone in the house," I say to entice him, hoping that the idea of some juicy gossip will make him all ears to my true life. "Not here, people will hear" I reply and move my head for him to follow me upstairs.

Once up there I pause and we just stand in silence. Matt looks over the balcony, me looking at my pint. Do I really want to tell him? "Right, what I've got to tell you has to remain a secret" I say, trying to be dramatic and suspenseful as I pause again for effect. I grimace with my face, like I'm holding back the secret to the cure of cancer because the government will kill me if I reveal it to anyone.

"Oh come on Steve, if you're going to tell me, you're going to tell me. I want to get back to drinking." His new substitute for the amount of dope he smoked. He's even started bringing pints into lectures, the tutors don't say anything I think they're all scared of him.

How do you put this into a conversation, oh hello by the way I'm..."I'm gay," I finally tell him. I study his face for any tighten of emotion or grimace, any posture movement away from me, I know all the signs of 'fuck, get away from me faggot' or as the late James said to me "never mention this again".

But Matt's face is complete expressionless and he doesn't even pause to think just replies instantly - "Madonna posters, pulling girls and not taking them back, Marilyn Monroe obsession, it was pretty obvious"

"Why didn't you say something? I've been nervous all evening about telling you. Working up the courage, worrying what will he think? Will he beat me up or something!"

"Makes no difference to me mate" he even offers his hand out and I shake it, then he laughs and says - "Just don't touch me again, I don't want to catch aids"

I can tell there is a hint of truth in the voice, a small fear. Everybody has their own way of dealing with the secret; Matt's is to take the piss. "I'm glad you're taking the piss, everyone else is so serious about it"

"Everyone else? How many people know?"

"James did"

"James is dead"

"Little Rob, Johnny he was the first person I told, Amy and Lauren. I'm slowly working up to my parents and sister"

"Can I be a fly on the wall? I can imagine your dad now, chasing you with the axe and chopping your dick off shoving it down your mouth shouting – 'you like to suck cock do you son'" We both laugh, but he doesn't realise how near the truth that is. He then decides to add a moments after thought to our entire conversation - "I just can't get over the whole idea of two guys doing it, I mean women fair enough as it's biologically impossible without added toys and instruments but two guys it just seems painful…"

Part 4: Madness

Out in town at HMV and Virgin Mega-stores with Matt, Lauren and Amy. Matt follows me round the gay and lesbian video section really intrigued by what type of films they offer. "I never knew they sold them in normal shops."

"It's strategically put by World Cinema, as no one ever buys or looks at that," I tell Matt. "Some of them are really good. They have a really good story lines, it's not just porn,"

"Of course not," Matt replies, holding a gay porn version of Batman and Robin.

"I've got some really good ones," I say, keeping an eye on the shelf where Matt put that video back. I'll come back and buy that later.

"You've got gay porn in the house?" Matt replies, for the first time looking disgusted.

"Yeah, I watch them most nights. Sometimes Johnny used to watch it as well, he was really intrigued like you about the videos"

"You mean, you're having a wank to gay porn, the room below me? That's sick!" Matt says. A guy is standing near us he looks at me, then at Matt and smiles. "I know him from Magnums" I say. I can tell Matt is worried about people thinking he's gay now.

The Batman and Robin video plays, the guy from Virgin sits with me, we're in his room. It is full of videos, a catalogue library of the A-Z of gay porn. I should feel turned on by this but I feel sick, this is going a bit obsessive with films for my liking. Even the wallpaper is of various stills from gay porn films. There's one normal poster, of Jarvis. "Jarvis embodies the spirit of Britpop," he tells me. The film begins and our heroes are stuck in a darkly lit cave. "It's the uncut version"

"Do you study these films?" Perhaps he's a film tutor and he's going to reveal that from next year gay porn will be an essential part of the syllabus to study. "We study black British cinema and got to watch Black Soul Rebels the other day" I say, hoping this will impress him.

"An important film but dated. So you study film?"

"Yeah, we get to make them as well sometimes"

He walks towards a closest. I'm scared what he's going to bring out. He better be willing to pay me. A large box is placed on the bed next to me. As he opens it, thoughts of horror films run through my head. He could be a serial gay rapist, who cuts the dicks off his victims and puts them in a box.

"What's in the box?"

"Patience"

"No, just tell me what's in the box please?"

"Close your eyes" For some reason I do as I'm told. If I'm going to die or have something cut from my body, I'd rather not be able to see it. "Open them"

As I slowly open my eyelids and await the horror of seeing him hold my cut off dick, then passing it to me, my eyes blur back to focus and he stands before me with a digital video camera. "You make films?" I ask relieved.

"I'm an auteur. I make homage's to classic films as porn. So far I've done Platoon, Star Wars and Singing in the Rain"

I'm lost for words. He just smiles and walks to another closet in the room. Jesus, how many closets does this guy jump out off? "Does one of those lead to Narnia?" I ask him.

"Lion, Witch and the Wardrobe, that's my next attempt" He pulls out a Batman suit, then a Robin suit and holds them towards me. "Recognise these?" I look at the screen and see that Batman has taken his mask of in the cave, and Bruce Wayne is in fact this guy from Virgin Mega-stores. "Its my film you're watching…" He then pauses in time with his character on screen and says –

"I'm batman."

'CARLA PART 2'

The streets are paved with gold. On each corner is a young lady of the night. Matt walks up to each girl, hoping to see 'her' face. The all beckon him towards separate rooms, separate roads. Finally at the end of the road he sees her, her long blonde hair, clear blue-sky eyes, and the look of innocence he wishes to recapture. But he doesn't run to her, or even walk, he stands still, caught in time, and watches her. Before his very eyes, she begins to turn to gold. The sun blazes across onto her alone, and the gold begins to melt, he holds his hand out, but she vanishes from him and the city of gold turns to the windy city and a storm that rains from the heavens.

"Carla"

Matt wakes up from his dream. He sits up in bed and surveys his room. The posters that protected him and let him dream of a new revolution to be part of, now hang torn and worn on his walls. In his state before Christmas he couldn't repair the damage to them, let alone himself. The floor is scattered with cans of lager,

Part 4: Madness

a new addiction, where once the rizzla's and tobacco spread across. Waking up, like this, with a hangover, seemed better punishment then waking up still asleep in his mind. This way he felt something, even if it was towards a more violent outlook.

The stereo is skipping, jumping on 'Lust for Life', he'd been listening to Iggy Pop for years, now he was the rage, the rejuvenation, cause of Trainspotting, the songs from the soundtrack had haunted every nightclub he'd gone into. His initial reaction to waking from his dream is to try and mend his posters, the sort of thing you can only think to do when in twilight, something that seems a necessity at... "4am" he says to himself, looking at the video clock, next to his stacked CDs, the Oasis 'Whatever' EP on the top, hoping that it will let him re-live memories of that period of his life.

The floor is cold. He cannot find his slippers, bare foot across the alcohol stained carpet, knocking into an half full can, it spills across the floor, running its own race against him. The sink basin in his room waits, with the mirror to reflect what he has kept trying to forget about all night, but his dreams wont let him go. Her. Carla. It was a year ago today. For those few hours he forgot about everything and everyone, he understood who he really wanted to be. Life is so simple when you make it that. The complications start when you begin to think, begin to make plans, set a routine.

This time the storm does not walk with him down the roads where a man looks to cast his shadow. Instead the dusk of the cold winters day is before him. A blinding sunlight in its hazy morning due, that kicks into his alcohol created headache, creating a colour of violence onto the very streets he walks blinded. No rain. It hadn't rained for a few days now. The sunlight had replaced it. The cold remained. A cold hearted sun that promised cities paved with gold from the security of inside your home. And that is what reflected from his dream, the windy cities streets for once looked paved with gold, and he knew that fate would draw him towards her. She would absorb his every thought, his every bout of excess until he could see her again. She had tasted just like a woman, made love and ached just like a woman. But she slept that morning with her eyes closed. With all that pain in the room, he couldn't stay in there. Since then nothing seemed to fit.

This was her world. Each corner ached with women of the night, waiting for their work number to be punched and sleep through the day with no regrets. He hadn't seen her since, he had avoided that part of the city, that part of the street. Not through fear of his own safety, but fear of himself and his own memories and feelings. How can you think you love someone you've never known, but for a few hours of bliss? They didn't even know each other's last names. The idea of being in love like this, holding onto a single memory, was more attractive than the ideal of being with someone permanently for him, always on the outside looking in.

Matt stands in the centre, like a year before to the second … waiting. It seemed like his dream; a circle of prostitutes had formed around him, either side of the street. He could now walk, passing each face. Each girl wasn't the face he looked for, he studied each one for a number of seconds, in case the year had changed her features, but each of these eyes were cold, and not innocent but betrayed by the debt they had to pay. Where was she? He reaches the final girl and studies her. No older than Carla looked that year. The final girl must always be the most inexperienced one, the one who would most likely talk to him and answer his questions. She had black hair down to her mouth, cropped, in a trendy pop style, a student style anorak on, underneath a one piece dress, starting from her shoulders, finishing at the top of her legs, like a belt. Long black boots.

"Hi" she says.

"I'm looking for Carla?"

"Sure, Carla"

"You know her?"

"Sure." She begins to walk. "I'll take you to Carla"

He enters a small box room with her, the same one Carla had been in the year before, the red carpet and curtains, but the bed seemed lifeless, no soul, worn, cold and bitterness of memories that she must have encountered in that room the last year. "Where is she?"

"She's right here?"

"Where's Carla?"

"I'm Carla" she sits forward, taking her jacket off. Her body was bony and frail without it, bruised arms. "Or I can be another girl if you want. Whatever you want to call me?"

"You don't understand"

"Sure I do, I can understand real good if you let me."

"This is Carla's room"

"Even better then." She brings him forward towards the bed and takes out a joint. "You want to get high?"

Part 4: Madness

"No."

"Why not you a Christian?"

"I prefer to drink"

"That's real eighties. You ever seen The Breakfast Club?"

"Yeah."

"You like it?"

"I prefer St Elmo's Fire. Look, we're getting away from the point, do you know Carla?"

"You look like the type of guy who likes to get high" she lights the joint.

"Long blonde hair, blue eyes, her name is Carla, she used to work this room"

"Wait let me see" She opens up a suitcase from under the bed and places a blonde wig onto her head. "This do? I haven't got any contacts." She pulls towards his jeans zip, and places her mouth towards the contents inside. He pulls her away and the wig comes flying off, pulling her hair. "What the fuck are you doing?!" she shouts. She grabs for her anorak and manically types into a pager. "You're going to get your arse kicked now fucker!"

The door breaks open, and a guy with a long black crombie jacket enters. Matt recognises him immediately as the pimp who he paid last year. Without a second thought, he brandishes a blade and steps towards Matt. "Wait... Wait! Don't you remember me?" The guy corners him by the window, the blade stopping his escape. "Last year, same place, same time. I was with a girl, a new girl... Carla"

The pimp looks long and hard and he begins to nod his head but the blade doesn't move from its intended destination. "Yeah. You paid me, not her. I'll never forget that, as it was her first day." He smiles, "After I broke her in."

"He kept going on about this Carla, then he got violent and pulled my wig off!" the prostitute on the bed screams out.

"I asked her if she knew where Carla was, she said yeah, then she took me back here."

"What about pulling my hair you..."

"Shut the fuck up Hope" the guy says. "You wanted to fuck with Carla again? You got habitual routines or something?"

"What?"

"I saw something the other day on TV, about this guy with habits who had to do the same routines every day of every year or he'd like combust through stress"

"I just want to spend some time with her, that's all"

"She don't work for me anymore"
"Where does she work?"
"You pay her time first"
Matt goes towards his jacket pocket, "My wallet" the guy backs of with his blade, he brings out some notes and goes to pay the girl on the bed.
"Not her. Pay me. Like you did before"
"What about my time? He's my notch," she cries out, still feeling her hair.
Matt passes twenty pound over to the guy. "How much more you got?"
"I was here for no more than five minutes."
"That's all it takes some people"
"All I want to know is where she is?"
"Must have been some fuck. I'm going to tell you where she is. But you got to pay me for it"
"I've only got fifty pound"
"You got a cheque book? You can write me a cheque. Thirty will be fine, but you'll need cash where she is." Matt begins to write a cheque for thirty pound and passes it over. He takes out a machine like he's in a bank.
"Very organised, you do this for everyone?"
"Regular customers. She's at a place called Nova Heights. You heard of it?"
"No"
"Its two streets down, right into the crack corner of St Mary's."
"What's she doing there?"
"I let her go. I don't like drug fiends on my roll call. Everyone thinks pimps are like what you see in the movies, big panderer hats, bright purple jackets, walking cane, get the girls hooked on smack, but not me, how can you run a business like that. It's all movies. I got twenty girls working the windy city for me, twenty four hours a day, seven days a week, it runs like a good accounts book."
"You make money?"
"If there's no profit, there's no point. I spend a lot on the red carpets and curtains for these rooms"
"How many rooms you got?"
"The entire building is made of seven rooms all the same. My room is the biggest, red as far as the eye can see. I love curtains. Doesn't mean I'm a faggot though" As Matt begins to walk towards the door he calls out "Just say you want to buy some skag"

Part 4: Madness

He didn't think it could get much worse than the street he was originally down, but this was the end of the town it felt like, the end of the road, where his dream would reveal its true nightmare. Buildings and houses boarded up. Litter along the pavement. Bars on both windows and doors. Glass across walls. Graffiti on smashed in cars. If the last place was originally what the windy city had forgot, this was the place the windy city never acknowledged existing in time. He reaches the building he was told. The door is open, ajar. He steps into the hallway, the smell of dry rot hits him immediately. The haze of people burning something illegal drifts down the hallway from a room with another door that is open. Matt stares into the room, he sees five people, one of them Carla, on the sofa. She is asleep. Wasted.

The others, two guys and two girls have tombstones in their eyes, oblivious to the fact a stranger stands in the doorway. Finally one of the girls catches his eye and stares at him, through the pale gaunt blizzard eyes he recognises her, Linda, he'd lived with her last year, her eyes were dead. Matt had been so stoned before Christmas that he knew that stare so well. Just go along with it. Don't want to break the ride. Break the silence. Break the sense of nothing. "Hey" he finally says.

"Hey" she replies and goes back to the pipe being passed round.

He takes this as an invitation to sit down. He sits next to Carla on the sofa. She is still, wasted. He wants to touch her and make sure she is still breathing, he then breathes a sigh of relief as he watches he face twitch in her sleep. He surveys the room; the two guys sit on sofa chairs, the two girls on another sofa, then him and Carla on the point where the circle forms itself. A pipe is being passed round. The smell is of strong weed, nothing more dangerous, for now. The room is full of hazy smoke. It is stuffy, no fresh air from the closed windows, behind the bars. The floor is littered with supplies of food and materials.

"What's up?" One of the guys leans over to Matt and passes him the pipe. He hadn't touched anything for nearly two months now.

To keep up the pretence he places his lips round the pipe and takes a little bit in, then passes it along, hoping they'd be too stoned to notice he hardly inhaled. He new all the right eye movements and paranoid hit expressions to make. It was just weed. If it had been 'crack' then he would have had to change course, think on the spot.

This had actually mellowed him and brought him to think relaxed. "Not much. Seeing if I could score?"

The guy nods his head. "No worries" he steps up and disappears into the adjoining kitchen.

Matt looks down at Carla, long blonde hair across her face, clothes baggy and unwashed. He wanted to see her eyes they would never lie.

"It don't agree with her," Linda said.

"The weed?"

"The skag. How's James?" she asks.

"He's dead" he replies, cool, speaking like it was an everyday conversation.

She nods her head like she knew it would happen. "What was it?"

"Suicide"

"He was a fucked up guy. Liked to do weird things in the sack"

"Like what?" the other guy speaks for the first time.

"Stuff you only do if you pay well enough"

The guy from the kitchen walks back in with a bag for Matt. "Alright"

"Yeah" he takes the bag, pretending he knows what's in it. And passes over the fifty pounds.

"Cool" the guy replies and sits back down on his armchair and re-lights the pipe.

Matt looks at the bag and then at Carla, and he sees two blurred blue eyes, slightly red around the pupils stare back at him. At first she is looking at the bag, then as she stares at him. He can make out a semblance of recognition in her eyes that can only happen when in this state, if they walked into each other in the street, they would have remained strangers.

"Hi" he says and smiles, trying to say it will be all right in that smile.

"Hey" she tries to smile back, but it comes across more as an embarrassed smile.

"You want to shoot in one of the rooms?" the guy asks before passing the pipe over to Matt.

He gently strokes Carla's hair over her forehead, her face hidden in the haze of the smoke. "Sure. Can I take Carla in with me?" he asks. But they don't reply, they have returned to their state of tombstone bliss, he could rob them blind and they wouldn't see him,

Part 4: Madness

or ever come looking for him, as they'd have to leave the house into the world that damaged them.

Carla steps up, and Matt follows her, in a wasted daze she slowly moves across the floor towards a room at the back and opens it, he follows her in.

There are no curtains in the room, and the hazy sunlight creeps a shadow of light through the bars into the room. He makes out Carla's silhouetted figure, standing like an Angel in that grasp of sunlight.

He turns the light switch on, knowing that the light is not true, that he has to see her in the true light. A bright light comes on, no lampshade, watts bearing down into her eyes. He can see her; drawn, frail looking, hair damp and unclean, eyes with patches of red around what was once clear blue, her face still young and innocent but sad, growing pale like the light that shines on her. "Turn it off, the light! Turn it off!" She tries to shout at him, but such is her weakness it comes across as a normal request.

She sits on the bed and stares at him. "Do you want to fuck me?" Matt just stares at her. He didn't want to fuck her. He didn't know what he wanted to do with her. "If you want to fuck me, you've got to give me the bag" she tells him.

He sits next to her on the bed. "Do you remember me?"

She looks at the bag. "Sure"

"No, Carla, do you remember me? This time, last year." He looks into her face, forcing her eyes to meet his, and when she tries to look away, he holds her face there so she can't escape. "Do you remember me?"

She looks at him; he releases his grip, leaving the bag on the bed and stands up. She looks away at the bag and opens it, then stops and looks at him. "Vampires, we spoke about vampire movies"

Matt turns to face her. "That's right Carla. Just you and me, in that room"

"You was nice to me"

"Go on"

"Then I shut my eyes and..." she looks over to him. "And you was gone" She shuts her eyes again and counts in her head and opens them. "You're still here. It wasn't a dream"

"No, it wasn't dream" he steps next to her. She gently touches his face. She then looks away again. She picks up the bag and takes out its contents, shooting some into a needle. Matt watches her struggle with the weight of the needle, the weight of expectancy what will arrive when she shoots it into her blood. He doesn't try and stop her; he just wants to watch her. She places the needle down, exhausted, out of breath, in pain. Beaten. "You'll have to do it for me?" she tells him. Matt looks at her, wanting to ease any pain she has felt in her life. He knew this wasn't the right thing to do, but what else were the options, he didn't know enough about it to help her. "Will you do it?" she asks, tears in her eyes. With those tears it clears the red from them, and he can see the blue skies about to rain. He places himself next to her and picks up the needle. She motions for where on her arm, keeping the environment tight around the impact.

"You'll have to tell me when to stop" he places the needle in, seeing prior tracks, it was less than he'd expected, she must have been new to the game.

"That's enough," she says and he presses down, the fluids inject through her body, he tries to take the needle out at as gently as possible. He watches her, a massive sense of relief and easing of pain in her face. She gently smiles at him. Her hair falls onto his shoulder and the rest of her head lays on him, like a pillow. As he studies her every feature, the sunlight begins to fully dawn through the bars of the window and it lights them both up as he holds her. He sees her in this natural light, and is amazed how with the injection of one thing, her face seems to brought back to life, the angel he originally saw at this point last year. "Do you want to fuck me now?" she says, laying her head across his arm and shoulder.

He holds out his hand and she places her hand into his. "No. I just want to watch the daylight"

"Me too" she says.

He gently strokes her hair and she makes the sound that two new lovers do, when they feel each touch of one another. Her eyes are asleep and her face starts to return to being pale and gaunt. He gently lays her across the bed and pulls the sheets over her fully clothed body.

"If I close my eyes, you'll be gone again" she says, her eyes open. "I don't want to close them"

"I'm not going anywhere this time" he replies.

She looks at him, as he watches the sun form a stream of light between the bars that entrap them in. "Go. I'll be here when you get back I promise," she says. She didn't want him to be part of this. She wanted that memory to remain pure. She didn't want to destroy her memory like she had his. She pretends to shut her eyes and can feel him stand up. She feels him pause at the door, a moment that feels like a lifetime. "We could start again. That's all I really want to start again."

"Me too" he replies.

"Not have to pretend to be someone different... just be them" Her eyes remain shut as she speaks. The door lingers open and then closes shut to her life. She continues to pretend to be asleep, with dreams of what her life could have been like before the windy city.

Matt dreams of a house with a million doors, each one he opens hoping to find Carla asleep waiting for him, but each room is bare. More panicked as he opens each door, the rooms start to get smaller, until he opens a door into another door that leads into a thousand doors. He jumps up with a start. It was 1pm. He'd only slept for two hours since he got back.

A grey cloud larger than the city itself replaces the blinding sunlight of the morning; it brings not rain, but the threat of things to come. Even the wind is still in the windy city for once, and the cold is hidden inside the eruption of the grey clouds closing.

He finds the street with ease, the grey cloud blurring the soulless faces on each corner, hiding inside every house between the bars, sniffing round broken buildings. They ignore him as he goes about his own business in a trance, the outside world cannot touch or harm him. The door to the house is open as before and he strides in. The two guys and Linda and the other girl still awake passing the pipe around the room. "Hey" Linda says, a repeat scenario of earlier.

"Where's Carla?" he asks, getting to the point. He had nothing to be afraid of; they were too fucked to do anything. The only thing he could be afraid of was himself and his addiction to something new, to her, Carla.

"She left. Packed her bags and went."

Matt's eyes spin round the room, expecting to see her collapsed, wasted somewhere, but to no avail. As he strides towards the room at the end where she had led him just hours earlier he hears Linda call out. – "Said she was going to start again. Like anyone can start again? Whose she kidding?"

He opens the door and like his dream, it is empty. She had left him this time. He would be the one waiting on the memories now.

'BLIZZARD'

Linda

The mirror never lies. That little girl, no more than eight years old, runs across my eyes, and the stream that begins to fill in them, reflects her by the water, playing with a future of memories to discover. Her parents watch her from the hilltop, living through the lives of their daughter, their only child. And like a camera that is showing me as the girl with each passing breath I try to catch inside the mirror I can hear her voice singing, but her voice isn't of the child, but of the woman, of me. "Well sister you're going to use more another year, You've earned everything you guessed was really borrowed, Your white rabbit habits leave you feeling hollow, Never smoked but your nose is a mountain of snow, Chasing all those red roosters looking for someone to follow" As I whisper the final line, her figure fades, her eyes become gaunt, her body older, and the young girl I was once, stares back as who I now am.

"You're eyes can never lie" Charlotte tells me.

Both of us stand by the mirror in the club toilets. Her face is heavily made-up but hasn't aged her like the last eighteen months have aged me. She was always in this blizzard she can control it. Mine is a hurricane. "When you phoned me, I thought you was suicidal," she tells me, not wiping at my eyes to ease the waterfall but watching the tears of the made-up clown next to her. Too much massacre on my cheeks too much hair gel and too much perfume. Too much to prove. When I phoned on her mobile, Charlotte was on a date. I knew the temptation of a cut line was sympathetic to my pathetic needs. "I'm alone" I told her.

"Haven't you got something with you?"

The cocaine queue waits at the last cubicle, the most classic of all English queues. For a self congratulating drug where I can invent the future and the little girl wont come and haunt me no more with memories of a past that was long gone, that was suffocating, that was boring. The excitement runs through my veins, my head starts pumping full of adrenalin. "Linda, you're shaking" Charlotte looks at me with worried eyes. She has been no better, but she handles her emotions, hides her past, and creates a different character for each new drug, a different wardrobe for each fashion. But I need seven different drugs for each new day, saying last weeks fashion is my wardrobes castaway. "This is the mid nineties," I tell her, "its our decade, the decade of no consequences".

"Sorry, didn't realise there was a queue" a guy tells us, a girl

Part 4: Madness

behind him in the cubicle. As the door opens, I push past them, much to their annoyance, grabbing Charlotte's hand. "There's plenty to go round all night," the guy shouts back at me; I slam the door in his face and lock it.

"Girl you need to slow down" Charlotte tells me, as the white powder she had taken out of her handbag disappears just as quick from her possession, into my possession, into my soul, accumulating numbers of thoughts in my brain. Silence. I fall back onto the toilet seat as Charlotte takes her turn. I watch her face, an expression of control, a mixture of delight and self-satisfaction at her own ego.

I can see the reflection of my own face, upside down in her make-up mirror, with dashes of the white blizzard to keep me hooked. It distorts my face across the mirror, makes me look tiny sitting on the seat, that the world is going to swallow me whole. "Fuck" I grasp my face.

"What's wrong?" She asks, a glow of control as she smiles. Bitch.

"Nothing" I try to say but it comes out as a panicked squeal, before I am put down. As the mirror continues to reflect me upside down, I feel a choking of breath inside my throat, something wants to come out... I throw up on the floor, just missing Charlotte's shoes.

"Jesus Christ, Linda, you should be able to handle it better by now" I say nothing but cough, running my hands through the water in the toilet, washing it over my mouth, they say it's the freshest water, fresher than a tap.

"We're going to look like first years," Charlotte continues putting me down.

As I push myself up, I hold onto either side of the walls and avoid the sick, she opens the door for the next membership of the longest queue of our generation.

"Oh fuck!" the next girlfriends say, stepping inside by the sick.

We push our way through various girls wearing cattle tops for their possession in the meat market outside. Staring in the mirror at painted faces, all whispering the word -"Bitches"- as we violently push our way through. I'm holding Charlottes hand so I don't lose my balance and remain in this hell forever. I can see the little girl in the mirror she is holding her hand out for me to leave Charlotte's hand and hold her's instead. I'm sure if I touch her hand, she will pull me into the mirror, back into a past that I was never really sure was mine or my parents wish.

Before I can hold my hand out, I'm into the black void of the outside... the dance floor. Where the drug is a friend that will sing a thousand operas. Dancing the snowstorm into its natural blizzard progression. I should feel untouchable; I should feel the most attractive person in the world. Nothing should be able to hurt me, but I'm starting to feel vulnerable, everything in my way of life is changing and it's all the way down. My vision distorts, as other people share the photo flash with me, then disappear into a horde of sweating souls, running on empty, dripping with their own nightmare tales of dreams from class 'A' substances. No come down, no come down, no come down. The music vibrates into my soul, playing a symphony I haven't heard before. Instead of the usual beats that would move my body to the dance of invincibility, each drum, each bass, is cutting into my ears, droning out a decibel of a high pitched tone, that falls into silence as the white photo flash takes my picture.

Silence...everyone is disappearing around me. I'm standing still but my body is moving in the shadow of the blizzard. I cannot hear anything. I can just make out Charlotte, dancing in her black playboy top, showing of her great arse for all around her. She seems to merge into the photoflash of white light, then reappear back into the blue blizzard in my sunrise. I grab at her; scared she may disappear for good next time. "What are you doing?" She asks.

"I think I need some more"

"Don't be stupid you took loads" she then looks into my eyes of the last eighteen months and the panicked expression on my face, "you've taken loads"

"Need more" I shout over the top of the silence I hear.

"What's wrong with you?" She looks at me for the first time in our friendship in real hatred, like she cant stand to be round me anymore "Get a grip" and she pushes my arm away and disappears into the next white flash of light, the imaginary beat all can hear but me.

Alone in a circle of strangers, trying to make eye contact with someone who might recognise me and help. All the faces seem to merge into one laughing guys head of disgust, as I stream past the band of brothers. The more I look around, the more the high pitched tone recoils across my ears, the white flash permanently across my features. "Help" I try to shout out, but nothing is coming out of my mouth, it moves but I can hear nothing but the tone of deafening silence, of being alone. I see myself in the crowded room and ignore me. I've run out of new ways to get close to me. I've run out of substances to say hello to me. Finally one face recognises me. "Linda, are you ok?" It's one of the guys I used to live with last year.

"I need to score" are the only words I can muster to him. I'm sure these are the first words I have said to the guy since I left that house.

"Ok" he replies.

I grab his hand. "Lets go outside" I pull him across the dance floor. The quicker I move across the dance floor to escape the same strangers faces and the white light, the more it leaves me behind, I start to feel better already...

...I cannot remember his name. "Come on..." he keeps repeating to himself, his body on top of mine. He has got it inside me, but he can't get it up, he's pushing faster and faster but it just gets more limp. Me? I feel nothing. Both physically and mentally.

The fresh air has brought my head back to a level ground. Sprawled back against the club alleyway, as romantic as the first time with 'that guy' whose name I refuse to mention - when he was sprawled across me on the boat, tasting the snow the first time, telling me 'how much he loved me' - and ever since then with each guy, could have been fifteen, maybe even twenty such is my nonchalance my feelings of nothings when they are inside me, I don't even fake grunts of satisfaction, or gasps of air when I was tighter down below and it hurt. I just let it happen to me, a consented rape in a sense. "I don't believe this..." He takes it out and starts to wank with his hand, hoping to get it harder; I can see in the corner of my eye how limp it is. "Come on, come on..." The fresh air of the windy city, blows down the alleyway, the bitter cold of a late Winter evening, punishing its inhabitants with the pouring rain, the alleyway shelters me. My legs are pale, white, freezing over. I'm so cold inside it makes no difference, each time he slobbers over my face the ice doesn't melt, his shaking hands leaving red marks on my pale legs. "Its too fucking cold" he says, trying to push himself inside me again. I think about helping him with some gasps, might get it harder, I open my mouth and only manage a depressed breath out. "Its harder isn't it?" he asks, thinking my breath as satisfaction not boredom.

I play the game, and gently rub his neck, watching my breath blow smoke into the cold winter air. A cat comes to shelter from the rain, it stops and stares at me. Seeing through its green eyes in black and white, no colour, like my life.

"Jesus Christ!" he yells out, and the cat scuttles away. He comes back out again, pulling his trousers up, afraid to look me in the eye. "It's the E, I cant fuck when I'm on an E" I just nod my head and like a robot pull my knickers back. Feel nothing. His eyes finally meet mine. "You wont tell anyone will you?" I just shake my head real slow and he runs back towards the club doors. His name finally comes back to me, Taylor. I stay in the alleyway, listening to the rain. As I attempt to walk, I can see my breath evaporating in the air, the high-pitched tone returns and all around the world of my eye is in silence. The white flashing lights take various photos and stream into my soul, I cannot walk, I cannot move, I can collapse...

What's that smell? Hospitals. The stench of bleach, like swimming pools. The fear of death. I must be lying down; as my eyes look upwards I can see faceless people strapped with masks in hospital uniforms looking down at me. They mumble words as they speak. I am being wheeled somewhere. Strapped down on a bed. I cannot move my arms or legs. I panic and try to move. One of the faceless masks holds me down. Another one puts a needle into my arm. My eyes settle back towards the ceiling. Mum and Dad peer down over me.

"You was such a good girl when you was young." Mum I'm right here. Listen to me. Why can't you hear what I'm saying?

"We had such high hopes" Dad. You can still have those high hopes. Help me to get back to normal. Why don't you hear what I'm saying?

"I still cant believe what they say, that you're like that, it must be some mistake?"

"That its outside influences?"

"Stayed at home forever, one happy family"

"Local job. Local boyfriend. Live down the same street"

"You can have your old room back"

The flashes of photo lights across my parent's faces each time they spoke, turns with the blink of an eyelid into my bedroom back home. I lay there trapped. Unable to move. The same sheets, teddies, wallpaper from when I was that young girl. And she sits at the end of the bed and sings to me. "Now you don't talk, now you don't call, Saw yourself in a crowded room and ignored you, You met your new friends, you saw your new life, You're running out of new ways to get close to you, You've run out of substances to say hello to you"

Part 4: Madness

There's knock at the bedroom door and the young girl I once was skips over to the door and opens it. One by one, each of the guys who fucked me in these last eighteen months, each dead piece of sex I felt nothing for, walk into the bedroom and surround the bed. I count seventeen in all. The guy I used to live with who failed to get it up who tried fucking me up the alleyway steps forward. "It was that E, it wasn't me. The E and the cold wind outside. I've never had that problem before. Maybe it was you. Yeah, that's what I can tell people."

Then 'that guy' steps forward. The one who took that little girl away that night on the boat at the fresher ball. I can still hear his words as he came - 'I love you, I really love you' and then remember the coldness he acted in my distance since then, him fucking Charlotte, "just a shag darling, just sex" he kept saying to me afterwards, "you're at uni, don't take it so seriously." How disgusted I felt when he fucked me, how I felt nothing, and all I hoped would be right, felt wrong. How I felt worthless when he discarded me afterwards, then I felt the need to feel that snow he had shown me, first to impress him, then to forget him, and finally to forget myself. "Its just sex, babe" he says holding out his hand to the little girl I once was, and they leave holding hands; he will take it from me again.

The room fades back into the white walls. Two doctors stand beside me, mumbling in their masks. They bring a golden bowl towards me, filled with snow. They push a golden tube towards my nose and tell me to - "snort away, it will ease the pain." The blizzard swirls in the bowl, towards the tube, hitting every sidewall inside, into the shooting carriageway of my mind and hitting the sound of silence. The blizzard begins its whirlpool in the cold air that ferments in my brain.

From out of my nightmare, the choice of reality stares before me. I'm in a room a living room, full of strangers, a big bowl of the blizzard laid out on the dining table, which we sit round in a circle. I am collapsed on a sofa, making me itch. I can make out posters on the walls, the 'Trainspotting' generation. There is the smell of nothing, it has the most distinct smell, cause once you've tasted it, everything has the same smell in places. "Where's Charlotte?" I ask, my head still blurry from my nightmare.

"She didn't want to come" a voice I recognise says. "Said she'd had enough of you tonight"

"How did I get here?"

"Saw you outside the club, you could hardly stand. Thought it best I take you back before something bad happens" The voice and face begin to blur into one. "Its cool Linda, you're at my digs. Why don't you relax babe" the voice says, it is him, 'that guy', the first one, the first time. His name I'm too afraid to say to him. He pushes the bowl towards me, the blizzard starts to evolve around, the storm a whirlpool of regret." You look awful"

"I needed something" It stares at me.

"Well, there it is. Take it" He sits next to me as I sit up on the sofa. Puts his arm round me, like we've been together for years. "Just like old times, what do you say?"

But this isn't a cosy relationship, where the boy and girl sit and watch TV, rent a video, snuggle up on the sofa with their arms around each other. I see the reflection of my face in the bowl, and he's right I do look awful. I need something one last time, something to feel better, then I'll stop I swear, I need closure. This is the perfect closure. The blizzard shoots its roller coaster ride up my nose, swirling round the blood pumping quicker through my body, I whisper - "The last time, then I stop"

"Sure babe, of course it is. You wanna fuck?"

"Closure, I want closure"

And 'he' leans in and begins to kiss me. "I love you, I really love you," he says like before, on that night that changed my life on the boat. And I let him put himself in me. I let the blizzard surround my heart. Its poetic I think as I pretend those fake gasps that closure begins at the original start. I start to feel better. The blizzard is keeping me warm. Better in the knowledge that this will be the last time. Better in the knowledge that I will stop. Honest.

ON YOUR BIKE

Alex

Oscar night. The night where one day I'll be accepting awards and plaudits and countless actress's on my black couch. "It's all for sex. I did it all for sex." I would reveal with my speech for my reasoning behind my analysing, "the more you analyse a woman, the more she wants to sleep with you, unravelling her demons whilst feeding your own." I wish Samantha would come and stay with me more, she's hardly ever here. Every time I try to get nearer to Amy she pushes me away. It's not working on her anymore, I went into her room, tried to lay on her bed and get into her pants the same way I did last year but she just left the room. I remained in there on my own for three hours. No one speaks to me. I've even been hiding the phone in my room so they'll have to come in and start a conversation with me to retrieve it. Last night I saw them all go out towards a phone box directly outside my room and queue to make calls rather than knock on my door. The phone began to ring in my room. "Hello?" I asked as I looked out the window and they all waved to me, putting the phone down, and the dial went dead on me.

"Never any gay issue films that's what I'd like to see" Steve says.

"Yes I would to. I think it would help all guys come to terms with their feminine side"

Steve looks at Amy. "Look you see Amy, Alex wants to be one of us"

"Maybe I am gay"

"You'd just want to be gay to be hip, so you can say you're a swinger because it'll be artistic. You got to be born with it, like me"

"I could say right now Steve that I want to sleep with you"

"Doesn't work like that Alex"

"Why not fuck me?"

"Cause you're not gay"

"Lets watch you're gay porn video of Batman and Robin"

"You'll only take the piss and it's important to me. It's a really good road movie"

"No seriously, I want to watch it, see if it turns me on" As we watch the film, I keep stroking Steve's leg, hoping he'll rise to my bait and ask Amy to leave, then I can experiment. I'd rather be the woman and let Steve be the man. Something anal could be just what I need to give me the push up in my life. The film is extremely boring and quite simply gay porn in a car that resembles the bat-mobile. At one stage the Joker joins in, and does some magic with a deck of cards and a plastic screwdriver. I wink at Steve, and stroke his thigh but he isn't rising to the bait. "Why wont any of you fuck me?"

I leave and go into Matt's room. He has borrowed Simon's Spectrum 48K and is playing some football game. "Have you moved at all in the last twelve hours?" I ask him.

"Can't. Move. Got. To. Complete. Season." he replies like a robot. His eyes burning red, a zombie, completely engrossed by the white light that shines two inches away from his face.

"Is this the same game?"
"Same. Game. Yes. Different. Season."
"What do you have to do?"
He stops and stares at his shoes for about three minutes, then finally turns and speaks precisely like a computer would if it could talk. "Its. Called. The. Double. You. Manage. A. Football. Club. Choose. Player. To. Buy. Or. Sell. You. Pick. Your. Team. The. Players. Have. Individual. Ratings...."
"Do you not even get to see the matches?" I ask
"No. Just. The. Results."
"Isn't it pointless then?"
He slams the computer and turns it off. "Yes. It's. Pointless. Like. Everything. In. Our. Lives"
"I'm worried about next year"
"What. About. It?"
"I get the feeling I'm not very well liked in this house"
"Well. There. Have. Been. A. Few. Problems"
"But if people could just make an effort they'd see I've changed, 'Slimy', it hurts when you all say it"
"I've. Stopped." whispers it...
"But you all still do it when I'm out of the room"
"Do. You. Eaves. Drop. Our. Conversations?"
Avoid the question. Change the subject. Find someone else to blame. "If Taylor wasn't here it would be much better. I've tried to talk to him but I know he turns everyone else against me. I don't understand why?"
"You. Shagged. His. Ex. Girlfriend. Last. Year."
"It wasn't just me"
"It. Takes. Two. To. Tango"
"I'm worried about next year, getting a house"
"I. Promise. You. Wont. Be. Left. On. Your. Own. You. Have. My. Word."
"Then why are your fingers crossed?"
"The. Game."
"I'm going to try and fuck Steve"
"I'll. See. You. After. The. Match. Boss"
"What does that mean?"
"The. Game."
I wait outside the room, looking through the keyhole and hear him load up the computer, with that horrible noise the spectrum 48k makes. It crashes. "C.U.N.T." He tries to load it up again. I can't

even see or hear him breathe, he's afraid to make even the slightest movement, afraid it will cause the computer to crash again. I bang up stairs purposely. The computer must have crashed, as I hear a massive bang sounding like a computer being smashed by a cricket bat and constant swearing. "C.U.N.T. F.U.C.K. B.A.S.T.A.R.D." I'll bang again in five minutes to make sure it crashes again.

I get into my bedroom and don't bother turning the light on, preferring to lye in the dark. As I lye on my bed, I feel something metal sticking into me. I jump up and see the shape of something in my bed – the Terminator perhaps? I knew I was John Connor that my plight in life is to save humanity. Finally ripping the duvet covers away, I see my bike has been put in my bed. With a Note hung up above the bed notches of my conquests.

'On your bike'

The bathroom water is running across the hallway. I take the bike and place it into the bath for whoever is going to get in. Leaving a note.

I'm drowning

TALES OF WHITE LIGHTING
(Episode 4: A White Lighting Hope)

Simon

There's no weed to be brought off anyone, Southampton's biggest ever drought. White Lighting has become the new drug of 'the house'. First time we spotted it, Taylor and I, went into the local office licence owned by 'Lucky', looking for extremely cheap alcohol before going out. The weather has changed from the fierce cold of winter, which left the house in a state of unrest, to a fierce blinding sunlight of cold morning springs. Everything about this 2nd year has been violent and blinding, the level of excess taken to the point of no return.

For some reason the course hadn't informed the authorities of me leaving, which has meant that I remain in Southampton, getting free money, paying 'student' rent and never having to go to lectures ever again in my life. Basically the same as I've been doing ever since I arrived. Haven't told my parents, they'll be so disappointed. I feel guilty as they keep sending me rent cheques. Go to tell them but have a drink instead and decide that I'll deal with it when I have to.

"Simon are you short of cash?" They ask me.

"Yeah"
"Do you need the rent paid for the rest of the year?"
"Yeah"
"How's the course"
"Yeah"
"What does yeah mean?"
"Oh you know, it's just a course, yeah"
"Do you need any other cash?"
"Yeah"

For now tomorrow never comes. 'Excess' is the tale of my year. Now I have met my match in the competition to die first in White Lighting Cider, a plastic bottle that has now become impious in our house and created a new religion around Southampton. The picture of the fierce lighting across a darkened blue sky, threats of storms and violence, attracted me on the label. "My life is now complete" was the only reply that made sense in a nominal life I've lived for twenty months.

At first 'Lucky' assumed this was a once off. Holding his baby daughter, as he passes over alcohol, cigarettes and rolling material, he calculated the bottle for us with a smile. "White lighting. You're brave"

"We like the label"

"So do the tramps"

As we stepped out of 'Lucky's' establishment, the eternal vision of the windy city had changed before my very eyes. Rivers of blood beckoned from each street corner.

"I've got a migraine," I tell Taylor as we step out the shop.

"Did you have one before you came out?" He asks.

"No, not until I brought this." Magic works in mysterious ways.

It tastes like it sounds – lighting, it rots your guts and gives you bad shits. But it gets you very pissed for only two pound fifty. After a while you don't even notice the acid taste and after effects that leave you wanting to kill someone, you get used to it.

"What do you think?" Taylor asked me, his eyes were so red with vanadium that they nearly burnt through his contact lenses, and it was like seeing a mirror image of my own side effects.

"Lets buy some more"

By the end of the week, Lucky was presented with the entire house. Even Alex getting in on the act to be hip, though he makes a bottle last over half a week, so I've started stealing it from his room.

We stand as the Magnificent Seven. "You know this stuff rots your guts?" Lucky tells us after taking our money, extremely concerned his best customers are spending only two pound fifty each a day. "It's what tramps drink."

Advice taken on board. "Seven two litre bottles, thanks very much."

Outside, the tramps stand ceremony by the subway wall that leads onto our road. They stare and nod their heads at us, in respect of choosing such a drink. The Irish tramp bows his hat and shouts out, "Walk my city paved with gold my friends, for I am king to this throne"

The Asian tramp with the limp, who I saw snogging a young college prostitute the other day, limps up with the girl on his arm and shouts "Nutter's, seven fucking nutter's!" he sees us holding the white lighting and bows, like a red carpet to walk leading to self destruction.

It's funny but seeing them drinking 'White Lighting', with their tongues hanging out, rotted teeth, smelly clothes, leering faces, a nod of acknowledgment of - 'Welcome to our club. She'll change your look and have you hooked.' This doesn't worry any of us. They say tramps can always tell future tramps.

Waking this morning from the hangover of hells drink, leaving food to thought for your will and testament to be made immediately, my mind begins to numb to the power. The tramps conversing welcoming us into the circle, we don't feel the cold, just the death in our lungs. Waking to the smell of fresh alcohol breath, clothes that hang drunk on a frail mind, another day nearer the abyss. Better to die young like your idols rather than grow old and die of something boring. Who wants boring? Life is boring. Each of us sits in our own rooms, drinking in our stolen pint glasses the entire two litres before leaving for a nightclub. As we each leave our designated area's of abuse, our cages of entertainment and fulfilment, we hold a 'crazy eyed' stare of distant oblivion, headlong rush into alcoholism. Sitting in our own personal rooms, caged up wanting to live and listen to our own music, ringing in our ears and tormenting us for years. Stumble through town, we've stopped going to pubs. Pissed already, sit on the dirty floors and get more pissed. Where we wont recognise the cold of early spring but just feel the heat inside our bodies. We wont recognise the faces that talk to us, three heads, slur my speak to the one in the middle.

"How are you more pissed then me, even before you arrived?"

Keith Reynolds's three heads ask me, blood on his white shirt, fangs hanging out. Nexus, vampire city.

"White lighting"

"What is that? An occult? Surely if its an occult I would have heard of it? Clem, have you heard of white lighting?" Keith turns to Clem, whose three heads stare at me cut off from his body where three massive train jackets circulate.

Sometimes, we smuggle the bottle of 'holy water' in the club with us and fill up our empty pints in the toilet. "What's that you're drinking?" a vampire asks me.

"White lighting"

"Have you ever tried your own blood?" He drinks in the toilet from a shot glass of blood. I don't tell him I've been shitting it since I've been drinking the 'holy water'. I pour some out for the vampire so he can taste it. I want everyone to share in this religion. "That's disgusting?" He waits for the after taste to kick in. "How much is it?"

"Two pound fifty for two and half litres"

"Fuck me, where can I get it?" His fake fangs fall out such is his excitement.

"Luckys"

"Here try this? It's my girlfriends blood, we want to form as one being," he tells me passing over the shot glass of blood. "If you like it, I can get her to bottle a regular order for you"

Welcome to the world of White lighting. You're life will never the same again. A close companion that wears its diaries hand in hand with all the silver that turns to gold.

(Episode 5: White Lighting Strikes Back)

Matthew

Fuck 'Common People'. 'Don't Look Back In Anger' is the song of our generation. Everyone thinks I'm a dealer Southampton is so dry. The windy city has got new 'Trainspotting' haircuts, bar me. I did my hair like that last year but started growing it back as I knew it was a mistake, as these people will. What's hip about trying to look like you take heroin? There was nothing hip in Carla's eyes as I shot up for her, just the look of despondency. There's a despondency creeping into our generation of people taking themselves too seriously. The idea is to not take ourselves seriously anymore; White Lighting has done the trick for me. What's the point in being serious about this? The decade. The music. The people. The drink. The Drugs. The course. Choose Life? What if I choose nothing? The music 'biz' and magazines want overnight sensation bands and fifteen-minute idols, there's no development for us to grow. Like the drugs before me, now replaced by the 'holy water', my middle name is despondency. I might as well destroy everything as I take myself down for the ride of nothing.

I drink a pint of white lighting in bed and throw up bile into the sink in the bedroom. This white lighting is killing me. I can feel my guts turning. My anger forming. Each drop of liquid is like a drop of the Hulk into David Banners blood.

The three worst people to have a white lighting drinking competition, myself, Steve and Simon. Even Taylor declined saying - "I would like to live to see the 3rd year." All three of us on our second two litre bottles, welcome to Jumping Jack Flash country. How do some fights start? Don't know but they all finish the same. It's like a kid's playground Steve wants some cigarettes. Simon won't give him any. "Give me some cigarettes"

"Buy your own"

"I deserve them!"

"Welcome to New Labour"

"Don't take the piss out of the Labour party, they're going to change this country when they get into power next year"

"Why? Cause Noel Gallagher mentioned Tony Blair at the Brit Awards?"

"They're the youth of today. Our vote matters"

"Then ask Tony Blair to give you a cigarette"

Only drunken accomplices with the same goal can go round the roundabout this many times. They start to fight. I see Simon's cigarettes and decide to throw them down the toilet and flush. Why? Only 'White Lighting' would know the answer.

"What the fuck did you do that for?" Simon says lunging towards me.

"I don't smoke, that's why"

Steve desperate that the cigarette situation is at an all-time low and he'll have no nicotine rush or know excuse to ask other guys for lights or storm into rooms when really stoned and say – 'Got any potatoes?' Says - "I'm going to top shop to get some cigarettes"

"Only the garage is open," I reply.

"Lets go then, all three of us," he says in defiant honour, like we're about the march into certain death. Those rivers of blood are drawing near.

I weigh up the decision; all three of us walking the streets this pissed, full of violence and pent up anger. "Sure, why not"

As usual, Steve cannot just go somewhere and leave the house automatically; he has to go into his room and 1. Dance to Madonna and 2. Shower, change his clothes and style his hair

Simon and I are waiting outside, threatening to beat up Steve if he doesn't hurry up. "JESUS FUCKING CHRIST" I shout back.

"What's the matter Matt, losing it?" A drunken Simon replies, and like me stares back full of 'White Lighting' viperous anger.

Two caged animals, where the city is the cage and it isn't going to be big enough to hold us both. Dark clouds form over the night sky. The lighting from inside my stomach hits the sky, and the storm of a thousand drunken nights of anger are upon us. We knock into each other's shoulders as we manoeuvre round, like two gladiators, or two tramps to the on looking world. Simon kicks out his leg and it hits my shin, "Oh sorry" he says and then does it again.

I trip Simon up with ease, I say I tripped him up but I just think he fell over he was so drunk. "I'll hit you properly next time," I say standing on top of Simon's chest as he lays on the pavement, my foot over him. Still he kicks his foot up with his big DM boots towards my groin; luckily White Lighting shrivels your dick up so I can't really feel it. I move off him. My patience snaps and I move towards him under a blood red sky. Either a push or a punch, a bit of both and too much of one - It's in slow motion; Simon falling backwards, the concrete step enlarging, Amy and Steve appearing outside, Simon's head hitting the steps.

"Oh my god" Amy says, as she picks up Simon's head, her hands are full of blood.

Simon hyperventilates when he sees the blood on his t-shirt. "It's the T-Shirt Noel Gallagher signed," he says, blood around Noels signature. "Wonder if it'll be worth more with my blood on it?" Even now he thinks of money and profit, penny in dogshit, lovely.

Once in the taxi to the Hospital, I read the White Lighting Label - Friend against Friend, Family against Family, Brother against Brother. Steve tells the driver our life stories. "We need the causality unit, he has split his head open, that guy in the back with him beat him up" Then turns to me, "I said it so he'll be scared and not charge us" he tries to whisper to me. The Taxi driver looks at me through the rear view mirror, I can see him reaching for a wooden club by his seat. "Stop at the first news agents" Steve says to the driver.

Part 4: Madness

"What?" I reply.

"I want those cigarettes" Steve replies. It makes perfect sense he ordered the taxi not for Causality but to get cigarettes. He pops out of the taxi and steps into a off-licence, he immediately goes back towards the taxi, "Can you lend me three pound?"

The taxi driver looks worried, and fondles the wooden club. "Have any of you got the money to pay for the fare?" He wants us to say no, so he can beat us to death. Perhaps he drinks White Lighting as well?

"I've got the money mate, look," I point towards a ten-pound note in my hand that was for a kebab.

"I'll take that," Steve says, but I pull it away.

"Its paying for the taxi"

"You fucking cunt, cant you see Simon's bleeding to death?"

"Then get back in and forget about the cigarettes"

"Fuck you. I deserve the cigarettes after today" Steve runs towards a cash point.

The taxi driver pulls out a flask and drinks from it. "I don't want no blood in my cab. Any blood being spilt is by me alone" What do you reply to that? Nothing. That's what. "Here, have some of this" he passes the flask over to me. I decide to take a sip, be rude not to.

I recognise the taste. "White lighting?"

"The cabbies best friend."

Steve rescues me from a conversation written by Satan in the depths of flames by coming back. "It's out of order, take us to a cash point mate and then back to the Off Licence?"

"What about your mate? He's bleeding, I don't want any blood on my car"

"He'll alright, he has got a flannel on his skull"

"White lighting I bet" The Cab driver looks at me and smiles like we're old friends, soul mates. "You ever thought of taking the knowledge son?"

"No" I reply, not knowing what the fuck the knowledge is.

Steve and I wait in the casualty department, the same place I was over eighteen months ago with my finger. It's the same chair I sit on.

The same TV channel programme on. I walk up to reception. "Don't you ever show anything else?"

"We have this on repeat for twenty four hours"

"How can you bear to watch it?"

"We don't" and she points to her own private portable TV on

the desk.

"Don't you think it's a little depressing to have this playing for the people waiting?"

"We like to inflict pain. Mind over matter. We're actually helping people like you"

"People like me?"

"Yes, addicts"

"I'm not an addict"

"Of course you're not" she pulls out a leaflet, "Acceptance is the first step"

I sit back down next to Steve who is smoking his cigarette at last. He even smuggled a pint of white lighting in his jacket. "I've won the drinking competition," he tells me.

"Shut up"

"Shut up" another voice beside me, says.

I turn to be greeted by the same mad guy who imitated all my movements and words outside the hospital that day with my finger. "Oh fuck"

"Oh fuck," he says.

"Do you know him?" Steve asks.

"No"

"No" the guy says.

"You've probably killed him" Steve says, forever the optimist. "He'll never be the same again, probably given him brain damage. We're all scared even say hello to you in the house now"

"Shut up you faggot," I reply.

"Shut up you faggot," the guy next to me replies.

"Look you see, there you go again, just like your father, good old math boy, couple of beers then beating the shit out of his mates. You'll have to tell his parents, ruined his entire life, he'll be a vegetable"

"Do you want to end up in causality?"

"Do you want to end up in causality?" the mad guy continues repeating my life.

I decide to play the mad guy at his own game. "I'm a fucking mad tramp, I stink of piss and eat my own shit"

"You're a fucking mad tramp, you stink of piss and eat your own shit" he replies.

"What's the fucking point?!" I lay my head in my hands.

"What's the fucking point?!" the mad guy lays his head in my hands as well.

Simon comes out; we expect news of a brain surgeon, a life-

Part 4: Madness

threatening cost of an operation that will leave me in Causality with the news of its expense. But none of the above, a stupid drunk grin, a bald patch on his head where the cut was, not even a stitch. Noel Gallagher signed T-Shirt blood stained.

In the taxi back, Steve tells the same taxi driver from earlier to - "Pull over, fast" - he begins coughing sick up towards his throat. He rushes out of the taxi, head down, coughing the sick as the door opens, then throws up violently outside on the pavement.

"I don't want any sick in my car" the Cab driver shouts at Steve and drives off without him.

"Karma baby, karma" I whisper from the windows at the departing vision of Steve, chasing after a taxi with sick coming from his mouth.

"Tales of white lighting." The taxi driver says, nodding his head. "You want a drink from my flask?" he asks Simon.

"Sure, fuck it, why not?" He replies and toasts Noel Gallagher's signature.

(Episode 6: The Return of White Lighting)

Steve

Before I went into Magnums tonight, I saw that 'nutter' Asian tramp with the limp, holding a young student girl against the subway wall, slobbering all over her. I pulled him back, away from the girl, pleased with my heroic actions. "Are you alright?" I asked her.

"Leave us alone, he's my boyfriend!" she replied.

He moved back onto the girl, young enough to be his daughter and continued his drunken slobbery. "Nutters!" he kept shouting, he must be some conversationalist. Only when drinking White Lighting can a world like this exist outside of the normal realm.

Why didn't I pull in Magnums? I don't understand it? I look like Damon from Blur.

I'm not a typical Queen but the cool kind of indie gay. A pretty boy style guru with model looks. There are guys in 'Magnums' that aren't gay and get chatted up by the guys I fancy. What's wrong with me? Dan 'not the man' followed me around all night; I almost kissed him but then told him I'd have to kill him.

"You still love me Madonna don't you?" I ask my Queen as I put on 'Who's that Girl' soundtrack and dance into the kitchen. Its just as loud in there, the speaker vibrating, that's what I need, vibration...

... And white lighting, there's a bottle left on the kitchen table, at least two thirds left... "Waste not, want not" I need some toast and cheese, some bread and some butter... ...Other peoples will do, as I don't have any, fuck 'em, they haven't had the night I've had, I deserve this.

Matt matrixes out of no-where and stands before me with his cricket bat in hand, hair all over the place, looks like Liono from Thundercats. "Steve turn the music down!"

"Fuck off Matt!" I reply, and drink from the stolen White Lighting.

"Help yourself to my white lighting then" he replies. "That cheese looks familiar as well, and my bread"

"I deserve it." I stand on tiptoes and push my finger towards him. "Are you homophobic!" Matt moves away, backwards like a pole dancer as I lean further in, tiptoes bent over, why do people do this when they're speaking to me? Do I smell? "I said are you homophobic!"

"Like all faggots, you're going to regret everything in the morning," he says walking away.

I try to follow him, to push him on the floor but loose my balance and grab hold of the cooker. "Coward" I reply and turn the music up even higher. "It always tastes good when it's someone's else's drink and food," I tell the Madonna album cover.

I can hear Matt's music the room up above, blaring out Oasis to drown me out. I stamp up the stairs and bang on his door, trying the handle. "Turn your music down CUNT!" I then stamp up the next set of stairs and knock on Simon's door. "Give me some cigarettes!" I demand.

I keep knocking, Alex steps out of the opposite room, I don't want to speak to him. "Hi Steve," he says. I just ignore him and he sheepishly dances to that imaginary music he always seems to have in his head into the toilet. I watch him have a wee, he has a strange dick, his foreskin is massive, he playfully shows me it and then dances back into his room and locks the door. I can't even pull that ginger nut.

I'll stamp back downstairs and wake everyone up I decide. "They deserve to listen to my life." I slip on the first flight down and fall, arse on each step, white lighting pint spilt all over me. I hit the bottom, between Taylor and Matt's room. No one comes out; I remain there for a full minute, hoping they'll see if I'm ok. But nothing. I get back up, making as much noise as possible, but by doing this I slip again... The pint glass smashes on the floor and

Part 4: Madness

I end up on the bottom of the stairway, face down, broken glass, I remain on the floor, having hit rock bottom in my life. Someone must surely come out? No one comes. My body begins to shiver. I feel a presence behind me. In a drunken state of despair it looks like James, as a ghost, smiling in the hallway. "Madness" he says then disappears.

THE ARTIST

Marie

Paintings that hang crooked on the wall, sending the wrong messages to send. But they all gather round like vultures to pick at pieces of my painted soul. The end of course shows. I'm a poet; I'm a preacher, an actress. They don't know it, they cannot reach me, I'm out of practice. I'm love with malice. I'm a thief; I'm a beggar, a con artist. I'm perfections artist Where once empty canvass's stood bearing naked portraits of what scares us most, no reflections, are covered in my four riders of the Britpop apocalypse;

The vampire queen hangs upside down in her nightclub of followers and victims. Pure white hair, painted in her wedding dress the day of her death and start of her life. She is the focus of the canvass, spiralling a web of life colours from her green eyes and sharp teeth that immerse around where she hangs. Followers at her head, both male and female, some with instruments of destruction, others with instruments of entertainment. The red floor carpeting of Nexus stripped from its events, and placed as a sculpture onto the painting of the souls who bow to her throne. The lights from the dance floor animate across her purity, painting the vision of an endless life that will live for centuries and feed on the instruments that those painted around her web bring as gifts for her resurrection.

"Yes, very, er, colourful..." the course lecturer says, Mr. Handcock. "Distorted images" he finally says. His name sums him up best. Hand to cock. Wanker.

My Mum looks at me very worried. She has turned white, like the birth mother of the student in the painting. "Is that meant to be you, Marie?"

"It is death," I tell them.

"What is it called?" Mr. Handcock asks, inspecting the body of the queen with a magnified glass.

"Marie" I tell them.

Mum tries to secretly swallow some pills from her bag, her

'mothers little helpers'. Dad doesn't say anything; two glasses of free wine in his hand, sunglasses glued on, a statistic on the motorway back waiting to happen.

An orgy of relationships; males and females in black and white masks, naked in their ambition and lack of inhibitions – Boys on girls, Girls on girls, Boys on boys - painted poster of the Blur singer watching on. Hetro and Lesbo, we're all the same fucked relationship painted on this canvass. But that tells only one half of the story. For that is only half the painting. The other half is an empty blank canvass but for the printed words 'Charlotte' made out of one of her cheap 'fuck me' belts that pass as skirts. Her name engulfed by emptiness.

"A take on relationships?" Mr. Handcock asks me, his forehead sweating, probably recognises one of the student boys in the painting.

"Those are all the people I have fucked in my three years here. Now they all fuck each other. And now I've fucked them all over."

Mum takes another pill. Dad takes another glass of free wine. And Charlotte whom I introduced as my housemate to my parents, not as my girlfriend, or even friend, much to her disdain, looks at the empty canvass around her name. Her eyes burn into the back of my head and a wry smile comes across my lips of satisfaction.

"Bitch" I hear her whisper.

"You fucked all those guys?" Mum asks, red in shame as my painting draws over her.

"And the girls" I reply as Dad lowers his sunglasses for a closer inspection.

Finally, the renaissance of the work, the perfections artist - Cartoon caricatures of the Britpop faces of my generation. Bands. Models. Magazines. Painted on the backdrop of the union jack flag. Red. White. Blue. With a queue forming of faceless people by a public toilet that is surrounded in a snow blizzard of white powder. The walls on the outside spell –

Thatcher's Britain
New Labour
Choice?
Future?
Same?

And I stand as a self-portrait with my back to them all, barenaked showing my behind, two fingers up in the air. A Monroe wig held in one hand, a Yoko Ono white sheet in the other.

Part 4: Madness

Mr. Handcock can hardly contain himself with his enthusiasm. "What's it called? What's it called?" he asks me twice such is his excitement.

"Don't look back in anger. Don't look back in anger," I say twice to appease him.

"Britpop" he says with pride to be the hipster student he never was when he studied.

And it is here where I decide to secure a first for my degree. "Britpop is just a reactionary of the original mod culture, through TV and a conservatism of music, creating a revival into a false reading of history, of dark weird pop culture of '66." Mr. Handcock is touching the picture, and then I feel him touch me with his other hand. "Take your hands off me you perverted loser," I tell him.

"God, I'm sorry its just the power of your work, it makes me want to fuck you"

Mum takes another pill.

"Have I introduced you to my parents?" I ask, as he stands next to them.

"Is that your naked arse Marie?" Dad finally speaks, lowering his shades.

Mum takes another pill. "I want to go home"

Dad takes a closer inspection with Mr. Handcock.

They all stand as the next generations Andy Warhol, seeking fifteen minutes of fame next to their portraits of life from three years of studying what the television shows us in one thirty minute episode. A nation of couch potatoes I fear for the day of reality TV. I have seen the future and its here, in this room - Art with no heart. I may not always carry a reflection in the mirror but at least I know I have a soul. An exhibition of sheer wasted minds that say they merit talent will doubtless emerge with their picture taken with the Mayor and his wife who have joined us in celebration of the windy cities artistic talent. Everyday he steps out the office it rains, what does that tell you?

"It's a true work of genius." The Mayor gasps at the family portrait one guy has created as his course masterpiece, done in a day over a Christmas drink reunion of members who hate each other. "Generations of life all in one room. One big family"

"Yes, its very profound, a statement of the nuclear family in today values in society" some ginger guy with big ears adds. I recognise him from the Institute, and the JFK crowd, Alex, he dances round rooms, a tune only he can hear in his head. Wearing the a-typical student necklace, he wants to be a hippy; his name is 'No Cred'.

On the next side of the room, a guy dressed up in a Major's army uniform stands six foot four, sandy hair, real in breed that only the rich can create, The Major and his horsy wife, part of the windy cities tea set. "Oh darling, look at this." The Major's wife is standing by a bed. "This is a marvellous sculpture." The bed moves. "My god, someone is in it!"

"Yes, that's the student whose creation this is" Mr. Handcock joins in the love of true art.

"How working class." She turns to her husband, the Major, as the guy in the bed begins to roll a joint on being woken up. "Lets buy it"

"I don't think its legal to buy people anymore dear"

"Do you have any roach material?" the guy asks.

"Well let's ask him at least." She turns to the guy in the bed. "How much for your work of art?"

"I'm not for sale. I'm an artist."

"We live in a mansion away from the windy city, we'd pay you a daily rate"

"What for?"

"Just lying in bed"

"You got a deal."

Finally, the group of art connoisseurs meet my heading of the four riders of the apocalypse.

The Mayor walks with his head down embarrassed to make eye contact. "Well this is ridiculous, where's the fourth one?" the guy in the Major's army uniform says.

"I'm the fourth one" I reply.

"So you're a painting? That's ridiculous!" As he peers further into the sex painting, of all my lovers engrossed in an orgy of self loathing with the empty half winking at Charlotte's personality, a disgusted look of eroticism fills his face. "That's disgusting!" he leans even further in. "None of these men have been Johnsend! They wouldn't get through the army training gates without the snip. How ridiculous!" He then studies the vampire's; "Stakes through hearts, and an M-16 up their arses would see an end to their world"

The dancing guy, Alex, is staring at it to; he is licking the paint of. "I'd love to be a vampire." His eyes then settle on the final 'Generational' piece. He holds his hands to his head and gasps like he has just seen the resurrection of Christ. "Britpop" he says. People, who you can't stand, can make you never like something again, by liking what you like. Their stigma becomes attached to it, like superglue sniffed up a spotty teenagers nose. I shall burn this work during the exhibition that will be a masterpiece. CHAOS I shall call it.

Waiting outside. Smoking. Waiting for the moment where I can set fire to the paintings and create a modern masterpiece even Damien Hurst would rival to match. The obligatory celebratory at these exhibition functions comes out and stands next to me, a joint burning in his hand. He is one of the music caricatures on my 'Britpop' painting. His fur jacket making him look big and bulky, hiding a staunch waist I'm sure of over exuberance, sunglasses on, unshaven with hair over his face. "You can smoke inside" he tells me

"I know that's why I'm smoking outside." He goes to pass me the joint but I decline with an arrogant look away. "Its too clichéd"

"I like you're work."

"Even the caricature of you? It made you look like a monkey"

"I thought it was very retro"

"Lets cut the crap. You want to fuck me, why else would you be out here?" Silence. He doesn't know what to say, so I say it for him. "I've always wanted to fuck in the ladies toilet."

As the fire blazes across the exhibition room, and punters run out with artists work, I put my parents into a taxi outside as the fire brigade storms past us. They are more wasted than I am or ever was. Mum with her constant supply of pills, making her slur her words, eyes wild and big as the sun, pale complexion. "Won't you come home with us?"

"I'm never coming home" I reply.

Dad sits in the back of the taxi, having smuggled out various half drunk glasses of wine. They spill over his shirt, as he begins to collapse. "Don't get wine in my car. I don't like wine" the taxi driver says.

"Are you a vampire?" My Dad finally asks me. Before I can answer, the taxi draws away. I have enough time to see Dad pass out in the back, and Mum pops another pill. They say are generation is wasted. These people are the real wasted generation that was left behind. We're just trying copy and emulate what they invented, through fashion, music and design. Our generation isn't Britpop. It's Retro. Retro means going back. Is nothing new anymore?

The final Nexus night, before I burn this place to the ground, not physically like I had done with the gallery exhibition with the aid of a Britpop luminary, but in my mental preparation to bid a farewell and unleash the chaos. A natural world, a world without the word 'freaks'. They asked for my paintings to be hung here as a muriel of student life. I burned them before they could take them and so they become attached to a stigma of a martyr. It is the unknown, the unable to see, that compels us the most. We hate not knowing.

The red carpet is stained with the generations' excess of youth'ism, of rebelling, of nothingness. Bodies inhabit the space with drink poured light, smoke inhaled high, and their sex questionable on a first glance. Lights swarm across the darkened areas, spinning with the retro to dark music the hordes feed on. Stylised homage's to idols of the Britpop years, dressed as front covers of music magazines holding 'what if' glances, mingle with the atypical student dressing down and then the dark knights of its culture, the 'want to be vampires'. If only they knew the truth. The occult 'gang', dressed in their dark cloaks, fake white fangs, blood stained white shirts, the art and film students who saw 'The Lost Boys' one too many times and believe it to be accurate. How wrong they are.

In the toilet is where the freaks stand by the mirrors and try to make themselves either more acceptable or unacceptable. Where you will stand under the influence of the night, and study yourself for a sense of sobriety, for a sense of what you should do when you return back into the night - Who you should walk home with, what you should take to keep up the pretence of the excess you've created for yourself. All of us clowns without the make-up. I study my straight jet-black hair; down to my shoulders it lays, like a queens layer. My green eyes, full of lost souls I have taken over the last three years. My retro clothes, brown chord jacket with fur lining, baggy shoulder cut top, with a crucifix that hangs down, a skirt that is as warm as the sun in its different colours down to my knees, the 'kinky' boots of an true avengers girl, meeting the skirt half way. Straight out of a fashion shoot from the sixties.

My skin can turn pale the further I look, and my tongue touches across my fangs that form. My green eyes, become jet black, like diluted pupils, and their is my reflection, it remains, like I said before, people live by what they see in the movies as the truth. Before I can fully transform, before my hair turns a beautiful white, and I become the queen in my painting, another reflection enters the mirror. That dancing guy, Alex, stands behind me, in the spilt second that I can see him, I return to normal. "Why are you constantly

Part 4: Madness

dancing?" I ask him.

"The tune of life" he replies, trying to be profound. "I guess you're wondering what I'm doing in the ladies toilet?"

"No. As I told you once before, you're very anal"

"I loved your work"

"That makes me hate it"

"I want to be a vampire"

"Doesn't everyone"

"I want to be immortal and live forever"

"Another deluded movie buff"

"Make me a vampire"

I finally turn to face him, having spent the entire conversation looking in the mirror at his reflection. "Do you truly want to die, Alex?"

"Not die, but live with no fear"

"That is to die"

"Just make me like that painting"

"Take you're clothes off"

He doesn't argue, he takes them off; he has a weird penis, long foreskin. As I approach him, I turn myself with each step. First my eyes from green to black. "Yes" he says. Then my tongue raps around my fangs. "Yes" he says. My skin turns pale. "Yes" he says. And finally my hair turns a beautiful white as pure as the snow. "Yes" he says.

"Close your eyes" I tell him. He closes them and I reach my breath towards his neck like in the movies. "You must not open them, only when you feel the humiliation"

And I slowly walk away from him, leaving the poor sap standing naked in the toilet. I leave a message on the bathroom mirror for him in bright red lipstick 'You just want to be hip' you cannot choose what to be in life. You are born with who you are. As I walk out the toilet, a girl passes me to go in. I hear her scream. I see in the corner of my eye as the door closes, a man's utter humiliation.

Bored with the night, with the club, with people, with university. I stand outside and think about causing the chaos that would make a true work of art. Burn the place to the ground. I watch from across the street as they all leave for the night; the retro 'gangs' the vampire 'gangs' the atypical student 'gangs' the townie 'gangs' And I decide to leave them and the Nexus to feed for another day on youth'ism. I have a better idea of a portrait to paint as my farewell gift to the windy city.

Creating art in the windy cities streets. A muriel to our culture. I scatter bins content down the parade of shops. Then finding 'Next' I throw the bin through the window and the alarm system rings bells for help that the police force in this city will take thirty minutes to arrive on. Picking up the next bin and returning to the scene of the crime to smash the windows of McDonalds and Burger King. Still know Police have arrived. The alarms ring out a symphony of different sounds. I am the conductor of the street. With a red, white and blue mixture in a tin of paint, I wash across the national flags colours over the windows of HMV and Virgin. Spelling the words of our middle decade

BritPop

                                                                  Retro

                      Sex

                                                                 Drink

Drugs

                    New Labour

New Lies

                    Revolution?

Finally, the Police Car arrives. Two helpless officers step out with stern faces and looks of new 'Hitler'. Give a man a badge and they think they have the same power as when they have their cock in their hand. I watch their reflections in my muriel's window as they run near me, holding out a baton and a pair of handcuffs not realising what fate awaits them. Law and order, sex and violence, they're all part of the same game. And as they touch my shoulders to pull me away, baton held high, like their sexual prowess on show, handcuffs about to be put on me for their sexual pleasure... I turn... In that split second... Eyes green to black... Hair jet black to pure white... Skin rosy to pale... And fangs... And I greet them hello with the face I hide behind in the shadows.

"Fuck!" they scream as I greet them with a vicious growl. Their hair turns white.

"Enjoy the art boys" I say to them and fly down the street.

Flying through the city I bid it a farewell through the parade of shops, nightclubs and late bars and finally to the ocean. I fly across the waves and breathe a fireball across the sea that only I will ever witness and wonder at its beauty, a true picture of art. The sea is the biggest empty canvass of them all, full of memories and wishes.

My future is packed into two duffel bags, the remnants of my life, of my past and of my present. I'm not too sure where I'm going

Part 4: Madness

to go. For now I sit in an early morning café drinking a cup of coffee.

It overlooks the ocean and I smile remembering the fireball I created and watched in the earliest hours of this morning, when all was still dark, and the shadows ruled the city. Across from me is another girl, long brown hair, leather jacket, I recognise her from the film course the year below. She too is drinking a cup of coffee and watching the ocean. "Do you mind if I join you?" I ask her.

"Sure" She replies. "I recognise you"

"I'm Marie."

"Clarissa... sorry, I mean... Clarissa"

"Coming home or going out?"

"Bit of both. You?"

"Leaving"

Silence, as we both drink our coffee and the sun begins to rise. Dusk upon us.

"I love watching the sun rise over the ocean" she tells me.

"Yeah, I've never really appreciated it before, it's beautiful isn't it"

"I saw the most beautiful thing last night. A fireball across the ocean"

I wonder what to reply. The truth. "I'm glad someone else saw it"

And the two of us sit in our private silence, watching the dawn set over the ocean, drinking from our coffees, both with our own secrets that the ocean keeps.

I see a truck driver pull into the dockland area, and enter the café, ordering a flask of coffee to fill up for his journey. Seeing this as my opportunity the hand fate has dealt me today, I stand to leave.

"Good luck" Clarissa or Clarissa says to me.

"You too" I reply, knowing each other secrets in silent stares as dusk drew upon us.

As the truck driver goes to get back in, I call out. "Hey, can I hitch a ride?"

"You don't know where I'm going yet?" he replies.

"I don't need to." I reply.

JUDAS

"You know it has to be done" Taylor takes a sip of his White Lighting cider and sits contented outside on the front porch of the self-destructive house. The sun shines down across them. Everyday this week the sun had shone on them these early evening hours, as they drank and smoked away in contented bliss away from the troubles inside.

"I know" Matt passes the joint over and basks in the bright sunlight. His pint of White Lighting needed re-filling, and for some reason in this hazy week of dusk and dawns, it had tasted nice. The joints hadn't made him paranoid. It was like sitting outside staring into their abyss on the porch outside. He figured he may as well take things to their natural conclusion for the education year, there was less than a week left. After the year of being wasted and madness, he could hardly remember anything, and the abyss they both sat and stared at in between the odd spoken line was the nearest he'd felt to content ness since last September.

"You don't owe him anything" Taylor takes the joint and smiles as the Verve tune kicks in. They played each of the original single EP's up to History. It fitted the mood perfectly, it brought out the sun, made all that was nothing seem like everything. The music letting them remain ageless to the faces that walk by.

"I promised him," Matt had maybe many unattractive personality traits but the one thing he'd pride himself on is not breaking his word. But as the sun glistened down into their wasted state and the truth is spoken in hedonistic emotions, it was words that fell away from him and meant nothing to his character anymore. "Wow man look at that." They look at the sun glow hazing across the city landscape, creating an early evening dusk, where even the clear blue sky turns a shade of red. And all is still and silent, time is frozen, and the world has become one. The trees sparkle in their bright green make-up; the horizon paints the picture of the windy city that is often left to the shadows that are awake at night and travel with the ghosts through the town. The town shines with reflections welcoming you. And the smog of the road is replaced by a cool glow of travelling into oneself. The summer had arrived.

"We're going to get a house without him. You're either with us or not?"

Matt ignores Taylor's question for a few moments. As faces of people he has seen, spoken to and known over the last two years

Part 4: Madness

walk past the painting that is the world in front of them, they don't notice him, perhaps it is he who is the painting? It's like him and Taylor don't exist for these early evening hours, they are Gods who sit on the veranda watching the earth breathe. Memories of the last two years flood through Matt. The warm colours and excitement of the 1st year, everyday seemed like summer. Then the insanity of this 2nd year, where the sun blinded them as they walked, the storm seemed everyday, and the windy city lived up to its name, colours of violence, a madness of excess that they'd wanted to live in the revolution of their lives.

"So, what are you going to do?" Taylor asks one final time.

"I just want to listen to the music, you know what I mean?" The music let him forget all this for these few hours. Where he could feel his soul as part of the city landscape, drifting over the parades of entertainment to the ocean where he'd ride the wave and finally sit on the shore. Where he'd sit until dusk and watch his past play a movie in front of him. Where he was on the outside looking in, not inside the madness that had taken over. Content.

"Yeah, I know what you mean." Taylor finally answers.

They'll be a new day at midnight. Tears are forming round Alex's eyes; he isn't dancing to a tune in his head any more, he's dead in the water now. "I'm sorry Alex, I had to tell you" Samantha says, keeping her distance from consoling him, she has only just put the knife in. What she says next will twist it and finish him off for good with great satisfaction.

"I don't believe it? Tell me again so I can try and understand it" Alex asks her. Even now he tries to analyse the bear facts, to see something profound and hip in being rejected by the entire house, being sold down the river.

"They got a house without you, and asked me to get you out the way for the day." Samantha looks at him in his torn red dressing gown, no underpants on. "Why do you always change into your dressing gown the minute you come back from anywhere?"

"It makes me feel comfortable." Alex replies. He loosens the belt as his back begins to shiver with the threat of bearing an over emotional brunt of tears. "Even Steve and Matt?"

"Especially Steve and Matt. Wake up Alex, play the game"

"I don't know the rules"

"The rules are there aren't any rules."

He places his hands, sweating with confusion into his head.

Thoughts as reasons for betrayal drive through the cloud storm in his mind; what did I ever do to these people? Wasn't I hip enough? Did I not listen to the right music? Did I not drink enough white lighting? Did I not inhale the joints properly? I don't want to be alone... "I don't want to be alone" he says to Samantha, holding his arms out, his belt loosening, and he shows his naked body to her.

"Its five in the afternoon, I'm fully clothed, I'm not having sex with you" And Samantha looks at his confused expression, the morgue of self-doubts that fill his grave, being dug by his own personality, a hole she helped create. It is now she decides that would be the best time to finish the game, stab him in the back at the time of ones greatest need. "I'm never sleeping with you again, Alex."

"What do you mean?"

"I'm leaving you Alex and I'm not coming back"

"But..."

"No buts this time. You can cry all you want, and beg all you want, like you have done before when I've said it, but this time I'm going"

"But they've all left me. If you leave me to then I've got no-one, I'll be alone"

"Exactly"

"Why are you doing this to me?"

"I said to you from the start Alex, it was a game to get at Amy"

"But that was nearly two years ago, it must have been more than that?"

"No. Just a game that I wanted to finish when the time was right"

"But I love you"

"I've never loved you"

"I don't believe you. You're not thinking properly" And as Samantha goes to leave for the door, Alex stops her, blocking her way, trying to hold her arms. She just pushes them away like the feeble man who she sees standing before her, broken by his friends and then killed by the girl he thought was his girlfriend. Tears are streaming down his face. "Wait. We could get a place together?"

"Why would I want to live with you?"

"I could leave Southampton and finish my course in Portsmouth"

"Why would I want you to come down there? I've got my own life now, I don't need you"

Part 4: Madness

He drops to his knees and starts crying, begging her. "Please, sleep with me and then decide"

"I told you, I'm never having sex with you again. Its called karma Alex, all the people you've fucked over. Now get out my way"

He followers her to the landing stairway, "I'll kill myself! I swear I'll kill myself if you go, I can't be alone…"

"Like I said Alex, there are no rules, only that you make your own." And with that she walks down the stairs, horns out of her head, dressed in red, a whip by her side, the devil in disguise.

As the door shuts on his life, Alex is convinced at the bottom of the stairs in the hallway is James, looking at his watch, a massive bloodstain on his shirt, where his empty lung breathes into the ghostly inhabitants. Alex walks back into his room. It is empty. He thinks about trying to dance to the tunes he hears, but the room is too spacious, a void of nothingness fills the air. He collapses onto his bed and looks at the empty space. Three things catch his eyes. A bottle of pills. A knife. A telephone. He can hear voices in the kitchen below. He decides to test the waters and goes down to make a cup of tea. In the kitchen stand the executioners, Matt, Steve, Taylor, Simon, Amy and Little Rob. "Hey" Alex says and does his pretend dance into the room, like nothing has happened, that it will take more to destroy him, when he is really dying with each passing second of humiliation in their company. They don't say anything. Ignore his very presence. Cowards too scared to look him in the eye, each staring into their own separate section of the floor or the wall. Alex realises he has never felt so alone in his entire life, and this feeling that grips him will never change, it was now the monkey on his back that only he alone could dismantle.

So when back in his room he begins the process to dismantle himself - All the kings' horses and all the kings' men wouldn't be able to put him back again.

Alex sits on his lonely bed and spaces himself out in a crucifixion pose. He had never realised how big the bed actually was. How empty the room is. It was too big for him. Left only with self-doubts and an analytical mind that prays on the defenceless, but this time he was his own chief subject, his own black couch. The light turns off and he switches the stereo on, Radiohead 'The Bends' album. This is what its like, he decides, suicide. An over the top emotional statement, the lights down, watching his own shadow dissolve with each breath, a Britpop luminary playing on the stereo, a death of a generation. He would become a martyr to those left behind, making suicide a statement of how to be 'hip' and understand the statements of this generation, of these bands. It was poetic. It made him feel immortal.

Another ghostly shadow moves across the wall and stands in front of him, James.

"What's it like James?"

"Death?"

"Suicide"

"I wouldn't know" James looks at his watch. "See you on the other side." The shadow goes.

In one hand he holds a knife. In the other hand he holds a bottle of pills. A suicide note for the generation of wasters. Poetic licence.

Matt wasn't sure what compelled him up towards Alex's room at that moment in the evening. A feeling of guilt? A need to explain himself? He was drinking, sitting outside with Taylor, passing a joint, listening to the Verve, but he felt a shiver down his back like someone had stepped on his grave. "I think its going rain" Taylor said, puffing on the joint, looking at the landscape of the city.

Next thing Matt knew he was going upstairs towards Alex's room. He pauses outside. "What am I doing?" he says to himself. But before he can answer he has opened the door and is greeted by Radiohead singing not to 'leave me high and dry', a stereo light that flickers across a bed, where Alex lays motionless in a crucifix position. "Listen mate, I know you're trying to sleep but I want explain a few things." No answer. "I understand if you don't want to talk, just let me talk, and you listen." No answer. "Now, I'm up here I don't even know where to begin. I don't even know why I came up here." No answer. "I'll go" Matt pauses by the door, and like before something moves his body against his minds wishes. He walks back over to the bed, controlled by an outside force. What greets him is a smiling face. Eyes closed. Bottle of empty pills in one hand. A note in the other hand. Blood drips onto the note. And his eyes settle on a slit wrist that has poured onto the bed sheets making them red.

One thing was for sure, Matt thought, if Alex was going out he was doing it in style.

The entire house, wait in the Casualty department, no strangers to these surroundings over the two years. Every revolution has its private casualties of war. No one says a word to another. The silence

Part 4: Madness

fills with each of their memories over two years. The guy, who imitates everything Matt does from his previous visits to Casualty, sits in silence, imitating him again, with his own private thoughts and memories to sit with. Even the receptionists don't speak to him this time, the same programme on as usual but for once this doesn't bother him, it made the place seem warm, to have at least one semblance of normal routine in an otherwise stop start life. He holds the suicide note in his hand. He hadn't the guts to show it to the others. This is something he wanted to punish himself alone for. He reads the crumpled note with dry blood spread over the words.

'Think we're playing a waiting game
Until the day you forget my name
With friends like you I better wrap up warm
'Cause a storms on its way
I'm going to have my day
Life is handing out everything you once craved
But you're left standing checking the price paid
It will be your sell by date that's running down fast
You're users, all users
Did you check the receipt?'

Alex had never been poetic in his life. He'd always tried to be hip. Now he was a poet of the deepest meanings, of the highest emotions. Suicide had given him what he always craved. Alex's mother arrives, no one was too sure who had called her. No one wanted to admit to doing the deed, or wanted to remember the conversation they had with her. How do you tell a mother that her only son had committed suicide? Where do you start? With the truth, always with the truth. And that had been the problem with this entire 2nd year. Too many lies. Too many drugged statements. Too many drunken outbursts. The smell of fear in excess in everything touched and taken. Excess of the generation where there was no end to the party line. They had forgotten where the line started. If it even existed.

The colours drained from the 1st year. The warmth and beauty around them turned to dark grey, bleak blue, and a threatening red. A stop start to each day and each new addiction. Nothing was too much. Everything had an edge to be explored and pushed over. Falling for eternity.

The educational year had gone so quick. One day merged into a month that merged into a semester that merged into a year. All the memories that engulf them as they wait are of a jigsaw. Nothing is complete. A face here... A night there... Something taken at... Too much said with... Sex... The smell of wasted rooms lost in a haze of smoke. Drunken rooms engulfed in violence later replaced that. Even the house fell apart around them, unable to cope with their life style. It seemed just one cold drugged and drunk roller coaster down the word excess. It was always going to take prisoners with its demands First James. Though only Matt and Clarissa knew the truth. Now Alex. What happened to the year? But now its over. And as they sit waiting to be put out of their misery...they remember that there is another year left. If they wish to come back. If they can survive this night...and themselves.

The Doctor comes out and walks towards the group. "He's going to be ok."

Matt begins to laugh and the others look at him like its very inappropriate. But he realises Alex had cancelled one suicide attempt out by doing another. Even in suicide Alex was still trying to be 'hip'. He can't help but wonder if Alex knew exactly what he was doing all along.

LONG HOT SUMMER

Matthew

Euro '96, our great chance, our World Cup '66, our new hero's. Taylor, Simon and myself have stayed in the house and watched it religiously, every match. Even Amy has joined us with her mates. These girls who had no interest in football before are now really interested, feeling like the rest of country, a feeling of euphoria, being part of something massive. Euro '96, Britpop, New Labour, it's all happening, the world is changing, the youth of today; Britain is the country to be in. White Lighting for the masses.

After the Germany game I feel gutted. It's like they gave us a chance to follow the holy grail, hold the taste of being someone, being part of something special to our lips and pulled it away at the last minute to remind us that we're just an island and we' re pieces of dog shit. I honestly thought that we were going to win it, but like everything with this country we are so near, yet so far. We celebrate losers, embrace them for trying but not being quite good enough and fear winners as they are looked upon as a law unto themselves. I don't think we'll ever win anything in my lifetime. I can't believe they let El Tel walk away, especially to that Cast song. Heroes in defeat, villains in victory. People we'd see in the street

Part 4: Madness

and say 'hello' to, strangers smiling, buying drinks, now they go back to being strangers, heads bowed down, a kind of recognised depressed stare, no 'hello', no drinks, back to normal life, back to being depressed, back to being an island.

Simon

It's just me, Taylor and Matt left in this city it feels like 'Day of the Dead'. The postman delivers a parcel. There's a massive photo of Johnny and a tape with a letter telling us to listen to the tape. We hadn't heard anything from Johnny since he disappeared last November, we've been placing bets to if he was alive or joined James in finishing life early. It starts and Johnny himself starts to sing. We sit and get completely caned as we listen to Johnny's very first album, recorded on a stereo in Manchester. I'm glad he's alive. Only a disappearing genius ala Syd Barrett could come up with this masterpiece.

The phone rings. It's my parents. I'm completely caned. They know about me dropping out of the course. That I left in Christmas. They knew then but wanted to give me time to be honest. They know I've carried on getting grants, which they tell me I've now got to pay back, and the rent money they gave me. I'm so caned. "Have you got anything to say?" they ask.

"Sorry" I reply more as a questioned answer than a statement.

They say - "Its best I don't come back for the summer." I get the impression they never want to see me again

Linda

Darren has a big supply coming in. I met him over Christmas; he's a local, used to go to the same school. I don't know if I'll go back in September, my final year. Its funny but despite all what's happened and now who I am, my grades are brilliant. The cocaine supply will be endless with Darren. I look in the mirror and see my face. The skin is slightly worn but with plenty of foundation it's ok. The hair is longer now and more split ends. With plenty of hair spray its ok. The rosy cheek girl, wild eyed and innocent of two years ago stares back at me and winks. As she fades, I see an old woman in my face and turn away needing a hit. "Where is it?" I ask.

But Darren is hooked up to something different. "Gotta move with the times, after Trainspotting, this stuff is the new cocaine" And as he pulls the needle out, a state of pure bliss comes across his face.

I run back to the mirror and pray for that young girl to fade back up smile and take me back in time. I admit it. I fucked everything up.

Alex

North London, Tottenham, isn't exactly the best area he could have left me. I would have preferred somewhere in Chelsea or Fulham, why couldn't it have been there? Still, the amount of money I'm going to make they'll all want to be my friends again. Revenge is a dish best served cold and this house is cold. There's an old record player and it keeps playing the same tune. The wind blows the curtains across scared faces that visit. Shadows run across and gentle laughing; it's a friendly ghost. It's James.

I phone the number. Her number. "Hello?" she asks. I stay silent down the phone. "Hello?" she asks again. I stay silent down the phone but let the ghost move the curtains and the wind gust through our souls. "I'm not coming back to you Alex" She knows it's me but I still remain silent. "Why don't you ever say anything, I know its you?" I remain silent.

She clicks the phone dead and I press redial. "Hello?" she asks.

Oh Samantha, you made a mistake making a fool out of me, they all did.

Taylor

In my parent's house before the Reading Festival, Matt and Simon came down today. I can't keep up with the pace of how those two drink. I need to stay awake and keep up, especially as they're smoking loads of weed but I need a little something to stay awake. Shall I make some coffee? I decide to eat it instead. I collapse on the kitchen table. Next thing I know, Amy's friend Samantha is looking pissed off as she wants to fuck me there and informs me that - "Matt is asleep in the living room so we need a room with privacy."

"Have you thought about the toilet?" I ask but then I realise the word 'toilet' reminds me of the coffee around my mouth and lips. I run to it and throw up over the carpet and everywhere but the sink.

I can't believe I've met this great girl. I wanted to fuck her in her tent with her friends but she just gave me a hand job in the end and I came in my underpants, which is a slight problem as I've got to wear them for the entire Festival. I wonder how old she is? She says seventeen, but the others when they saw her kept saying she

Part 4: Madness

must have been fourteen at the most. They're just jealous, she's great, she does look young for her age, but she's into so much good music for her to be that young, she must be seventeen. Even if she's not, it doesn't matter. I prayed it wasn't a one off and it wasn't. I get another hand shank in her tent and I come again in my underpants. When I get back, I decide that I've got to change them this time, they stink and I reckon I'll get another hand shank from her on Sunday, so I leave the underpants in the tent for whoever finds them first, and steal a pair from Matt's rucksack. He wears boxers, which I don't really like as if she tosses me off tomorrow its liable to go onto my jeans, so I'll have to be careful as I only have one pair of jeans. Her name is Zoë. She confides in me that she lied the previous two nights about her age. "I'm fifteen. But I'll be sixteen in August"

"So you'll be sixteen end of the month?"

"No, August next year" I decide not to tell anyone. I'm twenty-three, that's only nearly nine years difference, its like a thirty one year old going out with a twenty two year old, what's wrong with that? Nothing. We agree to see each other again after the festival. For the last two years any girl I've met at Uni has always been involved with someone or not wanting to have a boyfriend. Now I realise its better to go out with girls who aren't at uni but at school or college, even if she is my sister's best friend, though we haven't told my sister yet. She's in the fifth year of school. Perhaps they could share school homework together?

Matthew   'Knebworth' (August 10th & 11th 1996)

We formed as hundreds and turned to thousands. But together we are one. This is our time. And these are our kings. Silver, copper and gold we bring and they will sing. The largest standing concert in Britain, years of trying everything culminated here at Knebworth. For once the biggest band in the world were the greatest band in the world. Everything was leading up to this date. Something that would define what the music was all about, what the decade and its generation of followers wanted answered.

From one blade of grass that stood upright, now all is covered to the thousand miles of faces that we don't recognise. But words of songs that bring acknowledgement before the winter of discontent. I'm older than the people I see. I'm younger in the thoughts I keep. Refusing to burn away inside. Open air. Blue skies. Drunk and drugged, male and female. Somebody took the photo, where I stood. It's all been said and done. Show it round and I'm convinced, that

I'm down in this morning light. A revolution inside my head, they'll take the words I never said.

I'm turning in my head. I buy a headache. What did I take?. I just sit back. Trying to catch the line. Of my time.... The greatest band ever. The kings of rock and roll kingdom greet us with a sneer. Look at them Ma, on top of the world. We are rock n roll starrrrsssssssssssss. And we're so close that I'm a million miles away…(Things will never be this good again)

PART 5

September '96 to January 1st '97

Moving On

Moving on, you don't have a time of day. It's too late to call a name.
Must be pretty happy going back in circles again.
They'd go back to the same place they always meet. Still be scratching round feet. And feel like a fool when they get kicked in the teeth.
So many times we do repeat.

GHOST TOWN

Matthew

Final year. It's the start of September, arriving three weeks early before the term starts. I don't want to miss anything, flood my soul full of memories I can hold onto. I sat at my parent's home one evening in the summer and thought I had to go back and make the most of what time I had left. "I'm going" I told Mum.

"Will you be back for dinner?" she asked.

"No, you don't understand I'm going back"

"Back where?"

That's what I couldn't answer because I didn't know what to call it anymore, especially after that second year. I don't want that year again, I say that I didn't enjoy it but the truth is I can't remember any of it. Choosing to not recollect memories of James, Alex and Carla, each of them ghosts that will haunt my time in the windy city, whispering words of redemption across my soul as I walk the streets.

On the train to Southampton, my life packed into a Liverpool Football Club bag. Staring out of the window, for the first time on these travels the weather doesn't change; no clouds but no blue sky, nothingness as the two cities merge into one. Even the colours remain the same. Normal. I have arrived in a state of mediocrity in my mind.

"Hi" a girl says sitting opposite me. She has big rosy cheeks, blonde hair down to her shoulders, a fur jacket on, retro look.

For a moment I think its Carla. "Carla?" the first of my ghosts to haunt my travels.

"You don't remember me do you?" she says. At a closer inspection I realise it's not her, not Carla, and in my dejection I turn away and look out the window. "On a train travelling back two Christmas's ago." I look at her and then I remember the girl filling an application form in. "We spoke about university"

"Yeah, I remember. Where did you get into?"

"London"

"You enjoying it?"

"I'm loving it. That first year was the best year of my life"

"Mine too"

"I cant wait for the second year, I start in two weeks" With the look of excitement in her face I don't have the heart to tell her you cant go back, you cant recreate that 1st year, the second year will take casualties, friends, your mind, your soul.

Part 5: Moving On

"I'm going back to my final year" And I look back out of the window praying the colour and weather will tell me I have arrived but it shows 'nothing' but that which I already knew. Ridiculous isn't it, I make it sound like I'm going to die at the end of the year. In a way, I guess a part of me will be dying, I'll never have free money again, never have three years away from home in education again.

"Do you know what you're going to do when you finish?" she asks me.

" I didn't come to university to do work. I came to escape work." I reply. Maybe I got the idea of uni wrong; maybe I'm the last of my kind, the waster. I'm trying not to think about what will happen next summer, when it's all over. Do we all just pack up and leave, that's it.

"You got to think about the future, I'm already organising potential work placements. What have you learnt?" she asks me.

What have I actually learnt... "Nothing". Hoping later will never come. That this year will last forever. Now the fear of reality and work, going back home is playing catch up with me. By arriving early I can keep it from my door. Find out if I want to stay after the gold rush.

I step off the tracks into the daylight; the windy city engulfs me with its tales of pre-student months. There is no blinding sun. No hard rain. Even the wind is whistling a tired tune. It's strange, the town without any students, it feels like a different place... a ghost town. Full of faces that seem lost, a village that was damned of ghosts of students past, who out stayed their welcome and now wonder the streets searching all over again. It's a mirror of the future and it isn't pretty. Plenty of nutters shouting for no reason and following the nearest queue. Lost souls of former students, looking to find what they once felt. The streets are cold but the cold isn't in the windy city but in me. On each corner I see Carla, waiting for me. Each shadow is James, following me. And Alex, dancing round the city, his wrists bleeding dry, painting the pavement, pointing his finger at me, shouting 'Judas'. Ghosts of memories past.

September seems to be the month for the 'nutters', for the 'tramps', they are welcome in the pubs, before they go into hibernation, as do the 'local' community. Where do all these suspicious minds go once its end of September? During these summer months they crawl out of whatever coffin they lock themselves away and take the town back. Then the dark clouds arrive on the horizon, and - 'us, we, me,' - arrive as hordes of students on top of the hill, waiting to ride down into oblivion and they all retire again into the coffin, away from daylight and night, hibernate until it's all over again and the town can be safe and taken back. I walk the parade of shops through town but it's deserted. The town is dead. No students. Plenty of tramps drinking the last of their summer wine. "Why are you hear? Its not the end of September" Looking at me with suspicion. "Nutters! Fucking nutter!" "Here's ok, he drinks from the same holy water as us" and he raises the bottle of White Lighting in respect.

For the summer months there is a turn in fortunes and it is I who is made to feel the outcast, the tramp, the nutter, the unwanted visitor. In my favourite pub, the Tut N Shive, even the bar staff are different, looking at me with sceptic eyes. "A student in early September, its not time yet, how dare he?" I hear the locals whisper as I sit up at the bar, wanting to celebrate my return with a drink alone and get my mind round my future. As they continue to stare and whisper, evil eyes boozing in the back of my head, maybe I wont make it out of this week alive. So I leave the stall and pass them by without a sound. Is this what I will become if I stay in Southampton and not be a student? Drink up time to go. Go for good I decide to myself once the year is out.

The best bet is stay in the house. Feel safe here. Feel at home here. Feel like a student here. Hidden behind closed doors. This is the nicest house we have lived in the three years. Give it till Christmas and we'll destroy any purity it ever echoed out of its walls. The road is the start of the prostitutes walk. I'm nearer to my memories of Carla. For punishment or pride? I do not know as yet. As I stride my feet down to the house, two ladies of the afternoon greet me on the edge of my street.

"All right darling?" the older one says, looks late thirties, late twenties in reality, but her work as aged her by ten years. The short skirt that passes as a belt, black puffer jacket, gold earrings, the future Pat Butcher of prostitution.

"Alright" I reply, if they're going to be standing daily by my road I might as well get to know them. I can't look them in the face though. I'll only see Carla.

"Where you going?" she asks.

"To my house"

"Why don't you come into our house first?" the younger one speaks, her voice like that first time I met Carla and my eyes look up in hope.

"I think you've got an admirer," the older one says to the younger

Part 5: Moving On

one. I didn't realise I was staring at her, hoping to see Carla's face. Instead this girl is no more than sixteen, could even be the older ones daughter. Short blonde hair cropped to her ears, a pale skin, and heavy blue eye linear. She isn't Carla. "I've got to go and see my housemates" The older one pushes the young one forward and she puts her arm through my arm, like we're on a date and I'm walking her home.

"Bring them too, we can have a party" She starts to walk with me to my house.

"This is it. Thanks for walking me home" I don't know why I said that but it makes her laugh.

"You're funny. You going to get your housemates to come out?"

"Not tonight. Maybe another time"

"You make sure you do" And then she walks off, high stiletto heels, real short skirt, I'm sure she used to go to Kaos nightclub, a 'club' generation girl. As a car draws up, she is immediately pouring her work into the occupier. Both her and her older friend get in the car and they wave to me as their new client drives past. Nice Neighbours.

Amy, Simon and I seat ourselves in our new living room. The new nuclear family sit and watch Saturday evening TV, also known as 'nothing' TV. It's amazing how nothing seems to make perfect sense when you watch it like a couch potato unable to move. The Homer Simpson's of our generation, a beer sits in my hand. I've already started making an early Christmas tree of beer cans in the living room.

Simon had decided to come down to stay in the third year. The truth is he had no choice; he'd already signed the contract for the house that fateful day when Alex tried to kill himself, before his parents knew he'd been kicked out the course. Then it all came falling down after Euro '96. They didn't want him back home.

"Coming back seems to make the only sense in my life" he told me in the summer. "I cant go home. I might as well stay in Southampton. See it to the bitter end with all of you. It seems poetic, the right thing to do."

"What about the money?"

"I'll get a job or something. Besides, what's the worst they can do if I don't pay my grant back, send me to Vietnam?"

We hear the front door open. "It's the ghost of student past," I inform them. I'd seen them all day.

The landlord, my third, a different one each year, all the time very dodgy Asian guys who run mini cab firms, have big Mafioso families and never fix anything, Mr. Mandiar, big turban, big grin, big baseball bat, walks in. He stands directly in front of the television as we all hold are lottery tickets, waiting for our numbers to be called out and rescue us from the oblivion that awaits next year when all this is finished. "What are you doing here?" he shouts.

"We live here"

"But its not term time yet?"

"We've paid our rent. We live here"

"Not happy, no, no, no, not happy" he keeps repeating

"Why?"

"You shouldn't be here" he replies

I can see behind him is the prostitute from the corner, the young girl. "Alright" I say to her.

"So this is your house?" she says.

"My house. I own the house, they just rent" the landlord says.

"What are you doing here?" We demand to know. "You can't just let yourself in, there's laws against that," we threaten him. "Tenants rights," we get legal with him.

He makes something up on the spot. "I come to sort out business with you"

"What business?"

"I come back" And he leaves the house.

The young prostitute remains in the living room. The lottery numbers are called out and Simon tears up ten tickets. "What's the fucking point?" Even I had brought a ticket. I lost.

The young prostitute looks at the numbers, hurriedly puts her hand into her jacket pocket. She pulls out a mobile phone, a tampax, make-up and various assorted tasting condoms. "Nice condoms" I inform her.

"Yeah, if I'm going to suck someone's cock I prefer it to taste nice. This may sound racist but I don't like sucking an Asian guys cock pure." She finally finds what she wanted, a lottery ticket. Her face goes through the numbers. "I won!" she exclaims.

"You won?!" Simon shouts, jealous, looking to see if he can steal the ticket.

"I've never done it before, but its become compulsory at work to buy a ticket"

"Your pimp makes you buy a ticket?"

Part 5: Moving On

"Its part of the health plan, along with dental and eye check ups"

"You won the lottery?" Simon continues.

"I got three numbers, how much is that?"

"Ten"

"Ten what?"

"Ten, its only ten pound"

"Cool. You want to get drunk?"

"On ten pound?"

"I could buy some white lighting and we could share it," she suggests, nice girl.

There is a bike bell noise from outside, the kind of noise from a young schoolgirls bike as she rides across the pavement to warn pedestrians of the oncoming rush of youth. The landlord then steps back into the house proclaiming pieces of paper. "I have documents. I leave now. You fill in forms" He turns to the young prostitute girl. "You want a ride?"

"Sure. You got a car?"

"No a bike. I like to feel the wind through my turban"

We show them to the door. "If you let yourself in again, we're phoning the Police on you"

He gets on a little girls pushbike. "You'll have to go on the handle bars" he informs the prostitute, and they ride off into the night, ringing the bell as it scuttles across the pavement.

In Asda, another student is here early - Jenny O'Sullivan, the fit one of the O'Sullivan twins. Apparently she's in with Keith Reynolds's strange 'vampires' occult, but she's hot, flame red hair down her back, great figure, rounded, big breasts, great arse, she is someone I would really like to have a one night stand with on a regular basis.

I say nothing at first; embarrassed that she probably doesn't know my name. "Alright Matt" she says immediately on seeing I'm behind her in the queue and behind her in my mind but we're both naked.

"All right, Jenny" I reply, trying to act cool.

"You've come back early. I live here all year round now" she tells me.

"I was thinking about doing that" I lie.

"You should, be nice to see a familiar face during the ghost months"

"Its like a ghost town"

"Not if with stick together," wink, wink, nod, nod, "you should come down to our flat"

Thoughts of vampires and bats flying around come to mind. Could be fun. "Where do you live?" I ask my vampire hippy babe.

"It's a new apartment building. Here's my phone number"

"I don't have a..." but she writes on my hand, real gentle, and I wish she could have looked lower and written on my cock as it was standing tall and practically touching my hand out.

"Don't lose that." The number or the hard-on? "Hopefully I'll see you soon" As she walks away I picture going to her room straight away, glass of wine, no, white lighting, get her drunk and violent, loads of bats and vampires hanging from the ceiling, probably fucks in a coffin. Never sleep; never grow old, live-forever. She's out of my sight now and I realise I haven't got a clue how to get to those flats. Still I've got the phone number on my hand. Must remember to write it down before having a shower again, or alternatively, I could never shower again, and she'd be impressed, that I've kept the touch of her gentle hand on mine until we could consummate the meeting of our bodies. Maybe I'll just watch TV instead.

Open the door to the house the lights are off. You can tell when a house is empty, it whispers full of memories, haunting your present, in its darkness, in its stillness. Just an empty space engulfed by one person with a lifetime of memories to hide away from in the shadows. Every house makes its own sound. The last one was destruction. This one is emptiness.

Turning the light on in the living room, sitting on the sofa is Johnny. I don't jump, or scream. Just sit on the armchair next to him and turn the TV on. "Alright?" he says.

"Alright?" I reply. I didn't know what else to say. No-ones seen or heard from him in nearly a year, it just seemed natural that he would be there, waiting.

"Don't you want to know what I'm doing here?" he asks.

"Not really. Makes perfect sense." And it did. Everything goes full circle. He too must have felt that pull towards this place for the finality of it all, of our youth, of Britpop, of the generations failed revolution. We sit in silence for a number of moments as I scan the channels for something that will let me be able to think of nothing for a while. "I want to make an album with you guys. Finish what we started" Johnny breaks the monotony of nothing sounding bliss. "How did you get in?" I finally ask the question I should have asked first.

"I broke in"

"How did you know where we was? No-ones seen or heard from you in nearly a year" I seem to be asking all the questions backwards. These last two should have been the first two, the first ones the last ones.

"This was the fourth house I tried"

"You broke into three other houses?"

"I could smell the road, the house"

"You're not a dog"

"That's the problem with you people from down south, you've got no scent" Silence. I leave the channel on an Only Fools Horses repeat. "So you want to make an album?" he asks again.

"I'm not going back to that way of life again Johnny"

"What do you mean?"

"The holy trinity. I hardly smoke anymore. Just drink." I stare at him. "A lot"

He smiles and brings out a block of weed. "We'll see, we'll see"

The lost students sit in the living room. Blonde Paul sits has also returned, I haven't seen him for over a year, another lost face that returns to find the answer. "Don't know, it seemed the right thing to do," he tells us. "What's with the Jesus look Matt?" He says to me, thinking the second coming is standing before him. First the Bee Gees. Now Jesus. Next will be God. We spend the next hour filling both Johnny and Blonde Paul in about James dying, Alex trying to commit suicide, the entire madness of last year.

"Fuck" Blonde Paul says. "I never would have thought James would kill himself?"

"He was always fucked up when on drugs. I knew he was going to die" Johnny says.

"How?" I ask.

"The ghost in your hallway told me the night I left" As they recount tales of James and good times I remain quiet. Knowing the truth, the truth behind his death, the truth behind his life.

"As for Alex, that's not a surprise, probably did it to be hip"

"Where is he now?" Is he coming back?" No one answers, no one knows.

They put 'The Shining' on in the living room. A mattress taken out from the extension room, infested with fleas, for Johnny to sleep on and feel at home with. "I'm going to find my own place this time." He tells us, as he unpacks his belongings, turning the living room into his bedroom. He sees fleas jump around the mattress. "Least its not a hallway this time" he mumbles to himself, stamping the life out of the insect kingdom. I pretend to be asleep on the armchair, as they continue to skin up and talk about old times.

Things are always remembered fondly when they're in the past? I hear enough to remind me; "That last year was crazy" Simon tells Johnny. "Wish I could have been there for it all" he replies.

I must have been somewhere else during that year. Content that I didn't exist as days fell around me. As I sleep visions of ghosts past and future come to visit me.

WHO'S THE DADDY???

Taylor

I'm bored with Southampton it makes me feel empty. The city and house is constantly damp and cold. The first year breathed confidence into me, despite the psychotic relationship I had with Rachel. The second year can't remember much through the constant drink binge that White Lighting brought. All those one-night stands I had because I wasn't with Rachel. "You look like Johnny Depp," I was told on a regular basis. It's different this year, it's only October but I feel a distance from the City and all my friends. Now we all sit around and do nothing, waiting for the end to come. Trying to hold back the time on our lives. What should be a celebration has become a funeral parade. "Shall we go out?" someone will suggest. "We've been everywhere" "Done everything" "Its safer in doors" "There's something on the telly"

I want to return home, back to my clean house in Reading, back to my parents doing everything for me. I'm tired of this life now. My new girlfriend, Zoë, is back there; she's still at school, final year, and my sister's best friend. "When shall we tell her?" Zoë keeps asking me.

"Not tonight" I say as we fuck in her bed. I ignore her questions, as I have no answers. "Whose this playing?" I ask of the Nu-Metal on her stereo. I'm really getting into it, makes me feel dark and more like Johnny Depp. Mysterious.

"Panterea" she replies, "we need to dress you properly if you want to be a Goth"

"You're not a gothic?"

Part 5: Moving On

"Nu Metal. Gothic's. We all dress the same"
"Don't they have to kill themselves at twenty one?"
"I forgot you're old"

As for the Law degree what does it matter? I'm only studying Law because of my parents. They push us to do well, they wanted a family of lawyers, both mum and dad are top of that profession. "Family business" Dad keeps saying. Instead the more they pushed us the more wasted we became by default. They have two sons who are university wasters and a daughter who is a heavy metal gothic crossbreed. We never wanted for anything, everything has always been paid for, but no payment can take away the weight of expected burden. "You look like a fat Johnny Depp," I was told yesterday in the windy city. I need to lose weight, though –'A few extra pounds never hurts any lawyer. Adds weight when you approach the Bench,' Dad always says.

"You going into the course this week Taylor?" Little Rob asks me, mouth full of roast dinner.

"I don't know if I want to be lawyer" I tell myself more than him.

"I never wanted to be one in the first place" he replies.

"So you going to leave the course?" He can be my excuse - "If you do, I will"

"Don't know yet. I'll have to see how far I get on Lemmings this semester" He has just based his entire decision on a computer game.

Johnny is camped out in my room, using the stereo to record his new 'album'. The entire house is hanging onto Johnny making this album, in the hope it'll make them all rich and they can remain as students forever, sitting in this house doing nothing all day. I'm a prisoner battling for supremacy. "What are you doing Taylor?" Johnny asks me, plugging in his guitar.

"Sit ups are good for the stomach muscles." If I am to carry the family burden of added weight as I move into my twenties then I might as well tone it as a six pack, damn, that makes me think of drinking, and that makes me think of kebabs, I'll have to do at least hundred sit ups today just to work off my minds eye. The further I push myself, the more moments of joy come to me. Like that amazing blowjob Rachel gave me, I honestly never thought it was possible to cum like I did in her mouth, she swallowed the lot too, I shot what felt like a years load. My cock felt like an ice-cold lolly on the hottest summers day being licked and teased and finally finished and swallowed whole. Then I picture the last weekend I had back in Reading, with my sisters best friend, kinky sex with a gothic, she kept her glasses on, made me feel really dirty, like I should have been reading a book or revising instead.

Steve has caught on to the exercise bug, worried about his beer belly as well. We agree to run from the house, up to and round the Common and back home. "We promised to do this daily," Steve says entering my room, already in his tracksuit and limbering up like a ballet dancer on heat. He jogs in the most disgusting tracksuit top I've ever seen, trying to look exactly like Damon from Blur. But I doubt if Damon jogs around the city wearing a tracksuit top and bottoms that have obvious spunk stains on them.

As we get to the Common, I'm out of breath and we take a breather. "I've got a secret to tell you" Steve leans in towards me, coughing, checking his pockets for a cigarette, defeats the purpose surely?

"What's that?" I ask, happy for him to do the talking, as I pretend to be not out of breath but if the truth were known I'm thinking of giving up this running idea after day one.

"I'm gay," he tells me. I start to run. Run round the Common. Steve lagging behind, calling out for me to "Slow down." The more he catches up the quicker I run. I run all the way back to the house, into my room and lock the door.

There's a knock. "I'm getting changed Steve" I say through the damp vanish.

"Its me Taylor... Me and the baby." It's Rachel...her and the baby...

I open the door to be greeted by Rachel holding a baby, her new boyfriend behind her. "I didn't think the kid was due yet?" Is my first reaction as my mind starts to add up times and dates. There was a one-night stand when we broke up and then got back together for that one weekend. She was seeing the guy at the same time, so we both felt cheated. But she assured me that she fell pregnant a couple of months after that encounter.

"No" she says trying to cover up, "it's two months old." 'Its' two months old?

It's not the healthiest of houses to bring a baby into. There are the fleas in the living room. And the kitchen stinks...badly. The rest of the house keeps staring at the baby and then at me to see any family resemblance. But there Rachel is, with the father? Speaking to Matt with a baby in her arms like this is an every day occurrence

Part 5: Moving On

and the baby will be fine, used to unhealthy ways of life, probably the same in its conception. Better get used to it kid, if it was mine, it'll have the family jeans of putting on weight after your teens, a life of salads and exercises, where mates reveal they're gay is no thing for a young baby to wait for in sullen excitement. "Looks like you Taylor." Matt says as a joke. Even the guy whose kid I hope it is laughs at this, probably hoping it isn't his and then he can kick Rachel into touch like I did.

"We conceived 'it' the day we first had sex." Rachel states matter of fact. I like the way the baby hasn't got a name but is called 'it'. "It was amazing, we did it three times that one night, that's how I know its Darren's. I never did that with you Taylor did I?"

"Sex?" I reply

"No, three times a night." She has just shot my supposed idealised sexual prowess down. If that child remembers all this it sure is going to have a fucked up life. "Plus we were doing loads of coke as well, kept us going" She continues and the father just stands there with a broad grin. If the kid survives today, and its original conception story, it could grow up to be a great person of importance and sexual perversity, an MP. As I walk the proud mother and father of 'it' to the door, Rachel stops me once we're out of earshot. "I need you to come back to Reading"

"Why?"

"We haven't named 'It' yet?"

"You want my advice on a name? Be Godfather to it?"

I don't want to name 'it' until I know who the father is?" She tells me.

And the boyfriend smiles at me and then looks at 'It', as if to say – 'It could yours pal, if so, I'm outta here'.

"Its mine?"

"I don't know. Darren fucked me three times that night. You only ever got it up once a night. So the odds are more in his favour"

"You fucked us both that night?"

"Of course. That's why Darren was so randy, prove his sexual prowess." Again he stares at me with a stupid grin.

The next day, is Father's Day, and I get a letter through the post, hand delivered, pretending to be from the baby, saying - 'It was glad to finally meet its real dad and looks forward to its next visit.' I pack my bags and head back to Reading to be with my sister's best friend. Absence makes the heart grow fonder, but I don't think there's a pulse in that city anymore. It's like all of us are waiting for the death toll when the date moves to the final day and that's it, no more being a student. We're all waiting for our sentences for the rest of our life.

"Why are you back here?" Is what my parents greet me with as I step through the door? Both of them dressed in their lawyer suits. Hard-boiled. Hard cookies. Hard money.

"I thought I'd get away for a couple of days" I reply. I'm not going to tell them about the baby or that I'm thinking of leaving the course.

"Its bad enough having one waster son let alone two," they say and point towards the garden, where my brother is in the swimming pool enjoying the blinding rays of a cold late autumn day.

"We'll be back for dinner. Marietta is cooking duck. I want a course and grade up date then we'll drive you back. Family business remember son?"

"Family Business" I reply. I step out into the garden, where Roy, my younger brother by a miraculous nine months exactly, lays in the swimming pool, sunglasses on, as the sun blinds across the icy everglades of the land we own. He has a stereo playing 'Another Day in Paradise' by Phil Collins. "When did you get back?" I ask him.

"Start of the week"

I feel the water. "Jesus its cold"

"Good isn't it"

I see that he's naked bar his swimming trunks. "You'll freeze to death"

"Better out here than in there"

"How long you back for?"

"Indefinitely"

"You left your course again?"

"I walked straight out and got the first train back" It was the fifth time he'd left the course; my parents would drive him back within the week each time.

"When they driving you back?"

"Not this time buddy. I'm here to stay. Had all my stuff delivered by removal van back here on dads credit card"

"You've left for good? What about the family business?"

"I'm not part of that anymore. Besides, they've still got you"

I look at the icy grass, putting my hand through it, as a kid I'd play with it for hours, till I'd be dragged in by the maid, with frost bite.

Part 5: Moving On

"Or they haven't got you?" he says, peering down his sunglasses.

"How did they take it?" I ask in preparation for my fate.

"I'm still here but out of the will"

"They've cut you out?"

"Threatened, they'll never do it. Just tell them, you'll be fine"

"I never wanted to be a lawyer"

"A family of wasters. That's what you get with the modern nuclear parentage"

"You going to get a job?"

"What's the point? It will only please them"

"So what you going to do?"

"I figure laze around here in this pool until they kick me out"

"Then what?"

"Go back to university and start a law course"

"Then leave again?"

"You're catching on bro. You may be older than me but you're not wiser"

Then the phone call happens. "Its me." Me, being Rachel, she has a problem giving names to anything these days. "Ready to be a dad?"

Life is strange, one day you're at university, in a city that becomes your home, meeting strangers who become your friends and you share your experiences of the end of youth together. You're part of a scene, part of the decade that is talked about in magazines, sung about by idols we see on the screens, dressing and talking like it's a mirror laid before you with all the entertainment that is thrown onto you to consume and excess. Nothing means everything and everything is nothing. Then next day, you're standing in a hospital awaiting test results, with your gothic still at school girlfriend holding one hand, your ex-psychotic girlfriend holding your other hand, and her boyfriend. And all that seemed so important before means so very little, time stands still, as history dictates whom is the father of a child.

"What shall we call 'it'?" Rachel asks me.

"I haven't thought about it to be honest" All I can think of is I'll have to ask her to marry me if its mine. My parents would make me.

"How about Taylor junior or Rachel junior?" she suggests. "What shall we call it?" Rachel now turns to Darren.

"How about Darren junior or what's your girlfriends name

Taylor?"

"Zoë" she replies.

"Zoë junior"

"Wait, it's a baby boy isn't it?" I ask them.

"Yeah but names are two fold this decade, its trendy" Rachel tells me.

"Yeah a kid in ten years time without a double sex name will have the piss taken out of it at school by the next generation. It was on this documentary on channel four last night" Darren continues. They sure have put a lot of thought into it these last two months.

"How do you feel about this Zoë?" asks Rachel.

"Great. I can be its Aunt."

"But Taylor you'll have to marry me if it's yours"

The boyfriend smirks. "What if its Darren's?" I ask Rachel.

"No, we're not getting married. We'll continue to live in sin"

"Cool. I could live sin in the same house" Zoë says. "A marriage with two affairs under the same roof"

"A lawyers wet dream" I say. "My parents would have a field day with that case"

"Then we could have our own kids Taylor" Zoë continues painting her obscure gothic picture.

"Great" I reply. She's only fifteen. And she's already talking about houses and kids.

The Doctor with the results steps out of the door and my entire life, both past and future flash before my present…Hopes, dreams, drink, drugs, sex, responsibility, family – 'family business' - I can hear my dad say. The Doctor speaks and we listen, all is quiet, and though his mouth moves I cannot hear a word but for the faint crying of a newborn child. A newborn child inside me that is…

'It' is not mine.

The boyfriend, Darren, looks gutted. Rachel looks gutted. I'm sure they would have left it on my doorstep for me to bring up, then gone away together and fornicated like rabbits for future blood tests. Even Zoë looks gutted now that her dream gothic idealised future home has been destroyed. He is not mine… I'm not a father.

Back home in my bedroom I take out the assortment of gifts I had brought and hidden away. A big panda bear. Baby clothes. Small toys. I pull out the Father's Day card Matt had written as a joke. And I begin to cry. I'm not sure if it's through relief that he wasn't mine or the cold fact that I'm not a father – he wasn't mine, and part of me wished he was.

Part 5: Moving On

"Got someone up the duff then Bro?" My brother stands in the doorway. "Guys only cry like girls in such cases"

I wipe away my tears. "Rachel's baby, she thought it might be mine, but it wasn't"

"Close escape bro. Fate worse than death with that psycho"

"I'd brought all these presents, you know, in case it was…mine" I start to pack them away.

"What, you brought them out of your own pocket?"

"No, dads credit card, but the sentiment was there" Dad must rue the day he ever passed us his credit card details.

"Sometimes the little buggers go in first shot, other times they swim around for years. I'm mean look at us, I'm sure they've only ever had sex three times whilst they've been married and each time Dad hit the bull's-eye"

"He's a lawyer what do you expect?"

I hear mum and dad come back from their day at court. "Don't tell them," I ask my brother.

"Like they listen to a word I say anyway"

Dad walks up to the room. "Haven't you got a swimming pool to freeze in?" he says to Roy.

As Roy departs Dad catches an eye of the baby presents. "Are they for Rachel's baby?"

"Yeah" it could so easily have been my baby. My child. Part of me.

"You had a close shave there son. Bet you're glad you dumped her when you did?"

"Yeah" I reply.

"Pack your bags, Mum and I are driving you back after dinner"

I pack my bag. D-Day time. He comes into my room. I sit on the edge of my bed. Bag over my shoulder. Staring at the floor. "I'm not going back?"

"What do you mean you're not going back?"

"I don't want to be a lawyer dad"

"Look its bad enough I've got to put up with one waster, your brother, but not you. You're going back. Family business"

"I'm never going back" As I stand up to leave my room he blocks my path. "What are you going to do? Hit me? You're a lawyer, you know the law against parents hitting their kids"

And like all good lawyers, he looks at it from the lawyer angle not the parent point of view. That is why I don't want to be a lawyer;

I want kids, not cases. "You and Mum, you're not our parents, you're our lawyers"

"Don't worry" I hear Roy say as I leave, "he'll be back. He's a waster... just like me"

Arrive at the door with my bag over my shoulder. I have no idea what the reaction will be. As it opens I step inside and it feels right. The city is asleep. The future is mine.

"What are you doing here? I thought you was going back to Southampton, back home?" Zoë says not happy to see me. Then again she's a gothic, dressed permanently in black, she could be ecstatic but not show it.

"I am home," I tell her.

'TWINS'

O'Sullivan Twins

They stand in their naked glory by the window holding hands, formed as one like in their birth. Overlooking the windy city on the night of Halloween. As the lights turn a darker shade a sinister colour of unknown mystery beckons the walkers of the streets, mischief is upon us. Ghosts and lost souls attend a final dance along the ocean into the world they inhabited, a celebration of horror and all that scares us. "I love Halloween" Jenny says, naked in her purity by the window, long flowing red hair down to her shoulders, blue eyes like the naked ocean as dawn rises, and a figure of a fifties Hollywood starlet. Liana stood the same height as Jenny but she was bigger boned, black cropped hair rather than her sisters long flowing red, smaller breasts. They were twins but not identical. They shared a psychic link, a special bond that not even their parents could understand. What one felt the other felt. When either of them had sex, the other one would feel the pleasure, the pain, the nothingness, it was like sharing boyfriends, so in touch with each others emotions they were. One time after Liana had been screwing this guy from the course, she sat disappointed with him, in both the coming to early in sex and the boring relationship. Jenny walked in and summed up the situation. "You're getting worse at it each night" Jenny told her sisters boyfriend.

"How would you know?" he replied hurt.

"Cause I've felt nothing but bored for the last few weeks. I'm sorry its over"

The boyfriend laughed. "I'm not going out with you" He then

Part 5: Moving On

turned to Liana.

"You heard her" Liana replied. If one felt nothing then the other did.

They sit in the hot bath together, one at either end, like when they were children and as those years before them, they bathe each other innocently for the night ahead. Each touch of their silky skin, the other one feels, each drop of water, each run of soap, each pleasure point. Twice as clean now they have washed. They finish by kissing quickly on the lips, a peck for a second, and then giggle like schoolgirls. When they wanted to learn to kiss properly in preparation for their first boyfriends at school, they educated on each other. Nothing had ever felt as sensual and electric as the two of them kissing, for those moments they became the one being God must have intended them originally to be.

The O'Sullivan twins stand by the window now in their costumes reflecting shadows onto the courtyard for all the young people who roam the streets on this night of horror to gather supplies of sweets and terror on this relenting evening. Even the city landscape hovers with a dark grey cloud in the sky, but holds back on the rain, until midnight, when the chaos of 'mischief' is over. Each child's eyes glint with the thought it is their night of adulthood, the night where they hold the rules and dress as monsters that scare them any other night. All things must pass over the city. The sisters standing as guardians, move from the window and their protection of all that moves scared in the night, to the front door of their flat. Where standing awaiting them in costume is two of their three dinner guests. Keith Reynolds dressed in his obligatory black cloak, white blood stained shirt and fake fangs. "Sorry didn't have time to change," he tells the sisters. Next to him is Clem, in his usual train jacket, big woolly jumper and soiled trousers. "I've come as a train driver," he tells the sisters. "Nice costumes" they say in unison to the sisters, who stand before them in all their naked beauty, with only a large brightest green cloverleaf over their cunts, a pretty green long handmade necklace that hangs to the bottom of their breasts and rests perfectly. Their hair is filled with daises. They look the portrait of an erotic biblical story.

"We came as Eve" they tell them in unison.

Matt reaches the door, he checks the piece of paper he had originally written the address on, remembering Jenny's gentle touch when she wrote on his hand back in September in the queue in

Asda, how he got an erection when she did this and how most of all he thought I really want to fuck her. And since then he had kept contemplating phoning her, he'd see her in the pubs and clubs, they'd talk briefly, flirt, and for the first time since he'd been here, Carla apart, as that was different, he could see himself going 'steady' with someone, starting a proper relationship that lasted more than just the casual sweaty acutance in the night hours. There was something about her, something about their touch on one another. Flirting can be interpreted wrongly; he knew that better than anyone, cutting both ways in guilt of leading someone on and idiocy in leading yourself on.

"We're having a dinner party. Why don't you come round?" She had asked him.

"I don't know. When is it?" He asked he'd always like enough days grace to get ready and then talk himself out of going somewhere. He thought too much these days, rather than just acting on the instincts that had got him this far in life already.

"Are you doing anything for Halloween?" she asked him, pretending to change the subject.

"No"

"Then you got no excuse not to come" Jenny said tricking him into it. She smiled as he put two and two together that he'd been tricked. When he smiled back she automatically gave him a kiss goodbye on his cheek and he moved in at the same time. They were both still embarrassed enough to move the same way in order to get out of the way of each others lips, not wanting to test those waters yet.

Matt holds a bottle of wine in his hand. He thought about flowers as well, imagined her naked surrounded by a hundred roses he'd buy her, and they'd make love on the bed, crushing the thorns with their naked skins. The first cut of any new idealised relationship is always the deepest. But it was a dinner party, they'd be other people there, she may just have been being friendly, nothing more. At least with the bottle of wine, he could drink himself and get pissed if things didn't work out. Nothing gained. Nothing lost.

There's a knock at the door, Keith and Clem remain seated on the sofa, playing snap with a deck of cards, and the two sisters both simultaneously stand up like it's a mirror between them. Liana links to Jenny - 'Its Matt'. Jenny links to Liana.

"Hi Matt" Jenny opens the door welcoming Matt with a gentle

Part 5: Moving On

kiss on the cheek.

"I brought this" Matt says holding out the bottle of wine, and as Jenny pulls back from kissing his cheek he realises the vision of nakedness that is in front of him for the first time. Wondering, what kind of dinner party is this? As Jenny stands before him naked but for the flowers in her hair, the green cloverleaf below and then his eyes rest on where the long handmade green necklace lays. He averts his eyes, as she can tell he's staring there.

"Come on in, don't be shy" Jenny says, taking the bottle of wine and placing it on the dining table.

"Hi Matt" Liana O'Sullivan says, also standing in the same naked outfit as her sister Jenny.

'He's embarrassed' - Liana links to Jenny in there silence. 'Did you not tell him it was a fancy dress party?' 'No' Jenny links back to Liana in their silence. - 'I wanted to see his reaction.'

"Hey Mr. Oasis" Clem says as his greeting, sitting on the sofa, deck of cards in his hand, in his train jacket and underpants. Matt begins to wonder if he has arrived during a game of strip poker. If so, he was glad he was fully clothed in his brown suede jacket, flared jeans, black roller neck jumper, he'd have to lose quite a few hands to catch up.

"Nice costume Matt" Keith Reynolds comments, "the Jesus look, real retro for Halloween" Keith Reynolds says in admiration, fake fangs falling from his mouth.

"Costume? This is what I always wear," a confused Matt says.

"We came as Eve" The O'Sullivan twins say standing in front of him, holding hands, for a split second he's transported to the Garden of Eden, all he sees before him is forbidden fruit.

"What was you expecting - Bats, vampires, coffins?" Jenny asks him. "You know it's because of Keith and his occult that people get the wrong idea about us girls," Jenny tells him.

"Yeah, its just me who dresses up in the gear" Keith tells Matt, "I've got a coffin too"

"Great" Matt replies, now starting to feel a bit scared. Joni Mitchell plays on the stereo.

"You was expecting gothic darkness, 'The Cure', something suicidal, the soundtrack to 'The Lost Boys' " Jenny replies.

"You read my mind" Matt meets his eyes onto her body again, she looked great, he wanted to fuck her there and then on the dinner table.

"I can read everything you're thinking" Jenny smiles and Matt embarrassingly looks away.

He sits himself on the sofa next to Clem and wonders why he's in his underpants. "What happened to your trousers? Did you spill something on them?"

"No." Clem replies.

They sit at the banquet table like high court kings and queens, of ancient times. Two Eves, one vampire, one train driver and a retro Jesus Christ. The last supper. 'Lets play a game'- Liana links to Jenny. 'Trust me. It will be fun. What's the point in being twins if we can't use our link in situations like these?' - Liana looks at Jenny and then into her thoughts towards Matt.

'I wish you wouldn't do this?' - Jenny links in their silence. 'To late, I've got your thoughts'. - "So, Matt, do you have a girlfriend?" Liana asks him.

Matt drinks from his glass of wine. "No"

"No-one special?"

"There was someone but" he thinks of Carla, and then immediately blocks his mind from her, now wasn't the time. "It could never have worked"

"Do you like fucking on kitchen tables?" Liana asks Matt, then smiles towards Jenny, knowing its Jenny's favourite place to fuck.

"Jesus Christ!" Matt says and coughs some food, downing his glass of wine and refilling it.

"Answer the ladies question Matt, its rude not to" Clem states scratching his bare thigh, convinced he has been bitten by a flea.

"I've never really thought about it" He downs his glass of wine again and refills it.

"Would you if the opportunity arose?"

"With the right person, of course, yeah" Matt says finally relaxing, just go with it, the wine was going with it for him, the more he'd drink, the more he'd unwind, but he was worried of ruining it with Jenny if he had too much drink, he always acted a twat when drunk towards the women he liked.

"What have you been doing for Halloween then Matt?" Keith Reynolds asks, one of his fake fangs drops into the sweet dish.

Matt motions with his fingers to his teeth. Keith thinks he has got something caught and then Matt finally points towards the sweet dish. "Your fangs dropped in there".

"Answer Keith's question Matt, it would be rude not too," Clem says still scratching where he has been bitten.

"I don't celebrate it really"

"Why not?" Jenny asks like the inquisitive first date question, learning forward interested.

"Not since I watched 'Halloween Three', it really freaked me out"

"Is that the one with the TV show?"

"Yeah, that's right, six more days to Halloween, Halloween, Halloween, six more days to Halloween..."

"Then the snakes comes out of the kids heads?"

"Yeah that was the one" Matt drinks from his wine glass and fills it up again.

"Perhaps we should get the occult to watch it?" Keith mentions.

"Johnny told me your occult was an excuse to shag women." Matt replies.

"Johnny doesn't believe"

"So are you all vampires then?"

"Keith met a real vampire one time and ran away to Clem's room" Jenny replies, her and Matt laugh together.

"We're twins, can you tell?" Liana asks Matt.

"I can tell you're sisters" he looks at both their naked bodies, keeps his stare now his confidence is higher cause of the drink, doesn't matter if he blows it with Jenny, he has got food and wine here, he can be Henry VIII for Halloween night. "But you're not identical"

'He's drunk'- Liana links to Jenny. 'I know' – she replies.

"Close your eyes, I want to try an experiment," Liana suggests. Matt closes his eyes; as long as the wine was still in his glass when he opened them he didn't mind. "One of us is going to kiss you and you've got to guess which one it was"

"Ok" Matt says trying to act cool but the wine was talking and it can out smarmy, he has blown it already he thinks. Both Jenny and Liana lean over Matt, his eyes closed. As Liana moves her lips towards him, Jenny pictures herself kissing him. Soft, gentle, the promise of something more to their relationship, not just one night for them both. As their lips meet, Jenny feels herself as Liana, and feels the response she wanted back. "Jenny" Matt says softly, almost embarrassed by the quietness in his voice, like a kid asked whom he fancies most in class. He felt the same gentle touch on his lips he had felt on his cheek when Jenny greeted him hello. Matt opens his eyes and both Jenny and Liana are seated back at the respective parts of the table. Keith and Clem are laughing. "It was Jenny" Matt says to them convinced.

"It was me" Liana replies.

The five of them sit in a circle on the living room floor. Liana sits centre of the circle, a white sheet over her body, like a ghost ready to go out for mischief. "Every Halloween night, the spirits walk amongst us, it is their celebration of death"

Matt starts to turn pale. "I'm not doing a board, ok. I'm walking out if we do one" He didn't even know how he got talked into sitting on the floor in a circle in the first place. Then he has his reminders around him; the wine, the josh sticks hypnotising and relaxing his every chain of thought and of course Jenny, all but naked, sat next to him. He really wanted to be alone with her but he was so far gone through the events of the night that he'd pass out.

"We're not stupid, we'd never do one of those" Jenny assures Matt.

"No, we're just going to contact the dead" Clem continues, sat in his white underpants so his pride and joy was for all to see, his woolly jumper off as well, his train jacket remaining on.

Matt just stares forward, he doesn't want to look a coward in front of Jenny, but he doesn't want to leave either, a part of him intrigued to find an inclining of afterlife even if it cursed him eternally, he figured he couldn't be more cursed than the streets of memories he's forced to walk each day in the windy city.

"Join hands" Liana closes her eyes.

Matt links his hands with Jenny and Clem. He grips her hand tight. "Don't worry" he hears her say, his eyes shut.

"I feel such a prat" he replies, but then he realises his mouth hadn't moved and through a squint of his eyes he sees Jenny's mouth is shut as well.

'I wont let anything happen to you' she tells him without speaking, 'close your eyes'

Matt automatically closes his eyes, not sure if they entered the forbidden world already, how did he and Jenny do that? He squints his eyes open again, the glass of wine is full, and he wishes he could down it.

"They usually want to catch up with what's happening in the soaps," Clem whispers.

"Silence." Liana shouts. "Spirits of the night of celebration in your world, use me as your guide to speak"

Matt cant help but sneak his eyes open, and looks towards Liana, he wants to laugh as he sees her shake where she sits, watching her

Part 5: Moving On

head roll side to side, then her eyes shoot open.

"Who do you have a message for?" Liana speaks. Her eyes look around the room and she settles on Matt. "He wishes to speak to you Matt"

Matt swallows. "Can I have a glass of wine first?"

"You must not break the circle" She begins to shake again; her eyes shoot open as before. "He wants you to know that he's trying to get to heaven before they close the door"

"Who is it Liana?" Keith asks.

"He wanted to tell Matt as only him and the woman Clarissa know the truth"

"Who is it? Do they have glasses? What colour hair?" Clem asks like a game of 'Guess Who'.

"James"

Matt breaks hands with the circle, he stands up, kneeling back down to pick up the wine glass, downs it, leaving it on the dining table, as he reaches the door. The rest of the circle opens their eyes fully, like it's the first shade of sunlight through the curtains and it will burn them like vampires.

Jenny catches Matt at the door. "Sorry, it was just a bit of fun, we always do it on Halloween"

"Its ok, if I don't go now I'll never get home, that's all" he says trying to cover up the fact he is scared shitless at what just happened.

Jenny reads his thoughts. "Some first date hey?" She says.

"It was a date?" She leans in and kisses him on the lips; they hold the kiss together for a number of seconds. "It was you I kissed, I knew it was," he says.

"Yeah, it was me" she says.

As the door shuts, Liana remains seated on the carpet and links over to Jenny. - 'You really like each other don't you?'

'Yeah'

'What you going to do?'

'Nothing.'

'Why?'

'Doesn't make sense?'

'I think nothing rarely does for him'

THE DETECTIVE

Johnny sits on Simon's bed, both of them bored with the windy city and its final year of offerings. They look out the window and see the early November sky begin to set alight. Tonight was fireworks night and the city was erupting in loud explosions. It brought the city alive, away from the emptiness they had felt up to this point since they came back. "We should do something?" Johnny says, watching the fireworks explode and create a wheel of fascination.

"We're responsible members of the work place now" Simon replies. They both had jobs to stay in the city with the others, but he was beginning to think for what reason, they never did anything anymore, just sat and counted down the days.

"We need to put one day aside to relive old acid memories" Johnny says pulling out a bagful of acid he'd scored of Blonde Paul earlier in the week. "Here's some I prepared earlier." He loved watching the fireworks on acid each year. "The sabbatical is over, let's party"

They had been relatively clean for two months, so Simon reasons - "Let's do three each".

"What are you doing?" They ask Matt, stepping into his room.

"Writing the ultimate Detective story. 'Lacen's theory' that the Private Detective in Film Noirs is in fact detecting himself and is digging his own grave, a black hole he has to detect that is his personality and who he really is. It is this black hole that all private detectives eventually find and bury themselves in, the embodiment of their own personality. Arthur Fowler in Eastenders recently, he made his way up to that great allotment in the sky, but that's the point of Lacen's theory, he was in fact was digging his own grave throughout those final months, prison for a flowering wilderness campaign, digging the allotment as he died. Arthur Fowler is the embodiment of Lacen's theory. " He tells a startled Johnny and Simon.

"I don't know about Arthur Fowler, but we've got something to help you" And Johnny pulls out the bag of pills. "Its fireworks tonight"

Matt looks at the bag, he'd been good these last two months. In fact for the first time in these two years he had everything in the excess department under control. He knew when to stop, when to take. He even enjoyed the lesson earlier today on the course. His guilt to forget Alex, James, even Carla, seemed less every day by

Part 5: Moving On

staying away from the excess that brought them on in the first place. He wanted to see Jenny, not just see her but go out somewhere with her, yeah she lived a pretty weird existence in that flat with her sister but he could picture going to the cinema with her, going for walks in town, Christmas shopping, waiting for her after her lectures, a lifetime together in the final year.

"'The Singing Detective' was all about being off your face" Johnny motions with the pills.

"Old times sake" Simon says.

Then again he'd still be in control, one last time just to prove it, a sort of test, a celebration to his new life with his old life. If he was writing about a detective who was on acid, he needs to get inside the mind of his protagonist surely? He takes a single pill from Johnny. "A writer should experience what he writes"

Johnny's Acid Trip

Seaside resorts in November are great places to go. I stand in the tar pulling over the kid's roundabout. "Hi Johnny" Voices come from inside the tar pulling and I begin to push the roundabout round. It flaps about in the bleak sleety weather. "Why don't you let us see you Johnny?" The voices continue. I recognise them as all the girls I've had sex with. All the one night stands. "Come out then" I reply.

The clouds disappear and the sun comes out. As the girls show themselves under the tar pulling. All of them naked from the waste up. Big breasts. I'm in heaven. Perhaps the trip isn't that bad after all. "We've got something to show you Johnny" I can't wait.

The dark clouds come back from the horizon and the playground darkens. The hard rain begins to fall and the ground is driven in sleet. Each drop hurts my face. The girls are now naked from their feet up to their waist. I never wore any protection with any of these girls. As I look closer to their private regions they are deformed. "Oh my god" I say and begin to cough I can feel the sick hang in my throat hand over my mouth.

"What would happen if you had Aids Johnny?"

I throw up over the tar pulling. The girls have gone. I now sit alone on the empty roundabout. Hidden underneath the tar pulling... spinning round. Watching the sleet fall over the bleak playground.

The disused fair ground ride is across from me. I sit on the ride. My Dad is next to me. "I've got a present for you son" And he passes me over a black sheep.

I'm at the top of the ride now. "I can't get down," I shout towards my Dad but he is walking away.

"See you son"

The rain and sleet fall across my face. From here I can view every part of my life. Every city I've lived in. Every house I've deserted. Every girl I've had relations with. The wind hits up a great gusto. And I'm back in the windy city. Riding on the explosion of the fireworks. First thing tomorrow I'm going to the doctors…I know I'm ok but I just need to hear it said.

Simon's Acid Trip

I'm in a white room sitting down at a table in the centre. I have a glass of white lighting and a joint. My parents walk in. I try and hide the evidence but the room is as empty as my guilt I bare. "We want are money back Simon?" They demand.

"And not just us - The grant authorities, the student loans." They continue. "The entire world debt," they finish with.

Money begins to fall from the air, I try and catch it but it evaporates in my palm. "I'm sorry, I'm sorry," I mumble in a drunken slur.

My parents pick up the white lighting. "This stuff will kill you, rot your guts"

The mad Irish tramp sits beside me and winks. "Alright son"

My parents take the joint from my mouth. "Getting stoned all day?" A giant projection screen shows me getting stoned in a room, with the clock ticking over an entire twenty-four hour day and I hadn't moved. "What was the point of going to university?" they demand.

"There wasn't, I've wasted three years," I finally admit to them putting the white lighting to my lips.

"Do you actually want to do anything with your life?" they ask me.

"I want to get wasted" I reply, puffing on the joint. "It's the only thing I'm good at"

At the back of the white room, midgets with fireworks appear. "What are you looking at?" My parents ask me, ready for a fight.

"Midgets with fireworks" I reply.

As I look up at my parents my mum is dressed as a clown, my dad is a magician. "Pick a card son?" I take the centre card; it has a picture of me with the words… - 'I've got to get the fuck out of this town' my mum honks her horn and throws a pie into my dads face.

Part 5: Moving On

The midgets let the fireworks explode...

Matthew's Acid Trip

Now I'm in a dark gutter, a tunnel, water on the floor, a sewer. The smell of death and damp around my feet. There's a light at the end of the tunnel. I'm running down that tunnel. Pick up the mirror to see my reflection. Make sure I'm in my room. Not in that tunnel. Make sure there are no rats on my face chewing away like a cable wire. There's that spot. Don't pick it, makes it worse. It's like I've got a mole growing on the side of my chin. I haven't wet shaved for three years but I take some razors from Steve's room and shave over the spot. Opening the cut up, the spot out, it's a big red lump now. The tunnel is back inside the spot. I look in the mirror again. Ugly big spot, ugly big hair, ugly red face. Jesus Christ I need to find the light at the end of that tunnel. Keep on my running. That spot follows my every gaze in the mirror, waving to me.

There's a shadow blocking the light in the tunnel. Rats run round my feet. I can smell fear. "Alright Matt" the shadow says. It steps into the light. It's James.

"James, get out my way, I'm going to die unless I get out of this tunnel" I feel inside out. There's a fly around my head that keeps buzzing. James says nothing, he just keeps smiling at me, a big red stain on his shirt, his liver starts to fall out. A lizard dressed in king's clothes sits on the tunnels rooftop tail. There's a flash of a photograph light. James passes me over the picture. It's me in my room holding a mirror to my face. The mirror reflects the tunnel we both stand in. A picture within a frame. I'm running. I'm running.

My eyes blur across blue suburban skies. Next to me is Carla; I hold her hand, as I don't trust what's around me. Rain falls from the sky like tears. She has gone and I am crying from the heavens, tears leaving me strange. I thought I heard a fly, smiling pushing me out.

Alex stands in front of me, dancing to that imaginary music in his head. He has eggs in his basket that don't break when cracked. "How come you guys never come to see me?" he asks me.

"Didn't think you'd want to see us?"

"I'm still in Southampton, still on the same course as you"

"I prefer to keep a low profile"

"Scared your friends will stab you in the back?" I feel a sharp pain in my back and a knife drops to the floor. "Love thy neighbour when the room is smacked" Alex tells me before cleaning his knife then leaving. That apple hits my eye, thrown by that fly. Thought I head a fly, smiling pushing me out

Eyes closed.... Made the light at the end of the tunnel...never again...

"That's what they all say" a voice comes from the end of my bed. I'm afraid to look. I thought it was over. I thought I'd come down, hit my face on the pavement and be cut for days. "I think I've got a right to be here, don't you?" the voice continues. I don't recognise this voice, it's like a fake Irish American accent. I can smell cigarette smoke in the room, filling the air, destroying my lungs. "After all you created me," the voice continues. One eye opens and I make out the figure of a man sitting on the end of the bed. He stands up and steps out of my sight, forcing me to open the other eye. He wears a seventies flared blue shirt, a suede seventies jacket, floppy hair like Lennon, glasses like the man, his shadow is bent over, beaten. It is him - my Detective in the script - Jacob Angel.

"Why are you here?" I ask him.

"Because I am what you write"

"I can't write at the moment, I'm too tired, I'm trying to sleep"

"Each time you stop, you leave me alone and isolated"

"So? That's your character"

"I don't like being alone"

"You're a detective, its part of the genre"

"Fuck the genre. I want to be happy"

"It wouldn't sell," I tell him.

"You should see it round here" He continues his torment. "They're all here, Bogart, Chandelier, that singing guy"

"All in my room?"

"Yeah, though this isn't your room its Detective purgatory"

"How long have you guys been here?"

"Since you started writing, we can't leave until you finish the script"

"That could be years"

"Well you better get you used to it kid"

"Its just the acid talking"

"I'm as a real as the words you write. Guess I'm like the ghost of Detective past, present and future"

"What are you going to show me?"

"Nothing. The detective is always the last one to know anything, that's rule number one kid"

"Will you stop calling me kid!"

Part 5: Moving On

"You haven't given me any traits yet, I've got to have some kind of word I repeat"

"Let me sleep"

"You should count yourself lucky, your pals who you did the acid with, they got the ghosts of acid past, present and future and I can tell you, that is one nasty trip to take" He walks round the room and studies himself in the mirror for a number of minutes. "All I want to know kid is what happens at the end?"

"You end up in a mental asylum and fall into Pandora's Box"

"Don't I find the girl?"

"Yeah but she dies."

"No redemption"

"Pandora's box is your redemption"

"So I end up in a mental asylum?"

"Basically, yeah"

"Fuck that, I'm outta here" And he disappears.

My eyes open again... I'm alone in my room. My senses of hearing, sight and smell have returned to as normal as they can be after three years of this. The union jack duvet wrapped tight as a coffin round my shivering body.

If only I had Patsy next to me I too could be on the cover of Cool Britannia. The windows rattle with the wind and the continued firework explosions in celebration for another day we don't truly understand the meaning of. As the fireworks explode the colours reflect through my curtains and onto my walls. The posters of my idols, the pioneers of our decades stare back at me. "Not spelt Britpop But spelt Excess"

I can smell the revolution coming to its drawn out end.

BLAIR IN MAGNUMS

Steve

We stand outside Kaos nightclub after another night of 'true chaos'. The streets are freezing, badly lit, street lamps smashed in with the force of nature. The storm has brought a new breed of animal this year and its known as emptiness. Freezing below zero until leaving time approaches and the adult world comes knocking. "Will you come in with us?" I ask Matt and Johnny, they both look at each other unsure. No doubt thinking if the other does then they both will, then I can introduce to them a whole new world. They're both drunk enough to do it.

"Lets do it, pick up some blokes and have gay sex," Johnny says like it's that easy.

"You'll go down well with that attitude in there Johnny, be the queen of the ball" I reply.

"All three of us on the pull then?" I ask sarcastically but secretly hoping they say yes, and reveal their true identities. All guys are gay; they just need to be shown the way. I've tried for years to get anyone of my male friends to come into Magnums with me. They all say they will when they're drunk - "just to experience it" - that's how it starts. Then they all chicken out as the heat of their sexuality gets nearer the door. Step into the flames boys.

"Steve, I'm not going to pull some blokes, I just want to see what this kind of club is like" Matt gives out the typical A-Z hetro-sexual answer. Trying to prove his manhood whilst still being pc enough to get in touch with his feminine side, Magnums is full of these guys.

"Full of drag queens and really over the top gays isn't Steve, hey?" Johnny asks intrigued. I can tell he'll be disappointed if it doesn't have the 'over the top' ballroom drag artists. Another drug to add to his experiences. "The minute they look at you, they'll be eyeing up your arse, seeing if the hole fits!" Johnny jokes in his one-dimensional view of gay clubs. It's just a way of dealing with his true fears and desires. Trust me I know, I've been there.

"I'm going to turn back" Matt says, he keeps turning round, looking at Jenny O'Sullivan outside Kaos.

"It's not like that at all, just a normal club" I try to ease their fears before entrapping them in a lifetime of denial. "There's loads of straight couples and singles who go there" I don't tell them this is the worse aspect, the pc middle class student couples, wanting to experiment like Jarvis had told them. "Its really relaxing" Is my final selling line. Especially when you're passed the anneal nitrate and all your bones and muscles lose gravity for a number of minutes.

We reach their introduction into a new world – MAGNUMS. Situated round the back of Kaos nightclub, in between the garbage throw out and the street corner like a lady of the night walking the parade in the hope of picking a prince. I can smell the taste of too much perfume, too much garbage, mixed as a cocktail the most dangerous drug.

"Is Tom Selleck in?" Johnny asks the bouncers.

They don't look impressed. "That's original" I think they know these two aren't regulars and are coming to take the piss in a drunken state of oblivion denial. "Not tonight lads" the bouncer says and looks at me with a smile, meaning, get rid of your two mates and you can come in no problem, Steve.

"Why not? Are you homophobic?" Matt as ever goes looking for a fight.

"Yeah, we're as gay as the next man" Johnny then realises what he says and tries to back track. "Not that we're gay"

I take matters into my hands, hopefully it wont be the only thing in my hands tonight. I corner my two unwitting a-compliances and whisper my fire towards them. "They're not going to let us in." All guys are gay; they just need to be shown the path.

Back up to the door of Magnums. Alone. Its so cold out I'm shivering in my tight tank top and jeans. Didn't see the point in taking a jacket, I'll only take it off the minute I'm inside the heat. The bouncers let me in immediately being a regular at this time of night, 1.30am. "Alright" I say. "Got a light?" I test the waters with a dirty roll up I scrounged of Simon.

"All right Steve" they reply. I reckon they're gay.

They light the roll up for me, it burns into two immediately, looking like a deranged sculpture of a tree. "I'm giving up anyway"

The lights of red and blue erotica flash across the hall entrance as the old drag queen waits behind the counter to pass me a ticket. "Alright Alan?" I ask her, him. It has my dad's name.

"That's five pound Steve" the old queen replies not even looking at me.

"Five pound? Its nearly the end of the night, cant you let me in for free?" I worm my way into the drag queens affections, showing enough toothy smile and flirtation to get in for nothing.

"Terry, Steve wants to get in for free again" he, I mean she, it, shouts to the head doormen.

Terry steps from the door towards me, casting a shadow that makes the lights disappear and my own soul cast no shadow. "Pay or get out Steve"

Inside are the usual crowd. The typical queens that I cant stand, giving gays a bad name, dragged up the arse, made up like Lilly Savage. Then there's the over the top 'touchy' female guys, not made up in drag but obvious queens by the tight tops, the eye linear, and the way they walk, all with a fag hag in tow, I should have brought Lauren with me. I play the 'moody' closet gay, the guy who looks straight, and stands up at the bar, having a drink and rolling cigarettes, a wild west gay in a spaghetti western. The lights hit across me by the bar, reflecting my image like an idyllic angel across the roving eyes who want... The club is on one level and the bar I stand at in my created western saloon, stands at the start of the ballroom of ballerina's on the dance floor. The tables across the other end to get to you must cross the forbidden zone of the dance floor, where you come entrapped in a battle of wits to score. First to hit on me is Dean, or Dame, as he likes to be called. I met him a month ago, he's studying hair and make-up and he has promised to do this for the 16mm film I'm making, but I have to go out with him in return. Shivers went down my spine. I'll be choosing a very quiet, dark area, maybe Southampton Common. "Steve" he screams, big blue massacre and red lips, real Boy George look. He hugs me a big hello, in tow with his fag hag, Big Amanda.

"Hi Steve" Big Amanda says to me in her squeamish high voice.

"Alright, its busy in here tonight" I reply looking across the packed meat market floor, one table in particular has become centre stage, there's as many round it as on the dance floor.

"We've got a special guest," he grabs my hand and leads me towards a table where sitting at the head surrounded by twenty guys is 'that' TV personality from 'that' game show. I wish he'd have given me a clue; I'd have dressed for the occasion. This could be my big break into the TV and film world, by becoming Blair Larry's boy. And so the man from the decades Game Show and Royal Performances holds court. We as the court jester's hold onto his every word, laugh where appropriate, smile and look amazed at his showbiz stories and the truth behind his marriage and kids. "I like to swing, ever since the sixties!" he proclaims arms out stretched like a pantomime villain.

"What about your marriage, darling?" Dame, I mean, Dean, asks.

"She's my best friend, my fag hag" Blair replies.

"I know what you mean, I often think about going out with my fag hag" I tell the crowd thinking of the dreams I keep having where I'm fucking Lauren. "Just for show of course"

"I wanted kids. And you can't have kids as a gay couple"

"Not even adopt? Surely with your celebrity..." I ask.

"I'm a game show host not an MP" He replies.

"You mean there's MPs who are gay?"

"Why do you think they call it the shadow cabinet... Time to

Part 5: Moving On

dance" he then stands up. We all follow our gaze upwards wondering which one of us he's going to pick, me, me, me.... "Come on guys, let's form a circle and I'll pick" And like the pipe piper, we follow him onto the dance floor.

In the neon wilderness he looks good for his sixty years, dressed in his frilly white shirt, theatre jacket, and jeans. "I keep in shape," he tells us.

"You go to a gym?" we ask him.

"I have one in my house," he replies slapping his own bottom. Twenty guys dancing in a circle round Blair Larry, as he dances in the middle. One by one, he picks out guys from the circle to dance with him for a minute. He points his hand towards the next victim and sings - "Now you!" And they go into the centre of the circle and dance with him. Then he pushes the guy to one side. "Speak to the hand cause the face don't want to know" And points to his next special guest on the game show of his private life - "Now you!"

I'm getting nervous it will be my turn soon. I start dancing the best I've ever danced, real gyrating, Bruce Lee karate moves; enter the dragon as to enter my arse. There's no way he'll push me away. "Now you!" he points towards me. I sway my head side to side, a roll up in one hand, and a bottle of lager in the other. I dance like Damon Albern, hoping he can see the resemblance. I'm cooking, thoughts run through my head the Sun tabloids in a years time when I'm famous - 'The night I danced to win Blair Larry's heart' - 'It was the opening I was looking for and an opening he wanted that night' - 'I danced Blair into the west end'

Thoughts swell round my mind. I drink from the bottle of lager erotically to give Blair a hint of what I'm prepared to do with my mouth if required.

"Now you!"

WHAT? WHAT? He stopped me. His palm up in my face, and the next guy, bloody Dean, I mean Dame, is on the floor with him, he's even holding Dame's waist and dancing up against him. Fucking queers, I hate them.

Back up at the bar and I'm talking with Ed, who I've had the occasional sex with back at his house. And of course, like my shadow, next to me at the bar is Dan Not The Man. "He danced with me the longest," I tell Ed, sure hope he takes me home tonight; I'm so disappointed that Blair Larry turned me down.

"I'll dance with you Steve," Dan Not the Man interrupts the conversation. I just ignore him and turn my back on the poor guy, chubby, spotty, in his Southampton top, which says Le God. Can't believe I let him suck my cock in the toilets here last month, I was depressed though. I'm sure some of his spot puss came off on my dick.

"So what's the plan for tonight then Ed?" I ask lover boy.

"I'm going to have a shot at Blair, no offence Steve" and he runs off like a big girl towards the high court table of the round heads where Blair is king.

"I'll take you home Steve," Dan Not The Man says. I then run off like a big girl towards the high court table of the round heads to hang onto Blair's every word and touch of velvet skin. Only the rich have that texture. It can't be bottled.

Blair's party of roundheads, led by Dame, convene in the early hours in Blair's Hotel room after Magnums closes to relinquish its shadows of sexual deceit. It is December 1st this morning. "It's a celebration," Blair tells us as he opens the door to the Hotel room.

"What's the event?" We ask

"Life!" he replies arms outstretched conducting the orchestra of Gods.

What greets us is something out of a sixties advent garde pop flick. Hundreds of people gathered in what must be the biggest Hotel suite ever seen.

Midgets are walking round with bowls of cocaine and fireworks. "How very Freddie," Dame comments.

"It was all a lie, you know?" Blair tells us.

"The midget story?"

"There where no midgets with cocaine bowls. Just midgets. The cocaine bowls where already supplied in each room," He continues with his A-List gossip.

"What's with the fireworks?"

"I like my parties to go with a bang"

Fellow C-list celebrities from theatre, film and music nod their heads in acknowledgment to the guest of honour and his followers, as we set foot inside. "Isn't that the girl from that daytime soap?" My eyes celebratory spotting, stalker in the making.

"Yes, strictly C-List celebs here." Blair replies with a rich mans pride.

"Don't you know any A-List?"

"Of course but its not pc to have them at a party. C-list is the new A," he informs us.

"What about B?" I ask confused.

"What about it?" He replies in disgust like I've just spunked on his face.

The lady who is famous for being in magazines for doing nothing but going to such celebrations, being photographed with a nipple showing, stands on top of a glass table. "Not enough people are looking at me," she shouts.

The crowd round the table are cutting snow powders. "Get down you'll ruin the cut"

She strips off to her underwear. "How about now? All look at me now!"

"Cool a D-list strip show on the dry powder," the guys snort. And she begins to do her exercises on the glass table, her heels cutting into the fibre and kicking the powder. "What are you doing you crazy bitch?"

"I'm doing my exercises"

"The entertainment is here?" the guy taking the bowl of the midget proclaims pointing towards us, he is seated directly below the 'crazy' lady photographed 'twit' girl, so he can see right up her crack.

"Entertainment?" I ask Blair.

"You didn't think you was here cause I invited you did you?"

"What do we have to do?"

"Dance." And so the round heads, led by Dame in centre stage of the room, begin to dance. Somehow we work as a unit. All ten of us boy band material in our moves. Suggestions with bottles. "Strip" they all shout. Taken over by the adrenalin of an adoring public and Blair's advances, forever the showman I take centre stage away from Dame and begin my strip. Humiliation. Fascination. Both worlds collide in my soul as my body moves. I am a piece of meat to be looked and whistled at. "Bravo" they all clap at the end, as we stand in our naked corpses. Humiliation. Nothingness. Bare my naked soul to the masses who move onto the next slice of action. I am a male prostitute to adulation and humiliation. Both walk hand in hand across the gravy train of fame.

"What about me? Watch me" the 'twit' girl on the glass table starts to take her bra and underpants off and stands in all her skinny, bony, anorexic nakedness, beauty and the beast.

"You're so last year," the guy with the cocaine bowl says. "Another order of the finest dry cut please," and he places the bowl for the midget to take. "Oh, and leave me a firework"

"What happens now?" I ask Blair.
"You're finished"
"Do we just leave?"
"You're welcome to have a Jacuzzi"

Myself, Ed, Dame and my shadow, Dan Not the Man remain. Sitting in a hot bubbly Jacuzzi, like sportsmen after a hard day of trial and tribulations on the field, with midgets filling champagne glasses and private fireworks going off in the tub. Blair Larry steps out, in his naked glory. Well, I say glory; in this dark blue light he is trying to hide his wrinkled body. You can always tell how old a man is by his arse and his sags down to his thighs. I have to look away. The future is not bright. It is not orange.

"Do you know the right honourable Ronald?" Blair asks.

Out of the political wilderness stands a former shadow cabinet minister - Grey balding scalp, sullen whiskey eyes, saggy chest and stomach. The world of political suicide. "Hello, boys" Ronald steps into the pool and immediately sets his eyes on my aspiring political aspirations. "Who are you going to vote for?"

"Tony Blair, New Labour is going to change this world" I reply with pride.

"You don't fall for that youth bollocks do you?" He asks back in a condescending voice.

"He's one of us, one of the people" I reply.

"Stand disillusioned like a puppet on a string and watch his followers all sing" He replies.

"Very profound, who said it?" I ask him in my best Dylan Thomas voice.

"I did, just then. You learn a lot of poetry being the constituent of a wasted city"

A man comes out of the shadows holding a camera. "The entertainment boys" Blair commences with his hands and claps.

"Don't be shy in your performance" Ronald says to me.

"Why are we being filmed?" I ask.

"Just some home video entertainment, why else would I have wanted you all to stay?" Blair reasons for the second time tonight, and here was I thinking he wanted to be friends with me. The smell of rich breeding power breathes through the room as they begin their quests as kings to each throne with servants to their every needs. Rome wasn't built in a day and neither will my career be. Dame gets into the swing of things with Blair, there's no accounting for taste even if you are a game show host. Leaving Ed, Dan not the

Part 5: Moving On

Man and myself, to the tastes of Ronald. "What do you say then boys? Wish to sample the constituency?" He opens his arms wide for all of us to sample. Some things not even fame will buy a price for.

I had originally walked with Dan Not The Man back to his house. I contemplated being desperate enough to sleep with him. He held that stupid grin he had on his face as he held his hand out and grabbed mine. A COUPLE! I immediately threw up on the pavement. "Its alright Steve, I like the taste of sick" he tells me. I punch him the face and run away. He follows me down the road, gently jogging, "I love you!"

Back home, locked all the front doors. I can see his shadow up at the window. Up at the door. I've got to tell someone about this night. Lie about Blair Larry and say he invited me back and that I shagged him for fame. The truth is I left immediately when Ronald propositioned me, my shadow followed me out the bathtub; I was to ill to look at the remnants of hostility in the cameraman's lens.

I walk upstairs banging loudly, so it will wake some people up. I can hear laughter in Matt's room, so I knock on the door, there is a shushing and then - "Yeah?"

"It's Steve, can I come in?" There is a long pause, so I just step in Matt is lying in bed. "You wont believe who I just met in Magnums?" I go to sit on the bed and Matt almost turns white.

"Steve don't sit on the bed!" he shouts at me. "Its not that you're gay or anything, its just that I cleaned the sheets the other day and I don't want your dirty alcohol stained arse on my bed. Sit on the chair!" He screams at me, some people have no idea of people's feelings, it hurts man, it hurts. I ignore him and sit on the bed, but there seems to be a big lump under the sheets, must be his dressing gown and his foot kicks out at me. Must have a long foot, I never realised he was so tall. "Steve! Sit on the chair!" he shouts at me.

I finally sit on the chair and begin to roll a tobacco smoke. "Have a guess who was in Magnums tonight?"

"Tom Selleck?"

"No! I'll give you a clue... Game Show host"

"Bloody hell, not Michael Aspel!"

"Blair Larry"

"But he's married with kids?"

"Like I said, everyone is gay"

"Jesus, how long have I got until I turn?"

"I think you'll be alright Matt"

"Thank fuck for that. I just can't get over the whole physical aspect, having a dick shoved up your arse or wanting to shove a dick up some guys hairy arse and sucking cock, its not right"

"Thank you for your homophobic views Matt, they shall be noted."

"So what happened with Blair, did you suck his cock?"

"Nearly. He got everyone to dance with him in a massive circle."

Matt starts to laugh and there is another giggle, but I guess it must be coming from the TV. "It was like this" I get up from the chair and start to dance in Matt's bedroom, pretending to be Blair Larry, "Now you!" and I point my hand, "Now you!" and I move in a circle. "We each had a turn to impress him"

"And did you impress him?"

"Of course, he danced with me the longest and brought me a drink"

"So, what are you doing back here? Why aren't you in a hot Jacuzzis with the rest of the queens having a soap bath playing give us a clue"

"I was. We went back to his hotel room."

"What happened?"

"There where midgets with bowls of cocaine and fireworks"

"What happened?"

"Loads of celebrities there, like that girl from the magazines"

"The 'twit' girl?"

"Yeah, she was naked on a glass table full of cocaine doing her exercises"

"So what are you doing back here then? Why aren't you loving it up with Z-list celebrities sucking Blair Larry's cock?"

"I'm not like that, its fake. I'm going to make my money my way, not have to suck a has been cock, my talent will show through"

Matt just stares at me. "So he turned you down?" he finally says.

"Yeah" I reply dejected.

"If you've got no more dirt on Blair Larry I really need to go to sleep," he turns the TV off. "Night Steve" he says in the darkness. This is my motion to leave the room. I sit on the chair in silence picturing being in a hot bath with just Blair... After a few minutes... "Night Steve!"

I remain sitting on the chair for another ten minutes. Then I finally stumble in the dark and open the door. "Night Math Boy!"

Part 5: Moving On

I say to piss him off, as that's what his dad calls him. We hate our dads; we've actually made a deal, like strangers on a train, to kill them. As I shut the door, I hear some giggling again and I wonder where that came from. I look through the keyhole and I can make out someone that looks like Jenny O'Sullivan coming up from under the duvet. I open the door without knocking and search for the light switch, finally turning the light on. "Alright!" I say.

Matt is lying in his bed, a bulge in the duvet he just threw over, where Jenny O'Sullivan is hiding no doubt. "Turn the fucking light off!" Matt shouts. I walk over to the bed and pull back that part of the duvet, and there is...Matt's dressing gown. "Fucking queer!" Matt says.

I walk backwards, feeling embarrassed and turn the light off and shut the door. The giggling starts again and I can see what looks like Jenny O'Sullivan through the keyhole, coming up from under the bed.

'Merry Xmas everybody...'

Matthew

It's different being back home this last time. If I know where I'm going I don't know from where I came. When I come back in the summer that will be it, for good, until I decide on my next move. No education, there's nothing more left to escape into, no letters to add after a name that everybody seems to know but me.

Reflecting on the last two and a half years, I sit in my room, sober and not stoned. My Mum can tell the difference, she said she knew that I was doing a lot of drugs the previous years I came back. "Why didn't you say anything?" I asked her

"This was a path put before you alone" she tells me like a melodrama with Joan Crawford. She then pauses and a look into my eyes to see if a semblance of humanity has returned.

I have kind of stopped, not by any stretch of the imagination, but I do feel grown up, more mature. It's dawning on me that there's only six months left and then all I've known for three years will disappear and there's no going back. I look around Southampton now and see all the wide-eyed first years and see myself as I once was, but for the first time, I don't want to recapture that, I just... I don't honestly know it's time to look to the future. What do I really want to do? I'm twenty-two years old, going on thirty.

My friends from back in Hells Kitchen invite me out on

Christmas Eve. I go out with them, despite saying last year that I'd never come back again. Is this my future? The city of London is paved with gold I hear, maybe that's where the future waits for me. I'm bored on this Christmas Eve. I don't belong here. I don't belong in Southampton Am I grown up now? Is this what it is. Not belonging? Every addiction is a lonely one. My friends phone on New Years Eve. I make up stories that I've already got plans and going back to Southampton. Instead I lay down on my bed with a couple of cans and drink alone in my bedroom in my parent's house. I make a list of what I want to do. Where I want to be. All for this time next year…

1.

…. Can't think of anything.

Sometimes you wake up and you're going to have a day that will become a journey into your life. You don't plan it, you don't want it, but you can't stop yourself from fitting a lifetime into a day. "Where are you going?" My Mum asked. I had automatically got up, dressed, shaved, and even tired my hair back in a ponytail so I looked a little respectable. "Do you have a job interview?"

"I just want to get some fresh air" I replied and that is all that was on my mind. Air. Fresh. I walked with my head down to the ground, kicking at damp fallen leafs across the pavement, the naked woman of my dreams could have walked past in all her glory and I wouldn't have noticed such was my self-absorbed state. Like how this journey had started nearly three years ago, I had automatically wound up outside my old school gates. I hated school. I listen for the voices, the ghosts of my past to come and haunt my memories. Someone's in the playground, a young kid, I think about leaving, embarrassed that I'm watching, but I cant move, I'm frozen in the cave of my time. The kid is my ghost when I was ten years old; he stands on the opposite side of the fence and faces me, like a mirror. I'd forgotten how young my face could look before the excess of my personal addictions took their toll.

"What do you want to be when you grow up?" he asks me.

"I haven't got a clue" I reply.

"What are you going to do for money?"

"I owe over six thousand pound, I'll be in debt for the rest of my life"

"You better start making plans or you'll fuck us both up" The kid disappears and in his place stands the caretaker of the school. "If you don't leave immediately I'll call the Police"

Sitting in a coffee shop in town I see the young couples, the mums with prams, and the office workers, all grownups, no older than me. Makes me feel eternally young, makes me feel small. They all looked happy, perhaps that was the secret. I sit out of place, alone on a table that seats four. One customer a woman with a pram, she looks familiar, looks for somewhere to sit, and reaches the empty spaces around my alcove. "Do you mind if I sit here?" she asks.

"Sure," I reply and as I look at her we're both transported back in our gaze of recognition to nearly seven years ago, Sarah Hynde, my first proper relationship. My first, her first.

"Oh my God, Matt?" she asks, looking through the bleary red eyes of mine.

"Hello Sarah"

"I can't believe this. Wow, how are you?"

"Good... good. You?"

"Well..." she pushes the pram back and forth, "older"

"We both are," I say looking into the pram.

"How long ago was it?"

"Six years, eight months" I surprise myself with my exact date.

"You been counting? You never forget your first love or..." She replies

"First time"

It was messy, over too quickly, I was on top and I pushed myself in, neither sure what the correct motions should be, just going by our imaginations fuelled by TV film sex. It wasn't how you see it in the movies, it wasn't gasps of joy, but it was awkwardness of two bodies both trying to pretend they're doing the correct movements. I came. She didn't until I went down on her later that evening. Then we tried it again, experimented, and it wasn't embarrassing, it was enjoyable and we both came.

"This is my daughter, Adrian" she holds her up for inspection.

"Hello Adrian." And she grabs my finger. "How old is she?"

"Nine months"

"You married?"

"Living together. We're getting married start of next year."

"Wow, kid, marriage"

"You know I was thinking about you the other day"

"Really?"

"Yeah, when we used to talk about Prisoner C-Block H, I was

watching it with John, my partner, the other night in our house"

"You got a house as well?"

"Yeah, two bedroom place in Pyford. You know it feels like a different life when we were together at College that year. It feels like I'm a different person"

"Only seems like yesterday to me but then a lot of things do at the moment"

"What are you doing at the moment?"

"I'm at uni in Southampton"

"And you used to say you'd never go. You used to really hate education."

"I guess it was always an excuse to do nothing for a while"

"Are you enjoying it?"

"I graduate soon. This is my final year"

"What you going to do then?"

"I don't know. Maybe look for another loophole in the system so I can get paid for doing nothing"

"God, you haven't changed at all, it's good, I mean there's me all grown up with a kid and house, getting married, its good to see someone I know still living the dream"

"The dream?"

"Yeah of being young"

"Don't you feel young?"

"I feel happy"

"Must be nice"

"Look, here's my phone number" she writes it down on a piece of paper as I find myself holding the baby. "You must come to the wedding"

"I'd like that" I lie, I cant think of anything worse, being reminded how life moves on but I still stay the same. And then she leaves with the baby.

Standing in a phone box, I dial the numbers, seeing Sarah had got me thinking, what am I really doing? Just drifting on the ocean. Kids, marriage, houses, jobs, the population can't all be wrong. "Hello?" Jenny O'Sullivan answers. My tongue freezes over, what am I going to say? I just met the girl I lost my virginity to and she seemed so happy with life, all grown up, that I want to settle down with someone immediately cause it really freaked me out? "Hello?" Jenny says again.

"Hi Jenny" I finally speak, "its Matt"

"Hi Matt, I was just thinking of you"

"Two in one day," I say remembering what Sarah said to me.
"What?"
"Nothing." There's a silence. Filling with memories, both good and bad.
"I really enjoyed that night before Christmas," she breaks the silence with her thoughts.
"Yeah, me too." We had spent the night together in my room but we didn't do anything, we kissed and cuddled but nothing more. Not that either of us didn't want to, we did, but for some reason we just found ourselves holding each other through out the night, talking about our lives, both naked bodies across each other, and it felt better than any sex I'd ever had. Waking up and she was lying on me, music from the stereo playing, Northern Soul by The Verve. For the first time I felt contented but depressed simultaneously, because I knew it would never be this good again, another reason to mope around not being able to recreate each first special moment.
"When you coming back to Southampton?" she asks me.
"I don't know."
"Why don't you come back today, we could do something?"
"I'd like that"
"What shall we do?" She asks.
"Go for a walk maybe?" I reply.
"Makes us sound like an old married couple!"
"Be nice" My mind dreams of marriage, kids, houses.
"Are you ok Matthew?" she used my fall name in her serious tone.
"Yeah"
"Has something happened?"
"There you go reading my mind again"
"Sorry, I don't mean to, just you seem distant"
"Maybe it would help if I was there in person. I wouldn't be so distant then," I'm tired of being on the outside looking in.
"If we were together?" She really can read my mind, she always could.
"Yeah, together. I'll get the next train." And then I'll be honest with her and myself.
"Call me when you get to your house"
"Ok"
"Bye then till tonight?"
"Yeah, see ya later…" I pause and I can tell she's going to put the phone down "Oh and Jenny…"

"Yeah"

I can't say it. I can't say that I really like her and I think we're good together. "I'll see you tonight"

"Like we just said" and then the phone goes down but I hang onto my receiver. Like I hang onto everything in my life, for too long.

From the phone box I went straight to the train station, my body guiding me but my mind elsewhere, in a void of my past and present, a determined future. I didn't pack any of my clothes from my Mums house. I didn't go back, just went to the train station and left to Southampton. It wasn't until I got off at the windy city that I realised I had come empty handed, that I'd have to return at some point to pick up my clothes and work.

For some reason it felt like I didn't exist as I walked the parade of shops and streets, my own reflection wasn't there, I cast no shadow. Walking like this was a dream, I was in twilight and not in control of the events unravelling before me. I don't have the house keys. I knock on the door. It looks different. Some stranger opens it. "Yes?"

"Hi" I say and I realise that I've gone to my old house of the first year where I lived.

"Yes?" the Asian woman says again obviously one of my old landlords mistress's.

"Sorry I made a mistake." She goes to shut the door on me. "I used to live here," and then the door slams in my face and I see her opening the front curtain, holding a child, waiting for me to go as I stare caught in time of three years ago. It seemed adapt, that I'd try the house of the second year as well. I had to re-live all the old memories and ghosts of this town today. It was my fate. I don't even bother knocking on this house as usual the door was unlocked, whatever students moved in they had the same disregard for the house as we did regarding home safety. As I step in I'm amazed at how nice the house smells instead of the drink and drug fuelled rotting mess that greeted us for a year. The hallway is immaculate clean. I step into the kitchen, what was once 'Lord of the Flies', now is a shining new cooker, spotless surfaces and a curtain that cuts across where the open living room joins on. I step tentatively through this different house, this immaculate paradise and slowly draw the curtain rail back. Asleep on the sofa is some guy snoring away, his eyes open and he focuses on me. "Alright" I say.

"Alright" he says. I then pull the rail back and he goes back to sleeping.

It amazed me how different a house and stigma attached could be in the space of six months. When we lived there it was a crumbling shell, haunted hallways, a collapsing ceiling, the smell and breath of excessive self-abuse. What I stepped into today was normality.

Finally, I reach the house I'm meant to be living in. I knock on the door but to no avail. Simon must be at work. I walk round the back and try the kitchen door, it was unlocked, as I said, we have no regards for possessions in this house. We want to be robbed so we can claim the insurance and pay off debts. Sitting alone in the living room, the phone on my lap... Jenny, I should phone Jenny. The silence of the house freezes into my thoughts, the world starts to engulf me on this sofa, I hear a ringing noise through my ears, my vision becomes a roller coaster, going up and down, fast and furious, if I don't get off I'm going to be sick. I pick up the phone in my panicked state and dial the numbers... it rings and just before she can pick up, I put the phone down. I can't phone her, something is stopping me, that something being my personality and its natural regard to fuck things up when things are going right, a form of self-punishment and self-preservation. The phone begins to ring. She must have pressed redial. I leave it ringing in the living room as I walk back to the station.

"You're back then?" Mum says as I open the door to her house that same evening.

"I never went away" I reply.

Simon

New Years Eve I'm in Southampton on my own. They said they would all spend new years in Southampton for the long goodbye, but no one came. I went home Christmas Eve night and stayed till Boxing Day, less than forty-eight hours, I wasn't exactly treated with a hero's welcome. They're pleased I'm working now but don't understand why I'm staying in Southampton if everyone's going to leave in the summer. "It's the final year," I tell them.

"But you're not studying, there's no reason to be there" They keep nagging like old wives.

"It's a long goodbye," I reason.

"Are they staying next year in the city to work?" Good question.

"No." Is the only answer.

"Are you?" Playing Devils Advocate.

"No, I thought I could come back when it's over." Hands on knees.

"When what's over? I don't understand?" They never did. I don't tell them that I don't know either. Its like we're all waiting for time to run out. We all feel depressed as we know its coming to an end and there's nothing we can do about it. Rather than go out and enjoy these final few months of this life, we sit around and mope, feeling depressed about it ending, sitting in our separate rooms staring at ceilings, waiting for that end to come.

I decide to try the local pubs and see if there's anyone I might know, but at this time of year the town is dead. The locals and real townies have come out and reclaimed the town. All the students are dead. I sit up at the bar, trying to listen to a conversation, hoping I may get the opportunity to join in. But they all know each other and I know none of them. I'm left with some old guy, he kind of mumbles drunken nothings to me and I just nod my head, drink up and leave. Maybe the clubs will be different? Kaos, that's bound to be fun on New Years Eve, there's bound to be people like me, ex-students, who had to stay and seek shelter from the windy city storm of new years eve night in the shit'est club ever. Its not open...not even Kaos can afford to open on New Years Eve when the students are gone.

'Lucky' serves me in the Off Licence. Two bottles of white lighting. "Happy New Year!" he says to me, holding a baby.

"Happy New Year!" I slur back to him, holding tobacco and four litres of white lighting.

The mad Irish tramp and the 'nutter' Asian tramp with the limp, sit on the subway as I pass them, they make space for me. "Have a drink" the Irish tramp shouts out.

"Nutters! Many nutters!" the Asian tramp joins in festivities. Both hold the white lighting cider bottles up and nod to my bag.

"Maybe later" I reply and I walk back at a brisk pace, hoping the quicker I walk I might actually walk into a different life as I turn the corner.

Alone in my bedroom. Two bottles of white lighting. New Year celebrations outside and on TV. I've got to work tomorrow at 6am. Maybe if I listen to some tunes that will help. Read back issues of NMEs and Melody Makers. It's 11pm. I can only sleep when I'm pissed these days. I get into bed. Pint of white lighting on the side. I put The Shining on. It scares me, so I have to turn it off. What am I doing here? 11.45pm, I decide to pack my bags, I'm leaving.

Midnight, its January 1st, there's no trains. I unpack my bags. "Happy New Year" I say to the ghosts. I'll be at work in less than five hours. I've wasted three years of my life. What scares me the most is that I'd happily do it all over again. It's an old lost quality is comedy.

PART 6

January '97 to July '97

The Long Goodbye

Part 6: The Long Goodbye

CARLA PART 3

The streets are full of New Year resolutions being broken. The dread and depression of post Christmas, post New Years Eve, a new year upon us that will get quicker with each passing week, until it has gone full circle again and we look at what we've achieved. In every eye, in every face Matthew walks past, he looks for Carla in the busy windy city town, hoping that with each shop he will see her reflected, waiting for him like she had promised a year ago. The city seemed to have no personality left, nothing left to show him. It was like he himself had become immersed into the city and had become part of the weather, part of the colours. He'd see the warmth on first years faces, the look of a cold hell in the storm of the 2nd year faces, then finally the look of nothingness, of emptiness in faces like his in their final year, just a clock that was ticking to the end of an adventure they cannot change.

He believed fate would lead him to Carla, like it had done previously at the start of each year. He needed resolution; he needed an end to his consumed thoughts of the angel he'd met in a private part of his life. If there was an empty void, this was a part that would not let go today. But she is no-where in the windy city. If she even remained when she left that house last year. As he walks, seeing all these places where he was once afraid, with all the foolish things the streets hold of his memories, he wondered if they could see his hands where always tied.

At the end of the street walking back to his house, the rain falls like snow on a Christmas morning and lights the sky with a feeling of a city waiting for its inhabitants to leave. He reaches the top of his road and sees the young prostitute who works the route, who'd he often speak to on the way back from lectures, flirt with and converse about daily things. He saw a girl next to her also working the street, but she was new, and as the young prostitute turned and waved to Matthew, the girl next to her turned, and in front of him… Carla.

Once where he had control of his emotions Matthew now stood alone, waiting for her outside sheltered from his home, trying to find a place to shelter from the new storm. He tentatively walks towards the two ladies of the night, the rain feels warm as it falls on him, wetting his long damp hair down to his shoulders now, he gently pushes it back revealing a face of confused emotions.

"Alright how are you today?" The young prostitute asks.

"Cool," he replies and looks at the prostitute next to her, Carla.

Her face was not as pale as last year, more colour in her cheeks, more world wise and weary in her eyes, the look of innocent youth'ism replaced by a hard edge. And they stare in recognition at each other as the other prostitute keeps talking but he doesn't hear her words. "Hi"

"Hi," Carla replies, a harder edge to her tone of voice.

"...And then when I spoke to the doctor..." the young prostitute continues her conversation that has fallen on deaf ears.

"You want to go somewhere?" Matthew asks Carla.

"It will cost," Carla replies coldly.

"Six months and you've never asked me to go somewhere," the young prostitute says to Matthew. "What's so different about her?"

"Memories" he replies and takes out whatever money he has in his pocket, a twenty.

"That's not going to buy you a lot," Carla replies.

He enters Carla's flat, it's a one-bedroom mod cons; small kitchen, utensils, sofa chair, bed, table, all in one room. It is damp, but she's made an effort to make it homely, nice red curtains put up, tablecloths, a carpet between the bed and the start of the kitchen. "Nice," he says.

"Its home for now" she replies. "It's a start but I don't want to stay here"

"Where do you want to go?" He asks scared she'll disappear again.

"Look, you've only got twenty pound, its not going to buy you a lot of time so you might want to get down to business"

"Don't you remember me?"

"Yeah, I remember you." She looks away from his eyes.

"So why you being like this?" He asks confused in his blinded sight of unrequited love.

"Everything is business, you understand?" She replies coldly.

"What about your pimp?"

"I don't have one. I'm looking after myself. Its healthier." He looks towards her arms, as she takes her jacket off, and sees the tracks where she'd been shooting up when he saw her last. His eyes focus on one area, the track he shot up for her, she catches his eyes there. "That was the last one," she tells him.

"You don't have to tell me," but he keeps staring like it's her portrait that he painted.

"I want you to know you're not going to be fucking some smack

Part 6: The Long Goodbye

head"

"You never was to me"

She shakes her head. "Why do you speak like that? Like we've had some big romance?"

"Cause you're special"

"To me...you're just a punter." She meets his eyes with hers and stares with a cold heart.

"I'll go then, you can get a better paid punter"

As he walks to the door, Carla looks at her needle track and she remembers both encounters with him. "Wait" she calls out, holding her arm. "You've given me the money so you can at least stay for that time"

"Twenty pounds worth?" He asks smiling, contented.

"Yeah. Twenty pounds worth," she smiles back.

Matthew sits on the bed next to her and she moves to face him. "Does it hurt?" He asks and touches the arm where the needle track was his hit onto her, engrossed in the marks and the tracks of her tears that lay inside there. Something he helped create like an artist.

"It has been today." She moves her patterned arm away.

"So this is you starting again?"

She looks all-defensive. "It may not look like much to you but I'm my own boss, I don't use, I rent this room. It's just like any other person going to work and then coming home at the end of their day. I can live with myself, can you?" she looks at him.

"No, that's half my problem" And it was that which had brought him here.

"You're using up a lot of this money, don't you want to do something?" She asks.

"Yeah"

"Well, what do you want me to do for you?"

"Go on a date"

"What?"

"I want to take you out on a date"

She laughs. "You're crazy"

"I'm serious"

"Ok, where?" She decides to play along with his joke.

"It'll be an adventure"

"It will cost you and I don't know if you've got that kind of money"

"How about this, we go out and if after the first place you want

MJ Gunn

to go back to business then I wont stop you?"

"And you'll still pay me?"

"Yeah"

"You're crazy" But she smiles back at him in agreement.

The two of them walk through the shopping parade in town. The rain has stopped falling and the sun has come out for the first time that year, which leaves a picture across the horizon and the promise of a long day. Carla walks with her head down slightly, with each face she meets embarrassed it maybe a past punter as they look at her and leer. She wears her fur jacket, same work clothes on.

Matthew keeps her close to his side, he feels her looking down scared to look out. "Look at the sky" Matthew says getting Carla to look upwards finally. And the haze of a red skyline paints the truest portrait of the windy city either of them had ever seen.

"That's nice, but its still your money and I could still go after the first part"

"I know, but I feel untouchable" and he smiles towards her. "Lets do the first part, then its up to you"

"Good. Where to?"

"Here" and Matthew points towards Next clothes shop.

"Clothes?"

"Yeah, I want to see what you look like in a dress?"

"Its your money" As Carla looks in the mirror of the department store, long red dress on that has shoulder straps, fits across her slim firm figure perfectly, her long blond hair dropping across her shoulders, the light makes her blue eyes sparkle and she feels for that minute that she is someone different, that she is the girl she could have been, her youth given back to her, that she can sparkle and shine. She spins round her reflection like Cinderella. Matthew catches her doing this and she pretends to going back to being the hard nosed professional, a fake look of disinterest in her eyes. "I feel like an idiot"

"You look like an angel." And rather than keep the tirade coming back and forth, she studies herself in the mirror, wanting to see that angel.

"That's a brilliant fit," the lady assistant comes up to them.

"We can do without the hard sell" Carla replies immediately trying to make her sound streetwise but she is still engrossed by the different reflection in her soul to sound bitter.

"We get a lot of models come in and try stuff on," the lady continues.

Part 6: The Long Goodbye

"Models?"

"Yeah, that's right," Matthew says with pride and winks at Carla. "How much for the dress?"

"If we can say its someone whose endorsing our labels, who works in the industry we can get you a discount from the manager, its good business for us," the shop assistant replies.

"You'll have to ask the lady if she doesn't mind me buying her the dress?" He looks at Carla.

"The lady..." Carla says, spinning round the mirror and her new reflection.

They laugh and giggle as they step outside the shop. Carla still has the dress on, her work clothes now in a Next bag, her fur coat suiting the red dress. "Thanks".

"So, what do you want to do?" He puts the day's fate into one question.

She looks at him and then the faces that walk past her, not clients but guys eyeing her up. She puts her arm round his. "Well, I've got no choice but to wear it somewhere now, have I?"

He looks at her arm linked with his. This is all he'd ever wanted for the three years, a normal date, not drunk, not drugged, not one night stand, casual sex with a club acutance, but someone where he could just be content for a few hours at least, before the storm of his personality would demand more.

"Its beautiful this time of day" Carla says looking over the ocean, watching the waves gently crash to and fro, creating their own mystic of dreams and prayers.

"Yeah, sometimes I just come down here and stare, nothing more" Matthew replies and he touches his hand onto hers.

She looks at the hand, it promised so much. "Its just business remember?" she tells him.

"It's your call for the entire day, it always was" he replies.

She places her hand onto his. "Do you ever wonder about just going somewhere new, getting on that train and starting again, being someone different?"

"Everyday"

"Looking at the ocean, makes it seem possible" They stare for a number of minutes in silence at the ocean waking up to their presence. "Is this what its like when you take girls on dates?"

"I wouldn't know"

"Don't you have a girlfriend?"

"No, it never seemed to fit"

"With your lifestyle?"

"No, more with me, who I am"

"I bet you do this to all the girls, buy them clothes, take them to the ocean, you must be broke" she jokes.

They stay by the ocean for hours and speak, sharing a bottle of red wine.

Day turns to night in as what seems like minutes captures hours.

Carla spins round in her dress, dancing over to the ocean. "What's next?"

"You want to continue?"

"I thought this was a date," she says happily, the wine having gone to her head slightly, but the feeling of being someone different giving her the most rush. "You're not being a cheap boyfriend are you are making it only half a date?"

"Well, there is one more thing?"

"Lets do it"

"You don't know what it is yet?"

"I don't need to stupid" and she gently hits his arm and pretends to run away. "But you got to catch me first…"

After his final surprise, they return to the ocean that evening, lights of the city reflect over the stillness of the night on each wave of thoughts they reminisce of the day. And they hold each other's hands, it seemed natural, both of them away from their lives creating a new life just for this day. Watching the waves in a comfortable silence, happy to just watch the world wash away in front of them, oblivious to outside sources. "That's it," Matthew breaks the silence.

"Don't say that? There must be another adventure?" She asks but he walks over to the cash point. "What are you doing?" she asks, feeling insulted.

"Paying you"

"I don't want you to pay me. I enjoyed it," she says feeling hurt.

"I don't mean it to be insulting, its business, you've taken a days sick leave look at like that."

"I don't want it"

"I'd feel insulted, like you felt sorry for me if you don't. A gift for the dream."

She takes it, looking for any emotion of hurt in his face, his eyes, where she is solely reflected. "Then you've got to let me give you something…Take me home"

"I cant afford it"

"No, you don't understand, its my present to you, I want you to come back with me"

"Why?"

"Because that's what boyfriends and girlfriends do at the end of the date isn't it? I want it all to be right, special"

They step inside her shower washing away demons and join their dreams together. He gently touches her, letting the water cleanse them both of their past. She gasps gently as he puts himself inside of her and they don't shag, fuck or screw, but they make love, the shower washing their sins away. The first time for either of them that they truly understand what it is to make love, to feel as one when all is so right and everything else in the world doesn't exist. Just the two of them alive and their bodies forming as one, the world stands still for those moments and they escape into their dreams in a reality that makes no sense.

Their eyes are awake in the bed with their own thoughts and desires. Carla looks at the red dress sitting on the chair, its shadow engulfs the room and her sleeping spirit steps into the dress and spins round, curtsying for her naked eyes and then she goes. The dress remains back on the chair with its lived in memories of a day where no clocks were ticking. Matthew stares at the shade of light through the curtains, the day dawning in the early hours, scared that the time will come where he'll have to leave her room and go back to who he is.

"What are you thinking?" she asks him.

"I don't want the daylight to come," he replies.

"Why?"

"Cause then it means I've got to get up and go back to being me"

Silence.

"When I wore that dress I wasn't me, I was someone else"

"You still can be someone else"

"You never ask me about my past, about why I do what I do"

"I only know you from the minute I first saw you," he pauses looks away because of what he's going to say, he cant show his face, "I loved you, that's all I needed to know"

She visualises the ocean in front of them both. "When I looked at the ocean it made me think how easy it would be to just get on that ferry and start again, a different place, country. Somewhere no-one would know or recognise me. Don't you want that? Some kind of meaning?"

"I've never known any meaning, so if I had it I wouldn't recognise it"

"What about now? Do you feel any meaning now?"

"Laying here next to you, yeah, I guess I do. You?"

"I want to be the girl in the red dress again." She hears the ocean waves and the promise of a new life wash over her. "I'm saving money all the time so I can start afresh somewhere. That's what this has been"

"You don't have to tell me"

"I want to tell you. I want you to understand its for a reason, live a normal life"

"What's a normal life?"

"I don't know, like our day together"

"Boyfriend, girlfriend?" The past two years run through Matthews mind. "If you had the money would you go today?"

"Yeah. Would you?"

"Yeah," he replies to the answer he'd been searching for three years.

"We could go together one day?" She asks him.

"How about today?"

"What do you mean?"

"Leave together, both of us on a ferry"

"Where to?"

"Isle of Wight I guess to start off with, then maybe France?"

"Always wanted to go to Paris." She lets her mind dream and then settles back in the room and reality. "It's a dream we could keep?"

"We could do it today?"

"Stop saying that."

He turns to face her. "We don't have to love each other."

And the realisation then answers for her. "I love you"

"Do you trust me?"

"I trust you"

"Then meet me in a couple of hours by the ocean" He kisses her lips and brushes her hair back, "and we'll leave together."

"Just drop everything?"

"There's nothing to drop for either of us is there?"

And there wasn't but she couldn't believe it could be that easy.

Part 6: The Long Goodbye

"What about money? We cant just go somewhere with nothing, it will just be like being anywhere else, struggling"

"Meet me"

For the first time she can see the truth in his eyes. "You're serious?"

"Yeah, are you?"

"Together," she replies and holds his hand, hoping she doesn't wake from this dream. Carla sits up on the bed and thoughts of what she needs to do rush through her mind.

"Where are you going?" She asks him as he gets up.

"There's some things I got sort out; clothes, money, you'll need to do the same"

She places her head in her hands. "Its happening so fast, it was a dream something I thought wouldn't come real"

"Do you want to change your mind? Its ok if you do"

She looks at the red dress. "No, I want to go"

In his room, early hours of the morning, a bright blinding sun goes over his life in Southampton. Matthew packs what he feels belongs in his life into a holder. And with each possession packed away a memory rushes through him. But its to early to think about things, for once he was just acting on instinct and leaving the windy city behind, leaving the last three years to a different life, a different persona. There were no guarantees in life.

He scribbles a note for his housemates –

Sorry guys, see you in the next life, Cheers Matt

He stares at the room, one final look; posters left on the wall, the Britpop duvet, CDs of idols left on the desk and stereo. Before any more memories could engulf him he's down the stairs and out the front door, not looking back, just looking for Carla's face and a future they could have together. As he moves down the road away from the house, its like its all been a dream the last couple of years and this is him starting again, travelling from home to a new life, like that summer of '94. Oasis plays on his walkman - 'Live Forever'.

He's moving, walking, but it doesn't feel real that in a couple of hours he'll be elsewhere, a different life. This wasn't really happening the quicker he walked in the windy city the more unlikely this was true. The sun blinding his visions, his goodbyes to the city, he could feel a migraine coming on, his eyes were sensitive to any extreme brightness over the last three years, the abuse he'd put his body through had effected his sensitivity. The wind rustles up a storm that is erupting around the city; fallen winter leafs rush across his feet, down the shopping parade.

"Where you going?" The Mad Irish Tramp shouts at him as he rushes past.

"Nutter! Fucking nutter!" the Mad Asian Tramp with the limp shouts across the parade, pointing at him.

Matthew waves back. "Did you ever feel the pain, in the morning rain as it soaks you to the bone" he sings back to them as the rain hits across his face.

The storm has arrived but he was leaving it all behind. And as the sight of the ocean fills his eyes and a place away from his demons, the rain soaking him to the bone, there she stands, Carla, in her red dress. She doesn't see him, looking round, worried that he was just joking. Where was he? Has she made a pact to escape and nothing was really going to happen? Was it a game the two of them played whenever they met – disappearing on each other? She keeps wrapping the fur coat round her as the hard rain falls, she didn't want one drop to fall on the red dress she wore and ruin the sacred memories of her soul being alive. Out of the blinding sun that sparkles on the ocean in the hard rain, a rainbow forms on the horizon, she sees him and the relief cuts through her like when she came in the shower as they made love.

As Matthew reaches Carla, the smile on her face, the red dress, everything he'd always seen in her, he realises what he is doing. And as he steps next to her and she goes to kiss him, he stops her. And it hits him in the face, cold reality. Being so close to something that is so right and so beautiful at the same time it was wrong – he wasn't going anywhere. It all made sense to him now, the last three years, the tales of excess; meeting her, James's death, Alex's attempted suicide, his battle with his own demons – It all came down to this and doing something right for once in his life, something for someone else. "I'm not going," he tells her.

Her face drops to anger. "What do you mean we're not going?"

"I said I'm not going, you still are," and he passes her over a big brown envelope with money in it. Student loan money, overdraft, it was immaterial to him now. It was always was, just that he couldn't see it.

"My god, there's hundreds," she says counting through the notes.

"Over fifteen hundred," he replies.

"Where did you get it?"

"Its mine"

"What are you doing?" She asks him confused.

"Do you want to go?" He asks back.

"Yeah but not on my own"

"For once in my life I want to do something right. It all makes sense to me now, everything"

"I don't understand?"

"Neither do I fully"

"Why wont you come with me?"

The cold light of day hits him. "Because I'm not meant to, I got to see this out to the end"

"Then I'm not going"

"You said you're saving to go at some point, what's the difference? This way you can live that dream earlier, start afresh. Do it" He stares into her blue eyes one final time. "You're so close, don't blow it." He sees her look at the money then back at him. "You can pay me back"

"So I'll see you again?"

"I promise"

"When?"

"When I find out"

"Find out what?"

"I wont know till I finish it." He looks into her eyes. "You understand?"

And in the cold light of the day and the life she had lived, she did understand. "Yeah, I do"

"You got to hurry" he passes her the ticket for the ferry. "Its leaving"

"Why are you doing this?"

"Same reason you're going"

He runs with her through the rain, the sun still blinding, and the rainbow painting its farewell portrait and gets her onto the ferry walkway. "Wait" she says as she steps on board. But the ferry starts to move away from its port. As the windy city leaves her eyes and he stands on the side watching her go she shouts to him - "I don't know how to get in contact with you, a number or anything?" she shouts but to no avail as he disappears into a small figure.

"You didn't even let me kiss you goodbye," she whispers to herself. And as she sits herself down seeing the windy city disappear from her life once and for all, she realises with fear and excitement that she doesn't know what awaits her. She had enough money to turn back if it didn't work out, return and find him if she needed to. Go back to her old life back in the windy city. But as true as the rainbow that seemed to travel directly over her journey, she knew she'd be alright, that compared to what she'd lived through the last three years, this was nothing, this was a joy ride. Life was hers to live.

Matthew looks at the ocean and the rainbow that disappears along it. The blinding sun fading behind a dark grey cloud and a hard rain falls across him again. He'd changed his mind, he wanted to follow her, but he couldn't swim. "Love is hell," he whispers.

SPOT OF BOTHER

Steve

It stares at me like a separate head with a massive smile. Matt keeps saying its karma for taking the piss out of his spot, at least his one wasn't this big and was hide-able, but no-one can hide from this, my little Steve with its own face and features, forming half of my cheek and waving good afternoon to everyone. I can see a giant face winking inside the spot shouting 'karma, karma' with Matt's voice.

"Its massive" I say to Amy who sits in my room afraid to look at me.

"Its not that bad," she replies. "Let me have a look" I take my fingers away from trying to burst it and it smiles towards Amy; she turns away and runs out of the room, "Oh my god!" she shouts, I can hear her physically coughing.

"Amy, Amy, come back!" I shout after her and follow her into the living room where the three members of the stoned council sit, watching afternoon TV and smoking dope.

"What's wrong Amy?" Johnny is the first to ask.

I step into the room and all of them look towards my face. "Jesus Christ," Matt says and I can see him psychically leech sick up his throat then back down.

Simon cannot even bring himself to look.

Johnny is in hysterical laughter, "Its not that bad" I come closer to Johnny. "Oh, it is," he replies and goes to push my face away, moves his hand like I'm diseased.

"Bloody hell!" I cry and walk into the kitchen, the door wide open for all to see as I look into the steamed up stained mirror and the spots face stares back at me and winks. It has its own separate life. "Oh my god, its like that film with Richard E Grant with that head growing out of his neck" I push fingers trying to burst it and I scream in pain and turn to the others, a massive white pimple has come out on top, they all turn away sick.

"Jesus Christ Steve, you can't burst that, you'll die" Matt tells me.

Heat. Heat. Heat. I'm sweating. Burning. I push the water over the spot. Burn the bastard off. I can hear it crying as it dies. Burst baby, burst. As the heat from the shower descends I look into the mirror, and there it is, bigger than before, massive white head crying to put out of its misery. If I don't burst it I'm afraid it will consume my face entirely. So I head back downstairs to the disgusted looks in the living room into the kitchen mirror so they all have to witness it. "I'm going to burst the bastard"

"Steve, you'll die!" Matt cries back, well, laughs back.

But it's me versus the spot and if I'm to die whilst trying to get my face back to normal then I want these guys to witness it and be sick. And so I begin. I push. It hurts. I dig my nails deep in. I can feel it pushing out. Its almost like having a wank, masturbating, the joy of seeing it push further out, almost there, I wonder if this is what its like for a woman when she orgasms? It's too much though; it won't go through that final burst. I scream in pain. Amy arrives behind me with a needle, like a good nurse. Why? I'm not looking to sow something at this precise minute; perhaps she thinks it will need stitches? I can see the finger nail marks left in my skin; they already form a graze like I've cut myself on the pavement.

"Try the needle Steve" Amy holds it glinting in the light; this will kill it for sure.

The needle cuts into the skin but not much else. Fuck it, I push my two middle fingers either side and push like I've never pushed before, so this is giving birth? Giving birth to a mutant spot. "Aaaahhhhhhhh" I shout out, my breathing is stopping, its like someone's punching my cheek constantly..."FFFFFFFFFFFFFFUUUUUUUUUUUCCCCCCCCC CKKKKKKKK"

There is a massive release of pain... A massive sense of relief... I can see a white light... I feel like I've just come... I look up from my dizzy sense and see a mirror stained with white puss mixed with blood and there looking at me is an open war wound on the side of my cheek, blood coming out. "I've done it," I say like scorer of the winning goal in a football match. Running into the living room I'm greeted with a cries of lets have a look, like its some diamond ring and I'm getting married. They all soon turn away in disgust again, "the puss is coming out" they cry.

I return back to the mirror, "Oh know" I shout out, "I'm meant to be going out tonight." And the puss is pouring from my spot, non-stop yellow, wet spunk it feels like, so I continue to squeeze and it continues to flow. "It wont stop!" I cry out.

Matt kindly passes me half a loo roll from the doorway, afraid to step in; he sees the mirror, and the blood and puss on it, "Hope you're clearing that up?" he asks.

And so it continues, the puss will not stop. "I'll have a shower. That will stop the puss" Inside the shower again... My second in the last half hour... People can't accuse me of not being clean. And I let the hot water burn into the cut. Blood and yellow puss run down with the water. After thirty minutes I descend into the mirror and push the hot steam across my hand like in a film, to reveal a massive blood spot patch, a scab, its like half my cheek has been burst open and slashed. "I'll just say I got cut in a fight," I tell them. I look at the puss in the kitchen mirror and the blood, all dry and stuck together, someone else can clear it up. I can make it into a face, bits of little Steve's, I killed it, and now it killed my social life.

I sit in my room and anything with a reflection follows my burnt scarred tissue face. "I need to get wasted," I tell myself, checking my pockets for money, nothing but ten lottery tickets that didn't have one number. "I'm desperate, that's why I'm doing this," I tell myself as I sneak into all the bedrooms upstairs, whilst the inhabitants are watching TV below. I pause before entering Little Rob's room first, only to find that he is sitting on the edge of his bed face immersed over a computer game. "Alright" I say disappointed that he was in.

"What do you want? What do you want?" he shouts at me really fast as blocks fall from the computer game, his eyes never leaving the screen to look at my deformity.

"I just wanted to see what you was up to?" I'm good at lying on the spot. I'm a good actor. I should be a male model. "Haven't seen you for ages, what you been doing?"

"Playing tectrus...FUCK!" He screams. "You fucking made me lose my concentration!"

"Sorry, I'll go"

"Take that disgusting burst spot with you!" How did he see that?

Part 6: The Long Goodbye

Next room is Simon's. His bed is immaculately made, a bottle of white lighting waits on the table. There's no loose change or notes, I check his coat pockets, hoping to find a wallet; all I pull out is an old packet of Duma tobacco... that will have to do for his room. Entering Matt's room I'm surprised to see a suitcase open, half packed and a note scribbled on the desk - **Sorry guys, see you in the next life, Cheers Matt** - I'll use this as blackmail.

"What's this then?" I burst into the room and hand Matt the note of his intentions.

"What was you doing in my room Steve?" he turns the tables on me.

So I think on the spot again like a good actor... Can't think of anything so I start rolling a cigarette with Simon's Duma packet I stole.

"So you're in my room going through my personal possessions?"

I pause, not understanding how I've come out the villain.

"Is that my Duma tobacco Steve?" Simon asks me.

The phone starts to ring to rescue me. "I'll fucking get it shall I you lazy cunts!" I storm out the room, guilty and full of sin but still broke. I haven't even enough money to buy food this week. Let alone pay my rent. "Hello?"

"Steve?" it's my Mum.

"I'm glad you called I need money"

"What happened to chatting for half an hour before asking?"

"I'm desperate Mum"

"You always need money but you blow it on going out"

"I deserve to go out"

"And lottery tickets. I'm not sending you any more money. I'll pay your rent if you're really broke but directly to your landlord, I want your bank statements before I do so"

"Fucking hell! Even my own Mother doesn't trust me!"

"What do you expect Steve?"

"Some credit"

"I'm putting the phone down Steve"

"Wait...wait!" My finger keeps touching my scarred face. "The truth is I've had an accident but I didn't want to worry you... It's my face, I've scarred my face and I need hospital bills to remodel it"

"Remodel it? What the hell happened?"

What am I going to tell her, that I burst a spot? "I got in a knife fight"

"I've had enough of this Steve, I'll phone back tomorrow"
"But I need the money today!" I scream down the phone but it goes dead. Even my family think I'm a lying thief.

I test the waters in Asda. The others try to persuade me from going out or at least putting something over my face but I said I'm proud of this mark on my face. It's a battle of wills and adversity and say that it will become a talking point that I'll look very tough, getting slashed.
"But you look like a freak"
"It makes me look like a man" I reply.
"A man with a deformed spot growing out of his cheek" I can feel them all letting me walk a couple of yards ahead of them, so they disassociate themselves.

When I enter ASDA the stealing and criminal side of my tendencies cant help but come out. I need free food, this walk round will be my breakfast, lunch and dinner for today until I can either find some money to steal or find someone stupid enough to lend me some. I start on the fruit aisle and bite my way through an apple as I walk down the first aisle, a trolley in hand, mainly to push like a child as I race the other three. It's impossible to avoid people in this place. Everyone you don't want to speak to will be shopping at that same time. First to hit me as I try to duck down the aisle so he doesn't notice me is Alex. It's been awkward now he doesn't live with us, especially since his suicide attempt last summer. I make a genuine attempt to be nice to him, but I know with this massive mark on my face he'll want to psychoanalyse me.

"Hey Steve!" Alex dances towards us with that imaginary music in his head that seems to have been permanent for three years, wonder what tune it is? Sure gives him no sense of rhythm. He's smiling, ears sticking out, head moving side to side. 'Walking on the moon' maybe? And then he sees the side of my face as I put on a fake smile and can feel the puss coming out. His face turns white and he steps back. I try and smile towards Alex but puss and blood comes out like a vampire, those we've been hearing about roaming the windy city streets. Alex takes a couple of steps back and disappears, his head has even stopped moving, and he runs to the double exit doors and doesn't look back.

I can see a reflection of the spot in the silver foil of the ice cream I open up down the next aisle. It doesn't look that bad, though it's all I can see apart from smudged desert. Keith Reynolds is standing

Part 6: The Long Goodbye

beside us, appearing out of nowhere, rumour has it he's the main vampire, their leader. He is wearing work clothes not his vampire clothes, white shirt, no blood stains, and black trousers, looking like a grown up school boy. "All right Keith" I say biting into the ice cream desert I have no intention of paying for.

He doesn't care and opens one up himself. "Always wondered what these taste like?"

"Nice," I say and I lick my lips and with that one motion of human skin I can feel the puss again begin to drop from my face.

"What happened to your face Steve?"

"I got into a knife fight, they slashed me"

"I think there's blood coming down with that spot puss"

"Spot puss? That's impossible, it was a knife fight not a spot"

"Can I have some of the puss and blood drippings, for the cult?"

I decide to run this time, run from Keith Reynolds; afraid he might catch me being a vampire. I run smack into someone and knock the trolley over. "Sorry," I say and start to pick up the person's groceries.

"Hello," the guy replies and it's him; that guy whose cock I sucked in Southampton Common last year for money. Is there bad shit in the woods today or what?

"Alright" I reply.

He is holding his kid's hands, his daughter and son by his side. "I've been meaning to thank you for what you did that night, it revitalised my marriage."

"You could give me some money if you want?"

"Sorry?"

"I could always tell your wife and the course?" I turn evil; blackmail is easy when you're desperate.

"She knows, don't you darling." And up walks a beautiful wife, shoulder length brown hair, gleaming teeth, designer suits. "This is the guy who did the business for me that night"

"Pleasure to meet you." She kisses either cheek like I'm some favourite nephew she wants to have sex with. Then she looks disgusted and spits on the floor where her mouth had touched the spot. "Oh my god, what was that on your face?" This place is a madhouse. I've got to get out of here.

A trolley full of farm store savers, eight items or less to be precise. I haven't got any money to pay but I figure one of the guys will pay for me when it comes down to it, either that or I'll continue walking with my trolley after they've paid, like its one big order. The final members of 'look at Steve's spot' await us at the counter - The O'Sullivan twins. Johnny's face lights up, he has been trying to shag them both for three years without getting anywhere. "Alright" I say to them, big spot pointing towards them.

"Alright lads." They seem more interested in Matt though, why? He's full of hair, rough looking, he does have some nice groceries in his trolley though, must be after a cooked meal.

"Hi, Matt" Jenny says towards him.

"Hi," he pauses, looking at us, staring in silence at this soap opera moment and then back to her. "I'm sorry about the other day, I did come back but I left... again"

"I know. I saw you the other day, walking through town with some girl in a red dress"

We all look at Matt, waiting for him to explain the mystery lady. "Do you remember I told you about something I had to say goodbye too?"

"That was it wasn't it?"

"Yeah."

"Look, why don't we start again, maybe meet for something, two friends going out?" Jenny suggests to him.

"Is that invitation for me as well?" I say pretending to be interested and not gay. She smiles towards me but face drops as the spot looks towards them. "Yeah...." They kind of say and look away, wanting to leave very quickly. "See you soon Matt." She doesn't don't look back.

"If it wasn't for my spot it would have been me she asked out," I tell Matt.

The girl cashier in her white overalls with green stripes looking depressed on her day of from school totals up the items. "Seven pound twenty pence," she says and stares at me smiling, she fancies me, then sees my spot and seems to jump in her seat beginning to cough. "Oh my god!" She says hand over her mouth.

I look for the others so they can pay it for me, but I stood last in the queue like an idiot, they're all outside waiting for me in the cold winter air. "Er, my mates have got the money" I reply grabbing the bags of stacked food and walk hurriedly towards the door.

Just as I think I've made it, a large hand pulls me back, Terry, the doormen from Magnums. "Steve, you're coming with me"

"But Magnums isn't open till later?"

"Not Magnums you idiot! Here, I'm the security"

Part 6: The Long Goodbye

"My mates are going to pay for it"

"You were going to steal the food as well in the bags? You're just making it worse on yourself"

"Why what was you talking about?"

"The food you've been eating round the shop"

So I sit in the security office of Terry the bouncer, security man, massive shadow, and gay raffle ticket organiser at Christmas do's in Magnums. Next to me is a spotty teenager, he can't be no more than fifteen; he has a baseball cap, a football shirt, a bright gold earring in one ear. He smiles at me with his spots and I smile back with my spot. The room is darkly lit, a table lamp with a dark shade, shining into our faces, like an interrogation room, a big leather armchair that Terry swivels round like a Bond baddie to face us. "I want you two to watch this." Terry puts a video on we're treated to a ten-minute footage of Nazi's, atomic bombs, death camps, Beethoven's music, real Clockwork Orange stuff, all this with the light shining into our eyes. "Do you both understand now?" Terry says taking the video out.

"Yeah," the spotty teenager replies.

"Yeah," I reply back in the same teenage manner.

"I'm disappointed in you Steve, I don't want to see you in the club again."

"You can't stop me from going to Magnums, that's nothing to do with this."

"It's the only way you'll learn"

"Learn what?"

"Get out!"

The spotty teenager and I walk down a set of steps that leads to the back alleyway of Asda, the walk of shame. "First time?" I ask the kid.

"I'm a regular up there," he replies.

"Does he always show the same video?"

"Yeah"

"Does it help?"

"Of course it does"

"But you keep stealing?"

"I make a hundred pound a week flogging all the shit I steal. How much do you get a week spotty?" He asks me; even this kid gets more money than me.

"Do you need a partner?"

"I'm no faggot!"

"I mean with the stealing, I can get us into loads of student houses"

"Get a life you sad bastard" And he walks down the alleyway.

Dog shit and black bin liners full of waste surround me. Why did I become a student?

We get to the subway, beaten and bedraggled, the windy city coupled with the rain of a thousand storms that will not relent for anyone. The tramps in the car park between subways circulate their homes, forcing strangers aside to take different routes; there are different rules when God shits on us like this storm. I'm sure the city seems to be getting windier, like a hurricane that is blowing our final year into a whirlpool of madness that we cannot escape. Two tramps sit on the wet floor and are kissing. Going through the subway, a tramp is motionless on the floor, someone screams that he has no pulse and a blanket is put over him. The 'nutter' tramp stands a young student girl up against the rails and sticks his tongue down her throat. "Are you alright?" we say, pulling him off her, this could be a case of rape.

"He's my boyfriend!" she replies.

"Nutters, fucking nutters" the guy shouts out after us. The tramps convention starts to circle round us like high noon, we walk hurriedly through the rain and find the only empty subway from the storm and collapse onto the floor like tramps ourselves.

An American couple walk through. "Spare any change?" I ask, making sure they get a full glint of my spot.

"Get a fucking job!" They reply in LA accents. We even fail as tramps.

Hit the road outside and the wind pulls us back every yard we walk. The end of the world is nigh, wishing to take no prisoners. We see the American couple go into the Bookmakers. We decide to follow them in there. "Why are we here?" Matt asks.

"There's bound to be money lying around" I reply.

"It's a bookmakers, do you honestly think gamblers would leave money lying around?! Have you ever been in a bookmakers before Steve?"

Before I can answer, I see Mr Mandiar our landlord filling in a betting slip, holding what looks like our rent money. The young prostitute girl from down our street is with him. "Alright" she says.

"I want my rent!" Mr Mandiar says towards me, I still haven't paid.

Part 6: The Long Goodbye

"I'm getting it for you now," I reply and he doesn't seem bothered that I plan to pay with betting slips. If only there was a penny in dog shit. Lovely.

There was only one thing left to do when this desperate for money. Not even the banks would give me an extension, the lady just laughed at me. "Really Mr Reed you are a joker" they all pointed to me and laughed. "I'm serious, I deserve some credit!" I told them but it just made them laugh more. And so here I am again, over a year to the day. The fallen autumn leafs sit damp and heavy in the winter misty air, freezing the grass over, making it wet and squelching with each step you take across the Common. Dark clouds sit on the horizon awaiting my next movement. Those Hollywood kids have got it made, so lets party. I need the money. This time I'll go as far and dirty as the punter wishes. It means nothing else to me anymore. Those Hollywood stars have got to pay.

Across the walkway as I study the clientele, the new boys walking sheepishly round the wet winters evening, in and out of the shadows, I see Alex walking home. I hide behind a tree, the same tree I sucked the cock of that tutor I saw in Asda early. I watch as Alex keeps trying to put his arm round that young prostitute from the betting shop and she keeps moving it away, another suicide attempt by the end of the year I reckon if she keeps distancing his advances.

Alone and broke, standing in the Common, watching the new boys pick the fitter younger models, I once was perceived as. What's wrong with me? Why don't I get any action? I stand like a true camp queer once Alex and the prostitute are out of sight, leaning against the tree - my tree, my patch - the streetlight illuminating my shadow across the icy grass. Some guy comes up smiling, as I smile back he looks at the side of my face, where the spot has now scarred and walks backwards, holding his hands up like I was going to shoot him. Even a car drives past later, winds it window down, then as I lean in it speeds off without a word said. Its nearly 2am, I'm freezing cold and I've got no business. I've stood and watched everyone else be successful, even Dan Not The Man was prowling round, I hid because I didn't want him to be my shadow all night and watched in horror as the guy that walked backwards away from me, picks him up. The storm cloud reaches my spot, the wind blowing the hard rain into my face as I stand under my tree. There's only one thing for it...

...I'll have to break into the house, fake a robbery of all the possessions and claim on the house insurance.

'HIT WOMAN'

Clarissa

The body is wrapped in a black bin linear in the bathroom of my flat, it amazes me how still it is, how with each job I do the stillness remains outside, the weather is always the eye of the storm as I prowl the night, then after the killing there is a calm, as heaven and hell travel with a new lost soul. I've been waiting for 'them' to pick it up today, before that I had held onto to it for a reason, I wanted to feel sick for what I had destroyed in other people's life's. Sitting in the darkness of my living room, the bathroom door open and the bin linear propped up, looking at me in its darkness, reminding me of what I've become. Before I had always detached myself from the job. When I killed James, my natural instinct from all those years ago returned, it was a mercy killing, self-defence, putting James out of his misery for his pathetic life and the hurt he had coursed around the windy city. That's why the eye of the storm was my guide that night. Since then 'they' have taken my life from me without choice or reasoning. The bare facts don't complicate anything it's black and white, heads or tails. Life and death is that easily connected when we sleep through our streets.

I watched the guy in the park, Southampton Common, with his family on a daily routine. I couldn't understand what he must have done to deserve this, watching him with his kids, playing games with them, his wife so happy and full of smiles, on a winters day in late February and the first promise of spring started to creep through the icy grass. I sat on the bench with my course work from the film degree, like any other student, being the arty intellectual type, sitting alone reading my notes - Soviet Montage, the Russian political revolution through visual images, then music in film; a documentation of how music creates a dramatic effect as part of the film narrative. It sounds crazy but it was reading bullshit like this that was keeping me sane in this other world I inhabitant as a creature of destruction.

A football falls between my feet, as I stare up towards its owners the victims daughter runs up to me, she can't be no more than seven. "Hello" I say towards her and pass her the ball.

Part 6: The Long Goodbye

"What are you reading?" she asks me inquisitive like only an innocent child could be.

"My coursework, about music in films"

"I like musicals, Daddies going to take me to see one for my birthday."

"When's it your birthday?"

"Tomorrow." That was my deadline for the completion of the job.

Now the father comes running up, my client. "Come on Clarissa," he tells her, putting his arms round her like a protective father. Her name is Clarissa, same as me. "Sorry about that"

"Its fine she's lovely"

"She's a terror," he spins her round back to his wife and son. I watch them through the corner of my trained naked eye as the late February darkness comes upon their day, the natural light turns to street lamps that guide us home and for the first time since that day with James, I feel warm inside. The family walk away in the warm glow of the streetlights, making their shadows giants and strong, kicking the swept leafs as they travel back through the Common. The young daughter, Clarissa, turns to me smiling, her eyes the same as mine all those years ago, the world at her feet, and the excitement of her birthday wishes for tomorrow. "Goodbye," she says and waves to me.

"Bye Clarissa," I reply and wave back to her. It was like waving goodbye to myself all those years ago, when I was just plain old Clarissa, and not Clarissa, before my life was changed one night like hers will now be, all because of one person...because of me. The husband and wife smile towards me and nod goodbye, holding hands with their kids and each other, linked eternally as a family for his final few hours.

I may as well have been killing my own dad.

"Is there a problem?" the phone call asks.

"Are you sure it's the right person?" I reply.

"You have until midnight"

"What if I say no?" There is no saying no...I knew that.

"You have until midnight"

"I'll do it the day after tomorrow." After her birthday.

"You have until midnight" and the phone cuts dead. The choice was simple - Do the job, or become the job.

Waiting outside his house, a nice area of the rich part of the Polygon, family residences, if he has done something wrong, it must be a blue-collar crime; faked cheques or stolen money from the firm. Watching each of the lights turn off, shadows in the bedroom kissing his children goodbye, he doesn't realise how final each touch will be. His wife shows him to the door and they kiss like first night lovers at the entrance for the world to see in all their pride of being in love. He starts his routine walk to his night shift job, the shadow of death in front of his steps. I hadn't asked where he worked, just the route he took. He was a brave man who took the alleyway that leads into the subways where the tramps convene and talk tales of murderous nights in the city. Each person has a place of birth and a place of death, none is ever nameless, and this was his place of burial.

I stop in my tracks and feel his footsteps behind me slow down, his coat pulled tight around him. I turn and place the gun directly to his forehead and look into his eyes. I must see the expression in their eyes in that final moment, their final breath; it helps me sleep at night, joining the others round the dinner table of my nightmare. All with that final look off – 'TIME' - life flashing before them and the fear it had been wasted. But his look was different, he had acceptance and I stared what felt like an eternity into his clear blue eyes, his life flashing before me rather than him.

"Tell my daughter I'm sorry," he asks me.

"What?" I reply confused.

"The musical, she won't get the tickets for her birthday now." In his moment of death he felt guilt for ruining his daughters surprise. I pull the trigger such was the ridiculousness of it all. As the bullet hits his head, he stays standing, frozen in life, and he kind of smiles goodbye, like he knew it was coming, he knew it would be me, and his upright stance finally falls backwards and hits the alleyway pavement with a shuddering finality. I throw up for the first and only time.

"Bloody hit women, vampires and bats!" The mad Irish tramp stands next to me in the alleyway and looks at the body. "I'll be glad when you students have gone." He carries on walking down the alleyway to his subway paradise of escaped life, they had the right idea, don't choose life.

My phone rings. I know who it is. "Good job. Someone is coming down the alleyway now to take the body"

Out of the shadows steps SideBurns Pete, the meat man, big bin linear in tow. "Did he throw up before you killed him? What a poof!" he says. I remain standing, looking at the stillness of his dead face, still smiling directly at me, his blue eyes like the ocean. "We're going to have to keep him at yours for tonight, I've got a full shop to cut" He looks towards the moon, shining in all its beauty, a new soul opening the gates. "Full moon tonight, beautiful"

I sit alone in the Music in Film lecture room, Fiona and Keith Reynolds had made space for me to sit with them but I lounged at the back. My eyes open but my mind closed to all the surroundings and what was being taught. None of it really matters. Alone. The way my cards have been dealt. It's safer for the others that way, friends can't understand but I'm saving them by not being mates with them any more.

I sit at one end of the line; Matt has just sneaked in late and sits at the other end of the line at the back. I study his face and it's a male reflection of my blocked out surroundings, I try and smile towards him, but it just comes across as a stare, he returns the stare, both saying nothing but holding a moment together silently of how utterly redundant being in this room is.

The Long Goodbye finishes on the projection screen, as I stare across Matt has already gone. Fiona approaches me. "Why didn't you sit with us Clarissa?"

At first I don't answer forgetting who Clarissa is, then remembering she's me. "I didn't want to disturb anyone"

"Are you ok? We haven't seen you for a while?"

"Been working" I reply dead tone, seeing the guys face from last night on the projection screen, playing his last words about his daughter, "Coursework," I finally say. As the projection ends I see myself on the reflection dressed in the white cotton dress.

"You look pale Clarissa, not enough vampire action," Keith Reynolds says, with his vampire kit on. "We're going to Nexus tonight you should come with us"

I am the Queen of the underground. Fallen angels in nightclubs nights, I chase the highway of perfection where I only want to be free, in the pill I have swallowed to forget about me. The dance floor of Nexus is packed with faceless people. With each flash of neon light that flickers across my face, they become the eyes of 'them', the last 'breath' of 'them', nightmares and dreams in a passionate embrace. I let myself go, dancing to death, hair long, resting on breasts that bounce through the low cut top. My leather jacket feeling the heat across my body, water dripping from my head, the lights surrounding my every vision, the neon wilderness where I stand alone on a dance floor full of people. The more energised I become to dance away death with each movement hoping I'll return to who I originally ran away here to become. A faceless guy stands in front of me, dancing away, one of a thousand who all look the same. With my contradiction of alcohol and drugs, from one dysfunction to another singing just for me, I dance next to him as the Queen of the underground. "I want to fuck you," I tell him. Before he goes to speak I kiss him on the lips and when I pull away I tell him the score. "I don't want to know your name, I don't want to know anything about you I just want to fuck"

In my flat, where only a day before a body sat in my bathroom, the faceless guy slobbers all over me, too eager, too excited, he only has one person to please as he gets his weapon out and that's himself, the satisfaction is purely selfish for him. As he pulls my skirt down and I pretend to be in the heat of passion, where I lose my heart and come so slow, the drug brings its come down, and I get off here on the scene and re-live my dreams of night. Reality of what I'm doing kicks in, the reality of being disgusted. This isn't me. I push him away gently at first.

"What's wrong?" he asks, looking upset.

Without a second thought, like a wild lion running in the wilderness of the windy city, I kick him off me. He stumbles up and I double round with a kick into his chest and he fly's across the room, smashing into the wall and the film course books I have stacked on the shelf fall to the floor. "I don't want to" I tell him, eyes wild, like a vulture with its defenceless prey.

"Jesus Christ what's wrong with you?" he splutters out between regaining a semblance of his heartbeat. He crawls towards the door, as I stand over him ready in a kicking motion. I want him to feel pain. I want him to feel humiliation. I want him to feel what I feel when I take a life away. Nothing.

"It was a mistake," I tell him.

"You crazy bitch! It was you who picked me up!" And he crawls out of the front door I've kindly opened for him like a good host, showing him the hallway on one final blow.

My life is no longer my own, if it ever was. Clarissa died when she was thirteen in that white dress and no matter how hard I ran away from that life that became Clarissa, that's all it was running away. You can't escape your fate in life. The cards dealt... The ace of spades.

I lye in my bed and pray for a lonely beach in my dreams, where

Part 6: The Long Goodbye

a hide tide will knock that wall I preserve, bringing me riches. Then I see it, the air between each breath we take. "Is this forever?" "Can you see it?" "Is this forever" And as I dream of the ocean and the world underneath, there's a gap in my thoughts that could lead me away.

Setting sails to a different course, to the twilight of the night where your mind walks between dreams and reality. Confusing our addictions and desires. Scatters my thoughts. All I want...is to be shown time. Where forever...is so close. And I don't want...to dream alone. We're all the same when we sleep. A soul confession

In the park, Southampton Common, the due air of a cold March morning and the sunlight blinds through the clouds, as the leafs begin to return to the trees and the colour returns to the wind swept city. I sit on the same bench as that day last month, with my course work, as I have done every late afternoon since that day, hoping to catch a glimpse of his family and what debris I have left behind, only then can I move on. And there they stand - the Mother with her son and daughter. She tries to look involved in their playing but her actions are distant and she looks cold, her eyes staring into the distance for a number of minutes, hoping to see her husband appear again and it would be like before that night, before her family was destroyed. Her kids play with little enthusiasm, their heads down, forcing themselves for their mother. Even before the darkness appears in the early March late afternoon, she already brings reminisce of events to a close. She holds out her hands for her children to grab and walk with her, they both ignore her, caught in their own memories and she grabs their hands placing them in hers forcefully. The daughter, Clarissa, begins to cry; she sees me across the way, wiping the tears from her eyes and waves a hello in silence.

I wave back, whispering 'hello', and as they disappear from my life I begin to cry the tears of the daughter and the loss I gave her, which we have both suffered. In the way cards are dealt in life, and fate lets everything go full circle, I picture it will be her one day in years to come that will relinquish me from this life. Nothing happens in this world by accident, everything has its reason. When she spoke to me before, I saw it, my death.

I stand in the library surrounded by books that have no meaning for the dead. Looking for anything on musicals, that's what his daughter was going to see. I find a list in the local paper; an adaptation of 'Singing In The Rain' was playing in the theatre, that's what she'd be going to watch today as a birthday present. I imagine how she must have woken up early full of excitement, waiting to hear her parents get up so she could then rush to them and be greeted with love and presents. How the knock on the door came early that morning, and she rushed downstairs thinking it was her dad, but it wasn't him but news of him. And how the mum would have broken down in tears, as the young girl would cry for her present not understanding what had happened. A birthday ruined, a life taken.

The next day, as I begin my walk through town, I take a detour to that street. Placing the musical tickets for three in the envelope with a note – HAPPY BIRTHDAY - And I place the envelope through the letterbox. It's all blood money.

I walk the parade of shops forgetting about my lecture to attend, each person I walk by in the late winter morning feels a victim, none of them knowing how close to death they are standing. I open the palm of my hands and brush against them as they hurry past in their lives, hoping that touch will bring a vision of each persons role in my life. But all I can see in this bright March morning where silhouetted shadows walk the streets, we all start of with nothing and sing a lonely tune to ourselves until the day we find our bliss.

I sit in the café by the ocean, looking out onto the wind that brings a gust across the sea, the windows rattle next to me. Families fill the area up, mothers with children, the future generations. The table in front of me sits the ghosts of all I've had to kill. Crowded round with cups of coffee and tea, speaking tales of their demise.

James is at the centre with a newest member – the Father of Clarissa. "Thanks for the birthday gift to Clarissa" he says, raising a cup of coffee and winks at me. They continue in their separate conversations, I watch their reflections in the window as the ocean speaks in waves.

The ocean washes over my sins as I stand beside the rails, letting the gusty wind pull my hair back and wake me up to my life. The sun glistens across the crashing waves, forming the clear blue sea for today alone, the same colour I saw in his eyes when I took his sight away.

Across from me is Matt, standing in his own world, looking out over the ocean instead of being at the lecture we should both be at. He seems transfixed, looking at the ferries that go across, searching into the distance with his eyes for someone or something that is on another island.

"How long have you been here?" I ask approaching him.

"Not sure, feels like everyday since the new year," he replies.

"What do you see?" I ask him.

"Missed opportunities," he replies. "How about you?"

I look across, seeing the guilt of all the memories I've taken finally being swept away. "Rivers of blue..." I reply.

"How come you're not at the lecture?" He asks me.

"Same reason you're not," I reply.

"I'm just waiting," he says after a few moments of silence.

"Do you know what for?"

"Yeah but its never coming."

"Do you like the windy city?" I ask him.

He smiles to himself. "It feels like all I've ever known"

"What about before?"

"A different life, it wasn't me, still isn't now, just someone different," he replies not looking at me but the waves in his answers.

"Will you miss it when you leave?"

He turns to look me in the eye for the first time in our conversation. "Will you?"

Silence as the ocean waves bring forward the temptation in desires of what we're both looking for, having lost. I stare into the waves with him. "I just want to be the same as everyone else when I sleep"

INTO THE HEART OF DARKNESS

Matthew Part 1. Action!

Tales of Brave Ulysses and the end of the world, the storm of the havoc we have created over three years is coming home to roost. Standing in the centre of Derby Road, with a 16mm film camera shouting - "ACTION" Filming the rain drenched streets with ladies at work on each corner and punters interested in a service, as our films protagonist walks through his own personal nightmare of a day in the life – this is our Apocalypse Now. An overblown paranoid production that has wiped us out financially and mentally, makes no sense but is a great artistic achievement that only the director, me, will fully understand. Instead of burning jungles to the soundtrack of 'The Doors', there are burning streets of St. Mary's, not done for filmic effect but as they are always burning.

"What does this mean?" the crew of Steve, Blonde Paul, Johnny and Simon keep asking me.

"Nothing. It means nothing," I tell them and they all nod their heads in confused artistic approval that only bullshit can give a licence to.

As the day shoot ends and the rainfalls across grim faces that have been up since 5am to get the daylight shot rising over the windy city, I'm hearing that panic sound again. Everyone wants a piece of me sane, can't stop everything from building.

"You still owe me money for the film stock?" Blonde Paul tells me.

I brush him aside with a hand held high to block out the pressure of the outside world of the individuals around me. "I cant pay what I haven't got but feeling"

"What does that mean?"

"It means I'm going to get wasted and create a masterpiece"

"What about the hundred pound you still owe me?"

"You'll get it at the end of the shoot, I'm an artist"

"I want it now"

"Jesus Christ," I cry out, the hard cold rain falling into my eyes, wiping tears down my cheeks, "Cant you see what I'm trying to create here?" I hope he can because I sure as hell can't, maybe he'll let me in on the secret of our apocalypse?

I'm having a nervous breakdown caught in a world that exists only visually in my mind, a world from a camera lens, motivations of performers stuck inside a mind that's had too much excess. I've got the fear. I've got what I always wanted and the reality of that was rubbish. You live your life to a certain point for twenty-two years and then all the experience and everything counts for nothing and you can't do anything anymore. The world is supposedly opening doors for you but its actually closing them. The only way to deal with my creative nervous breakdown is to get as hammered as possible. You never hear about creative masterpieces without taking shit loads of drink or drugs. Never hear the public say – "Well, since he stopped taking drugs he has really come out of his shell and blossomed" I'm an addictive mess again for the first time in months making my creative statement, I wouldn't have it any other way. Unopened letters wait for me in the house, bills, rent due, its

Part 6: The Long Goodbye

all immaterial whilst I'm filming. Reality? I am reality. What's that letter on the floor? Who's that knocking on my door? They're taking my soul. They want me cold. But the windy city beat them to it. I'm as cold as the narrative I'm creating... ...An author in hell.

"White lighting?" I offer to the rest of the riders of the storm.

"I'm rolling, I'm rolling" Johnny breaks his record of rolling a joint in less than a minute.

"Is this the after show party?" Amy sits on the sofa watching four drenched filmmakers having nervous breakdowns.

"It's the end of day film party" I reply.

"But haven't you been doing this all week?" She asks me.

"Before filming, during filming and after filming" I reply.

"How do you know what you're filming?"

"Its best not to know. Do you feel or are you an I am?" I ask the world.

White lighting downed to create the edge. Joints smoked to breathe fire. Who needs sleep? When the tales of a city have to be told. Who needs food? When you feed an empty sleepless body with addictions. "Is this how Exile on Main Street was made?" I ask at 3am.

"What time we filming tomorrow?" Steve asks me.

"4am" Simon replies.

"That's good got a day off," Steve says.

"No. In an hour it is tomorrow"

"Tomorrow Never Comes" I tell them. "John Lennon"

"You need to get off your John Lennon trip man" Johnny warns me of unhealthy idolised habits. We sit in a stony drunk silence for the hour before we begin to film again, eyes pretending to sleep upright on chairs. Feet sprawled across tobacco and rizzla scattered tables, pint glasses of white lighting to strike with each taste to keep you awake.

"Steve" Blonde Paul's voice speaks in the silence, "You still owe me three hundred pound for the film stock"

The rustle of early deliveries outside as the gate opens with footsteps off landlords with baseball bats to claim back his house and rent due from Steve and myself, stops by the door. "Landlord?" I stare towards Steve.

"Milkman," he replies as the sound of the bottles hits the doorstep.

"But we don't have milk delivered?"

"So?" Silence.

"Steve, you still owe me three hundred pound for the film stock," Blonde Paul continues.

Steve jumps up like a startled rabbit in the headlights of a car that's been on-rushing him for three years. "Fucking hell I know Paul! I fucking know! You'll get your money ok?"

"Ok, calm down I'm just reminding you"

"If you don't mind I'd like to get some sleep in my wasted state before we have to get up and film again." Silence for a full minute, then an alarm goes off. "Time to get up for filming." A week into the heart the darkness.

Matthew Part 2. This is a Robbery!

Where is everyone? The house is empty. It feels like bliss. I sit on my bed and collapse. Leaving all the lights off in the house. Continuing the 'Heart of Darkness' though the filming finished over a week ago now. I could lay in this silence and wait till the end of the course and the end of the windy city. Each of my muscles and bones relax, I can feel myself sinking as light as a feather into the bed. Wondering if this is an out of body experience. "Feels so good" I whisper alone in the darkness.

There's a bang downstairs. And I hear someone say - "Shit". I thought the house was empty? Then there's another bang and further movement. I slowly move my head towards the semblance of the doorway but there are still no lights on. Who would come into the house without turning the lights on? I did. But I'm having an out of body experience. We're being robbed. "Oh, well, my room will be alright" I whisper to myself and go back to resting my head upright trying to recapture the feeling of being as light as feather. All my stuff is in my room, I'm too tired to move downstairs and be a hero. Fuck the others, they would me. "Its their own fault for going out and not telling me" I whisper to myself, content in my excuse.

There's loud running up the stairs, a noise of someone tripping and a "Fuck" the voice sounds familiar. What kind of burglar runs up the stairs making as much noise as possible? My bedroom door opens wildly with a crash and bang, the light turns on and I move my head in my tired state of oblivion into nothingness, to see Steve staring at me with a big black bin linear round his shoulders like a student father Christmas. "Fuck, I thought everyone was out?" Steve exclaims.

"Steve, why are you robbing the house?"

Part 6: The Long Goodbye

"I'm not." He pauses and the reaches for one of his scabby ready rolled roll ups that burn in two the minute the fuel hits them. "I'm just tidying up"

"In the dark? I'll ask you again, why are you robbing the house?"

"Why are you sitting in the dark?" He retaliates with a question for an answer.

"You could have at least worn a mask or tea cosy over your head. You're not even wearing gloves. Don't you know anything?" I pity the fool.

He places the bag down. "So? We're insured aren't we?"

"Do you know how many failed insurance scams students pull each year in this city?

Hundreds. And you know why? Because they're not professional about it."

"I thought you just claim the house insurance?" Steve says innocently.

"They don't just turn it over, they investigate it, Police, the whole state tax paying money of civil servants get involved. We're students, they're the last people they're going to turn anymore money over too."

"The police get involved, shit?"

"What did you think? You just rob the place and then claim? Then some Jon Doe comes round in a suit asking you to fill in a form?" He says nothing. "Your silence speaks volumes Steve"

"Alright fucking brain box how come you know so much about it?"

"Its my job to?" I reply.

"Your job?"

I finally reveal my private out of body thoughts - "Yeah, I've been thinking about doing the same thing"

We burst into the living room wearing tea cosy's on our heads, goblin masks over them, black gloves on, dressed in clothes we brought from selected charity shops around the city. "Everyone on the fucking floor now!" I shout at my housemates and good friends on the sofa. Little Rob, Simon, Amy and Johnny remain nonchalant and go back to playing cards. "I said everyone on the fucking floor now!" I wield the cricket bat against the 'food' table and it collapses underneath.

"You want some of that?" Steve shouts through his mask, standing on tiptoes.

"Oh great, we'll probably lose our deposit now" Amy says.

"You two are paying for that," Little Rob says.

Steve and I look at each other, unsure what to do. I motion with my head for him to approach the sofa and get nasty. He strolls over in typical Steve fashion; it's so obvious it's him by his townie walk of body swaying side to side. "This is a robbery!"

"Sit down if you're going to join us for cards, if not stop ruining the game," Simon says.

"Just sit down Steve," Johnny say as Steve looks over standing on his tiptoes.

I lay the cricket bat down and sit on the sofa. "What you playing?" I ask.

"Gym rummy" Amy replies.

"Nice mask Matt," Simon comments.

Steve still stands on his tiptoes and picks up the cricket bat wielding it high in the air. "I said this is a fucking robbery!"

"Steve just sit the fuck down!" I shout at him.

He looks confused still, bouncing on his tiptoes, and then slowly his bouncing comes to a standstill and in his goblin mask he looks towards Simon. "Can I scab a cigarette Simon?"

He takes his goblin mask off and then his tea cosy. "Nice mask Steve," Simon comments looking at his face. "If we're going to rob the house for insurance we got to do it right. Have a house meeting to total up the money and possessions"

"Is there anyone who hasn't thought about robbing this place?" Steve asks. "What do you mean nice mask, I took the thing off?"

After the house meeting, we each run into our private rooms to do whatever we decide with the 'now' stolen possessions. I take my TV, Stereo, my least favourite CDs, and my imaginary video, placing them into a cupboard, figuring I'll decide what to do with them once we fill in the application claim. For now I'll leave them in the cupboard. After an hour of boredom, where I'm sitting on my bed realising that without music and Television life is pointless, Simon steps in. "I just checked, we haven't got any house insurance"

"Thank fuck for that," I reply "I was bored shitless"

A red flicking light of sparks comes across my window; both Simon and I go across to investigate. Steve is outside a small fire around him, burning his possessions. "What's he doing?" Simon asks.

"Have you not told him about the insurance?"

"I thought you had?"

Part 6: The Long Goodbye

"But you've only just told me…" I run downstairs, through the living room, past Amy's stir-fry in the kitchen and out the back door. "What are you doing Steve?" I ask standing next to him, the flames engulfing his stereo, television, records and clothes.

"I thought I'd burn the possessions, that way they'd never be able to trace them." I don't have the heart to tell him, standing watching his life go up in flames. "Even my Madonna records, they'll be worth a bomb, original vinyl," he says with pride, standing on his tiptoes throwing in 'Who's That Girl'.

Matthew Part 3. I'm a Made Man!

Hate is a sentence that has no parole. The wind is blowing the mullets of hair backwards, rain damping the spirits of the warmest men, soldiers marching to a war they no longer want to fight - That is drinking all day - Death by midnight. Our Irish haven waits for us at the end of the road. Entering this place of warmth and friendless we are greeted by suspicious stares by the 11am regulars who don't like there space – an entire empty pub, being invaded as it cuts down their limitless choices of seats.

The first drink is always the hardest. There's not enough metaphor in music today.

Even I, the greatest advocate of Britpop, is sick of the countless bands coming out with the same haircuts, the same tunes and no talent, enough is enough, we've all been giving those that matter a bad name with our antics. Even the essays at college have got me analysing film, analysing myself is the most dangerous aspect, after nearly three years I actually find I'm enjoying learning something other than a prowess absorbed in my body and deflated mind. Big words keep spilling from my mind and keep me from boredom and self-satisfaction enough to want to learn more. I've turned into a pretentious prat. I decide to get drunk, the only answer to demons that lay awake during the night, its better to pass out than try to study and reason the big questions.

Up at the bar sits the local of all locals in fact I've never seen him move from his stool. Sitting with his leather jacket on, rings on his fingers, short-cropped hair, I'd say around fifty, built short and stocky. Now I'm a recognised face in the pub he nods in acknowledgement to my presence. I'm now a made man. "Alright?" I ask.

"How's it going?" he asks me in a strong Sheffield accent with a hint of Irish.

"Good." As the bar lady approaches me before I can realise what I've said I ask him, "What you drinking?"

"Pint of carling" he replies.

"Two pints of carling" I order.

"Bernie Hughes" he offers his hand.

"Matt Ryan." He shakes my hand with the strongest grasp I've ever felt. "Strong handshake"

"You can always tell a man by his handshake"

"That and what films he likes"

He laughs at this. "I'm a McQueen man"

"De Niro"

"Nice."

"I hope you don't mind me saying but you look a bit like Ian Hendry." He looks at me worried like I'm taking the piss, ready to thump me, "You know the guy in Get Carter?"

He pauses, his mind thinking back. "Oh yeah," he says with pride. "Great film"

"Best British film ever made." I tell him "That and The Long Good Friday"

He nods his head in approval. "You know you're films"

"I'm studying film"

"Student," he says and nods his head with an element of disgust.

"I'm in my final months." Then sleep for a thousand years.

"Been trying to find Bullet and Getaway on video for years but I cant find them anywhere"

Out of nowhere my bullshit starts running. "I can get them for you" I lie.

"Yeah. How much?"

"No money," I wave my hand away, turning into Arthur Daley. "Its easy for me" I lie again.

"Nice." He replies and starts to roll up a tobacco smoke. Some large guys come into the pub with strong accents; they're greeting him up at the bar, surrounding him and cutting me out. I decide to walk away. "Hey Matt," he calls out and they make room for me to step back towards him, which I do automatically summoned before royalty. "When you get those videos I'll be in here." He shakes my hand a firm bone breaking grip goodbye.

Across the road tonight in Lennon's, is something I reckon the great man would be proud of himself; maestros Simon and Johnny are an impromptu gig, they have been rehearsing for the last two

Part 6: The Long Goodbye

weeks, well I say, rehearsing, been getting stoned to such an extent that Simon wasn't going to even perform tonight. He got so nervous saying they hadn't practiced enough, scared of making a fool of himself that he hid in his room and Johnny had to coax him out, then he has been throwing up all day. Apparently it's going to be a free form style of music. Sounds like my life, make it up as you walk and talk. The entire film course is here to cheer the impromptu session on and nod heads. Even the 'Rich Bitches' are here, Lyn, Saskia, Victoria, I didn't think they walked into this part of town; they only went to New York's and mixed with guys whose dads pay for holiday homes and fast cars. They probably brought some tissue to put on their seats, as they are worried about dust. Dark shades on in case they are recognised. "How long we staying?" I hear Lyn ask.

"Until the gig is over," Saskia replies

"Best to show our appreciation in case they become famous," Victoria says.

"Plus, it makes us look retro," Saskia reasons. These are the type of girls who get in the back of other people's black cabs when at traffic lights. The fakes of our generation, its all a smoke screen, where nobodies real and people who sit and tell it like it is get slagged off. The truth is always in the end of a scene and Britpop is know different I have discovered.

Enter stage left, raise right eyebrow, as the two-man act come onto to the stage, Simon looking extremely white, Johnny wearing shades and a tracksuit top of course. The guitar starts up and the organ follows, neither knows what the other one is playing but they just spiral down their own visions in their heads. I fear this will be their one and only gig, as most people only want anthems for pubs these days.

Even the mad Irish tramp is here, dancing on top of table. "Bring it on boys" he shouts. His mate the Asian tramp with a limp next to him. "Musical nutters!" he points towards the stage dancing with his limp.

As I survey the area further I see Bernie Hughes with his cronies and he raises a pint glass and he winks at me. I am a made man. Blonde Paul, who is going to do his jungle DJ act after, sits at the front of the stage like he's part of the band, head down looking at the floor and nodding up and down, like he really likes the music. He is completely out of place, too embarrassed or too wasted to move, the comatose Bez of the band. Finally the guitar and organ wind up and cheers even from the 'rich bitches' are heard and then they disperse to New York's and their playboys. They unfortunately miss Blonde Paul take the microphone, scratch some records, thump out a mad bass line, as he speaks sweet nothings into a microphone, so quick it sounds like his rapping on speed, the faster he goes the more incompressible, swinging his arms like a guerrilla "dgfgadn lksdkjkdjkksfdgloi" he keeps repeating, followed by the immortal words - "I'm an artist"

A guy is scribbling on a note pad next to me, he wears a badge saying musical press. "What did you think of the gig?" I ask him.

"What gig?" he asks.

"Why are you here if you didn't come for the gig?"

"I'm waiting for the band to come on"

"They were just on," I inform him.

"Supergrass were just on? I was told they're a three piece who play retro 'Who' style rock?"

"This is Lennon's," is the only reply I can think of.

"John Lennon is here?"

"No the place is called Lennon's"

"This isn't the Joiners Arms?" He asks me perplexed. "I'll have to make it up...Again"

"Who do you write for?" I inquire so to never buy the magazine.

"The Melody Maker"

"That figures," I reply and leave him scribbling down his views on a gig he never saw next to his daily shopping list.

As I lay in bed later that night, I'm surrounded by three years of posters who fill in as idols; it feels like the end of an era. I wonder what Jenny is doing now, if she too is looking at posters of memories? I wonder if Carla is happy in her new life? It's bittersweet on your own, full of memories of our friends smiling at the sun before the winter of discontent. I'm older than the people I see...I'm younger in the thoughts I keep... Refusing to burn away inside.

Matthew Part 4. Ginger's Porn

The only reason I've turned up for all the Music in Film lectures is because of the eye candy, our tutor, a Geri Halliwell dirty filthy woman, late thirties I'd say. This is her first teaching job and everyone turns up not for the lesson, she hasn't got a clue what she's doing but to look at her and go for a drink afterwards in JFKs. She's at the top

Part 6: The Long Goodbye

of the table holding court, all the guys looking at her face wondering how much make-up she has on and what her real colour between those legs is. She's one of these 'loopy' people I discover who reveals way too much of herself after three glasses of wine, telling Steve and I her life story. "I've been married twice." "Divorced Twice." "One husband used to beat me." "I used to be an actress in light porn films" "I hate my sister as she stole all my boyfriends and roles" Her entire life story is played out to us in a drunken broken woman slur. She wobbles up from her chair, spilling her last glass of wine. "Does anyone want a lift back in my mini?" That's like asking would you like a trip to casualty after being wrapped around a tree like Marc Bolan, least he was famous. Mark Gammond our course leader is immediately standing up with her.

Then Steve who thinks is Gammond gay and wants to find out tonight says. "Yes me too"

I have no choice but to say "Me too" as I don't know the way back without Steve, after three years I still get lost.

In the car, I sit in the front with 'Madam Porn Actress' Music Teacher and general drunken slut, whilst Steve sits in the back with Gammond the convinced his theory that everyone is gay is going to come home to roost and he'll get a 1st.

"Oh shit," she says as she takes a drunken turning nearly hitting the Asian tramp.

"Fucking Nutters!" he cries out.

"Fucking shit," she cries out again as the Police pull us over. They walk towards the car, it's the same two guys it always is - they *are* Southampton's Police Force, it explains a lot. "Sorry officers I cant get used to riding on this side of the road," she says in a poor America accent.

"Have you been drinking?" Bad cop asks.

"Wait a second," Good cop says and motions for his partner to follow him back to their car.

"Shall I drive away, I could out run them?" she asks me.

"You're in a mini," I reply.

The two police officers walk back and she smiles at them in a drunken guise, her lips and mouth stained from excessive red wine drinking, she's going to jail.

"Can we have a look at your drivers licence?" They order rather than ask, look at her photo and then back to her.

"Its her I tell you, its her," The Good cop keeps repeating.

"We're massive fans" the Bad cop says.

"Can you sign some videos for us?" The Good cop runs back to the boot of his car, like a child whose won a prize, pulls out some porn videos and returns them to her.

"What would you like me to sign them as?" she asks, and I look at the titles, *'Ginger girls are more dirty' 'Hard Cheese'* and *'Hard Cheese part 2'* each one has her on the front, with tits and cunt out.

"Sign them er..." the Good cop pauses, "I know, I know..." he gets all excited "to my favourite boys in blue, you guys can handcuff me again any night..."

"Big knob" the Bad cop replies.

She finishes signing them and passes them back. "Drive carefully" they shout as they speed off down the road to find their next student victim to beat up.

Mark Gammond is dropped of at his wife's house, annoyed that she didn't invite him back and pleased to leave the car after I saw Steve touch his knee as we took a tight corner and go "oh, sorry" letting his hand linger there. In her house, she has put on one of her porn films telling us "You should pre-sexualise the music, it's a really good example of music in film" As I watch a long object being put somewhere the sun don't shine and is miles too painful too ever happen without the help of a wide-angle lens. "Method acting" she comments and she touches Steve's knee. Too disgusted to look at the screen and too disgusted to look at her obvious manoeuvres on Steve, I shift my eyes through her essays on the desk hoping to find my masterpiece on Apocalypse Now. I wrote about how the film shows through music the Americans hatred towards the Vietnam War and the idea of it being sold as a consumerist tool, through songs like 'Satisfaction' and 'The End'. This was the best essay I've ever written, a true masterpiece into the heart of darkness. I find it and read through it with pride and then find her mark....

"50%!" I scream towards her, noticing she wears allot of make-up and is a disgusting whore.

"Oh no, its all me, you have to be very athletic," she replies.

"50%!" I scream again and throw the essay paper towards her.

"Oh that." She thought I was talking about her porn work.

"But it was a masterpiece"

"It started ok, then it was like you went on some big acid trip about the Vietnam War and consumerism and drugs"

"An acid trip! An acid-fucking trip! Have you even seen the film?! Its about the heart of darkness"

"What my porn film? You've seen it before?"

Part 6: The Long Goodbye

"AHAHAHAHAHHA!" I scream out, my heart torn out, what's the point in doing essays I just want to make films. "I don't give a fuck what you think you stupid bitch!"

"You're a scary guy" She tells me, I grab her hair and her wig comes off, I knew it, she was bald. "AHAHAHAHAH" she screams.

I leave the house with Steve sat there awkward. "I'm gay," he tells her immediately.

THE GREAT GIG IN THE SKY

Portsmouth, Wedgwood Rooms

The Band

It's the end of the road, the final leg of the journey in this country. Started north and travelled south, until we couldn't get any further unless we play on a riverboat. A generation of madness, the best ideas form for centuries. Absolutely knackered, it's been a long tour, could do without this final gig. Never been here before, not even when starting out. The 'Wedgwood Rooms' sounds like something that happens in a playground by your mates. Pain is a musical barrier. Acceptance is a speech when you retire. Probably just go through the motions, play for an hour. Get the crowds thinking and then get out of dodge. Look what we've all done? Making fools of everyone. Hopefully they'll be some nice girls, groupies to share on the van back up to the airport. They could even fly back to the home country with us. Haven't had any good groupies for a long while, not since the Seattle days. Days where the sun never went down, dawn to dusk in the night air that silhouetted our career.

Bad news is there's no real groupies out there… Again. Who books these dead end men only venues? Good news is the crowd are the best of the tour. To my surprise they know all the old tunes. They're getting the vibe that we bring back. The old days awake each morning in my drunken daze. Different places, different names, same faces. There are always a couple of wasters in the crowd who shout bollocks at us. One guy constantly shouts "FUAST" I know he means the German Krout rock band but I just play along and make up some tale, "Umm, Nazi crisps, you can get them for free." A couple of the wasters keep shouting "Johnny Baker" They even start singing some of this man's supposed songs in-between our set list - 'This song is for walking down the street' Sounds good. The crowd have been brilliant, even the wasters shouting intrigued me. Two hours and thirty minutes of low-fi mystic. Haven't done those since the days of Seattle and our chequered youth. BritPop? What the fuck is that? A cereal?

After the gig, we go to the side of the stage, pretending we want to chat to the fans for a while, hoping to see if some possible girl action was hidden at the back and will now show themselves. Unfortunately we're faced with four wasted guys who keep saying, "Listen to Johnny Baker he's the new Beck." And then ask for a lift back as they had missed the train back to Southampton.

"We're going in the opposite direction." I lie to them, trying to be sincere.

One of them doesn't take it too well. "You fucking cunt Barlow! We came all the way down to listen to your music, you came on late and played an extra long set and 'cause of you we've missed our train! How the fuck are we meant to get back now?!"

The next freak show on the list of side events is a young guy who keeps giving me his card, dressed in a suit saying, "I own a studio. You should come down and record some songs"

I politely take the card and pretend to look at it. Doesn't this guy know who we are? We've got five commercially released albums in the last eight years, two of which have been successful. We're singed to a major indie label. Why the hell would I want to come down to some student's university studio? Only in England does this happen. They're deluded.

Back on the coach, travelling back to the airport. The three of us sit on our separate bunks and relax. As I look out the window I see those wasters who asked for a lift back walking the streets. I get the card the suit man gave me and throw it out the window. It drops to the feet of the abusive waster. I can't wait to get back home, back to our country. As I read my music mag, I have to ask – "What the hell is a spice girl?"

Southampton, Civic Hall

The Fan

'Torn and Frayed' it's rare you hear such a good song being played in a venue before the band comes on. 'The Mood'. You have to be in 'The Mood' with gigs. Everyone here seems in 'The Mood'. Students from all parts of town, there's a defiant buzz and

Part 6: The Long Goodbye

expectation around. Maybe because in this windy damp dark city these bring with them a ray of light of what can be achieved if you listen to the music. Like a swarm off bees towards honey, we roam towards the stage when our guests arrive. Children, male and female, we all fight for conversancy, for territory. The closer you are the more inside yourself you feel. Let the tunes vibrate your soul. Take you flying. Up above is where I stand. Falling from the stage. Surfing on heads and hands. Lying crucified and carried like Jesus to the end of the line. I am king and I am love. Lights are hitting me. The trips kicking in. The beats crash like waves in my ears. I'm alone inside of me. Let the rhythm carry the beat. Sound surrounding me. Lights another place. Another time. The edge is the trip that these mushrooms bring to me. I can float and hear and see the wave of euphoria inside this floor. We're all coming together as one. Let the rhythm carry the beat. Come feel me. I want it to last forever. Don't let go off me.

Outside, strangers nod and smile, part of something that is theirs alone in their soul. Embrace the different sexes and fluids for a few seconds of joy. To recapture a moment that will never be lost in the archives of our soul. We keep stored away like a video in our minds. Little did we know, that in a few weeks down the line, this would be Rob Collins Last Stand before the great gig in the sky called him.

"That's the best gig I've ever been to" I proclaim wasted by the music alone.

I'm asked - "Do you want to get stoned, Matt?"

For once I decline. I don't need to get high or feel wasted. I am as high as I can get. No drug can do this for you, only the drug of music. That is the drink of the soul, the wine of our minds. In bed words of my mind fill the paper that holds my dreams…

I'm rising up back to dreaming, I'm sparking up back to sleeping
Feelings, feelings are gone, Feeling, feeling I'm free, The world inside of me
Love the sound I can hold, Hollow sounds light my sky
Lights trailing my bodies cold, Ocean rides shoot my eyes
I can't stop laughing, Dance a naked lifetime through this drugged fountain
I can't stop laughing, I shall follow, I shall follow, They're walking my way
No sleep as I promise the last time, Don't need no reputation
Nothing down I feel the edge, Found love in repetition
Come, come, come for me, The perfect finish to the best day
Lazy morning is my gift…

LONG GOODBYE

Part 1. Who's your course rep?

The clock is ticking. Matt sits outside Mark Gammond's office, looking at the sectaries the course leader has no doubt shagged, told them the Bowie on acid story in the seventies. Probably hasn't even seen Bowie or brought any of his albums, which in some respects is a wise move. Mark Gammond sticks his head out the door and his face drops when he sees whom his next 'discussion' group is with – the last of the wasters, the king on the throne. "You better come in," he says with disdain, wondering how Matt had made it to the final weeks of the course. It was a bleak room, with no natural light from any sources, permanently dark and cold. There is a portrait of Gammond with what must be his wife and kids hanging on the wall.

"Nice portrait" Matt says.

"David's got the same one," Gammond replies and Matt looks next to the family portrait and sees a larger portrait of Mark Gammond with David Bowie.

"This the famous concert where you took acid?" Matt holds a ticket encased in glass that names a Bowie concert in LA in the seventies with an acid tab inside.

Gammond's face turns red with anger and he puts his hand in the draw where he keeps a gun. "Put the glass encasement down and take you're hands off the desk"

"Bowie was shit in the eighties." Matt enlightens him with his musical taste.

"Where's Steve?" Gammond asks not even looking at Matt, long hair dangling down, unwashed, crinkled, and unshaven.

"He's late," Matt replies, "Probably sucking some guys cock, he's so unreliable. Has to have a shower and shave just to leave the house these days he's so paranoid about getting worms" Matt pauses before his final all important statement "He's like a girl."

"Then you alone can tell me what you guys have done for your documentary presentation"

"Documentary presentation?" Matt replies confused, then he remembers the reason for sitting in this Nazi interrogation room, Steve mentioned something about doing a presentation about Madonna. "That's why we're meeting with you is it?"

Gammond reaches into his desk and secretly loads some bullets.

Part 6: The Long Goodbye

"You people expect me to do all the work for you. Perhaps if you turned up for class you wouldn't be wasting my time"

"Madonna," Matt replies "We're talking about In Bed With Madonna"

"Oh very pc" Gammond sarcastically comments. "Well tell me about what theory you want to go down with Madonna..."

"Well I'd like to fuck her"

Gammond already starts his next sentence not taking in what Matt said. "You don't know do you? Because you've done none of the readings have you? All you people want to do is make films!" He slams the desk draw shut, holding the gun in his lap.

"Well, it's a Film Course, that's the point of the degree isn't it? Is that a gun in your lap?"

Gammond fondles the gun ignoring the question. "You have to learn about the theories behind films, the analytical aspects to understand. That's what people like you always fail"

"All this theory is bollocks, everything is gay fucking sub texts"

"Have you read my theory on Dead Poets society?"

"Yeah, its another gay fucking sub text."

Gammond bangs his hand on the desk. "These people are professors in their field!"

"Doesn't a waster have as much right as the next person to an opinion?"

Steve walks into Mark Gammond's Reception Room, his face drops with sounds off a verbal fight erupting. Steve immediately knows that it's Matt; he'd pick a fight with a nun. Steve pictures him standing over the mutilated body of Mark Gammond, his dick out and pissing in his open mouth, with Johnny sitting on the carpet rolling joints. As Steve opens the door he closes his eyes. "Oh fuck, there goes my degree."

His eyes open to see Gammond standing up with his fists banging on the table, Matt leaning over the table about to lump him one. "Alright," Steve says, bouncing in like Damon from Blur praying he still got a degree, all he can hear in his head is Damon singing 'Parklife'. Thoughts of having to explain to his axe-wielding Dad why he didn't complete the final week go through his mind. "You idiot son! You only had five days couldn't you even keep out of trouble for that long?" his dad would shout at him.

"It wasn't me it was this twat I was living with"

"You're living with another fucking guy?"

"Four other guys actually"
"Are you fucking queer?"
"Well yes, I am"
"Here's Alan!" he shouts wielding the axe towards Steve's head.

"Don't you have an office?" Matt asks the Head of the Student Union, standing in a toilet.

"Not yet, but they're working on it for next year. Besides its quite handy, a lot of students are hungover when they come here and need to throw up." He points to the toilet sinks. "Excuse me one moment." And he rushes over to them and throws up. "Please take a seat" and offers for Matt to sit on cubicle toilet seat. "About you're problem, with that Nazi, have you gone to your Course Rep?"

The Course Rep was Alex. "No." Karma, baby, karma, he thinks. "It's difficult with the guy in person… He tried to commit suicide last year and part of it was my fault"

"You fucking arsehole. Get out of my toilet!"

"What?"

"Us Union Reps stick together man, suicide for one is death for all of us…get out!"

"Do you even know the guy, Alex Page?"

"Oh, that dick, well, sorry, sit back down." He waits for Matt to sit back down and then leans in. "Is it true he used to watch his girlfriend fuck other guys behind his back?"

"What's the got to do with why I'm here?"

"Do you want my help or not?"

"Yeah, he watched Samantha fuck guys behind his back, sat in a car and masturbated over it. Now will you help me"

"Sure, that's what I'm here for isn't it. I'm not one to listen to idle gossip. How long is left of the course?"

"We're in the final weeks"

"The final weeks, are you an idiot! No-one can get kicked off on the final week, its like an enlist paper to Vietnam"

Stepping into the Dorchester, Matt finds the man his looking for immediately, Bernie Hughes sat up at the bar, pint of Carling roll up hand. "Alright Matt, what you drinking?"

"Got those videos for you," he replies taking out the Collectors Edition of 'Bullet' he'd stolen from Steve's room and his own collector's edition of 'The Getaway'. It was a small price to pay for what he wanted done.

Part 6: The Long Goodbye

Bernie looks at the videos with gleam, touching the front cover, staring idolised at pictures of McQueen. "McQueen, the cooler king" he keeps repeating. "All I need now is a video"

"No, problem, I'll sort it." The one in Johnny's flat would do fine, he'd take it as payment for free rent over various stages in the last three years.

"There must be something I can do for you?" Bernie asks.

"I wonder if you can organise a little welcoming party for someone" He'll arrange a little graduation party just for Mark Gammond. Revenge is a dish best served with a transit van, some ski masks and baseball bats. Recreational activities.

Part 2. A Political Landslide

Even the NME and Melody Maker get in on the act. The Britpop generation voice wants to be heard by Tony. Stars pictured with Tony being taken for a ride. They'll be dropped immediately after the victory, all a pretence that they're interested in what our idols have to say. They'll be taken through the front door and then shown to the exit door. Even as a student you can't slag off New Labour without getting a slap. BritPop. New Labour. Matt was starting to have his doubts about both - Faceless people who sing anthems in pubs. He often wondered if people all stood up and said whom they'd vote for if who would actually get in? Answer - Lord Such (The Monster Raving Loony Party). This is the party times of the decade after all.

"Do you not want to know who I voted for?" Steve says with pride to the entire house.

"No." Simon replies.

"Don't you care about this?" Steve asks his working class comrades.

"Care about what?" Matt asks.

"That's not the attitude of New Labour is it?"

"I voted for the Tories," Amy reveals.

"You Tory scum! A political landslide they're calling it" Steve says with pride. "One hundred and seventy-nine majority"

He stands up, whilst the Television shows the stars going into 10 Downing Street to suddenly become muted and shown the exit door. "They'll be loads of street parties tonight"

"Why?" Simon replies.

"Because the country has changed for the better that's why"

"What do you thinks going to happen to Steve? You'll wake up tomorrow and Tony would have paid off your overdraft?" Matt asks him.

Steve looks up and down the street with Amy, in the late spring evening, a still night, with a clear blue sky. Even the wind had taken a rest to watch events unfold. "I don't see many parties Steve?" Amy says.

"They just need someone to start it, that's all." And he steps back inside the living room to be the court jester and party organiser of the street for his beloved Labour party.

In the middle of the road, with a banner reading – **NEW LABOUR NEW BRITION** - Hung between two lamp posts across the centre of the street, Steve sits alone with a table of white lighting, burnt hamburgers and Farm Stores fish fingers, a mouldy loaf of bread and a poster of Tony Blair. Curtains open and stare at the madman who sits alone in the centre of the street. He waves to each of them shouting "Celebrate New Labour with me"

"What the fuck are you doing blocking the street?" The young prostitute, Janine, who works the road comes up to Steve.

"Would you like a glass of white lighting?" He offers the lady of the night.

"You're costing us business!" She screams at him.

"How about a fish finger sandwich?" He passes her the plate of farm-stores specials.

"My clients are having to go round a different route to avoid you."

"Don't you care about today?"

"I'm calling the Police"

"How can a prostitute call the police?"

Five minutes later the resident Good cop, Bad cop, arrive. "What is this?" Bad cop asks.

"A street party to celebrate New Labour's victory," Steve replies with pride, chest out.

They both look up and down the street and see no one else. "Where is everyone?"

"They're getting ready"

"At 3am?"

"Yeah, it's a street party"

The Good cop takes a taste of the pint glass and spits it out. "Ahhh! White lighting"

"Its quite nice once you get used to it," the Bad cop replies.

Part 6: The Long Goodbye

"We're confiscating all this stuff"

"What about my party?" Steve cries out.

"We've got one down the cells if you really want to party," Bad cop replies

"Fish fingers, farm stores," Good cop says biting into the sandwich.

"Hamburgers as well," Bad cop says, picking up the entire plate.

Steve sits in the back of the Police Car, with Good Cop, Bad Cop, as the two of them eat his food and drink his White Lighting. "Good party mate." Good cop tells him.

"Yeah." Bad cop lets out a loud burp. There's a noise on the radio.

"Bloody robbery taking place," Good Cop says.

"Where is it?" Bad Cop asks.

"Derby Road," Good Cop replies.

"That's just the next street down," Steve says hoping he'll get to go for a ride in a police car.

"Isn't there any unit closer?" Bad Cop inquires.

Good Cop speaks into the radio. "No."

They sit in silence for a couple of minutes finishing of the food and drink.

"Shouldn't we be going there?" Steve asks them.

"Don't tell us our jobs son. Get out!" As Steve steps out the car, they pass him the empty plates and finished bottles of White Lighting. "Clear this mess up. We don't want to see your face round here again, got it?"

"But I live here"

"It's a new government, new rules."

And the car speeds off, away from Derby Road and the robbery.

Part 3. For some it will always be Tuesday

The lights flicker down and the cinema becomes a world of self-abuse for final year students.
TUESDAY
'For some it will always be Tuesday'.
10minutes later -
The end…
Titles.

Fades to black.

'Jimmy', 'Jimmy' whispers of his name…

Three years of being wasted accumulated into 10minutes for Matt. Mark Gammond catches up with him, speaking in stringent tones of pain. "Great film, well directed Matt." He sits in an electric wheelchair, neck cast on, two broken legs. Matt continues to walk away, glowing in the satisfaction that Bernie had repaid his gifts and given Mark a private end of course party.

"Did you not hear what Mark said, he congratulated us," Steve says.

"He can suck my cock," Matt replies grabbing the drinks in the foyer.

Even the guest of honour in Harbour Lights Cinema by the ocean, 'Mr. Tommy', woke up for that one. Wearing his slippers and dressing gown, prepared for bed, he'd been asleep during all the 'issue' films. Then his younger bird wakes him up at the first sign of nudity and suddenly the man himself is eager and staring at the screen, salvia dropping from his mouth. "Was yours the film with the nudity in it?" the guest of honour asks Alex, chosen by Gammond to have his photo taken with 'Mr. Tommy' for paper.

"Yes that's right." Alex lies.

"Some of those films were utter crap. That one about the boy wanting to meet Rod Laver at Wimbledon and then meets a prostitute and kills her pimp," the guest of honour speaks about Alex's film, as he smiles towards the camera, "utter bollocks!" Alex places an arm round the guest of honour and his mouth opens laughing at a fake joke as the guest of honour continues, "I should introduce you to Ollie Reed, he'd love that bath scene you shot."

Matt stands at the back of the foyer in the shadows with a glass of wine, desperate for a beer. He notices one of the 'rich bitches', Lyn, looking at him, that kind of 'I'd like to get to know you now after watching your film, you intrigue me' look. He puts on a fake smile. She walks over to him. "Great film" she says.

"It's a fucked film," he replies.

She puts on a fake laugh. "Expressionistic views" and she brushes her hand onto Matt's brown suede jacket. "We're all going to New York's tonight, why don't you come?"

"I'd rather drink my own piss"

She puts on a fake laugh again and keeps her hand on his arm. "You're crazy"

The photographer walks up to them; the same reporter from

Part 6: The Long Goodbye

the gig in Lennon's. "Alright, thanks for that tip the other night," he tells Matt

"This going into the Melody Maker?" Matt asks.

"The Melody Maker?" The guy replies.

"Yeah, that's who you write for isn't it? What's it going to be, the Britpop generation of retro films that are boring bullshit like their predecessors?"

"Good angle, I like it." He starts to scribble in his pad next to his shopping list. "This is for the local paper"

"So you don't write for the Melody Maker?"

"I write for a quite few publications" he passes over an article from Gardeners Monthly. "Loved your film, sex, drugs, rock 'n' roll. The guest of honour had salvia dropping from his mouth"

"So maybe you should ask why you took a photo of some guy who had nothing to do with my film?" He motions towards Alex.

"Photos and interviews are taken with the wrong people all the time, its clichéd to actually interview the proper person these days." He takes his camera out and frames Lyn and Matt. "Any quotes about your film?"

"Oh very pc," Lyn says and puts her arm round Matt.

"I want to get wasted," Matt states as a fact and the camera flashes.

"Great quote, real generational," The reporter tells him.

The end of course party seeks acceptance in redemption. Happy in a web of disillusionment, shadowed in an illusion of a tomorrow that never comes, Matt looks around the party, it begins to dawn on him – what happens when you can't party anymore? Looking at all the faces of faked excitement, when they all felt the same, scared of what was awaiting them outside in the real world, he could see a hollow vacancy, where nothing had come along to replace the hedonistic Britpop, which in the end went no-where. False dawns and triumphant nights all return to the sound of silence

Matt rolls a joint, Jenny O'Sullivan moves next to him. "Alright," he says trying to play it cool.

"I'm going to miss you." She smiles towards him, reading his thoughts, wondering why he just didn't say them.

"Yeah, lets stay in touch." Why don't I just say that I want to be with her he wonders?

"I'm going home now." And she looks at him waiting for him to stop her.

Silence. And he realises its not that he's in love with her, it's the fear of never seeing her again, or any of these people whom he has only just got to truly know, if we ever get to know people at all behind our masquerades. As he stares at her, he realises that he's never truly loved anyone whilst he has been here he never even loved himself. It seemed to go all so quick, but it was over, he had no Courses Left, the Degree was finished, he had a week left on his contract in the house and they were still hiding from Mr Mandiar over the three hundred pound gas bill that they will never pay. He doesn't want it to end.

Jenny kisses him goodbye. "Jenny, wait," he finally calls out. She walks back over to him. "You staying in Southampton?"

"Yeah its my home now," she replies.

"I'll still be here for another week." He wants her to take control, he can't bring himself to stop trying to be laid back, stop trying to act cool.

"So?" Just tell me how you feel she thinks, trying to send a signal to his mind.

"Maybe, we could meet up, with the all the others, a kind of farewell?" He finally suggests.

"The long goodbye?"

"Yeah, the long goodbye." And he watches her walk away. There was always tomorrow he decides, he could put himself on the line tomorrow. When deep inside was full of plans, he'd leave them to tomorrow to face, someday leaving nothing left. If he could read books full of love, he'd be ready to start. But in the end he knew that human nature meant we're always in and out of love. What was real love? "Someday I guess we all need to start," he whispers to himself as Jenny leaves the party. And like a shadow that kept him warm, she's gone leaving him nothing, not even a catch of her breath.

He passes the joint to Johnny, the guy who fought against the bullshit of the Course like he did, but remained the last one standing. Johnny nods his head and they both look at the party from the outside, standing inside.

Johnny offers the joint to Mark Gammond in his wheelchair. Matt looks at Johnny in disgust, "What the fuck are you offering that cunt a joint for? He's one of them, one of the enemy." Matt then looks closer and sees it's the roach of the joint, the cardboard, and he nods back to a smiling Johnny, as Mark Gammond inhales cardboard,

"Oh yeah, that's good. Just like Bowie on acid," he says as the cardboard cut out burns onto his wheelchair.

Part 6: The Long Goodbye

THE LOST SOULS

Alex

The contracts are signed today, by the summer the money would have gone through. Not all the money in the world can take me back again, to when I first came to the windy city nearly three years ago. How life can change who you are and what you believe in that time. Samantha. Amy. Rachel. The house that fell as we slept inside in the madness of the second year... Then my hospital visit.

"Why did you do it Alex?" My mum asked me about my suicide attempt.

"Because it made sense," I replied.

She looked at me with the same eyes she'd use for my Father. "Did you do it on purpose?"

"I'm tired," and I shut my eyes pretending to sleep. The truth is I didn't do it on purpose knowing I'd be found, I actually did it to die, to experience something I could then be hip above all the others with. Be a martyr like James was held in esteem for those few months. Now he's just a name that pops up in past tense in certain conversations. Taking one final look round my house in North London before the sale makes me rich, James ghost stands before me in the empty dining room.

"You're just last weeks fish and chip paper," I tell him.

"What can you do?" he replies.

"Should have left a suicide note like me," I tell him.

"There was no suicide to write a note for," he replies. "What happened to you anyway? I kept a place at the table for you?"

"Those Judas's saved me."

"Did you plan that Alex?" Even the ghost doubts me.

"I'm more loved now than I ever was. I am Resurrected"

"You're not Jesus. Besides, there's plenty of time for you to do it right."

"Alex who are you talking to?" Amy has come into the room. I invited her down this weekend to help sort out the contracts and paper work on the house with me in the hope she'd relinquish her cold exterior to the idea of 'us' as a couple, and open the barriers.

"James." I say as his ghost disappears.

"James? James is dead, Alex." She walks over to me concerned look in her eyes. "Have you taken your pills this morning?" It was working a charm, all girls' love playing Nurse.

"I don't like taking them alone," I reply.

"Give them to me," Amy says holding out her hand. I take the pills out of my pocket placing them in her hand with a gentle touch. I'd been given pills to take since that incident last summer. Prescribed medicine to ease what the doctor said was "Depression"

"I'm not depressed," I told the Doctor, "I'm happy"

"You're socially isolated Alex," he replied.

"I've got loads of friends, girlfriends, boyfriends, I'm the Course Rep"

But he wouldn't listen to me. "You're afraid of being alone, most of us are." And he wrote out a yearly prescription of these pills. They ease my headaches, create a big black couch that I sit on and try not to analyse anymore, but just relax and let the world pass me by for a while.

"Do you still need the pills?" My Mum asked me last month.

"Yes of course," I replied. Taking my daily dose of two, though I'd forgotten to mention the two I'd taken earlier to help me get up.

"Its just that you seem fine."

"That's because of the pills"

"You're not becoming dependent on them are you Alex?"

"They're just pills" I replied. And that's all they are. Just like life is only life.

Amy takes two out and I open my mouth, she places them in there, passing me a glass of water. "There, you'll feel better soon"

"I feel better already when you're with me," I tell her and she walks away.

"We've been through this," she replies.

"I'll stop taking my pills"

"Look Alex, you're not going to blackmail me into going out with you again." She storms towards the front door before shouting back up, "I'll wait for you in the car."

I keep seeing the exit sign in front of me, maybe its time to set sail and jump out on my bail? I always wanted to be a revolutionary of this time, surrounded by wasted opportunities of others who tried to catch me blinking that early summer evening last year. As I take the bottle out again and pop one more pill, I hear a mad man outside shouting. "Every dog has his day"

I run to the window and rhyme in encouragement to the man. "Who will be the first to pay?"

"Shut up and take your pills suicide boy," he shouts back.

And revenge in my thoughts of vengeance start to consume me. Plans for the summer when all this is ended. All the money I'll have in my pocket - I could be anyone. I could go traveling and become

Part 6: The Long Goodbye

talked about as the hip martyr I attempted to be. See the world and sit on the biggest black couch of them all. "I'd like to get some brochures about traveling" I ask on the phone.

"Where to?" A woman sales rep replies back.

"I want see the world," I tell her theatrically in reply.

"You're taking a sabbatical?" She asks me.

"I've done that for three years. I want to live"

"How long would you like to travel for?"

"As long as it takes." I don't need any of this anymore, these false promises of friendship, the false dawn of a revolution. I am my own island, my own black couch. I wonder how many prescribed bottles of pills I'll be able to fit in the suitcase?

Linda

Sweating. The room is white. The sheets are bare. Crumpled over me as I move their entrapment off me. Posters of pop stars who I've fancied over my teenage years stare at me from the walls. I can't breathe. "Help me!" I scream. I hear footsteps outside my door and then a pause before entering, an argument between two people and then the footsteps descend away. "I'm suffocating," I scream out, as the sheets wrap over me and I writhe in agony to take it all away. I just need a little something. Then on the bed she appears. "Go away, you're not real". She smiles and pushes my hair back, wiping the sweat from me. "I just need it one more time" I beg her.

The young girl with the innocence of the world covering her every pore puts her fingers to my lips and starts to sing. "Through my diseased eyes I can't stop seeing, Shut doors familiar faces as I'm bleeding, And if I could still see what you see, I guess I'm on fire and you're still killing me...In my burnt out mind I'm feeling insecure, In this one horse tribe I'm feeding to score, If I could lose this way and find some faith, If I could hit this floor and feel so safe, I'll be turning back no more...I love, I see, I cry, I need, I feed, I die...If I could be so better, I wouldn't be insecure, If I could just get better, You'd come to me to score"

Black out.

Daylight. The sun blinds my eyes of the heavens through my curtains. I must be dead. I am pale as an angel. My mouth is dry. My mum and dad sit on my bed. "When is it?" I ask.

"June"

"How long have I been here?"

"A while"

I jump up. "The Course, what about the Course?"

"Its ok," my mum says and turns to face a shadow that steps into the light. "Isn't it?"

"It's ok Linda, you can repeat the final year." The psychiatrist I saw in the first year is here. "You're not alone in this," he says, in his hand are leaflets, phone numbers, recovery groups. All I can think is great - I get to repeat my three years of uni again, all the addiction, all the wasted memories and blizzard noses. That's what the pure white is through my room - the mountains of snow outside waiting to take me back into the eye of its blizzard. I close my ears waiting for them to leave.

"I need fresh air," I tell Dad, hoping he'll leave the window open slightly, as my strength has been sapped, I wouldn't be able to push it open. I'm not even sure if I can walk. "I'm suffocating"

"She'll be alright," Dad tells Mum's worried look as he leaves it ajar. "We've got to start to trust her again."

"She can't get far without any money," I hear my mum say. Little does she know there's other ways of paying.

I close my eyes. The fresh air breathes life into my legs again. And I shiver in my room when my eyes open…As I crawl on all fours to the window trying to find the strength to stand up…All I can think about is – why didn't they take me to a proper hospital? Because of their social standing that's why. Because I'm still their little princess in their eyes, that's why. I'm sure they all think it's been a big mistake, that after a few days or weeks in my room I'll be ok.

As I push myself out of the window…Crawling on all fours naked like a trained solider across the garden path…I tell myself I will be ok. I just need one little taste to get through the rest of my life. One little snort to remember the pain to stop fully. Then I'll be ok. Then I'll stop. I collapse my body's strength by the gate. Hoping someone will take pity on me and feed my diseased eyes. The sunlight burns onto my naked pale skin. I see a shadow next to me. It is she again. The innocent child I once was in a past life. The innocent child I never was in this life. She sings her final song to me - "Little scarlet keeps walking two steps back, Trying to catch the night in day, And every side carries a weight, And everybody wakes too late, She takes another hit out in the street, Takes the poor money from her feet, Now silly scarlet drop your hat and take a bow, Didn't you always wonder that all the sisters knew how? Do you sleep at night knowing how you got rich? A sweet smell of

Part 6: The Long Goodbye

success drops from your lips" And as she finishes, her shadow in the sunlight expires.

My eyes close as my parents rush screaming from the house to suffocate me back in my room again. "Just pay the fucking hospital," I mumble, "Who gives a shit what the street thinks"

Christina

My mobile rings as I park the car in the shopping parade, wanting to have one last walk down the aisle. It's my boyfriend. "Where are you?" he asks.

"I'm in town"

"I thought you was driving back?"

"I am." I look around at wonderment at how quick the three years went as I see the same look of excitement on faces of new strangers to the town who will replace my time and me. "I just wanted to say goodbye" I walk the parade of shops broad smile on my face life has never been better. This guy approaches me he looks familiar.

"Christina?" He asks me, long curly hair down to his shoulders, brown suede jacket, flared jeans, looks like the epitome of Britpop.

"Matt?" I ask. He nods his head. "What is that a wig?" I ask him, last time I saw him he had hair no longer than mine, cropped to the eyebrows.

We sit in a coffee shop overlooking the parade of shops and new people, both with a sense of farewell in our eyes over the city.

"Just feels like yesterday that I met you, the first person I met in Southampton." He tells me.

"That's right, you was the second person in the house after me." And my mind flashes back to him standing in the doorway of his bedroom with his parents, a different complexion in his face and eyes. "You've changed quite a lot"

"Is that a compliment"?

"Depends whether you still want to look innocent or not?"

"You look exactly the same"

"I'll take that as a compliment" I tell him.

"I guess I can tell you this now but I always wanted to fuck you," He states bluntly, and then begins to laugh to put me back at ease. "We all did in the house. Me, Alex, Taylor"

"How are they? Do you still see them?" I change the subject for my own benefit.

"Taylor went back home at the start of the third year."

"What about Alex? Is he still trying to analyse everything?"

"I don't know really, I don't see him"

"I thought you two were mates. What happened?"

"Madness"

"Madness?"

"Yeah, a wasted madness. I don't think any of us ever fully recovered. What about you?"

"What about me?" I reply.

"This reminds me of when we first met, answering questions with questions"

"I'm not sleeping with you"

"I know you're not, you don't have to keep telling me"

"Well, I just wanted to get that straight." We smile at each other still flirting like we did those three years ago back in that house in the 1st year.

"What course were you doing again?" He asks me.

"Media Studies. Yours was film wasn't it?"

"Yeah, you got a good memory"

"Its surprising we've never bumped into each other our lectures are in the same buildings"

"I didn't always attend"

"You got anything lined up for when you leave?"

"I just feel like I need to sleep for a few years, you know what I mean?" he asks with the look the city has carried in us all for three years of an emotional roller coaster ride.

"Yeah, I know what you mean." I wouldn't change the last three years for anything. None of us would, we've been part of something special.

"Where you off to?"

"Back home to Oxford but I wanted I'd take one final look round the windy city"

"You're not coming back?"

"I wouldn't want to live here not being a student."

"So you're going back to Oxford to live for good?"

"I couldn't go back home now, could you?"

"Not really. I guess I'll have to though, for bit"

"I'm moving to London with my boyfriend"

"The city paved with gold"

"That's what they say. How about you, you got a girlfriend?"

He pauses before answering, he was always secretive. "No."

"Why not?" I ask.

Part 6: The Long Goodbye

"It never seemed to fit with me"

"Too busy getting wasted and stoned right?" My phone rings and its my Mum seeing if I'm on my way back. "Sorry, I've got to go" I stand to leave.

"Me too." We step outside into the gust of wind that carries memories in the city.

"You want a lift somewhere?" I ask him.

"Thanks but I'd rather walk, take it all in before its gone"

"I know what you mean," I tell him, as I walk away I turn back. "You know the one thing I wont miss?"

"What's that?" he asks.

"The wind" Whenever the wind speaks to me now, I'll see that Town's face at my door.

In my car I drive past the parade of shops and people, including Matt, and they all become strangers. Faces I will never see again in my lifetime. These memories shall fill our time for us alone; no one can take them from us, not ever.

OASIS

Matthew

The radio comes on; early in the morning, it's the day I leave. An Oasis song plays, the new single - 'Do you know what I mean'. I scramble for a tape and press record and collapse back under the duvet. It started with Oasis 'Live Forever' and its ends with them. The sound of a bunch guys on coke in the studio, not giving a fuck in a blizzard of noise, long songs and air guitar rifts. The three years have gone full circle. Like them I have grown and progressed, bitterer, more acid tongued.

What had been planned for the final night was always going to be an anti-climax. Too drunk to go onto a club, Steve was inviting everyone back to the house, and as I stepped into the living room that night, I found the entire stormtrooper population sitting on the sofas and chairs. Upstairs Amy, Simon and Johnny hid. I soon followed them. For some reason I was coherent but unable to move due to the drink, the fact that three years had to come to an end had finally hit me and I was scared to move in case I lost all the memories I had gathered, then the end would come. I was left in limbo, left in the abyss.

Others soon joined us upstairs. And there sat Jenny, it could have been a final glorious fuck to end this part of my life with but the chair wouldn't release me.

"So I'll see you then?" Jenny said preparing to go. She knew I didn't want her too. All I had to say was the truth; that I wanted to go out with her, not just tonight but every night and see what happens. But I'm too wasted in this chair to move. "Stay in touch" she says.

"Yeah, you too," I reply. Do something you idiot? I kept telling my mind but my body wouldn't move. I don't say anything. I let her walk out of my life, like everything else I've ever wanted. It's easier that way, more poetic.

Once we all started to go to bed I trembled downstairs, hoping that I wouldn't find all the stormtroopers building a death star, but it was empty, apart from one person...Alex, he was asleep on the sofa. I guess he felt it too, the full circle of events and he wanted to sleep that final night in a house with the people who he had lived with for two years before we left him high and dry. I still hadn't forgiven myself for what happened to Alex that second year, this final year I was seeking some kind of solace, some kind of redemption and here it was that final night - Alex asleep on the sofa, wanting it to end how it started. Staring at him for those final moments I transported myself back to meeting him in the kitchen, nearly three years ago. Where did it all go?

Pull the duvet tight around me, I want to close my eyes; the world can wait for a few minutes more. I know I have to get up. I know its morning. I know today I travel back. Back to where though?

We came.

We saw.

We conquered.

We go home.

But where is home if our parents wonder where home is themselves? Are we forever searching? Forever growing? Home is where the heart is but what if you have yet to find your heart, or understand how it beats?

How long had I spent lying in bed like this in these three years? Clouded over in mind, duvet was like a security blanket, keeping all my dreams and worries of the future away; I could have slept for eternity. That first year it seemed all I did was sleep during the day and wake at night. I was a vampire. Now I'm getting ready to be an adult, if there is such a word.

Laying in bed the world would pass me by and I was contented for it to. The world was other people's problems, other peoples

Part 6: The Long Goodbye

dilemmas, other peoples goals, all that concerned me was what time to get up, go out and spend. For a few minutes more I want to see if I can relive that feeling, find myself transported back and feel it like I did that first time of discovery. But you can't go back and I feel nothing but the little voice saying - 'You got a train to catch'

My CDs are already boxed up. So many times and memories tied up when each one was brought. When I first listened to them, the soundtrack to my life. Mazy Starr - 'Riding on high' sleeping the day away. For each month a different sound, a different hole in my wallet, a different voice of Britpop, a different promise to a new Britain, a different member to the membership of these three years and a club that is exclusive to us only. Each album cover signifies a changing of the outlook of clothes, of styles in our appearance, the substances we'd chase our demons away with, and we are left with these memories with each song that cries out to hold on. The NME shows the Verve returning. A sound of frustration, of bitterness, of still being lost but maybe there was a false hope given that we can build on. Ashcroft stares at me and smiles our spiritual leader for the times ahead. 'Bittersweet Symphony' plays as my farewell to the guardian of my room. The Verve's soon to be released album 'Urban Hymns' is the bible at the end of these times, our redemption. Like anything at the end a massive vacuum will be left to be filled. It seems at the end they all came back to bid us farewell - Verve, Oasis, Echo and the Bunnymen, the assemble set piece of Spiritualised with 'Ladies and Gentleman' and RadioHead's 'OK Computer'. As the new kids grow into adults these will be their anthems, compared to our 'Parklife', our 'Live Forever'.

A broad union jack covers my bed sheets. To what debt do I owe this country? Something in the region of five thousand pounds on loans they shall never see. Nightclubs and pubs all sang our anthems. It's funny how each year changed with a song, with a certain line, with a certain style, but how much did we essentially change? Just killing time, I guess we all were.

Jump up and pull the union jack duvet off me...No more. The curtains open and I take one final look from my bedroom window, which has been my binoculars in one form or another for three years in various guises. It is windy of course. It is raining of course. And the truth is, I wouldn't have it any other way, the windy raining city all year long. In that first year it was warm, everything was colourful. The second year was a haze of violent colours in a despair of excess. The third year it just seemed to rain all the time, waiting for us to leave. Out stayed our welcome. Excess. SsecxE. It sounds like success. And that is how we would measure ourselves here...

It's amazing how your entire life is packed into two suitcases. I'm yet to decide if this is a good thing or bad thing, it depends on how quickly I might need to run back here if I cant stand it back there. They're both heavy as I put them outside my room, and like a hopeless romantic that I hide so well from others, I give one final look round my room, my prison cell at times, escapism and paradise at other times, and bid a final goodbye. "No change, I can change, I can change... in my soul"

Shut the door.
Then open it again
Had I left something?
No
Has something fallen down?
No
Had I left the window open?

No. I just thought that maybe if I opened it again, it wouldn't be today but the start of the first year again. God, I really don't want to leave. All that moaning this year.

All that can't wait to leave, and when it dawns you want time to go backwards - the moon becomes the sun and night becomes day... You can't go back, only forward... If I stayed I'd only moan. I've got to find a place where I'm happy. Where I don't wish for the grass on the other side. Take my experiences and learn from them. From out of every negative is a positive.

Knock on Amy's door, Steve is already in there, he too is packed and she is crying. She's got another year left in this place I don't know if I'm jealous or if I'm envious? The two go hand in hand. I give her a cuddle and kiss her goodbye. I give Steve a cuddle and a pretend kiss - "See you later fagot!" It's a nice goodbye.

Next is Simon, he's asleep in his room, he lives near me back in Hells Kitchen, so I'll be seeing him soon enough. "Make sure you bring a baseball bat back with you, you're going to need it in Hells Kitchen."

"Yeah," a drunken slur calls out.

The living room, I take a glance around from the doorway. I put the cases down and decide to try out every seat in the room. Always preferred the armchairs, the sofa always made me itch. Alex has disappeared and vanished from the sofa, maybe he wasn't here at all last night? Maybe it was my conscience wanting it to go full

Part 6: The Long Goodbye

circle for my sins.

Front door.

Open.

Slam shut.

Pause.

Mad Nutter tramp "One nutter!" He shouts and points at me.

"Two nutters!" I shout back and point at him.

"Three nutters!" He shouts and points at an invisible friend. This could go on forever so I walk hurriedly along the road, forgetting one last glance at the orange house, as it became known as. I don't want to encourage the tramp to join in, trust a tramp to ruin my farewells.

I go over to Johnny's flat, he opens the door with a joint in his mouth and cup of coffee; this really could be anytime in the last three years. I even hug him goodbye, and this surprises him, hope he doesn't think that I'm gay now.

It's a twenty-five minute walk to the train station through town and all the old haunts. There are still students walking around; some like me going back to the future with a question mark, some walking aimlessly around, wondering what they are meant to do. Oasis plays on my walkman, 'Definitely Maybe' album and it hits me how no-one looks like rock stars now, as the tune I came in with guides me out - *'Live Forever' was the nineties.*

The rain hits me and the wind blows me backwards as I grip for my life on the suitcases. If I let go, I wont have anywhere to go, this much I understand.

As I wait at the station, no expectations pass through me again. The train stops and people get off, this isn't my train but I can't help but wonder what would happen if I got on it, one-way ticket and start a new life, like Carla had. I've done it before, three years ago; it's easy when you haven't a choice but where it's demanded you are.

What happens if you faked who you was and wanted to be someone different? All it takes it one step on that train. Faces get off, and I'll never be one of those again getting off to journey round the windy city and lay my hat as home. The train pulls away and with it the danger of being someone else.

I put myself on the right train and realize I won't be coming home again. Sitting on the train so many faces that all passed me by. As the train starts to leave, the girl with the rosy cheeks I always see sits herself opposite me. "Hi, we meet again"

"Yeah" I reply.

"I'm always visiting friends in Southampton"
"I wont be any more"
"Have you finished you're course?"
"Its over," I reply more as a statement of these last three years than the course.

And she starts to ask me various questions that I have no answers for –
"Where you going back to live?"
"What you going to do now?"
"How much money do you owe?"

I turn my walkman discreetly back on, 'Cigarettes and Alcohol' blares out as my response. I stare out the window as the windy city rushes past and disappears as just another memory; it is that simple when you make it so.

Traveling back home a change of direction could change my life again. Writing down all the thoughts in my head, I wanna be famous, I wanna be known, I wanna be someone…

…Who isn't tame? Life's so tame

TALES OF BOBS BARBECUES

2005

? ?

Bob stands alone at the barbecue. Untouchable and un-talkable "Give the man his space," they all whisper. "For he has the answers" For Bob it was a barbecue not a statement. He puts the red pork chops onto the fryer and turns them to there dripping crispness. His big white hat like one of the seven dwarfs pulled over his head. A butchered once white apron. "They can serve themselves," he wheezes out, and like a fast food vender he opens up various buns, places the food on plates and then onto tables outside in this bright American sunlight. The dusk before dawn, this truly was beautiful. Why we had to share it with so many strangers didn't make sense.

"It's served they cry." And the vultures run over to the tables where they sit like kings devaluing tales of how they met the man. But where was the man I wondered?

A roadie makes space by the benches and plugs in an amplifier and mike, starting a sound test. The whispers are of an impromptu gig, hand held DV Cameras are taken out and tapes running. There is a tap on my shoulder and it is Marty, waving a super 8film cam in my face, I thought they were extinct but this guy still champions the course like the record collector champions vinyl, 'We will not let it die'.

"He wants to speak to you?" Marty tells me, camera lens in my face. I am pulled by the hyper Italian saint inside the house towards a darkened sitting room, where on the floor cross legged sits Bob, opposite him on a sofa passed out is Robertson. The TV has the shopping channel on. "I love this channel" Marty waves the camera around the room, running up and down, mumbling to himself.

"You like the barbecue?" a wheezing voice comes out from Bobs shadow.

"Not really" I reply honestly, it was shit, I wanted to go home, and I didn't care who this guy was.

"Why not?" he asks.

"The people. You know these people?" I ask disappointed by the man's taste in friends.

"No."

Silence again and Robertson begins to snore.

Marty runs round and waves the camera to the walls to catch

our shadows.

"Amazing, amazing, amazing morals, sins, churches, shadows, life is real, a reel of film, film is an expression of art, art is what…"

"Hey man, shut up" Bob wheezes out, he turns the channel over to QVC. "That's better, I like looking at the fit presenters". The shadow beckons me closer. "I heard about you. What did you study man?"

"I studied nothing for three years."

"And you think that's enough to get you an invite here?"

" It's the best schooling in life, cause once you know nothing, you then understand everything"

The shadow laughs and throws me a barbecue rib. "You wanna jam?"

"No, I want to do nothing"

"Me too"

The shadow and I sit and talk about nothing into the dusk hours of the sun, until the vultures have dispersed and his impromptu gig is played to an audience of three.

STINKIN THINKIN
A Novel by MJ Gunn

Paranoia. London, city of broken dreams and nervous breakdowns leading up to the year 2000 turns into schizophrenic insanity for Isaac a drink and drug addled young writer, stuck in chemical generation of getting wasted, clubbing, tripping, watching Soap Opera TV. A walking time bomb waiting to explode… he takes on the persona of his new protagonist, James, to life threatening effect, the answer for both his own bored personality and writing a masterpiece.

What happens when you begin to live life as the main character in your new book? Marie, 'the perfect art student girl' could be the first step towards achieving his goal. But if he wants to play this dangerous game, he'll be stuck with a dangerous female partner who couldn't care less about him. Life begins to imitate art in famous faces, musicians and writers, secret packages, films, petty crime, violence and finally a gun. Events spiral out of control in his double life as two worlds collide - Isaac Versus James for control of his mind and personality.

THERE ARE NO INDIVIDUALS ANYMORE.
Isaac wants to be one, whatever the cost…

COMING AUTUMN 2007

Printed in Great Britain
by Amazon